TARIZON
Civil War

Acknowledgment

A special thanks to my son and law partner, James Manchee, whose hard work and long hours at the office have made it possible for me to spend the time necessary to write and promote my novels.

Tarizon: Civil War

Book II

By

William Manchee

Top Publications, Ltd.
Dallas, Texas

Tarizon: Civil War
Volume II

© COPYRIGHT
William Manchee
2009

Cover Design by Dan Silverman

Printed in Canada

Top Publications, Ltd.
3100 Independence Parkway, Suite 311-349
Plano, Texas 75075

ISBN 978-1-929976-52-2
Library of Congress #2009921759

    No part of this book may be published or utilized in any form or by any means, electronic or mechanical, including photocopying, recording or information storage and retrieval systems without the express written permission of the publisher.

    This work is a novel and any similarity to actual persons or events is purely coincidental.

Dedication

The Tarizon Trilogy is dedicated to my grandchildren, Joshua, Alex, and Isabella.

1
The Battle of Tributon

The PT22 streaked across the treetops of Southern Tributon hoping to avoid radar detection. Aboard the small transport jet was Captain Leek Lanzia on his way to join up with the 3rd Loyalist Army, the new name for the old *mutant army*, which was about to engage the enemy along the Rini River. On Earth Leek Lanzia was known as Peter Turner, and many on Tarizon believed he was the one the Prophecy had predicted would come to save Tarizon from the tyrant, Videl Lai. Nobody knew the source of the Prophecy, but it first surfaced shortly after the unification of Tarizon under the Supreme Mandate by the holy one, Sandee Brahn. The Prophecy forewarned of dark, desperate days for Tarizon and the rise of a ruthless dictator who would enslave anyone who refused to abide his will. Thirteen cycles later a series of super volcanic eruptions enshrouded the planet in dark poisonous gases that killed billions of humans and other life forms and threatened the very existence of life on Tarizon. Fortunately the Prophecy promised an eventual end to the planet's doom.

> *When the sun and the moons align,*
> *amongst the Earthchildren will come*
> *one wise and pure in heart.*
> *A man of humble birth,*
> *who'll tame the savage rhutz,*
> *unite those who'd have liberty*
> *and justice restored to Tarizon,*
> *and rid it of its evil tyrant.*
> *Known as The Liberator,*
> *he'll restore the Supreme Mandate.*

Tarizon: Civil War

*and free from bondage
The mutants, seafolken, and nanomites.*

Even though the enemy outnumbered the Loyalists ten to one and they'd likely be slaughtered in battle, Leek's mind was not on that imminent peril, but on his mate Lucinda who'd recently fallen into the hands of the enemy. Since that tragic event he'd been scarcely able to think of anything else but the urgent need to rescue her and the baby she carried in her womb. He played the words of Videl Lai's closest confidant, Rupra Bruda, over and over in his mind. *"... you'll never see your darling Lucinda again. Videl plans to parade her through the streets to show the citizens of Tarizon how impotent you are. The crowds will spit on her, and then they'll hang her in a public place so everyone will know what happens to traitors! ..."*

He had learned that Lucinda was being held in the capital city of Shisk on the continent of Turvin. He had lived there for a while when he first came to Tarizon and knew it well. To rescue Lucinda in the deepest, most secure part of the enemy's territory would be suicide, yet it had to be done, because, to Leek, death would be preferable to a life without Lucinda and their child.

Joining Leek on the PT22 were Lt. Loonas Levitur from Merria, known by his friends as Red, Lt. Tamurus Lavendar from Serie, who everyone called Tam, and Rhin, a life form known as the rhutz, who had bonded with Leek soon after they first met over a cycle earlier. Their destination was a small town called Gulh where the 3rd Loyalist Army had hastily built a military base.

"So, how do you plan to take command of this army when you know nothing about it?" Red asked cautiously.

"Oh, I'm not really going to command it. I'm sure they have capable officers who can do that. I'm just here to reassure the soldiers that the Prophecy is real and that Sandee is behind them."

"I don't know," Red replied. "While you were off giving speeches at the investiture, I spoke with several mutant officers and, believe me, they have higher expectations of you."

Leek sighed. "Well, they may be in for a disappointment. The only knowledge I have of the mutant army comes from the memories Threebeard gave me during my brief telepathic training."

"Well, that's a start. What do you remember?"

Leek closed his eyes. "The army's been in existence for less than a cycle."

"You're kidding?" Red gasped.

"I know. It gets worse. There were only about ten thousand seasoned soldiers with military training when they began to organize it. Out of necessity these ten thousand were made officers and given the task of training the other 990,000 or so soldiers. Since the TGA didn't allow mutants to be officers, none of them had leadership or advanced training of any sort."

"Wonderful," Red moaned.

"The biggest problem, though, has been outfitting the soldiers. Videl Lai has been monitoring all military supply outlets, so Threebeard had to go to the black market to get uniforms, equipment, weapons, and supplies. As a result, most of what they have to offer is old, outmoded stock."

"What kind of weaponry can you get on the black market?" Red asked.

"Rifles, pistols, power knives, impact grenades, gravel mines, bayonets—occasionally a portable Muscan missile launcher, if you're lucky—that's about it," Leek replied.

"No lasers?"

Leek laughed. "A few—a thousand or so if we're lucky."

Red shook his head. "We're going to get slaughtered."

Tam, who'd been sleeping, sat up and stretched. "You forget that many mutants have gifts and powers that will be more valuable than any laser."

"That's true," Leek said. "They did an excellent job of getting us into the TGA detention compound to rescue Lorin and General Zitor."

"That was an elite group that assisted us," Red noted. "You won't see that kind of talent throughout the mutant army."

"Maybe not," Tam replied, "but we must carefully assess those kind of skills and use them to our advantage."

The pilot's voice came over the intercom. "We've got a couple TGA fighters on our tail. Taking evasive action."

The jet abruptly began to climb, banked sharply starboard, and then dropped into a narrow gorge.

"How much farther, I wonder?" Leek asked evenly, not seeming to notice the plane's violent lurch and downward plunge.

Tarizon: Civil War

Tam looked down at his data pod and said, "Just two or three loons according to my calculations."

"Where'd you get a data pod?" Leek asked.

"Lorin gave it to me before we left. I've got one for you and Red too."

"Good. They will come in handy."

The pilot's voice came over the intercom. "A missile has locked on! Ejecting decoys."

Red peered out the portal and swallowed hard. "Oh, Sandee! Have mercy."

There was a explosion from behind them. The plane accelerated and then rocked wildly. "Hold on," the pilot's voice said. "Prepare for landing."

The three soldiers braced themselves as the small jet hit the runway hard and rolled to an abrupt stop. They were up on their feet quickly as it was apparent the base was under attack. Leek pushed a button, the cabin door retracted, and a disembarkation ramp slid into place. Rhin rushed down it to the ground and began sniffing around. Leek stepped out and gazed over the battle zone.

A small contingent of mutant soldiers rolled up in personal transporters, normally referred to as PTVs, and jumped out. "Captain Lanzia! You must leave immediately. The base is under attack and the enemy is less than a kylod away."

Leek looked out at a panorama of explosions, burning buildings, and heavy smoke billowing into the sky. "Where's Lt. Leode?"

"He's in an emergency meeting with his command staff trying to keep them from taking their men and fleeing to the Doral Mountains."

"Why would they do that? Are they a bunch of cowards?"

"No. It's just that we're not ready. We weren't expecting an attack for thirty days. This has taken us completely by surprise. I'm afraid if we try to engage them, it will be a slaughter."

"What's your name?"

"I'm Sergeant Hawkh."

"Well, Sergeant. I appreciate your concern, but we came here to fight."

"The situation is hopeless. Can't you see that? If you don't leave now you'll be killed and, with you gone, the war will be over."

"I think you overestimate my importance. I'm just but one soldier."

William Manchee

Sergeant Hawkh looked at Leek and then back at the battle scene. "All right. I'll take you to Lt. Leode, but he'll be angry. My orders were to get you back on your plane and out of danger."

"Thank you, Sergeant. I'll tell the lieutenant it wasn't your fault."

Sergeant Hawkh shrugged as Leek, Tam, and Red disembarked. Just as Red stepped onto solid pavement, a low-flying fighter, bearing markings of Tarizon's Global Army, or the TGA, streaked by dropping a string of cluster bombs. About twenty feet off the ground the cluster of twenty bombs shot out in every direction. Fear gripped Leek as a bomb narrowly missed him and his companions. There were explosions all across the runway turning it into a heap of concrete and rubble. Leek turned and looked on in horror as the last bomb headed straight at them.

"Run!" Leek screamed just before the bomb hit the PT22 and it exploded. Red, Tam and most of the soldiers managed to dive into a ditch beside the runway, but one of the mutant soldiers was hit by shrapnel from the exploding plane before he could find cover. The piece of mangled metal severed his spinal cord, killing him instantly.

Sergeant Hawkh ran over to him and felt for a pulse. Leek dusted himself off and staggered over to help out. "He's dead," the sergeant said.

"I'm sorry, Sergeant," Leek replied softly. "Is there anything we can do?"

"No. The medics will be here in a few tiks and they'll take care of him."

Leek nodded and then looked over at the burning PT22. "So much for turning around and going home."

Red suddenly appeared out of the ditch holding a blood soaked handkerchief on his arm. He was sweating profusely and breathing heavily.

Leek rushed over to him. "Are you okay?"

"It's nothing. I'll live. What are we going to do now?"

"Whatever we're ordered to do," Leek responded.

"Sorry about all this," Sgt. Hawkh said. "You're lucky you got here at all with the number of fighters the TGA has in the sky today."

"How long has this attack been going on?" Leek asked.

"The fighters have been softening us up for two days now. Command expects two armored divisions here in a few kyloons and six infantry divisions right behind them."

Leek's stomach turned. He looked at Tam and Red and shook his head. "I sure hope Lt. Leode convinced his men to stay and fight."

Tam and Red didn't respond but just stared out over the vast camp of mutant soldiers readying for battle. There were endless rows of camocubes, transport vehicles, piles of armaments and supplies of every sort. As they were surveying the camp, a PTV pulled up and Sergeant Hawkh motioned for them to get aboard. Rhin jumped in and the others followed. The PTV began to move slowly along the crowded roadway that led through the base for some time until it finally reached a large bunker. Sgt. Hawkh got out and led Leek and his friends inside.

They went down several flights of stairs until they were deep underground. A soldier met them at the bottom and escorted them to the battle room. Lt. Leode was talking excitedly to one of his junior officers when he spotted Leek step inside.

"Captain Lanzia! What are you doing here? I told the sergeant to send you home."

"I'm afraid the TGA has destroyed our PT22 and your runway as well."

He shook his head. "You've come at a bad time. We're about to go into battle. There's no time to deal with you."

"Deal with me?"

"Right. I can't be distracted right now. Sgt. Hawkh will have to look after you until this battle is over."

"Can't we help?"

"There's no time," he replied angrily. "The enemy is pounding at our door."

"Of course," Leek agreed. "We'll stay out of your way."

"Thank you," he said and then rushed off.

Leek scratched his head and looked around. Many of soldiers were staring at Rhin.

One of them asked, "This is your rhutz?"

"Yes," Leek replied. "Meet Rhin."

The soldier raised his eyebrows and backed away.

Leek smiled and looked at Sgt. Hawkh. "I don't think Lt. Leode is happy about our arrival."

"No. I'm afraid not. He's not a believer in the Prophecy, but the soldiers will be glad to hear you have arrived."

"Yeah, a big help we're going to be. All our gear blew up in the plane."

"Don't worry," Sgt Hawkh said. "We'll have you refitted immediately."

"Thank you. It's doesn't sound like we have much time."

"Yes, I'm afraid not."

"So, do we have any chance at all of stopping the TGA's attack?"

Sgt. Hawkh forced a smile."Well, now that you're here the morale of the troops will go up a notch. I'm sure we'll give them a hell of a fight."

Leek glanced over at Red and Tam, then back to Sgt. Hawkh. He wasn't surprised by Lt. Leode's obvious resentment at his arrival on the eve of battle. He knew he'd feel the same way if the circumstances were reversed. He wondered if there really was anything he could do at this late date to change the mutant army's fate. "Can you give me a quick assessment of the situation?" Leek asked.

"Certainly," Sgt. Hawkh said, strolling over to a map of southern Lamaine Shane. He pointed to the southeast border between Tributon and Quori. "We are here near Gulh. Just to our south is the Rini River. It runs from the base of the Doral Mountains some two hundred and fifty kylods to the Coral Sea. About a quarter million troops are positioned along that border. To the north, the Liehn River runs approximately fifty kylods from the Doral Mountains to the Dark Sea. We have about a hundred thousand troops there. Another fifty thousand troops patrol the Doral Mountains. The rest of the army is in Northern Tributon and Southern Rigimol."

"What about the TGA?" Leek asked.

"They have nearly a million soldiers along the Rini River and another half million north of Gallion along the Liehn River. Troop concentrations suggest a three pronged attack in the north across the Lienh into Rigimol, just below the Doral Mountains across the Rini River toward Rizi, and in the southeast across the Rini River toward Gulh."

"What kind of armor do they have?"

"Their standard armored vehicle is the Lutzva Hovertank. It's very fast, equipped with a long range turbo laser blaster, twin Muscan missile launchers, and with its lemdinium shell is nearly indestructible."

"What about air power?" Leek asked.

"The TGA has a squadron of two thousand fighters based in central Quori near Mapi. They have another smaller one near Gallion to the north."

"What do we have?"

Tarizon: Civil War

"Ah, not much, I'm afraid. Just the fighters you and your friends stole from Pogo Island and the ones that made it up here after the battle of Lortec. I'd say a hundred at best."

Leek felt sick but tried not to show it. He forced a smile and asked, "So, what's your command structure?"

"Colonel Shanziba is in charge of the 3rd Loyalist Army. He's touring in the north today. Like I said, we didn't expect the attack to begin so soon. Major Linz is the second in command and is on his way here to meet you."

A wave of despair washed over Leek. He wondered what he would say to Major Linz when he showed up. He'd expect brilliant ideas and insights into how to meet the TGA's imminent attack, but Leek didn't think he had any. He wondered what Tam and Red thought about the situation.

"While we are waiting for Major Linz, is there somewhere we might get a bite to eat?" Leek asked.

"Of course, I apologize for not offering you anything."

"It's no problem. I just think better with a full stomach."

Sgt. Hawkh led Leek, Rhin, Tam and Red to the officers' dining hall where he excused himself to go arrange to get them outfitted. A sober-looking chef gave them the day's standard rations and a cup of luri. Leek stared at the red liquid in his cup.

"What's this?"

"Luri," Red advised. "It's a drink made from the luri berry which is very common in these parts."

"Hmm." Leek said as he cautiously took a drink. He raised his eyebrows. "Not bad. Kinda like our cranberry juice back on Earth."

A loud thunderous clap shook the building. Red and Tam looked up nervously.

"So, you think they're going to run over us?" Red asked.

"Not necessarily," Tam replied. "You keep forgetting the mutant's extraordinary abilities."

"Oh, I doubt being able to read someone's mind is going to stop a hovertank."

"No, but being able to strangle the driver with your thoughts might do it," Tam retorted.

"Sure, but not every mutant can do that. I've only heard of a few with that kind of talent."

"Stop it," Leek said angrily. "I'm sure the command staff will be putting the mutant's talents to good use. We can ask Major Linz about it when we see him."

"Speaking of hovertanks. We need to learn more about them," Tam said. "They must have a weakness. No hardware I've ever seen is perfect."

"We'll ask Sgt. Hawkh about them when he returns," Leek replied.

"What are we going to do when the battle begins?" Red asked.

"Maybe they'll let us borrow some fighters," Tam replied. "We'd be a lot more help in the air than on the ground."

"I don't know what plans Major Linz has for us," Leek said. "I guess we'll just have to wait and see."

When they got back to the battle room, Major Linz was waiting for them. "Captain Lanzia, it's so good to finally meet you. I heard your address at the investiture. It was quite moving."

"Thank you. It was such a shock to have the Chancellor assassinated right in front of our eyes. I'm afraid I went a little bit crazy."

"It was just what was needed to keep the people committed to resisting the TGA and defeating Videl Lai and the Purists." He looked at Rhin and smiled. "And Rhin. How remarkable it was that she sensed the traitor and stopped his attack."

"Yes, she's done that more than once."

"Remarkable!"

"So, Major," Leek asked. "How can we help when the TGA forces get here?"

"You've already helped. Your presence during the battle will give the soldiers great confidence and hope."

"But we want to fight."

"No. No. That would be too dangerous. Sgt. Hawkh has a vehicle with your gear packed up and ready to go. He's going to take you out of the battle area until we can arrange transport out of here."

"We'll do as you order, of course, but we'd be happy to fight. We're all pretty good pilots. We thought we might be of greater value in the sky."

Major Linz shook his head. "No, your death would be a disaster to our war effort. We can't afford for anything to happen to you."

Leek let out a sigh of disappointment. Major Linz shrugged and said, "But we do need pilots, so your comrades would be welcome to take up fighters."

Tam's eyes lit up and Red smiled. Leek gave them an envious look. "Well, can I at least get a briefing on the enemy's armaments and equipment, so I'll know what we are up against?"

Major Linz gave Leek an irritated look then managed a smile. "Of course. Sgt. Hawkh will see to it. But you've got to leave soon in order to ensure your safety."

"I will. Thank you, Major."

"Now your friends will need to go with Lt. Virga to inspect the aircraft they'll be flying and be briefed on our battle plan."

"Sure," Leek said, turning to Tam and Red. "I'll see you two after the battle. Good luck. Give 'em hell for me."

The three embraced as Major Linz motioned to a soldier standing near the door. When he got up close Leek noticed he had four ears, two on each side, and a lumpy spike on his forehead. He glanced at Tam and Red and noticed them stifling smiles.

"Gentlemen, this is Lt. Virga. He'll escort you to the airstrip that's being repaired as we speak."

"Very good, sir," Tam said. Red nodded and they both followed Lt. Virga out of the room.

Major Linz spoke into his communicator and a moment later Sgt. Hawkh approached.

"Take Captain Lanzia to see Sgt. Mohr for an intelligence briefing. Then get him out of here as we previously discussed."

The Sergeant saluted, turned and they left the room. Sgt. Hawkh led them through a maze of corridors until they reached a small waiting room. Inside a tall, lean soldier with very large green eyes stood up.

"This is Sgt. Mohr. He's attached to our intelligence section and can tell you what we know about the enemy's arsenal of weapons. I'm afraid you won't have much time, though. I'll be back at 0600 kyloons and then we'll have to leave."

"Thank you. I'll see you then."

Sgt. Hawkh nodded and left. Sgt. Mohr moved quickly to the door and motioned for Leek to follow. "My office isn't too far from here. Come on. We have a lot to cover before you go."

Leek hustled to catch up. They went to an elevator and went down two levels. Sgt. Mohr said nothing as they left the elevator and turned left down a long corridor. When they were nearly at its end, Sgt. Mohr stopped and peered into a retinal scanner mounted on the wall. There was a beep, a click, and then a sliding door opened and the two soldiers walked into Sgt. Mohr's office.

The office was furnished with a steel desk at one end and a small conference table at the other. Along the far wall were computers and other electronic equipment. Maps and aerial recognizance photos covered most of the exposed walls.

"So, what exactly do you want to know?" Sgt. Mohr asked.

Leek took a deep breath and replied. "Well, I'm particularly interested in the hovertanks, because I understand they are the biggest threat to our army."

"Yes, that's a fair assessment. A hovertank can destroy anything in its path and they're difficult to take out."

"Do you have pictures of them? I don't think I've ever seen one."

"Yes, pictures, schematics, specifications, reports—we've got it all."

Leek poured over the voluminous information as Sgt. Mohr pulled it out and placed it before him.

"So, what makes the hovertank so invincible? These pictures and specifications don't mean much to me."

"Unlike a conventional tank that moves quite slowly on the ground, the hovertank travels above the ground on an air pulse. It doesn't need roads or even a hard surface and travels quite fast."

"A missile will still take it out, won't it?"

"Well, a direct hit would, but the hovertank comes with an array of defensive abilities that make missile destruction difficult."

"Like what?"

"It has a detection device that tells it when a missile has locked on. When that happens the tank can accelerate or change course rapidly. It has an incredible ability to maneuver itself behind cover too. And, as a last resort, it can shoot out decoys to draw the missile away from it. In the few encounters we've had with the hovertank, less than two percent of our missiles have destroyed their targets."

"What about their crew? Doesn't it take many men to run a hovertank?"

"No. The few that we've captured have had but two or three men inside. We suspect one operates the craft, one handles weaponry, and the other keeps in communication with command."

"So, if missiles are not effective, what about disrupting their communications?"

"We've tried that, but they have a very sophisticated communication system that we haven't been able to jam or disrupt."

"What about their air pulse. Can't you break that somehow and make them crash?"

"I don't know. Like I said, we've only had a few encounters with them."

Leek looked at his watch and frowned. "Well, I guess I'm out of time. Now, at least, I have something to think about. Thanks for your help, Sergeant."

"No problem. I hope you come up with something."

They returned to Sgt. Mohr's quarters and found Sgt. Hawkh there waiting anxiously. He shook his head.

"There you are. We must leave, the enemy has penetrated our perimeter."

They rushed outside where a PTV was waiting. It reminded Leek of one of the monster trucks that he watched on TV back in Texas. A driver and one soldier rode in the front seat, Sgt. Hawkh and Peter were in the crew cab, and two more soldiers rode outside on the rear cargo bed.

As they sped away planes screeched overhead, bombs fell around them pelting them with debris, and the smoke was so thick it was all Peter could do to breathe. But soon they reached the opposite perimeter of the camp and were leaving the battlefield behind them. When they reached the top of a nearby hill overlooking the base they stopped and watched the TGA's assault on the loyalist army.

To their horror a line of hovertanks swooped in and decimated everything in their path with bullets, rockets, and streams of fire. They watched as thousands of soldiers were ripped apart by the barrage of bullets, blown up by the rockets, or torched by endless streams of fire. Those few soldiers who were still alive after the hovertanks passed ran for their lives. Nothing the mutants threw at the hovertanks seemed to phase them as they advanced forward with hordes of TGA infantry in their wake. Leek watched in disbelief as the command bunker where he'd met with Major Linz and Sgt. Mohr exploded into a fiery inferno. He wondered if either of them were still alive.

Within an hour the battle was over and TGA was marching

northward without resistence. Leek and his escort pressed on to the northwest toward the Doral Mountains where they'd planned to hide from the TGA. As they pressed on, Leek looked toward the sky wondering what had become of his friends. Had they been able to get airborne before the enemy assault or were they lying dead in a ditch somewhere? He prayed to God they'd somehow survived.

2
Earth Shuttle Rendevous

Tam and Red followed Lt. Virga outside relieved and excited that they'd be able to participate in the battle from the air. Neither officer relished a direct confrontation with the TGA ground forces with their overwhelming superiority. From their T-47 fighters they'd have the weaponry and firepower to seriously hurt the enemy and, if they got in trouble, they had a much better chance of escaping and returning from the battle alive. Not that they were cowards but they were young, having only recently graduated from officer training school on Pogo Island, and still had a lot of living to do.

The T-47 wasn't the most sophisticated fighter on the market. It had been the workhorse of the TGA, however, since it was much cheaper than the more technologically advanced fighters. The T-47 was powered by a combination pulse detonation engine and kerosene fueled ramjet which gave it both atmospheric and limited space flight capabilities. Its skin was made of lemdinium with sirilic leading edges which allowed it to withstand the extremely high temperatures experienced in reentry from outer space. In addition, it had the ability to change its skin color using electrical charges. By emitting light through a series of slits, the aircraft could match the luminosity of the surrounding sky, making it nearly invisible to the naked eye. Its shape and absorption qualities made it impossible to track on radar as well. Since it flew at mach-8 it outpaced its own sound waves and arrived at its target without warning.

The noise level outside the command bunker was worse than when they'd first arrived. Enemy fighters streaked across the sky dropping bombs and firing missiles at will. Tam wondered how any Loyalist fighters could have survived such an aerial assault. Presently, however, Lt. Virga led them down a flight of stairs into an immense underground hangar.

Tam quickly tried to count the aircraft that stood before them, but gave up when he realized he didn't have a high enough vantage point to see them all. Most of the aircraft were fighters but he saw at least one transport plane and a couple of PT22s.

"You have more PT22s," he said to Lt. Virga. "We could have still gotten out of here when ours was destroyed."

Lt. Virga stopped and looked back at him. "True. But the runway was destroyed, remember. Even if we could have sacrificed one of these PT22s we wouldn't have been able to get it off the ground."

"How are we going to get in the air now without an operational runway?" Red asked.

"Ever since you came we've had a construction crew working on a temporary airstrip. As you can see we're about to be overrun, so we have to get all of these aircraft out of here in the next few kyloons. It's lucky you came, actually. We were short a couple of pilots and since we couldn't leave any of these aircraft for the enemy, we'd have had to blow them up."

"Where are our planes?" Tam asked.

Lt. Virga turned and pointed. "Over there. I think you'll recognize them."

Red gasped. "That's the plane I stole from Pogo Island."

"Yes, and Lt. Lavendar's is behind it."

Tam and Red rushed over to their planes and gave them a cursory inspection. "They look like they're in good shape," Tam noted. "Just a few new scratches here and there but otherwise just like we left them."

"When do we go up?" Red asked.

"Soon. Right now we need to go to the battle room for a tactical briefing. It's about to start."

Lt. Virga led them to a corner of the hangar where pilots were streaming into a conference room. Maps and charts covered the walls and three solders sat to the side manning computer terminals. Major Linz and another officer stood in front of the pilots waiting to begin. When the last pilot stepped into the room, he shut the door and the briefing began.

"Ladies and gentlemen. As you know too well, we are under siege and it is unlikely that we will be able to hold our position. It is no secret that

16

the enemy's forces are far superior to what we have been able to muster here in such short order. Just a few moments ago I received a communique from General Bratfort, Commander of the TGA's 4th Army. He has demanded our surrender within one kyloon or he will order the complete annihilation of our forces. He says no prisoners will be taken.

"Obviously, we cannot surrender. To do so at this stage of our struggle for freedom would be a disaster. We must stand our ground and do as much damage to the enemy as possible. Our only hope is to slow them down so that the forces to our north will have time to strengthen themselves before confronted by the enemy.

"Soon you will be ordered to battle. You will be outnumbered in the air at least ten to one, so it is imperative that you avoid direct contact with enemy aircraft. Fly at top speed and in stealth mode. You'll only be attacking hovertanks. We must destroy as many of them as possible if the assault on Tributon is to be stopped. Find your targets, attack them, and then disappear. Don't hang around to see if your target was destroyed. With so many enemy aircraft in the air it won't take but a few tiks for one of them to lock onto you. Get in and out quickly, then disappear. Any questions?"

Major Linz looked around at each of the officers, but nobody said a word. Finally, he raised his fist and yelled, "Then man your planes! The destiny of Tarizon is in your hands!"

The pilots responded with cheers of approval, and as they scrambled out the door, one of them screamed *Seama lo dante*, which in Tari meant *death to the tyrant*. Tam and Red started to follow them when Major Linz called them back.

"I have another assignment for you two," he said.

"What's that, sir?" Tam asked.

"I understand you've been up to the refueling docks that service the shuttle craft coming and going from Earth."

"Yes, sir, we have," Tam replied.

"There's a shuttle that's just arrived from Earth. It's manned by Loyalist forces and needs to be escorted to the surface. Can you two handle that?"

"Well, we were kind of looking forward to knocking out a few hovertanks," Tam replied, a little disappointed, "but whatever needs doing is fine with us."

"Good. It's important this Earth shuttle be protected so it doesn't get into enemy hands."

"You can count on us, sir," Red assured him.

"Your planes are ready and your flight plan has been programmed into your computers. The shuttle is waiting for you before it attempts reentry."

"Yes, sir," Tam replied.

Major Linz returned the salute and then turned away from them. Tam and Red made their way quickly to the door and then ran double time to their planes. The ground crew had the two planes fueled, loaded to the hilt with Muscan missiles, and fully stocked with food and survival gear since it was unknown where they'd be going once their mission was complete.

By this time planes were starting to line up for takeoff. Tam and Red got into theirs and taxied into the long line. The ground rumbled from the bombing that was going on up on the surface above them. Tam wondered how much of a beating the underground hangar could take before it caved in on them. He prayed he and Red would be long gone before that happened. Finally the fighters made it to the tunnel that led to the surface.

Red gave his fighter full throttle and it lurched forward into the tunnel. By the time it reached the tunnel's end it was going three-quarter's speed and immediately lifted into the air. Tam followed right behind and urged his fighter to climb quickly before the enemy could lock a missile onto it. A stream of hot bullets flew by him. He held his breath, praying to God and Sandee that none of the bullets would find its mark. None did and soon he and Red were high above the clouds heading for the edge of space.

"Renegade 3. You read?"

"Loud and clear, Renegade 2."

"You get away clean?" Tam asked.

"Not a nick," Red responded.

"Me either. I'll take point, you watch our back."

"Acknowledged, see you at the pumps."

When they got close to the refueling station Tam checked his radar and saw nothing but Red following him. Without hesitation he pulled up and locked onto one of the big hoses. Red came up a few tiks later and locked onto the hose next to him.

"Be sure she's filled up," Tam said. "It takes a lot of fuel to break out of Tarizon's gravitational pull."

"I'm kind of nervous about this," Red replied. "We've never taken one of these birds into space."

"Don't worry. The computers do all the work. We're just along for the ride."

"I know, but what if they fail and we have to go to manual pilot?"

"Has your computer ever failed you in the past?" Tam asked.

"No, but I've heard of it happening before."

"Just relax, we'll be there in a flash."

The two fighters disengaged from the refueling drone and sped off toward their rendevous with Earth Shuttle 26. They looked back and noticed Tarizon getting smaller and smaller as they plunged upward into the darkness of outer space. Once they'd escaped Tarizon's atmosphere they sped toward the tiny speck on their radar screens which they knew had to be the Earth shuttle.

"Approaching ES 26," Red reported. "Rendevous eleven loons. Attempting radio contact."

"I've got your back, R3."

"ES 26, this is R3, do you read?"

Static came out of the radio for a moment and then abruptly cleared. "ES 26 here."

"R2 and R3 ready to escort you to the surface."

"Did you encounter any traffic coming up?"

"No. Skies were clear."

"Good. Let's take her down."

The ship's powerful rockets came to life and the big shuttle began to move slowly at first, but quickly picked up speed. Tam and Red circled the ship looking in all directions for signs of the enemy. Tam wondered where the shuttle would be landing but didn't dare ask over the radio. He didn't have a secure channel and he knew anybody with a military receiver could be listening to them.

The Earth Shuttle reentered the atmosphere and descended quickly. Tam and Red followed it closely, continuing to keep an eye out for trouble. As the three crafts descended toward the surface of Tarizon, Tam quickly calculated in his mind that they were heading for the coast of Lemaine Shane near the Quon and Rigimol border. As they descended, the shuttle's speed increased to an alarming level. Tam wondered if the pilot had lost control of it.

"R2 calling ES 26. Is everything okay?"

Tarizon: Civil War

There was no response so Tam repeated his question: "R2 calling ES 26. You're going too fast, decrease your speed or you'll crash!"

But there was still no response, so Tam hailed Red, "R2 to R3, do you read?"

"R3 here. What's going on?"

"I don't know. Can you see anything wrong from your angle?"

"No. Not a thing."

"What in the name of Sandee is going on?"

As Tam and Red looked on in helpless horror, the shuttle continued its perilous descent until finally the radio crackled to life. "R2 are you there? R2 are you there?"

"R2 here. What's your situation?"

"We've lost our rear thrusters. Attempting to re-engage."

"Can we help, ES 26?"

"I don't see how."

Tam couldn't believe what was happening. He'd never heard of a shuttle crashing during reentry. What was going on? Then just as the ship was about to crash into the Coral Sea it veered sharply in a northerly direction. Tam swooped down behind it and saw it dump tons of debris into the ocean. Then it went stealth. Suddenly, Tam knew what was happening.

"Oh, God and Sandee. No! No! It's crashed. Oh, my God! . . . R3, did you see that?"

Red didn't immediately respond. He hadn't seen the shuttle crash but he saw the debris in the water.

"R3 did you see that?" Tam repeated.

"Ah. No, but I can see where it hit."

"Do you see any survivors?"

"No. Not a soul. . . . I'll circle around and look again."

"I'll join you but I doubt anybody could have survived a crash like that."

Finally Red caught on. "You're probably right. It sank so fast. I can't believe it."

Tam and Red circled the area where the debris had been dumped, pretending to be searching for survivors. Then their onboard computers received a communique changing their flight plan. They put both fighters on autopilot and relaxed. Soon they were flying over northern Quon and the Doral Mountains. Several loons later a flashing light told them they were near their destination.

As Tam took back control of his fighter he looked below for a landing strip but saw nothing but trees and rugged terrain. He began to worry as it was starting to get dark and he was low on fuel. Finally, coming over a ridge he saw a valley below and noticed landing lights flickering on and off. He switched to a secure channel and hailed Red.

"R2 to R3. Do you read?"

"R3 here."

"I think our destination is below. Does that look like a landing strip to you?"

"Affirmative."

"Then I'll see you on the ground."

Tam broke off and headed for the strip. It was a dirt runway that had obviously been hastily constructed. When the fighter hit the ground the plane shook so violently Tam feared it might break apart, but finally it came to a grinding halt. Red rolled in a few tiks later in a cloud of dust and nearly collided with Tam's fighter.

As they climbed out of their cockpits they noticed a squadron of soldiers had come out to meet them. They were wearing the uniform of the mutant army. Their leader was a seafolken who stood a head taller than Tam and Red. Seafolken were a race of amphibious humans who lived in or near the sea. They had been enslaved and persecuted by Vidal Lai and the Purists and were allies in the Loyalists' cause.

The seafolken introduced himself as Sgt. Ponde. "I have orders to bring you to our commanding officer."

"That's fine, but we'll need to camouflage these fighters first."

The seafolken nodded. "Can we help?"

"Yes," Tam replied. "We could use some help putting on the nets."

Tam and Red pulled out the nets and Sgt. Ponde's men helped cover the planes. When they were done they followed Sgt. Ponde up the side of a hill. When they got to the top and looked down at the valley below they saw Earth Shuttle 26. It was an enormous vessel but it appeared to be partially buried in the ground.

"What happened?" Tam asked. "Did it crash?"

"No. It comes equipped with its own drill that allows it to burrow underground. That's how it was able to keep from being detected while it was on Earth."

"So, why bury itself here?" he asked.

"Ah. You'd better ask Captain Shilling about that. Come on. She's expecting us."

"*She*. Captain Shilling is a woman?"

"Last time I saw her she was."

Tam looked at Red, shrugged and then followed the sergeant down a narrow path that led to the valley below. It wasn't that women weren't the equals of men on Tarizon, but since the great eruptions women were generally barred from anything that interfered with their childbearing. So, it was unusual to find a woman in the military, particularly in a command position.

When Tam and Red got to the shuttle, Sgt. Ponde left them and the guard on duty escorted them to the bridge where the captain was waiting. The captain still wore the uniform of a TGA officer minus the TGA insignia. The Loyalist army was young and uniforms hadn't been a high priority. Tam and Red saluted.

"Gentlemen, be seated."

They took a seat on a bench across from her. She gave them a motherly smile.

"Thank you for escorting us in. I'm sorry we couldn't let you in on our deception. We couldn't risk communicating our plans with you. I thought you'd catch on and you did, quite nicely."

"Yes," Tam said. "I was a bit confused there for a minute, then it suddenly dawned on me that you wanted it to appear the shuttle had crashed."

"Really?" Red said, squinting. "Is that what all that was about?"

The Captain and Tam laughed.

"That's all right, Lieutenant. At least you went along with the charade even if you didn't know what was going on."

Red shrugged.

"So, Captain. Have you heard how the battle turned out? We missed it since we had to escort you in."

The captain's face turned somber. "Well, as we feared we were no match for the TGA Army. They broke through our lines and are half way to Rizi by now. We're going to make another stand there and hope we can stop them."

"Have you heard from Captain Lanzia since the battle? As you may know we went to boot camp together."

"Yes, the Liberator. I've heard you two were close to him. Unfortunately, we haven't heard from his party yet. We're trying to make contact now, but haven't had any success so far."

"What became of all the soldiers encamped at the mutant base we were at?"

"A good many were killed. The ones who survived were ordered up here to the mountains to regroup. That is why we landed the ship here. We are to be the new Loyalist Army headquarters for Quori and Tributon."

"I've never seen a shuttle before. I didn't realize it could bury itself."

"Yes, the shuttles were designed for the Tarizon Repopulation Project on Earth. Since most of the population wasn't aware of the project, the shuttles had to be hidden. It's not easy to hide something this large, so our engineers built the bottom of the shuttle like a drill bit. When a shuttle landed it simply started rotating until it had buried itself. When it was time to leave it simply reversed its spin."

"That must be something to see."

"Well, you're in luck. We're about to commence rotation right now. We don't want the TGA to find our new headquarters."

Suddenly the ship started to move and vibrate slightly. There was a jolt and then the rotation picked up speed. Tam and Red looked around nervously. The Captain smiled. "Don't worry. We do this every time we land. It's quite routine. We scan the terrain before we land to make sure we get a soft spot."

Red looked at the Captain skeptically. Tam leaned forward and asked, "Can we refuel and then go help defend Rizi?"

The Captain nodded. "Yes, that's what I'd like you to do, but first I want you to meet someone."

"Someone on the shuttle?" Tam asked.

"Yes, a returning guide. She's got news she wants you to convey to Captain Lanzia when you see him."

"Why doesn't she tell him in person or tell you?"

"She's being sent up to Rigimol and may not see Captain Lanzia anytime soon. Apparently what she has to say is of a personal nature and she thought it better she talk to someone close to the captain."

Tam nodded. "Okay, where is she?"

"I'll have someone take you to her. She's in the dining compartment right now. I'm sure you two must be hungry. You can eat while you talk. In the meantime, we'll have your fighters refueled and readied for battle. You can leave tomorrow at dawn to join the battle at Rizi."

"Thank you, " Tam said.

"Oh, and one last thing. She's part seafolken. Be careful."

"Be careful?" Red replied. "Why?"

Tam nodded thoughtfully. He'd heard stories about seafolken women and their uncanny ability to seduce unsuspecting human males into unwanted relationships, often to the victim's great peril. It was said that seafolken women once swam in the seas on Earth and were known as *mermaids*. One of the ways these seafolken women were able to seduce men was on account of a small stinger on the tip of their tongues. The stinger's natural function was to paralyze fish so that they wouldn't thrash around in the seafolken's mouth during feeding, but it was also used on males during mating for intense sexual stimulation.

"I will," Tam said.

"Why should we be careful?" Red asked puzzled by the warning.

"I'll tell you later," Tam replied.

After they'd gone Red asked, "What was that all about?"

"You don't know about seafolken women?"

"Ah. . . . Well, I guess not. What about them?"

Tam laughed and then told him. "Wow! We need to find us a couple of them and have a party. Do you think there might be some on board?"

"Maybe, I saw some male seafolken."

"Where there are males there are bound to be females, wouldn't you think?"

Tam was grinning as he hailed the guard who'd escorted them to the captain. He asked him to take them to the dining compartment. A beautiful young lady sat alone eating when they arrived. The first thing that Tam noticed was that she was pregnant. He looked for signs that she was part seafolken but couldn't see any. He and Red walked over to her.

"Hello," Tam said. "I'm Lt. Lavendar and this is Lt. Levitur. But you can call me Tam and we usually call this brute, Red."

The woman smiled and replied, "Oh. You can call me Tehra."

"So, Tehra. The captain told us you had a message for Leek."

"Leek?"

"Ah. Perhaps you know him as Peter."

"Yes, Peter Turner. So, he's changed his name?"

"Yes, he's called Leek Lanzia now. It was the name he used when he was in officer training school at Pogo. It was the name most everyone knew him by, so it stuck."

"Of course," she said, nodding. "What I wanted to have you pass on to, ah, Leek, is that while I was on Earth I met his father. In fact, I spent a good amount of time with him."

"Really? Leek will be so glad to hear that. How is his father?"

"Fine. Now he's fine. He went through some rough times, but when I left him everything was okay. His mother is doing better now as well."

"How was it that you knew Leek's father?"

"Commander Kulchz, the Tarizon officer in charge of the Repopulation Project, assigned me to him as a guide. It was my job to help him adjust to the difficult task that had been assigned to him."

"Really. What task was that?"

"Oh, that's too complicated to get into right now and it's not what's important. The thing Leek needs to know is that his father helped destroy a TGA shuttle and saved, not only my life, but many others as well. He's already a hero to our cause and I'm going to report his heroics to the Loyalist command in Rigimol when I get there."

"Is that so?" Tam laughed. "That's incredible. Leek will be flabbergasted."

"How did he save your life?" Red asked.

"Well, after I'd been taken prisoner by Kulchz and his men, he came to rescue me even though there was no realistic way he could have done it. He risked his life coming to the shuttle and probably would have died trying to rescue me, but fortunately, he ran into some of my Loyalist compatriots. Together they managed to stall the shuttle's takeoff and eventually free everyone held hostage. Once we'd escaped he took us to a place to hide until we could be picked up by a friendly ship."

"Why would he do that?" Tam asked. "Men don't usually risk their lives just for the hell of it."

Tehra nodded. "Yes, you're right about that. I suppose over the few months we worked together we became close. And then there was the baby . . ."

Tam and Red looked at Tehra's large belly then they looked at each other. It appeared she was nearly term. There was an awkward moment of silence and then she took a deep breath and exhaled slowly.

"So, what Leek needs to know," she said proudly, "is that he will soon have a brother living on Tarizon!"

3
Succession

The control panel next to Lorin Boskie's door buzzed. She went over to it and switched on the video. General Zitor's face appeared. She pushed a button and the door lock disengaged. General Zitor quickly entered the compartment. His face confessed great weariness. Lorin locked the door behind him, turned and smiled expectantly.

"So, did you hear anything?"

"The delegates are close to a decision."

"Close? They've been debating who should succeed my father for three days now. In the meantime the enemy is advancing with impunity on every front. They must make a decision now!"

"I know. I've been assured the decision will come very soon."

Lorin took a deep breath and began to pace. "They've got to elect me, General. We've been planning this war for almost two cycles. Everything was coming together just like we'd planned. Videl Lai is such a coward. He knew he couldn't outmaneuver Father, so he sent an assassin. But he forgot about me. I will see to the TGA's demise. I'll avenge my father's death!"

"I know you will."

"If I'm given the chance. What if they don't elect me? What will I do?"

"You'll help whoever is elected. That would be your duty."

"Sure, but they wouldn't listen to me. They'll want to be the architect of their own victory. But it's too late to start all over again. The war will be lost if we don't act now. Every moment of inaction brings the TGA closer to victory."

"They'll make a decision before the sun sets. I've been assured of that."

Tarizon: Civil War

"I hope you're right for the sake of Tarizon."

A beep came out of General Zitor's communicator. He stopped talking and listened intently to the caller. He smiled and said, "You've been summoned to the chairman's office."

"Finally," Lorin said, grabbing her coat and rushing to the door. The knot in her stomach tightened as she feared the delegates would cast her aside and go with a more seasoned politician to be the next chancellor of Tarizon. They rushed outside and walked quickly across the street to the building where the delegates were meeting. After going through a tedious security check they were escorted to a conference room where the chairman and a handful of delegates awaited them.

The delegates stood when she entered. Lorin didn't know what to make of the summons. Had she been elected? The chairman smiled and motioned for her to sit.

"Thank you for coming, Madam Boskie. The delegates have asked the executive committee to ask you a few questions about your plans should you be selected to fill your father's position as chancellor of our new government. To be fair, I'll tell you that the list of candidates has been narrowed to you and Senator Mammett."

"Thank you, Mr. Chairman. That's encouraging."

"Just so you'll know, the full delegation will be listening to what you have to say here today. They will, of course, be listening to Senator Mammett as well."

"What questions do you have, Mr. Chairman? Whoever is chosen must get to work immediately or all may be lost. I understand TGA troops have already pierced our lines in northern Quori."

"Yes. So, let's get right to it. Many of the delegates are concerned that you have no political experience. You've never been elected to public officer nor do you have any military training."

"That may be technically true, but I have devoted my life to assisting my father in his many elected and appointed positions. During that time he has entrusted me with great responsibility which has given me an intimate knowledge of the inner workings of the Senate and the Council of Supreme Interpreters. At every stage of his career I was right there with him, helping him carry out his responsibilities. Therefore I think I have as much or more experience in government as Senator Mammett."

"What about your lack of military experience and training? Senator

Mammett is a veteran and served six cycles in the TGA."

"As you know, my husband Jake Boskie was a Lieutenant in the TGA and has joined the Loyalist cause. He is in Quori today helping to defend our southern perimeter. For the past two cycles Jake, General Zitor, myself and my father have been carefully planning the civil war that is at our doorstep. Senator Mammett was not a participant in these planning sessions and it wasn't because he wasn't invited. We contacted him and many other senators asking them to help us fight Videl Lai and his Purist movement, but most, including Senator Mammett, felt it imprudent to associate themselves with our cause. They feared we'd fail and then they would be subject to Videl Lai's wrath. Do you want a coward as Chancellor?"

One of the delegates stood and yelled, "I beg your pardon, Senator Mammett is not a coward. Mr. Chairman, this is outrageous."

"Sit down. Everyone here knows Senator Mammett and can decide for themselves whether he's a coward or not. Now, Madam, one last question."

"Yes," Lorin replied.

"If you are elected to complete your father's term, what exactly would you do to defeat Videl Lai and the TGA?"

"I'm glad you asked that, Mr. Chairman. As I said, over the past two cycles my father, General Zitor, my husband, myself and many others have been carefully considering every aspect of a military operation against the TGA should Videl Lai be elected Chancellor. We were certain that if he were elected he would try to suspend the Supreme Mandate and strip the legislative and judicial branches of all authority. We also had intelligence reports that he was in the process of seizing control of many of the state governments throughout Tarizon. He in fact accomplished that objective through bribery, intimidation and murder.

"Of course, we would have preferred to keep him from getting elected Chancellor, but he had such powerful friends and allies it would have been suicide to openly confront him. All we could do was get ready for the moment when his true self was unmasked. Then we knew a majority would rally behind us to protect the Supreme Mandate and the rights and freedoms of the inhabitants of Tarizon."

"Yes, I understand that. But, what specifically will you do if you are elected Chancellor?"

"I'm getting to that. One of the responsibilities that was given to me

Tarizon: Civil War

from the outset was to develop an intelligence network throughout Tarizon. This required me to make contacts on every continent, in every state and as many cities and towns as I could. The intelligence network would have two jobs. First, it would provide us information on Videl and the activities of the Purist Party throughout Tarizon. We could also use it to send out information about the Loyalist movement throughout Tarizon. Secondly, the members of the network would begin to create Loyalist cells that would be used to recruit members and soldiers to fight against the TGA.

"As we speak there are over 8,000 cell leaders waiting for instructions. If they don't hear from somebody soon they will assume we've already lost and be forced to abandon our cause and step in line behind Videl Lai. Since I personally set up this organization on behalf of my father, I know the cell leaders and communicate with them regularly, the moment I give instructions they will be followed. If you don't elect me, of course, I would encourage them to cooperate with the new Chancellor, but what I fear is that Senator Mammett would not immediately set this organization in motion. He would want to study it and decide if it would be useful to him. Or, if he did immediately set it in motion, I fear the people would not respond to him as well as they would to me."

"Thank you, Madam Boskie. I think you have answered all of our questions. If you would like to go to the main hall now you can watch the delegates cast their ballots."

Lorin took a deep breath and stood up. "Thank you. May God and Sandee be with all of you in this hour of great peril."

The guards escorted Lorin and General Zitor to the main hall where 350 delegates waited to cast their votes. Lorin felt relieved that it was out of her hands now. For a few moments she could relax and do nothing. She sat in the gallery and watched the delegates milling around. Many friends and supporters stopped by to offer her encouragement and wish her good luck. She thanked them appreciatively. Finally the chairman took the podium.

"Fellow delegates. It is time to consider the matter of electing a new chancellor to fill the vacancy caused by the assassination of Robert Garcia. Please cast your votes."

Lights suddenly flashed on a large screen to the right of the podium. The two names, Senator Zenor Mammett and Lorin Garcia Boskie, suddenly appeared. Numbers started flashing beside each name. Mammett 23, Boskie 14. The delegates broke out in conversation. There were screams of delight and despair as the numbers changed. Mammett 39, Boskie 37. Lorin looked at General Zitor and began to tremble.

"It will be all right," General Zitor assured her.

"Ah! No!" someone screamed as the tally went to Mammett 72, Boskie 67.

Lorin put her hands over her eyes. She couldn't bear this. What would she do if she lost? It couldn't happen. She couldn't bear it. The number changed again. Mammett 139, Boskie 141. Lorin's heart soared. General Zitor put his hand on her shoulder and squeezed it gently. She smiled up at him. "How many votes left?"

"280 voted, 70 to go," General Zitor replied.

"Oh, God. Please. Just 36 more votes."

Once more the tally changed. Mammette169, Boskie 171.

"Only ten more votes. You're almost there," General Zitor assured her.

The board was quiet for a moment. Everyone looked around to see who hadn't voted. The chairman stepped up to the podium. "Last call for votes. If you want to vote you must do it in the next 100 tiks."

The number 100 appeared on the top of the vote tally. It began counting down 99, 98, 97. The tally changed again: Mammett 171 Boskie 172.

There were screams of anxiety from delegates all around as the countdown continued—67, 66, 65. The tally blinked again. Lorin stared at the numbers: Mammett 172, Boskie 172. Her heart sank. General Zitor stood and exclaimed, "For the sake of Tarizon you must elect Lorin Boskie!"

The chairman frowned at General Zitor, but said nothing as the countdown continued—37, 36, 35. There was a flicker and Lorin looked up anxiously at the tally. Mammett 173, Boskie 173—21, 19, 18. Lorin closed her eyes. She couldn't stand it—11, 10, 9. The general shook her. "Wait. It's going to be okay!" Finally, there was one last blink as time ran out. Mammett 176, Boskie 174.

Lorin collapsed in her chair, tears flowing from her eyes. There were screams and jubilation from the Mammett supporters. General Zitor just stood there in shock. A delegate muscled his way through the crowd and sat in the seat next to Lorin.

"I'm sorry, Lorin. I did everything I could to convince the delegates to vote for you."

Lorin looked up. It was one of her father's friends, Senator Marcuzzi. She sighed. "I know you did, Senator, and I'm very grateful."

"I know Senator Mammett very well and I fear he will be no match for Videl Lai."

"I hope you're wrong," General Zitor said. "We have too much at stake to let him win."

Lorin got up. "If you'll excuse me, I'm not feeling well. I'm going back to my compartment. If Senator . . . I mean . . . Chancellor Mammett wants me he can reach me there."

"What are you going to do now?" Senator Marcuzzi asked. "Do you have any plans?"

"Yes, I have a funeral to plan. It had to be put off due to the urgency in selecting a new chancellor, but now it must be done. I hope I will see you there."

"Of course," Senator Marcuzzi replied.

A guard escorted Lorin back to her compartment as General Zitor and Senator Marcuzzi continued to talk.

"We must convince our new Chancellor to act quickly. What Lorin said about the urgency of the situation is true. Any delay will be disastrous."

"Yes, I agree. Let's go see if we can get an audience with him."

The two men attempted to approach the new Chancellor but he was surrounded by guards and well-wishers. They waited for an opportune moment to get his attention but were thwarted at every attempt. Finally, the new Chancellor was taken away to the Chancellor's quarters. When they asked one of the guards if they could speak to him they were brushed off and told to contact his appointments secretary the next day. They both retired to their compartments bitterly disappointed and fearing the worst.

The next day General Zitor attempted again to contact Chancellor Mammett but was told the Chancellor was in conference, so he went to see how Lorin was doing. She was glad to see him, as she wanted to thank him for all he had done for her.

"I didn't do it for you, necessarily. I did it for your father and because it was the right thing for Tarizon. You should be leading this war, not Mammett!"

"Yeah, well. We just have to hope he'll be up to it. I just wish he'd contact me. I need to tell our cell leaders something."

Just as she spoke those words her communicator chimed. She

picked it up and said, "Boskie here."

A few tiks later she put it away and looked at the general.

"We've been summoned to the war room."

General Zitor raised his eyebrows. "Well, it's about time."

Moments later they were strolling into the hastily constructed war room. Most of the Loyalist command were assembled to brief the new Chancellor on the situation and give him their recommendations. A huge map of Tarizon was mounted on one wall and a large VC monitor on another. General Lugwin stepped to the head of the table.

"Ladies and Gentlemen, I'd like to introduce Chancellor Zenor Mammett."

The officers stood and began to clap. The new Chancellor shook everyone's hand, smiling proudly as he worked the room. When he got to Lorin he took both her hands in his and said, "That was a great interview you had with the executive committee. You almost had me convinced to withdraw my candidacy."

Lorin smiled wryly. "Well, it's not too late."

Everyone within earshot who heard the exchange laughed heartily, but the Chancellor remained focused. He moved quickly through the line of well-wishers until he came to his chair. After he'd taken his seat, he motioned for everyone to sit down. "Thank you, but we don't have time for personal tributes. I need to know what's going on. I've heard many conflicting reports and I must know what the facts really are."

A tall, grey-haired general rose. "I'm General Rosz. If I may, I'd be happy to bring you up to date."

The Chancellor nodded and then whispered something to his aide. General Rosz signaled to an assistant and the lights dimmed. A map of Tarizon appeared on the big screen. Lortec was highlighted. "TGA forces from Ock Mezan have initiated a heavy assault on Lortec. They seem bent on retaking the island. So far, we have repelled them but if they keep up the assault they will likely be successful."

The Chancellor nodded grimly. "I see. Do we have reinforcements that we can send there?"

"Not really, sir. Our main army is in southern Rigimol and the mutant army is facing the enemy in northern Quon."

"I see."

"As you know, our base in the Beet Islands was destroyed after we took Lortec. A freak clearing of the atmosphere allowed the TGA to pinpoint our position. We were lucky to get our forces off the island before it was obliterated by enemy missiles."

"Pogo and Muhl, of course, remain in TGA hands and the enemy continues to use these two islands to train their troops."

"General," Lorin said. "Leek Lanzia was able to enlist the support of the seafolken on Lortec. Are they being utilized in any capacity in the defense of the island?"

"Not to my knowledge. I'm afraid only Captain Lanzia knows how to summon them."

"Then we must contact him and ask him to summon them again. We can't afford to lose our foothold in the Coral Sea. As long as we are there the TGA will have to watch their back as they try to move north into Tributon."

"Does anyone know how many seafolken there are?" the Chancellor asked.

"It's difficult to know exactly since they live in the sea. There's never been a census, but I know for sure there are millions worldwide," Lorin replied.

"Well, why don't we mobilize them? I've heard they are great warriors."

"The problem," Lorin replied, "is that they don't live in cities and towns. They are free and independent and always keep moving, particularly now since Videl Lai has ordered them to surrender for military service or be shot."

The Chancellor shifted in his chair nervously. "Well then, how was Captain Lanzia able to summon them?"

"I don't know exactly, but Threebeard taught him how to do it. Some kind of mental telepathy, I believe. Even then only a few with the gift can communicate with them."

"Where is Captain Lanzia now?"

"He's with the mutant army," Lorin replied.

"Yes," General Rosz interjected. "The mutant army's morale was bad, so we thought if the Liberator was sent there it might help in the upcoming battle."

There was snicker from several of the officers and Chancellor Mammett smiled. "You mean, that was a good excuse to get him out of your hair."

"Well. Yes, that too."

More soldiers laughed and Lorin scowled at them.

"Although we acknowledge Captain Lanzia for his skill in the air and courage on the battlefield, he is still but a novice in the art of war. I seriously doubt he'd have a prayer against Videl Lai if he were in command."

"You know, General," Lorin said. "I used to feel the same way about Captain Lanzia. How could this boy from Earth be the fulfillment of the Prophecy? But at every turn he has astounded me by his ability to adapt and learn just enough to be successful. If you want my opinion, Liberator or not, he will be a key factor in this war."

"Your opinion is so noted," the General replied. "But so far Captain Lanzia's presence has done little for the mutant army. The reports we've been getting indicate the mutant army is getting slaughtered. The TGA has broken through at three critical points along the Rini River and there's nothing between them and the capital city of Rizi."

"Well, you can hardly blame that on Captain Lanzia. We all know the mutant army is inexperienced, poorly equipped and lacking in seasoned leadership. We knew they'd be no match for the veteran TGA forces. Besides, Captain Lanzia's only been with the mutant army two days."

"True enough. I guess we were hoping to be astounded."

Chancellor Mammett and many of the other officers laughed again. Lorin shook her head and looked away. She had grown fond of Captain Lanzia and hated to see him ridiculed. If only her father were here, she thought. He'd not put up with this outrage.

"Anyway," General Rosz continued. " The mutant army will make another stand at Rizi in a few days, but unfortunately there is no reason to believe they will be any more successful there than they were on the Rini River. We just hope they can at least slow down the TGA to give our regular army time to prepare for an assault on Rigimol. For if Tributon falls Rigimol will be next!"

The door to the war room opened and a messenger rushed in. He handed a letter to General Rosz. The general opened it, read it and then passed it to the Chancellor.

"What is it?" Lorin asked.

"It seems that Videl Lai has ordered the genocide of all Nanomite swarms. He says it's a preemptive strike to prevent them from joining in the

Loyalist movement. Apparently the operation has begun and is expected to take only thirty days."

"Oh, God and Sandee, no. What are you going to do?"

The Chancellor shrugged. "I don't know. Are we to send troops to every Nanomite swarm? That would be an extraordinary commitment. I don't—"

"You must protect them. They have been invaluable already to the war effort. We've got to protect them."

"Yes, of course we will," the Chancellor said evenly. "General, look into this and give me your recommendations by midday tomorrow."

"Yes, sir."

Lorin was stunned by the Chancellor's apparent indifference to the imminent genocide of the nanomites. She looked at General Zitor. He rolled his eyes. Lorin folded her arms and glared at the new Chancellor. Finally, he said irritably, "So, what would you have me do?"

"If you can't afford the troops to protect them, then you should move the swarms and keep them hidden. That way they will survive and when we need their help we'll be able to find them."

"Fine. General Rosz. Consider Mrs. Boskie's comments when you report to me tomorrow on the Nanomite matter."

Lorin gave the Chancellor a cold stare. He turned to General Rosz and said, "What about the Loyalist cells that apparently are waiting our orders?"

"Well, I think that's going to take some study. I'm not sure exactly what to do with them at this moment. We've got to concentrate on defending Rigimol."

Lorin stood up angrily. "Well then, you won't need me any more today. May I leave to plan my father's funeral?"

The Chancellor stood up. "Yes, of course. Thank you for all your help. We'll be in touch."

Lorin bowed slightly and made her exit. She rushed across the street and ran up the stairs to her compartment. Once inside she went to her GC and punched in a code.

"R1, come in! R1, come in."

There was a momentary pause and then Leek's voice came through. "R1 here."

"R1, this is base."

"So, am I talking to the new Chancellor?" Leek asked expectantly.

"No, I'm afraid not," Lorin replied somberly.

"Oh, no. What happened? I thought you'd be a shoo-in."

"The senator's a better politician, I'm afraid."

"I'm sorry. You'd have made a great Chancellor."

"Listen. We just heard that Videl has launched an all-out attack on the nanomites."

"What?"

"He means to exterminate every last one of them. You've got to warn them. I don't know if they can do anything to protect themselves, but you've got to give them a chance."

"Well, I'm in a bad spot right now. We're running from the TGA. They've broken through our lines and our troops are in retreat."

"Oh, Leek! Don't let them catch you. Can you get away and hide somewhere?"

"We're trying to make it to the Doral Mountains. There are vast forests there where we can quickly get lost."

"What can I do to help the nanomites?"

"I don't know. When we stop for the night, I'll sneak away and try to make contact with them. I'll tell them you're ready to help in any way you can."

"Leek. This new Chancellor is a joke. He has sent you to Tributon just to get you out of the way. He doesn't believe in the Prophecy."

"Hmm. Well, you didn't either."

"I know, but I know better now."

"Well, that explains why they whisked me away just as soon as I got here. At least they could have given me a plane like they did Tam and Red."

"They're fighting?"

"Yes."

"Jake's down there somewhere too," Lorin groaned.

"Really. I'll keep an eye out for him."

"Thanks. Please contact the nanomites as soon as possible and warn them. We can't let Videl Lai carry out this genocide."

"I will. Don't worry. I'll get through to them."

"Thank you."

The sound of an exploding bomb came over the GC. "Oh, jeez. I've got to go. There's a hovertank coming at us. I'll talk to you tomorrow."

Tarizon: Civil War

The GC went quiet and Lorin took a deep breath. She was worried sick about Leek and Jake. And now she had to add the nanomites to her list. At least she'd done something to try to prevent their genocide. She wished she had telepathic powers like Threebeard and Leek. Then she could summon them herself, warn them of the imminent attack and offer her help. But now all she could do was hope and pray that Leek would somehow escape the TGA pursuit and be able to contact them. But even that might not be enough. Even if the nanomites were warned they still had to figure out a way to defend themselves against the full wrath of the TGA army.

4
Genocide

Lorin's news shocked Leek. He couldn't imagine an intelligent and creative life form like the nanomites being exterminated like common house flies. He recalled the magnificent Hall of the Interpreters in Shisk where he worked for Councilor Garcia when he first came to Tarizon. It was an incredible architectural masterpiece built entirely by the nanomites. He recalled his first dramatic encounter with them. To demonstrate their substantial talents and abilities they cut his lights and sealed off his room like a tomb. He thought he was going to die. When the lights finally came back on there was a message on the wall assuring him that he *was* the Liberator and letting him know the nanomites were counting on him to fulfill the Prophecy. Since then Threebeard had taught him how to communicate with them telepathically and he'd had several fine conversations with Allo, one of their swarmmasters.

The big transport vehicle lurched to one side, sending Leek hard against the door. Rhin flew off the seat onto the floor where she scrambled to get her footing. Leek struggled back into an upright position only to be jolted the other way into Sergeant Hawkh. Bombs were falling all around them and a hovertank had a beat on them.

"It's got a lock on us! Abandon ship," the driver said slamming on the brakes. Leek opened the door and he and Rhin jumped out just a few tiks before it exploded into a million pieces. Leek hit the ground and rolled into a clump of tall grass. Rhin scampered in after him. *Lie down, girl. Don't make a move.* They sat there for a moment taking advantage of the cover. Leek knew if they were spotted by the hovertank's gunner they'd be killed. Hovertanks killed everything in their path without exception. He peered out of the grass and saw the hovertank's machine gun mow down their mutant driver and two soldiers. Leek rolled back on his back and didn't move. *Stay down.* While he was lying there he noticed Sgt. Hawkh between him and the fiery inferno that used to be a transporter. He wasn't moving. Leek wondered if he was alive.

The hovertank finally moved on but Leek knew the infantry would be close behind, so they didn't have time to lose. He crawled over to Sgt. Hawkh and shook his shoulder. "Sergeant! Sergeant! You okay?"

Sgt. Hawkh stirred. Leek rolled him over and was glad to see his eyes open. "You okay?" he repeated.

Sgt. Hawkh sat up and dusted himself off. "Yeah, I'm okay. Just a few bruises. That was close."

"We've got to get out of here. The infantry will be here soon."

Sgt. Hawkh glanced behind them nervously. There was a cloud of dust on the horizon and the sound of vehicles approaching. "But where?" he asked.

Leek looked east and saw nothing but grassy plains. To the west he saw the snow-capped Doral Mountains. "Our only hope is to get up into the mountains out of the way of the advancing troops. We're sitting dirkbirds out here."

Sgt. Hawkh nodded and scrambled to his feet. Rhin sniffed the ground and then took off to the west. They followed after her and had to go double-time to keep up. The mountains were several miles away and they knew they were in a life or death race to get there before the TGA came through. The advancing troops were in a wide horizontal formation leaving nowhere to hide while they passed by. The only escape was to reach the mountains before the TGA troops got there.

Halfway to the mountains it became apparent to Leek that they weren't going to make it. The far eastern flank of the line of advancing troops was moving faster than the rest. Before they'd be able to get to the mountains they'd be spotted and quickly killed or captured. *Over here! Follow me!*

Rhin often interjected her thoughts into Leek's mind. He'd gotten used to it. He looked ahead at Rhin and saw her dart down a ditch and disappear.

"Follow me!" Leek yelled to Sgt. Hawkh as he started running as fast as he could toward where Rhin had disappeared. The sergeant followed, wondering if Leek had gone out of his mind. Then as he watched Leek dart left and right, Leek disappeared. When he got to where Leek had vanished he saw why. There was an above-ground pipeline that ran across the valley. Sgt. Hawkh stopped and searched for any sign of Leek and Rhin. Finally, Rhin came running out of a drainage hole that went below the pipeline. He quickly ran to it and went inside.

"Come back in here. I don't think the TGA soldiers will come searching down here," Leek said. "We can hide a few hours until they've passed."

"I don't know. If they're good soldiers they'll be all over this place," Sgt. Hawkh cautioned.

"Maybe, maybe not. I think they'll be tired and anxious to get on to their destination. There's no reason to suspect anybody would be down here."

"Well, I don't know that we have any better options. If we go on toward the mountains they're going to spot us. At least down here I can get a little shut-eye while we wait for them."

"Yes, something tells me it's going to be a long time before we get a good night's sleep again."

Sgt. Hawkh, Leek and Rhin retreated deep into the drainage pipe and settled in to wait for the TGA forces. Sgt. Hawkh fell almost immediately to sleep. Leek was too wound up to sleep. He was worrying about the nanomites and how he was going to contact them. He wondered if he could contact them from a distance or if had to be close to them to make contact. The one time he had communicated with them he was in close proximity, but he knew the swarmmasters communicated over long distances. He decided to give it a try.

He closed his eyes and thought of Allo. He knew he had to purge himself of all other thoughts to make contact. Unfortunately that wasn't easy to do since he was still sick over Lucinda's capture, upset that he was being excluded by Loyalist Command from any meaningful role in the war, and had a hundred thousand TGA troops breathing down his neck. Just when he thought he'd purged his mind of all those thoughts, he thought of Lorin's defeat in the vote to replace her father as Chancellor. He wondered how the delegates could fail to realize that Lorin was the only person who could lead the Loyalists to victory.

There were noises above them—vehicles, soldiers marching, and an occasional burst of gunfire. He wondered if the TGA front line was passing overhead. He didn't dare go up and look. He'd just have to wait and hope they wouldn't search their temporary hideout. Then there were voices. Rhin jumped to her feet and disappeared into the darkness. Her thoughts flashed through his mind. *Stay here. I will keep them away.*

Leek readied his weapon and then waked Sgt. Hawkh. "There's someone coming down here. Rhin's checking it out."

"Huh?"

"She's telepathic. We communicate without words."

"Right. I heard that. Is it the TGA?"

"It must be. Who else would be coming down here?"

In the distance they heard Rhin growling. "Should we go help her?"

"She said to wait here," Leek replied. "She'll tell us if she needs help."

There was more growling and then gunfire. *I'm leading them away. Go to the mountains. I'll catch up with you there.*

"Come on," Leek said. "She's distracting them so we can get away."

Sgt. Hawkh looked skeptical but didn't argue. He grabbed his gear and followed Leek outside. To the north they could see the front line of the TGA pushing onward. To the east they saw several soldiers chasing Rhin. She was a good distance ahead of them and moving at an incredible pace. Leek wasn't worried about them catching her. He figured the soldiers would soon give up the chase, so they'd better get away while they had the chance.

As darkness fell they reached the mountains and followed a stream a few kylods before setting up camp. Exhausted, they rested awhile and then Leek made a fire while Sgt. Hawkh managed to kill a rabbit for dinner.

After dinner, Leek peered out into the darkness nervously. "I hope Rhin is all right," he said.

"It didn't look like she was in any danger from those TGA soldiers who were chasing her," Sgt. Hawkh replied.

"No, but Videl Lai has ordered the death of all rhutz. They may have called for help. I hope she shows up soon. She saved my life once."

"She did?"

"Yes, when I first came to Tarizon. My guide and I were stranded in a bad part of Shisk. While we were waiting for Central Authority to send someone to pick us up, we ran into a street gang that had ugly plans for us. I thought Lucinda and I were done for until Rhin showed up and took a bite out of one of their thighs. The rest of them scattered in a hurry."

"Wow! I can see why you're so close to her," Sgt. Hawkh said. "It still seems strange, though, to see a man with a rhutz. I know they say Sandee walked with the rhutz, but I always thought that was a myth."

"No. I don't think so. A rhutz once saved Sandee Brahn's life too."

"Hmm."

Leek suddenly remembered he had to somehow make contact with the nanomites. "Listen. You don't happen to know where the nearest nanomite swarm is, do you?"

"Nanomite swarm?"

"Yes."

Leek explained to him about the ordered genocide of the nanomites and his need to warn them. "I tried to contact them earlier but it didn't work. I think I need to be close by a swarmmaster to have any luck."

"Well, there is one near Rhule. It's at the foot of the Doral Mountains about twenty kylods from here. It was the main source of nanomite swarms for construction in the capital city of Rizi."

"Good. Just as soon as Rhin returns, I must go there and try to warn them."

"That could be dangerous. There'll be TGA patrols in the area."

"We'll stay in the cover of the mountains as long as we can and then sneak down to the farm while it's dark. Hopefully no one will see us."

"Okay. That might work. Why don't you get some sleep? You'll need your strength tomorrow if you're going to be able to communicate with them."

"You sure? I could take the first watch."

"No," Sgt. Hawkh replied. "I can sleep later. You've got to have a clear head tomorrow."

"Thanks," Leek said. "Wake me when Rhin returns." Then I'll take the watch and you can sleep."

Sgt. Hawkh nodded as Leek lay back and put his head on his backpack. He was asleep almost immediately and began to dream. He was in Rhin's head and could hear her growling.

This isn't going to work. If I confront them they'll shoot me. If I retreat they'll discover Leek and Sgt. Hawkh and either kill them or take them as prisoners. There's only one thing I can do. I must lure them away so the Liberator can escape to lead our armies against Videl Lai.

Rhin lunged forward and before the two soldiers knew what had happened she had bolted past them, traversed the length of the drainage pipe, and was sprinting across the prairie.

"Was that a rhutz?" the first soldier said.

"I think so," the second soldier replied.

"Come on. We can't let it get away. We've got orders to kill any rhutz we come across."

"But it's so fast. How are we going to catch it?"

"Call in some air support. We'll get a copter to cut it off and drive it back toward us."

"Understood. Will do," the second soldier said, grabbing his GC. He barked in his request and then the two soldiers began jogging after Rhin. Several loons later two copters could be seen approaching in the distance. Rhin stopped and perked up her ears.

What is this? They called in air support for a lone rhutz roaming the prairie? Videl Lai is such a coward and a fool. He should know the rhutz are a peaceful species. We have never been a threat to humans nor did politics interest us in the least. It is only when we are left no choice do we take sides in a conflict.

Many cycles earlier, when the world was in conflict and found itself on the brink of self-destruction, the great Sandee Brahn took up the cause of unification and the institution of a world government under the Supreme Mandate. Since all would have been lost had Sandee Brahn failed, the rhutz stood beside him and helped him restore stability to Tarizon.

After unification, the rhutz retreated once again into the background, not caring to have any sort of relationship with the human race. The rhutz only sought to be left alone to live in peace. Twenty cycles later the great eruptions came and as a matter of survival of the planet the rhutz joined with Central Authority to respond to the global crisis that threatened the very existence of life on Tarizon.

Forty cycles after the great eruptions, the rhutz was again forced into an alliance with humans. The Purists, who had recently seized power under Videl Lai, ordered the genocide of the rhutz as they did for every other life form on Tarizon that refused to be subjected to slavery. They preferred not to be involved in the conflict as it was against their nature, but the survival of their species was at stake, leaving them no choice.

Videl Lai is a fool to force us to be his enemy. Does he not realize that every rhutz is connected to every other rhutz on Tarizon and will act collectively to protect one another? This was because each rhutz had two levels of consciousness.

They had an individual consciousness in which they lived their daily lives independent of each other. But above that primary consciousness there was also a collective consciousness that was common with every other living rhutz on Tarizon. The collective consciousness was rarely invoked but when it was, it interrupted the rhutz' primary consciousness and put him in direct communication with every other rhutz on Tarizon.

This was how he'd been recruited to befriend the Liberator. When Threebeard told him that the Liberator had arrived on Tarizon all rhutzs knew through their collective consciousness that he must be found and protected. *Since I came across him first, it was my duty to befriend him and become his protector.*

And now through the collective consciousness I will summon help from my pack to thwart the pitiful attempt of Videl's lackeys to destroy me.

The two soldiers stopped to watch the copters swoop down to finish off the rhutz. Suddenly one of the copters veered to the left. The two soldiers squinted to see why it had done that. To their dismay they saw another rhutz running away from it. Their attention was then drawn back to the other copter as it had veered off in yet another direction. The two soldiers suddenly realized there were three rhutz now running away from each other. The confused copter pilots took off after their new targets only to see more rhutz appear darting in and out of the tall grass, and running in all different directions.

As the two soldiers stood watching in dismay they heard a menacing growl from behind. When they whirled around two rhutz were on them before they could position their weapons for a shot. Their teeth sunk into the soft tissue of the soldiers' necks, severing arteries and spraying blood in every direction. They clamped down on their throats with a vise grip that made it impossible for the soldiers to breathe. Within a few tiks they were dead. When the rhutz looked up they saw in the distance the copters spinning out of control.

Rhin looked on with satisfaction as the two copters continued to spin until they finally hit the ground and exploded. *You have taken us for granted, Videl. You assumed we were a helpless life form, but you should have studied us more before you made us your enemy.*

Rhin thanked his fellow rhutz who had come to her aid and then bounded off to find the Liberator. She had been forced to leave his side to protect him, but she was anxious to find him to make sure he was okay.

When she got to the drainage pipe she picked up their scent and began to follow it. It was nearly dawn when she found Leek and Sgt. Hawkh sleeping next to a fire that had long since died. Leek woke up, sensing Rhin's return.

"You're back," Leek said, rubbing Rhin's head affectionately. "You had quite an adventure, girl."

Sgt. Hawkh opened his eyes and then sat up abruptly. "Oh, Sandee Brahn! I must have dozed off."

Leek laughed. "It's okay. Nobody knows we're here. It's good we both got a good night's sleep. We've got a big day ahead."

"Thank you, but falling asleep on watch is inexcusable. I don't know what happened to me."

"It's all right. Make us some breakfast and I'll forgive you."

After breakfast they set out for the nanomite farm. It was slow going across the rugged mountain terrain and through dense forests without a road to follow. Although it was only 20 kylods away, it was late in the afternoon before they saw the farm in the valley below. It looked more like a dry lake than a farm. There wasn't a speck of green or any other color for that matter in the whole place. Up closer they saw many white mounds which they assumed were individual swarms. The only sign of a human presence was a huge garage with several large trucks parked around it. Leek assumed they were used to transport the nanomite swarms to construction sites. There was no sign of the TGA anywhere.

"You should wait up here, sergeant," Leek said. "I'll go down and try to make contact. Rhin can watch my back and you can keep an eye out for the TGA from up here where you can see for many kylods in all directions."

"Okay," Sgt. Hawkh said, pulling off his backpack. "I could use the rest."

"Don't fall asleep."

"No. Don't worry and good luck down there. I hope you can make contact."

"Thanks. We'll give it our best shot," Leek replied as he took off down the mountain with Rhin at his side. As they walked, Leek wondered how he was going to get through to the nanomites. He didn't know their swarmmaster's name, so it would make it difficult to channel his mind to one single nanomite. When they reached the perimeter of the farm Leek looked around for any sign of a headquarters or primary mound that might be larger than the others, but each one looked exactly the same.

As he was pondering the situation, Rhin began walking toward the center of the farm. Not knowing what else to do, Leek followed her. Directly in the center of all the mounds was a smooth area of crystal, diamond shaped and glistening in the morning light. Rhin stopped in the middle of it and lay down. Leek looked at her and said, "Okay, I guess this is a good a place as any."

Leek sat next to her and crossed his legs. He took a deep breath, closed his eyes and slowly exhaled. The key to telepathic contact, Threebeard had told him, was to channel all of his thoughts toward the one who he wanted to contact. Since it was impossible to see a nanomite he had to imagine what one would look like. In his mind's eye he painted a white ant and focused on it.

Great swarmmaster of the nanomites, I come with a message of great urgency. Videl Lai has ordered the extermination of all nanomites on Tarizon. TGA soldiers are probably making plans now to implement this edict. You must evacuate all of your farms immediately and hide from the TGA until the Loyalist forces can destroy Videl Lai and restore law under the Supreme Mandate.

Not feeling any response, he repeated his message in his thoughts. After doing this several times he opened his eyes and looked at Rhin.

"I don't think I'm getting through."

Keep trying," Rhin urged telepathically.

Leek closed his eyes and concentrated even harder on the little white ant he'd conjured up in his mind. Midway through his message the little white nanomite came alive.

"We are honored by your visit to Nanomite Farm 2279, Peter Turner, Liberator of Tarizon. Your warning is most appreciated. We will convey it to our brothers and sisters throughout Tarizon."

"Do you have a name?"

"Not like humans. You can call me Master 2279 or Thine, if you prefer a more intimate name."

"Okay, Thine. You can't delay this evacuation. I'm sure the TGA attacks will start very soon."

"Unfortunately, as you probably know nanomites can only live in a controlled environment. This will make it difficult for us to evacuate our farms."

"I know. We figured as much. Lorin Boskie is waiting to assist you

Tarizon: Civil War

in any way she can. She has a network of Loyalist supporters all over Tarizon. They will be mobilized immediately to assist you as needed."

"Thank you. We'll need drivers to load our swarms on the transport trucks and take them to safe locations."

"I'm sure that can be arranged. In the meantime we saw a garage and motor pool complex on the outskirts of the farms. I've got Sgt. Hawkh with me. Perhaps we should start moving your mounds right now, if you know of a safe place we could take them."

"Yes, take us to the Cathedral of St. Robbith in Rhule. We built this cathedral several cycles ago and it would make an excellent place to hide. If we're discovered there we could ask the church for political asylum."

"Excellent! It will be done. Get your swarms ready for transport."

"Yes, Peter Turner, Liberator of the nanomites, seafolken and mutants of Tarizon. No preparations are necessary. We have been awaiting your commands."

"You have?"

"Yes. You must tell us how to help you defeat Videl Lai."

"Ah. Okay. I will. Just as soon as I get you to a safe place."

Leek stood up and immediately got on his GC. He first contacted Sgt. Hawkh to see if there was any sign of the TGA. The sergeant said there wasn't, so Leek told him to come down the mountain immediately to help move the nanomite swarms. Then he called Lorin.

"Good news. I've gotten through to them."

"Oh, I'm so glad. Do they need our help?"

Leek relayed his conversation with the nanomites and told her to alert her cells to be ready to move.

"I've got a list of all of the farms. I'll have them start lining up drivers right away. You'll need to find out the transport locations so I can pass them on."

"Right. We're going to start moving Farm 2279 now. I'll call you back just as soon as I'm given the information."

When Sgt. Hawkh arrived, they went to the motor pool and began surveying the equipment. Neither of them had ever participated in the transport of a swarm and had no idea how to operate the equipment. As they were looking around the yard they spotted a small shack. Smoke was billowing out of the chimney.

"I bet whoever is in that shack can help us out," Leek said.

"True enough, but what if the TGA has already contacted them?"

"We'll just have to chance it."

They approached the shack cautiously. Sgt. Hawkh went around back and Leek went up the front door. Ordinarily he didn't think there would be any danger in knocking on the door, but if the order to kill the nanomite swarms in Farm 2279 had already been sent out, the assigned assassin might well be right inside the door. He held his breath and began knocking gently. There was movement inside and then Leek heard someone grumbling.

"Can't a man sleep in on his free day?" a voice said as the door opened slightly. "What do you want?"

Leek relaxed when he saw the man was a mutant. His pointed chin and contorted nose made that quite clear. "Sir, my name is Captain Lanzia. I'm here—"

"*The* Captain Lanzia?"

"Yes, the one and only."

He extended his hand and Leek took it. "I'll be a cross-eyed prickeltern. You're the last person I'd expect to find knocking on my door."

"Well, yes. I bet that's true. What's your name?"

"Ernee Swanh."

"Glad to meet you, Mr. Swanh. I've come because we desperately need your help."

Leek explained the situation and the urgent need for immediate action. Swanh grabbed his hat and coat and rushed outside. "Come on. I'll show you how it's done."

Mr. Swanh gave them a short tutorial on operating the equipment and then let them watch while he loaded a swarm onto a truck. The hives lived in a hard but brittle substance that was most conducive to their growth and productivity. Each hive was held together by a wooden frame which made for easy transport. The hives were delicate, though, and had to be handled with care. If they were dropped or jolted too much, the hive would shatter and the swarm would have to be relocated. Even if relocation were possible it had to be done quickly and many nanomites inevitably died in the process. If evacuation was not possible, they would all die.

There were 121 hives and each truck could transport eight hives at a time. That meant they would have to make five trips to the Cathedral in Rhule to get the job done. Since it would take a little less than a kyloon per trip they'd be lucky to be done by nightfall. This concerned Leek because, by his calculations, the TGA could show up at any moment. Remembering how effective Rhin and his fellow rhutz had been against the copters and TGA soldiers, he asked Rhin if she could muster up a pack of rhutz to help guard the nanomites while he, Sgt. Hawkh, and Mr. Swanh were gone.

"Yes, just as the nanomites, we are at your command," Rhin assured him without speaking a word.

Leek smiled, still not quite used to having such a devoted following. He enjoyed the respect and loyalty shown to him, but it was a bit overwhelming to have so much responsibility. But he knew he couldn't give that more than a moment's thought. There was too much to be done and time was too short for indecision. He just had to have faith that God would make him strong enough for the task.

5
The Battle of Rizi

Red and Tam were in a daze after their meeting with Tehra. The news she'd brought was shocking and seemed surreal. They were anxious to find Leek and tell him the news about his father and Tehra's baby. But nobody had heard from him since the battle at Rini. They'd been informed that the TGA army was about to launch its siege of Rizi, the capital city of Tributon. The assault was expected at dawn. It was no secret if Rizi fell that the border city of Khor would be next.

It wasn't generally believed that the mutant army could stop the TGA, but it was imperative that they inflict serious damage on them if the regular Loyalist army was to have a chance when it was confronted by the TGA at Khor. The air war at Rizi would be particularly important. The mutant air force had to be able to control the skies or its troops would be decimated by cluster bombs before the battle ever began.

Even if they kept the TGA fighters away from the front line, they'd still have to deal with the hovertanks. Tam and Red had been discussing that problem all night, but much to their chagrin, hadn't come up with anything. But when Tam fell asleep that night he immediately began to dream.

For a while he didn't know where he was, then he realized he was inside Leek's head. He'd somehow made a connection with Leek and was getting his thoughts about dealing with the hovertanks. Leek believed the hovertank was vulnerable. The key was to disturb the pulse it rode upon. If the pulse were interrupted the hovertank would be forced to the ground where it would be as vulnerable as a conventional tank. It was true the hovertank had numerous defenses, but its most potent defense was its agility and ability to change positions quickly. If they could interfere with the hovertank's pulse generator, they might have a chance at destroying it.

Tarizon: Civil War

The dream then shifted to a vast prairie and Tam saw Rhin being chased by two TGA soldiers. The scene shifted to a copter spinning and lurching out of control. He saw the fiery crash and wondered what it meant. Why had it crashed? Had Rhin somehow caused it?

A pain shot through Tam's head. He turned over restlessly. Then he was in the middle of a telepathic exchange between Leek and someone. He wasn't sure what it was all about but he knew somebody or something was being evacuated. He awoke with a start and looked at his digital readout. It was time to get up.

He shook Red. "Red. Get up! It's time to get ready for battle."

Red groaned but finally rolled over and sat up. They dressed quickly and went to the dining hall for a quick breakfast. While they ate, Tam filled Red in on his thoughts about the hovertanks.

"So, what you are saying is that we shouldn't try to hit the hovertanks directly but create an explosion beneath them," Red summarized.

"Yes. You program your missile to explode under the hovertank and interrupt the pulse. Then when it hits the ground I'll be right behind you to nail it while it's vulnerable. It will take precise timing to be effective."

"Well, we can try it. It can't hurt anything. If it works we'll pass on the technique to the other pilots."

Just as the sky began to lighten in the east, Red and Tam got in their fighters and started their engines. They were each loaded with sixteen Muscan missiles, six cluster bombs, and 25,000 rounds of heat-seeking bullets. Tam was advised that the main body of Loyalist fighters and bombers from bases in Rigimol and northern Tributon were already in the air and the assault on Rizi had already begun.

"R2 ready for takeoff," Tam advised.

"R3 ready as well," Red added.

"R2, you're cleared for takeoff. R3, follow R2 after 30 tiks."

"On my way," Tam advised as the big fighter lurched forward and accelerated down the makeshift runway. Thirty tiks later Red's fighter burst forward and was in the air quickly heading north over the Doral Mountains on a collision with the with Tributon's capital city of Rizi. Tam looked down at the grey forest below and imagined how it must have looked fifty cycles earlier before the great eruptions brought darkness and despair to the planet. The dark green evergreens that had survived the climate change were now pale and sickly looking. The shrubbery and underbrush were a mixture of greys and pale yellows and flowers were a rarity. Tam wondered if he'd ever see the sun again in his lifetime.

When the two fighters broke out over the plains of Tributon they could see billows of smoke rising in the distance. The battle was on and they could scarcely wait to join in. To their left they saw a Loyalist fighter approaching.

"L21 calling R2, is that you?"

"Affirmative, L21. How's the battle going?"

"Badly. Very badly. We were ambushed before we even got into Tributon air space. It was a disaster."

"How many of you are left?"

"I'm not sure. Fighters were exploding all around me. It was a miracle I was able to escape. You should go back to your base."

"No way!" Tam said. "We came to fight. Why don't you come with us? They won't be expecting company from the south."

"What use are three fighters against three thousand." L21 asked.

"We've got some ideas on how to put a hovertank out of action. We need to at least try them out."

"I don't know. It sounds like a suicide mission."

"Don't worry," Red chimed in. "We got these ideas direct from the Liberator."

"Captain Lanzia?"

"Yes, he wants us to try them out. We could use your help," Red said.

"Affirmative then. If the Liberator needs my help I'm in."

"Let's go then. When we see our first hovertanks, L21, you go in low to distract them. Red, you come in next and aim for the pulse."

"The pulse?" L21 asked.

"Yes, directly beneath the hovertank. We'll explain later. Then I'll come in for the direct hit. If we're successful we'll repeat the drill on the next one."

"Affirmative," Red said.

"All right," L21 said. "Let's find us some hovertanks."

As they flew over the battle scene they saw utter and complete devastation left by the hovertanks and infantry following behind them. Dead mutant soldiers were lying everywhere, thousands of them piled one on top of the other. Tam muttered his disgust as they flew over the ravaged landscape.

"Up ahead," L21 said. "I see them."

"Right. There they are," Tam replied. "Okay, L21. You're up."

L21 broke off and swept around to make a run going west to east. Tam and Red broke off following him, spacing themselves to facilitate the 1,2,3 punch they'd planned. As L21 flew by the first hover tank it jerked around and shot off a missile, but it was off the mark. Suddenly Red was on top of the hover tank. He fired his missile, but decoys flew out of the hovertank and the missile locked onto one of them and exploded.

"No! Don't lock on the hovertank. That will activate its defenses. You've got to hit the ground beneath it."

Tam aborted his flyby and the three fighters regrouped for another run. "Let's try it again. This time let's get it right."

"Sorry," Red replied. It's hard to intentionally miss."

"Okay, L21. Let's go. We'll soon have company."

"On my way," L21 replied. "Follow me."

L21 broke off again and flew across the path of another hovertank. It jerked around again but L21 was long gone before it got a shot off. This time Red came in low and locked his missile on a truck directly beneath the hovertank. When the truck exploded the hovertank dropped like a rock from the sky. Before it hit the ground its stabilizer rod engaged as if it were going to fire its cannon. At that moment Tam locked on it and fired. Decoys immediately shot out and the missile locked onto one of them and exploded harmlessly in the distance.

"Skutz!" Tam yelled.

"Its okay," Red replied. "I've got an idea. L21. After you streak by, circle back around to follow R2 with a second shot."

"Affirmative. Good idea. Let's try it."

After they'd regrouped, they found another hovertank destroying everything in its path. L21 flew by just as he had before but then circled back in for a final shot. Red found a target below the hovertank and locked onto it. When it exploded the hovertank plunged to the ground, causing it to automatically engage its stabilizer rod. Tam immediately launched his Muscan missile and, as before, a flurry of decoys flew from the hovertank luring away the missile, but this time another missile locked on the big hovertank and there were no decoys this time to divert it away. The hovertank took a direct hit and exploded into a giant fireball.

"Yes! We did it!" Tam screamed.
"Affirmative. We have a kill," Red said.
"The first one of the war," L21 added.
"All right!" Tam said. "That was fun! Let's do it again."

L21 banked off and found another target. With perfect precision the fighters executed yet another coordinated attack, and a hovertank exploded and plunged helplessly to the ground. Soon dozens of hovertanks were burning across the Tributon prairie. Unfortunately, the three fighters were running out of fuel and ammunition, so they had to leave the battlefield and head back to their secret base sooner than they would have liked. Nevertheless, they felt good, like they had really accomplished something. Although the TGA won the battle of Rizi and took Tributon's capital city, for the first time they'd suffered some significant losses and it was clear they were not invincible after all.

When Tam and Red got back to the shuttle, they introduced themselves to L21. It turned out he was Lt. John Sillmar, an Earthchild who'd grown up in Lower Serie. Sillmar had graduated from officer candidates school in Pogo a cycle before Tam and Red. He'd also been in Sgt. Baig's platoon and had studied under Lt. Londry. While they were reminiscing, Captain Shilling walked in for their debriefing. She was in a somber mood.

"So, I see two birds left and three returned. Very interesting."

"Yes, Captain. This is Lt. Sillmar. His entire squadron was wiped out so he joined up with us during the battle."

"I see. I understand you had an excellent day—the first hovertank kills of the war. Very impressive. Unfortunately, that's about the only good news coming from the war front today."

She described how the mutant army had been totally annihilated during the battle and how the Loyalist air force was severely crippled. Only one hundred and twenty planes had made it back to their Rigimol bases—a loss of over one thousand planes. This meant when the TGA and Loyalist army met in just a few days, the TGA would have complete air superiority and the few planes that remained would have to be used strictly in a defensive posture.

When Captain Shilling asked Tam for a detailed report, she listened intently as he described how they'd experimented and finally figured out how to destroy the first hovertank and then went on to knock out a dozen more. "Unfortunately," she pointed out, "without an air force it was a moot point." Nevertheless, she said she'd pass on the information to Loyalist headquarters for analysis. Tam then asked about Captain Lanzia.

"I've been told he's helping to evacuate nanomite farms," she replied. "Apparently Videl Lai ordered the eradication of all nanomites and Captain Lanzia went to warn them. Now, I think he is helping with the evacuation. You probably flew over him on your way here. The farm is located in Rhule."

"Permission to join him," Tam asked.

"Affirmative. Tomorrow morning you should go find him and bring him here. He's been ordered to take command of what's left of the mutant army."

Tam smiled broadly. "What happened to Colonel Shanziba and Major Linz?"

"They were both killed. Captain Lanzia is the highest ranking officer surviving at this time, so Threebeard has appointed him commander of the 3rd Loyalist Army."

"What about you? Don't you have seniority?"

"Yes, but I'm a shuttle commander. I know little about ground warfare. Besides, I'm not the Liberator."

"So, you believe the Prophecy." Tam observed.

"Indeed I do. I'm anxious to meet your friend Captain Lanzia, so don't let me down. Find him and bring him back here."

"Will do, Captain."

"And while you are looking for him, I've got a few strategic targets I want you to destroy."

"Sure. What kind of targets?"

"There's a road stretching from the Rini River through Rizi and up to the TGA front line. It's the TGA's main supply line. I want you each to unload a double load of cluster bombs on it. If we can create a little havoc along their supply lines it could slow down the pace of their forward movement."

"Sounds like fun," Tam said.

"Good, then. Now there's a party waiting for you in the lower deck. You better get going?"

"A party?" Red asked.

"Yes, it's estimated each of the TGA's hovertanks have killed over four thousand of our fine soldiers and today you've taken out thirteen of them. I'd say saving the life of 50,000 men is worth celebrating."

A feeling of great exhilaration swept over Tam, Red and John as they made their way to the lower deck. When they got there the entire crew of the shuttle stood and applauded them. When the applause ended, the music started and the party began. The shuttle had an abundance of female guides who fought over the privilege of taking care of the three heroes. After Tam, Red and John each selected a companion for the evening they ate, drank and danced the night away. It was a night they'd never forget.

Although Captain Shilling had authorized the party, she had banned alcoholic beverages because of the following day's mission. Hung over pilots couldn't very well fly a dangerous mission over enemy territory. And if the pilots couldn't drink she didn't think the crew should either. But the lack of alcohol didn't seem to dampen the party or slow it down in the least. It went on until the early hours of the morning.

During the party the three heros were dubbed "the Three Avengers," as Captain Shilling wanted to make sure word about their heroics would spread throughout, not only to the Loyalist territories, but all of Tarizon. She knew the Loyalist forces needed hope and the TGA army needed something to worry about.

The next day the shuttle's doctor gave the Three Avengers a specially formulated energy drink to combat their fatigue from the previous night's celebration. After they'd drank it they felt as wide awake and alert as ever and were anxious to go out on their mission. When they got to their fighters they were shocked to see the incredible number of cluster bombs attached to them. They wondered if they'd be able to get off the ground.

"Don't worry," Captain Shilling said. "Your thrusters can handle the payload. Since we only have three fighters to work with we have no choice but to load you to the hilt."

"I don't mind," Tam said, "just as long as she'll still fly."

"She will. Don't worry."

Tam was skeptical but didn't question the Captain. When he started down the runway he held his breath, but his concern wasn't necessary as the fighter took off effortlessly as usual. Once they were in the air they headed southwest toward Rizi where they picked up the supply line going north to Khor. They flew as far as they could in stealth mode to avoid detection. Since there were enemy fighters patrolling the supply route, once they were over their target they knew they'd have to come out of stealth mode, drop to the desired elevation, and then quickly unleash their cluster bombs. At that point the enemy would know they were there and any TGA fighters in the area would close in on them in a hurry.

John came in first with his load of cluster bombs and took out a dozen trucks loaded with supplies and ammunition. The ensuing explosions left giant craters in the roadway. Red came in next and took out a two-kylod stretch of the road a little farther north. They seemed to have taken the enemy completely by surprise as there was no resistance to their assault. At least until Tam made a third run a few kylods to the north. As he was approaching the road, two TGA fighters suddenly appeared and took up chase. Just as he released his cluster bombs one of the fighters locked on him and fired a missile. Tam immediately fired his decoys and took evasive measures. The missile, however, wasn't fooled by the decoys and kept on his tail as he dived down and circled back toward the fiery inferno he'd left in his wake. The missile had almost caught up with him when he plunged into the smoke and flames billowing from the convoy he'd just bombed. When the missile hit the draft of heat from the burning trucks it suddenly began spinning and jerking erratically until it finally flew straight down and collided with one of the burning trucks.

Tam breathed a sigh of relief only to realize the two TGA fighters had followed him through the smoke and were still on his tail. He gave his bird full throttle hoping to outrun them, but they managed to keep up with him and he feared they'd lock on him again. He didn't know if he could outmaneuver another Muscan missile. Just as he'd about given up hope he noticed Red and John had sneaked up behind his two pursuers. He saw two puffs of smoke as two missiles were launched. The two planes suddenly plunged downward and a slew of decoys shot out in all directions. One of the missiles took the bait and followed a decoy out of sight. The second one, however, went straight through the debris and hit its target. The big fighter burst into flames and plummeted to the ground below. The second fighter came around one more time for another look but apparently decided three against one was more than he wanted to tangle with.

"R2, are you okay?" Red asked.

"Yeah. I'm fine. Let's get out of here."

"Amen. Let's go find Leek."

"Setting heading for Rhule. Last one there is a dirkbird," Red challenged.

The Three Avengers gave their fighters full throttle, leaving a chaotic scene behind them. Twenty kylods of the Rizi roadway lay in ruins cluttered by hundreds of burning trucks, transport vehicles, and dead soldiers. Tam felt good as he figured it would take them several days to get traffic flowing again. In the meantime the TGA would have to ration their supplies right when they were ready to confront the regular Loyalist army.

When they got to Rhule they kept a lookout for the nanomite farm. When they saw the clear white area in the midst of the prairie they knew they had found it. They circled around looking for a spot to land and discovered the entire area was infested with mounds where the swarms had been kept. It didn't appear there was any suitable place to land until they found the caretaker's shack and a clear patch of ground behind it. Once on the ground they looked around for any sign of life. The swarms were already gone and the place looked deserted.

"So, now what?" Red asked. "He's obviously gone."

"Yes, but where did he go? Where would he have relocated the nanomite swarms?" John asked.

"Why don't we ask him?" Tam said.

"What? You gonna take a nap and dream about him?" Red said.

"No. Lorin gave us a data pod, didn't she?"

"Oh, right. Can we contact him with that?"

"I believe that's why she gave it to us," Tam said and pulled his out of his pocket.

The device looked like a small calculator but had no number or letter keys. Tam held it up to his face and said, "Leek. Where are you?"

The words he spoke were displayed on the face of the pod. A moment went by and then there was a reply. "I'm at the Cathedral in Rhule. Are you close by?"

"Yes, we're at the farm. We'll come find you."

"No, I'm about done here. Wait there. Sgt. Hawkh and I are leaving now. Watch out for the TGA. They're looking for the nanomites."

"Okay. We'll keep our eyes peeled. See you soon."

Tam looked at Red. "Pretty nice, huh?"

"Yeah. How does it work?"

"It's just the cheap version of the GC. It bounces its signal off of orbiting satellites. It's only good for communication between a limited number of people. In this case it will allow Leek, you, and me to communicate with each other."

"Doesn't the TGA control all of the satellites?"

"Yes, but they can't keep us from bouncing our signals off of them."

"Yeah, but can't they intercept the messages?"

"True, but they are encrypted, so getting the message won't do them any good."

"They don't have code breakers?"

"Yes, but it will take them time to break an encryption and they are changed randomly each time you use the device."

"That's impressive. Can I get one?" John asked.

Tam shrugged. "I don't know. We'll have to ask Leek when we see him."

Less than a kyloon later they saw a cloud of dust in the distance. They got in their fighters and readied them for takeoff in case it was the TGA. As the dust cloud got closer they saw it was just a single transporter. Two men were in the cab and one on the bed watching over a single crate containing nanomite swarms.. They relaxed, figuring it must be Leek, and got out of their planes. The transporter came to a stop in front of them and Leek, Rhin, Sgt. Hawkh and an old man got out. Tam and Leek embraced.

"It's a relief to see you. When those hovertanks came blasting their way through the base, I was afraid they'd catch you. I've never seen anything so destructive."

"We managed to hide from the hovertanks and with Rhin's help escaped the infantry and a couple of copters."

"Good girl, Rhin," Tam said, starting to pat her on the back, but then thought better of it when she gave him the evil eye. "You'll have to tell us all about it later. Right now, we need to get out of here before the TGA spots us."

"Good idea. We'll need to load that crate on the plane."

"What's in it?" Tam asked.

"Nanomites."

"Really. Why are we bringing them with us?"

"If they are going to help us against Videl, I need to be able to keep in contact with them."

"Makes sense."

"Where are we going?" Leek asked.

"To your new headquarters. You're about to take over command of the 3rd Army."

Leek frowned. "What?"

Tam smiled. "Come on. I'll tell you about it on the way."

6
Saving the Nanomites

Lorin had been told not to activate her worldwide web of Loyalist cells until told to do so by the new Chancellor, but it was an order she could not obey. If Captain Lanzia were able to make contact with the nanomites she knew just warning them would not be enough. They would need help in relocating to safe havens where the TGA couldn't murder them. This would necessitate activation of the cells she and her father had so carefully cultivated all over Tarizon. She pondered what the Chancellor would do to her when he found out she'd disobeyed his orders. Her GC beeped and she picked it up.

"S1 here."

"R1 reporting."

"Were you able to warn them?" Lorin asked.

"Affirmative. We're in the process of relocating them to a safe location."

"Oh, that's wonderful. I was so worried you wouldn't be able to communicate with them."

"I've warned them and they've passed on the warning to all the other swarms, but they'll need help relocating."

"Yes. I know. I'm about to pass the word down to our cells."

"Good. They're scared and I promised them we'd protect them."

"There's just one problem," Lorin said hesitantly.

"What?"

"The new Chancellor isn't on board with using my father's network yet."

"You're kidding?"

"He's had twelve hours to consider it and has done nothing."

"We don't have time to wait!" Leek said angrily.

"I know. The nanomites will be dead by the time he gets around to doing anything."

"But, if you disobey them they'll kick you out of the government, if they don't lock you up and try you for treason," Leek said thoughtfully.

She sighed. "I know, but we must do something."

"Let me activate the network. You can disavow any knowledge of it. I'll just say it was an emergency and the Chancellor had told me to use the network if I ever needed it. They won't dare challenge the Liberator, right?"

Lorin laughed. "You're getting the hang of the political game, aren't you?"

"Well. I've had a good teacher."

"Okay. Where are you now?" she asked.

"At the Cathedral. His holiness has lent me his office."

"Good. There are four global cell leaders you'll need to contact. They will pass your information on down through the network."

"Good. I'll need the location of each farm so I can have them start looking for safe havens. As they find them they can report the location to me and we can coordinate transport. It's going to be a monumental job relocating thousands of farms."

"Is it safe for you to stay in Rhule? Now that you've relocated the swarms, they'll be looking for you."

"No. I can't stay here. Tam and Red are coming to take us up in the mountains. We're going to try to reorganize what's left of the 3rd Army."

"But how will you communicate with the nanomites from the mountains?"

"I'm going to take a hundred swarms with me to our headquarters. They're going to help us construct a new 3rd Army headquarters."

"Excellent. It may become the new Loyalist headquarters if Rigimol is taken."

"Well, let's hope that doesn't happen."

"What should I do now?" Lorin asked. "They may not believe that you had the contact information for the cell leaders. They may arrest me."

"You're right. You should come to the mountains too. Come right away, but don't tell anyone that you're leaving or where you're going."

"I've got my father's funeral tomorrow."

"Right. Leave right after the funeral."

"But how will I get there?"

"Tell General Zitor to arrange it. Tell him I requested your assistance. I'll contact him with a location to take you and then I'll send someone to pick you up."

"Pick me up?"

"Yes. My father once told me that if you wanted something kept secret, don't tell anyone about it."

Lorin chuckled. "Smart man."

"Yes, he is. So, I don't dare let anyone know the location of our new headquarters. I trust General Zitor but I don't want to put him in a position that might compromise him."

"Okay. We better get started. Get a cable and plug it into the computer. I'll send you the contact information along with the location of each of the farms. Do you have anyone to help you?"

"There's an old man here who helped me with the relocation and I'm hoping Tam and Red will be here soon. Either way we'll get it done."

"Good. I'm sending the data now. Call me if there is anything else I can do."

"Affirmative," Leek said plugging in the cable and watching the printer come to life.

Lorin hung up and breathed a sign of relief. She was surprised but grateful that Captain Lanzia had agreed to activate her father's cells. At every turn Peter Turner had shocked and amazed her. When they first met she was unimpressed by this teenager from Earth. He seemed so unlikely to be able to lead the Loyalist movement, but now she was convinced he was the one described in the Prophecy. She just had to make sure he got all the support he needed to pull it off.

There was a knock on the door. She got up and looked out through the peephole. It was General Zitor. She opened the door and let him in.

"Well, you're not going to like this."

"Why, what happened?"

"Chancellor Mammett has been told that nothing can be done to protect the nanomites. His military advisors have told him he needs to focus on defending Rigimol. Apparently in just a few days there is going to be a great battle on the Khor River. He's been told if we lose that battle the war will be over."

"I figured as much," Lorin spat.

"They've also tabled activation of your cells. They want you to give them a complete list of all participants along with any information you have on them."

"He's crazy. If a list like that were to get in the wrong hands everyone on it could end up dead."

"I agree. But you've been ordered to turn it over."

"I can't do it. I don't have the list anymore. I destroyed it after I sent it to Captain Lanzia. He's in process of activating the cells right now to get help in protecting the nanomites."

"What! The Chancellor is going to be very angry about that."

"I know, but he insisted I give it to him."

The general smiled. "So, what will you do now?"

"Captain Lanzia wants me to join him. He's trying to reorganize the 3rd Army. He's going to contact you soon with a pickup point where you can take me."

"A pickup point? Can't you be taken directly to the base?"

"No. He doesn't want anyone to know where the base is located. He thinks the TGA is monitoring our communications."

It was a lie, but Lorin didn't want General Zitor to think Captain Lanzia didn't trust him. Her mind started to race thinking of all the things she needed to do before she left for Tributon. She had a strong base of support in the new Loyalist government. After all, she'd only lost the election to become the new Chancellor by a few votes. She didn't want to lose what support she had, so she'd need someone to keep her supporters solidly behind her. She thought of Senator Marcuzzi. He'd been one of her father's friends for many cycles and she trusted him implicitly.

"General, Senator Marcuzzi doesn't think our new chancellor will be much of a match for Videl Lai."

"He's not the only one," the general snorted.

"If he's right, there may be an opportunity to bring a no-confidence vote. If that happens we'll need to be ready."

"Yes, absolutely."

"So, I'd like to you and Senator Marcuzzi to keep my supporters together while I'm gone. I'll keep both of you fully informed as to what Captain Lanzia is doing and you can pass it on to those you can trust to keep it confidential."

"That will be a bit dangerous but, you're right, a most critical line of communication in case future opportunities materialize."

"Good then. Will you talk to Senator Marcuzzi for me? I doubt I'll be able to speak to him before I leave."

"Yes, of course."

She smiled, took a deep breath, and said, "Well then. I guess I better get packed. I'd like to leave right after the funeral. I think I'm safe until then."

"True. I doubt the Chancellor would be so bold as to arrest you during your father's funeral even if he finds out what you've done."

"Thank you, General, for all your help. You've been a good friend."

"It's been my pleasure to know your father for so many cycles. I hope our relationship will be as long and as strong."

"I'm sure it will. Good luck at Khor. May God and Sandee be with you!"

General Zitor left feeling relieved that Captain Lanzia was asserting himself and that he'd have the capable assistance of Lorin Boskie, but he was in a delicate position as General of the 2nd Loyalist Army. He had a duty and an oath of loyalty to the new Loyalist Chancellor, no matter how pathetic a leader he might turn out to be. If he failed to pass on any information he received about Captain Lanzia's activities, it would be a breach of that duty and he could be help accountable. Of course, his army was loyal to him. That had been demonstrated when he opted to join with the Loyalist movement. His men had stood by him even though they were considered traitors by Central Authority and the TGA. But would they stand behind him if he were accused of treason by the new Loyalist government? That would be confusing to his officers and soldiers. He hoped it wouldn't come to that.

The next morning thousands of mourners arrived at the Cingellic Cathedral located in northwest Shini. It was one of the largest and most ornate churches in Lemaine Shane. Lorin was still reeling from her father's death, but her mind was too preoccupied with her imminent departure to Tributon, Jake's whereabouts, and the nanomite situation to properly grieve. She felt so alone. Her mother had died when she was quite young and she had no siblings. There were no grandparents, uncles, or nieces. Of course, she and her father had many friends, but they were not family. She wished the funeral were over so she could get on her way, but there was an endless line of mourners waiting to give their condolences and she could scarcely afford to be discourteous.

Lorin smiled at the man who stepped before her. They embraced.

"Your father was a great man. It was a privilege to serve with him," Councilor Shilline said. He was a member of the Council of Interpreters and served with her father for many cycles.

"Thank you," Lorin said. "My father thought highly of you as well." As he stepped aside, the next mourner came into view. It was Chancellor Mammett.

"Ah. . . . Chancellor. It was so nice of you to come," she said nervously. "With the army about to engage the TGA, I didn't expect you to make it."

He stared at her for an awkward moment and then cleared his throat. "Well, I wanted to speak with you and I was afraid this might be my last chance."

Lorin's stomach twisted. She wondered if he could have already discovered her plans. She looked at the long line of mourners behind the Chancellor. "Well, Mr. Chancellor. I don't think I'll be done here for hours."

"I don't need but a minute of your time. I'll be brief," he said coldly.

"What's on your mind, then?"

"I knew your father well. He was a stubborn man and once he got his mind set on something there was no stopping him. I see the same qualities in you, so I assume you're going to try to get what you want whether I approve or not."

A rush of anger welled up in Lorin, but she bit her tongue. "Are you accusing me of something, Chancellor?"

"Nothing yet, but I just wanted you to know I'll be watching you closely and I will not tolerate anyone undermining my authority."

"Don't worry about me, Mr. Chancellor. I'd worry about Videl Lai and the TGA. They're the ones with two million troops about to cross our borders."

The Chancellor drew in a deep breath and was about to reply when an aide rushed up and whispered something into his ear. He glanced at her one last time and then rushed out of the hall with his aide. Lorin closed her eyes for a moment while she composed herself and then shook the next mourner's hand. Quite a while later she saw General Zitor at the end of the line. When he finally got to her he told her it was time to leave.

"The TGA have crossed the Khor River. I've got to go to the front. You can come along and after my pilot drops me off he'll take you to the rendevous point."

She nodded. "Good. Let's get out of here."

General Zitor took her out a back entrance where a PTV was waiting. Soon they were on their way to the transport station. Lorin thought of Jake. She hadn't heard from him for two days. That was unusual as they normally talked daily. He had gone to Rini to help out the 3rd Army which was short on pilots. She knew he had gotten there safely because they had talked by GC. But after the battle she hadn't been able to reach him.

"You haven't heard from Jake, have you?" she asked.

General Zitor frowned. "No. I'm sorry, Lorin. I've put out the word for everyone to keep an eye out for him, though."

"Good. Thank you. Did any of the pilots from Rini make it back?"

"Some did, but they went right back out to help defend Rizi. It's a good thing Jake wasn't with them. They were ambushed before they got close to the battlefront. Only a handful made it back alive."

"What about his E-box? If he'd crashed wouldn't you be getting a message from it?"

"Yes, it could be emitting a signal, but unless someone is searching for him it wouldn't matter. Right now we only have a handful of fighters and those must stay back to guard Shini. I'm afraid Jake's on his own unless Captain Lanzia can put together a search party."

"I plan on asking him to," Lorin said softly. She wiped a tear from her eyes. "I hope he will."

"Well, if anyone should sympathize with your situation, it should be Captain Lanzia. Has there been any word about Lucinda and the baby?"

"No. Leek thinks she's being held in Shisk. He's working on a plan to rescue her. She's probably had the baby by now, so that will complicate matters."

"What do you mean?" General Zitor asked.

"Well, I doubt they'll let Lucinda keep the baby in her jail cell. The way they treat prisoners, she'll be too weak to nurse the baby. They'll probably take it to an orphanage or keep it at a hospital. So, even if they are able to rescue Lucinda finding the baby is another matter."

"I'm not so sure it's possible to rescue either one from Shisk."

"It isn't possible, but I didn't have the heart to tell him that. He'll figure it out for himself as he tries to put a plan together. It's not easy to face reality, particularly when it's so bitter."

"Yes. How well I know."

"Did you get a chance to talk to Senator Marcuzzi?"

"Yes, he's on board. Feel free to call either of us if you have news or need our consultation."

Lorin felt the plane start to descend. She could see the anxiety on General Zitor's face as he looked out over the countryside beneath them that would soon be the scene of unimaginable horrors. She was glad she'd be far away when it happened. The plane hit the ground hard and skidded to a stop. General Zitor stood up, grabbed his carry-on luggage, and nodded to Lorin.

"The pilot will take you to Gallion where you're to rendevous with Captain Lanzia."

"He's going to personally pick me up?"

"Yes, all of his pilots are busy disrupting the TGA's supply lines. Gallion is far enough away from tomorrow's battleground that neither of you should be in danger."

"I've never been to Gallion. It's a seaport, isn't it?"

"Yes, there's a big naval air station there too, but it should be deserted tomorrow with the battle going on."

"Good luck, General. My prayers will be with you."

The general smiled and left the plane. After they'd refueled they were back in the sky heading west over the Doral Mountains. Lorin couldn't help but think of General Zitor's comment that even if Jake's E-box were broadcasting a signal nobody would pick it up because nobody was looking for him. She worried that he might be lying injured somewhere hoping to be rescued before he bled to death. She knew if the TGA found him first they'd finish him off. She remembered how Leek had rescued her and General Zitor when their plane had been hijacked by one of Videl's spies. He'd been able to find them by searching for the plane's E-box transmission. Perhaps he'd do the same for Jake. She prayed she could convince him to try.

7
Rini

General Zitor stepped off the plane into a cold rain. An aide held an umbrella over his head. They rushed to the waiting transport vehicle and climbed in. Threebeard, who was waiting inside, smiled at his old friend. "Welcome, General. Get in." They embraced and Threebeard asked, "How was your flight?"

"Not bad, but I prefer being on the ground. I could never have been a pilot."

"So, how is Lorin after her defeat?" Threebeard asked.

"Why don't you go ask her? I'm sure she'd love to see you."

"I'd like to give her my condolences. I felt bad about missing the funeral, but any meeting with Lorin Boskie now might make it look like I supported her rather than Chancellor Mammett."

"So, it's a free country. Isn't that what we are fighting for?"

"Yes, of course, but if our new chancellor doubts my loyalties he might remove me as defense minister. Since I'm not a modest man, I can say that such a move would be a disaster for the war effort."

General Zitor laughed. "No, nobody would ever accuse you of being modest."

Threebeard motioned to his driver. He started the engine and they left the airport. The road to the base was clogged with traffic and troops moving south. Enemy planes flew overhead and occasionally one would venture down for a closer look.

"How long do you think it will be before they try to cross the river?"

"Sixty to ninety days is my guess. Maybe longer. They've just been through two major battles, so their soldiers must be exhausted. They'll have to regroup, resupply their divisions, and plan their attack."

"Plan their attack? It's pretty simple, isn't it? They just line up the hovertanks in front and let the infantry back them up. It worked well at Rizi and Rini."

"But that was against the young and inexperienced 3rd Army. It won't work against the regular army, I won't allow it."

General Zitor laughed. "I like your confidence, Threebeard, but how do you plan to deal with the hovertanks? They seem invincible."

"Nothing is invincible. Did you know that three of our pilots destroyed more than a dozen of them at Rizi?"

"I thought our air force was wiped out at Rizi."

"This was the remains of the 1st Airborne Division."

"Of the mutant army?"

"Yes, I don't know how they did it, but it proves the hovertanks can be destroyed."

"If we had an air force," General Zitor reminded him.

"Yes, if we only had an air force."

"So, what is your strategy? How are we going to defend Rigimol?"

"I've talked to Captain Shilling who has set up a base of operations for the remnants of the 3rd Army. She's hopeful she'll have fifteen or twenty divisions ready when the offensive begins. Since we don't have an air force and the hovertanks will destroy anything in their path, my plan is to only place token opposition against them. We will let them blast their way through our lines and then launch our attack from both flanks. Once we are in between them we'll have only the infantry to deal with."

"What if the hoveranks turn around and come back at you?"

"I've studied the last two battles very closely and have noticed a wide gap between the hovertanks and the infantry. The gap widens as the battle goes on. If we don't oppose the hovertanks I believe they will be so far ahead of the infantry that, even if they come back, it will be too late. The two armies will be so intermingled that the hovertanks would kill as many of their own soldiers as ours, should they try to intervene."

"That's a very bold plan, Mr. Defense Minister," General Zitor said. "But even if your plan works, what makes you think we can still win?"

"If the 3rd Army comes through and attacks from the west, I think the enemy will have its hands full. My objective is to hold the enemy at the river. We *must* hold the enemy at the river. If we do that, the morale of the army will falter and ours will soar like a dickel."

"You think we might get a few defectors?"

"Precisely. Videl Lai didn't let his men choose sides in this war. He pressed every TGA soldier into service, and they remain there not by loyalty to him, but for fear for their lives."

"So, where does our Liberator fit into your scheme of things?" General Zitor asked.

"He's to be promoted to Commander General of the 3rd Army."

General Zitor's eyes widened. "That's quite a leap from Captain to Commander General. How do think the 3rd Army's command will take it?"

"Ordinarily, it would be an absurd thing to do, but right at this moment the 3rd Army is in shambles and there isn't any command structure. We are only in contact with a few divisions and most of the officers are dead or missing. In light of that, I'm promoting our Liberator so he can rebuild and command the 3rd Army."

"But will Chancellor Mammett stand for it?"

"He will for now. He has no choice. He cannot afford to challenge his Defense Minister on the eve of the greatest battle in the history of Tarizon. After the battle is over he'll likely get rid of Commander General Lanzia any way he can, unless—"

"Unless what?"

"Unless, our Liberator proves himself in battle."

General Zitor laughed. "Well, as much as I am a fan of Leek Lanzia, I don't see how he could possibly be a factor in the upcoming battle. I mean—"

"Well, I guess we'll find out if there is any truth to the Prophecy, because to be honest with you, General, it will take the intervention of God and Sandee to win this battle and save Tarizon from Videl Lai's tyranny. I believe in the Prophecy and I have done all I can do to make it happen. I've thrust the Liberator into a position where he can fulfill his destiny. If I was wrong in doing this, then you and I and millions more will die, and Tarizon will fall into utter darkness."

General Zitor swallowed hard and prayed Threebeard knew what he was doing.

8
Summoning the Seafolken

In order to keep in constant contact with the nanomites while the war was being waged, Leek had decided he needed to have a nanomite swarm close at hand. While they were moving the swarms to a safe haven he had recalled Colonel Tomel's recount of the Nanomite Wars and how formidable an adversary they turned out to be. He also remembered their offer of support in Shisk when he first came to Tarizon. So, he asked through his thoughts if some of them would be willing to come to his headquarters to coordinate the nanomite participation in the war.

"Alo of the nanomites once offered his help in fighting Videl Lai. Is that offer still open?"

"Alo spoke for all of us and as long as Videl Lai walks on Tarizon, we are at your command."

"Then I'll need some of you to accompany me to my new headquarters so I can keep in constant communication with you."

"We've anticipated your request and have selected one hundred swarms to go with you. They will be our delegation to the Loyalist government."

"Excellent. How will I transport your swarms?"

"The elected ones will gather in one of the mounds. You can carry it in one of the transport crates."

"How about air pressure? Is it all right to fly you to our base?"

"Yes, we're not that fragile. The only real danger to us is if we get too wet. Nanomites need air and we don't swim."

"Okay, I'll keep that in mind."

Leek, Sgt. Hawkh, and the old man found the transport crate and loaded it on the bed of the truck. Then they gathered their things and drove back to the farm. In the distance they saw Tam and Red's fighters waiting for them. As they neared the makeshift runway, Tam and Red got out of their planes and came to greet them. They embraced and exchanged pleasantries, but with the TGA expected anytime they didn't delay in loading their cargo and getting underway.

Since the T-47s needed only one pilot Leek, Sgt. Hawkh, and the nanomites had to fly in the cargo hold. As Leek sat cramped in the small compartment he thought of Tam and how much he had hated it when he had to ride there after his rescue from Pegaport.

Eventually he felt the fighter touch down. When Tam opened the door to the cargo hold he heard the sound of heavy rain. Panic struck him like a jagged rock.

"The nanomites can't get wet! Tell Red to keep the door to the cargo hold closed until we can get something to cover the crate when we take it out."

Tam nodded and ran over to Red's fighter. After a few moments of scratching their heads they pulled the big camouflage net out and used the bag it was kept in to cover the nanomites' crate. Then they carried it carefully down to the Earth Shuttle 26 and loaded it aboard.

Captain Shilling met them in the room she had made ready for her visitors. "Captain Lanzia, I'm so glad to finally meet you. I've heard some impressive things about you from Tam, Red and . . . well . . . other admirers."

Leek blushed. "Well, I've survived so far, but I don't know about tomorrow."

"So, you're a realist. That's good."

Tam introduced the captain to Sgt. Hawkh and told her about how he'd been assigned to keep him out of danger.

"Well, you've done well. It would have been a great loss had we lost Captain Lanzia. I wonder if you're up to a new assignment, Lieutenant."

"Lieutenant?"

"Yes, you'll need to be an officer for the task I have for you."

"Of course. I'm at your disposal."

"Good. The remnants of the 3rd Army are scattered all over the Doral Mountains. I need someone to find them and reestablish communications."

"Sure, no problem. I'm quite familiar with the 3rd Army and I'm anxious to find out what happened to everybody anyway. When do I start?"

"First thing in the morning. Get a good night's sleep and I'll have a transporter and crew ready for you right after breakfast. We need to get the 3rd Army back in operation just as fast as we can."

Captain Shilling called over one of her staff members and told him to escort Lt. Hawkh to his quarters, then turned back to Leek.

"We've got so much to do and so little time. Forgive me if I seem distracted at times."

"I quite understand," Leek said. "These are difficult times. Tam and Red have told me how impressed they are with you and your ship. It's a pleasure to be aboard."

"Thank you. . . . So, I understand you've brought me nanomites. That's wonderful. I'm honored to have nanomites aboard my ship. I just wish I could talk to them and welcome them."

"I can do that for you, if you'd like," Leek said.

She smiled. "Please do."

Leek closed his eyes and tried to see an image of a nanomite in his mind's eye. When it appeared he conveyed the Captain's greeting and translated for her.

"Welcome to Earth Shuttle 26. It's an honor to have you aboard."

"Thank you. It is our distinct pleasure to be aboard such an amazing craft. It is hard to imagine that your ship travels through space to other worlds."

"Yes. That is quite amazing. Is there anything I can get you now? Are you comfortable?"

"We are fine for now. In a few days we will need food. We'll let you know when that is required."

"How are the relocations going? I know Captain Lanzia and Lorin Boskie were helping coordinate things."

"Yes, thanks to Captain Lanzia's warning and with the help of the Loyalist organization throughout Tarizon most of our swarms are safe for now."

"Wonderful. Now, promise me you'll let me know if you need anything?"

"We promise and thank you for your hospitality."

"My pleasure. . . . I'm sorry, but I must leave you now. Captain Lanzia, I'd like to see you in my office at 1800 to give you your orders."

Leek saluted. "Yes, Captain. I'll see you then."

Captain Shilling left and Leek said his goodbyes to the nanomites, promising to return each day to check on them. Then he headed for the dining room where he was to meet Tam, Red, and John. On his way memories of his abduction from Earth and trip to Tarizon came flooding back through his mind. He thought of his mother and father and the siblings he'd left back on Earth. What were they doing? Did they miss him? It seemed like a lifetime since he'd come to Tarizon. In the dining hall he found his friends and took a seat.

"Leek, this is Lt. John Sillmar. He's a pilot from the 2nd Loyalist Air Force. He was one of the few survivors of the ambush."

Leek smiled and they shook hands enthusiastically. "It's great to meet you."

Tam told Leek about the techniques they'd been developing for destroying hovertanks. "So you were able to connect with me through your dreams? That's pretty handy," Leek said.

"I must have, because I didn't know anything about hovertanks, but you were studying them and trying to figure out their weaknesses. I just took your ideas and experimented with them."

"That's excellent. You'll be getting a lot more practice here soon when the TGA crosses the Khor River."

"Yeah, but what good are three fighters against three thousand?" Red asked dejectedly.

"You're right," Leek replied thoughtfully. "We've got to figure out how to get more planes."

"The last time I checked," Red replied, "we didn't have any aircraft manufacturing facilities operational."

"No. We don't. I was thinking about stealing more planes."

"We're going to walk onto an air force base and steal planes?" Red said, shaking his head.

"It isn't like we haven't done it before."

"Right, but that was different."

"Not really. This is the same concept, it's just a bit more complicated," Leek said. "I have to travel up to Gallion and pick up Lorin. I'm going to scout out the TGA air force base and the naval yards while I'm there."

"May I speak frankly, sir?" John asked.

Leek laughed. "If you don't, I'll see to your court martial."

"Good. Your plan seems . . . well . . . insane."

Leek shrugged. "I agree it might appear that way, but in my mind I can see it working—quite well actually."

"How many planes do you think we could steal?" Tam asked.

"I don't know. We need to find out how many pilots we have. That will be the deciding factor."

"But the base will be heavily guarded and the planes will have ignition keys and security codes," Red pointed out. "You can't just jump into a plane, start the engine and take off. What if they have self-destruction devices?"

"Those are all legitimate points that we will have to take into consideration. I know it won't be easy, but I believe it can be done. More importantly, if we don't do it, I don't see how we can stop the TGA from taking Rigimol."

Red swallowed hard. Tam raised his eyebrows. John said, "You're probably right about that. So, what can we do to help?"

"You all need to locate pilots, assemble and train them here, and teach them how to destroy hovertanks. In the meantime, I'm going to be working on our plans for acquiring planes. We're going to need a lot of help to pull it off, so I'm going to summon the seafolken while I'm near the ocean. It's about time they got into the fight."

"Summon the seafolken?" John repeated with raised eyebrows.

Leek explained to John how three seafolken generals had come to him in a dream and offered their help. Then he told him about the seafolken rescuing them during the battle of Lortec and escorting their boat out to sea and away from danger.

"Red and John can get the pilots assembled," Tam said. "I'd like permission to assemble a special tactical squad of mutant soldiers—soldiers with extraordinary abilities that will be useful to you at Gallion."

Leek nodded. "Good idea. Permission granted."

After they'd finished dinner Tam decided it was time to relay the message from Tehra. He wasn't sure how Leek would take the news, so he was a little nervous as he started.

"Ah. There's one more thing," Tam said.

"What's that?" Leek asked.

"Ah. Well. When we first got here to the Earth shuttle we met a guide returning from Earth."

"A guide, did she know Lucinda?"

Tarizon: Civil War

"I don't know. We never asked her, but she did know your father."

"What? My father?"

Tam explained what Tehra had told them about her working with his father and becoming very close. He told him about how his father had helped destroy a TGA Earth shuttle in service to the TGA and then hid her and other Loyalists until they could be picked up by Earth Shuttle 26. Leek was thunderstruck.

"You've got to be kidding me. This is some kind of joke, right?"

"No. I don't think so. Tehra seemed quite sincere. She was going to make sure the brass in Shini knew what your father had done for the Loyalist cause."

Leek didn't know what to say. He just sat there in stunned silence for a few moments. Finally he said, "So Dad and Mom are okay?"

"Yes, she said your mother had taken your death very badly but when she found out you were alive she recovered quickly. There's something else too."

Leek's eyes narrowed. "What?"

"Ah. We told you Tehra was pregnant, right?"

"No, you didn't mention that."

"Well, you know that's why women go to Earth."

"So I've been told."

"Well, ah . . . it turns out that . . . ah . . . well, how should I say it?"

Leek laughed. "Just spit it out. I'm dying of suspense."

"Well, pretty soon you're going to have a brother on Tarizon."

"Huh?" Leek said, not seeming to comprehend what Tam had said. "A brother? What are you talking about?"

Suddenly Leek understood the implications of Tam's words. "That's not possible," he said angrily. "My father would never betray my mother."

"I got the impression from Tehra that she kind of tricked your father into it. You know how those seafolken women can be."

"She was a seafolken?"

"Well, part seafolken. I'm not sure how much."

"Oh, my God. I'm going to have family on Tarizon. That's incredible. When is she due? I'll have to go to Shini for the delivery!"

Leek was on the verge of tears. Tam and Red just looked at him in astonishment. They hadn't expected him to be so happy about Tehra's pregnancy. Sensing their feelings, Leek said, "You don't know how lonely it's been here for me. The idea that I'll have a real family again is—." He turned away, trying to regain his composure.

"Yeah. It's good to have family," Red said. "I'd feel the same way."

Leek turned back, wiped a tear from his eye, and sighed. "Yeah. Hey. I'll see you guys tomorrow before I leave, okay?"

"Sure," Red replied.

"Oh. Where's Rhin? Have you seen her?"

"I saw her run off into the woods earlier," Tam said. "I haven't seen her since."

"Too bad. I could have used the company."

They nodded and Leek left to go to the cabin that had been assigned to him. It was compact but had all the amenities that he needed including a bed, shower, closet, entertainment center and computer. He even had his own GC with a monitor so he could see who he was talking to.

Leek lay down on his bunk and thought about Tehra and his new brother. He wanted to spend time with him since his father obviously wouldn't be able to do it. He knew it was particularly important when a child was very young to bond with a male. Those were the formative cycles that would determine his character and ambition.

He wondered what kind of a mother Tehra would be and how she'd feel about him. Then it struck him that Tehra would probably have a mate who'd act as her baby's new father. Leek didn't know how he felt about that. He didn't know if he wanted to share his brother with another man. Finally, he thought of Lucinda. How would she feel about Leek's new brother? She'd love him, he was sure. She'd be happy to learn that Leek would have a blood relative on Tarizon. She'd be happy about anything that made Leek happy. He was sure of that.

Leek's thoughts turned to Lucinda's desperate circumstances. He hadn't even begun to plan her rescue. Fate was coming at him so fast he hadn't had time to even think about it. His immediate goal was stopping the TGA before they took over all of Lemaine Shane. If that happened the civil war would be over and Videl Lai wouldn't have any reason to keep her alive. He had to figure out a way to stop the TGA advance. There was no other option!

The alarm on his data pod buzzed. He'd set it so he wouldn't forget to report to Captain Shilling as requested. His mind had a way of wandering off and often he'd discovered that hours had gone by without him realizing it. When he got to her office, her assistant, a Lt. Shuvin, told him to wait. Lt. Shuvin was human but had an odd quality about her. Leek wondered if she was a mutant. It didn't matter to him, of course, but he wondered if she had any special powers or abilities.

A green light blinked on the lieutenant's desk and she nodded that Leek could go in. He smiled, strolled past her into the captain's office and stood before her. Captain Shilling was writing something in a file. When she was finished she looked up and said, "Have a seat, Captain."

Leek took a seat and looked around the captain's office. There were photographs and paintings of beautiful landscapes. He didn't recognize any of them, of course, since he'd actually seen little of Tarizon and what he had seen was brown and blighted. Captain Shilling caught him eyeing her display and smiled.

"These are all pre-eruption era photos and paintings. I like to think ahead to the future. They say in ten more cycles we may be able to see our sun again. The landscape should recover quickly then."

"Yes," Leek replied excitedly. "It's already happening on Lortec and the Beet Islands. Even as far north as Mulh the forests are quite magnificent. Not that I even want to go there again. They have a nasty bird there called a Drogal."

"Yes, I've heard of them. They're similar to your dragons back on earth."

"Yeah, but dragons aren't real. At least I've never seen one."

"I believe they actually did exist many Earth centuries ago. I'm kind of a history buff, as you call it on Earth—Earth's history as well as Tarizon's. I know quite a lot about Pharidon, our mother planet, as well."

"Really?"

"Yes. It is believed that many animals from Pharidon were brought to Earth and Tarizon. They were raised and nurtured by the first settlers and then released to live and evolve on their own."

"Wow. That's very interesting. Is there proof of that theory?"

"Not really. There is much evidence to support it but no irrefutable proof, I'm afraid it's been lost over the ages."

"Hmm. That's too bad. It would be kind of a cool theory."

A smile broke out on her face. "Cool. I've heard that term on Earth. It's used by teenagers, right?. . . But, I guess you are still a teenager."

Leek shrugged.

"It's hard to believe God has given so much responsibility to one so young."

"Oh, you mean the Prophecy. Well, there's no irrefutable proof that I'm the Liberator. In fact, I think Loyalist command wishes they'd never ordained me with that title."

"Well, that's politicians for you. They use people like bullets. When they're loaded and ready for use they'll cherish and protect them, but once they're spent, they toss them aside like common garbage. The only reason you're still alive is that you still might be useful to them."

Leek was a little startled to hear Captain Shilling talk about her superiors the way she was. He wondered if she was testing him—trying to get him to say something treasonous.

"I don't know Chancellor Mammett, but I don't think Lorin or her father were like that," Leek replied carefully.

"No. Chancellor Garcia was no politician. He was a visionary, a man of great wisdom and integrity—qualities rarely found in politicians. Unfortunately, Chancellor Mammett is a pure politician with few redeeming qualities."

"Maybe so, but he's our commander in chief, so I guess we're stuck with him."

"He's not my commander and chief," Captain Shilling said.

Leek frowned. "But, didn't you join the Loyalist movement when you brought your ship back to Earth?"

"No, in fact Loyalist command thinks the ship was destroyed during reentry. Officially everyone aboard this ship is dead."

"What about the guide, Tehra? I thought she went to Shini."

"She did, but she wasn't an official passenger on this vessel. She was one of many marooned Loyalists we picked up before we left Earth. She knows not to mention Earth Shuttle 26."

"I'm confused. What are you planning to do with the ship now?"

"It's going to be your new headquarters. You're going to take command of the 3rd Loyalist Army and eventually, if God wills it, all the Loyalist armies. We've got everything you'll need aboard this ship to do it."

Leek just looked at Captain Shilling in disbelief. He couldn't believe an entire army was being dropped in his lap. He knew eventually he'd be given a real command, but he'd hardly had sufficient training or experience for it to happen now. He struggled to respond.

Tarizon: Civil War

"Yes, but the 3rd Army has been destroyed. And even when it was fully operational it was no match for the TGA. So, even if we somehow bandage it together, without the support of the new Loyalist government and the 1st and 2nd Loyalist armies, what could we possibly do to defeat Videl?"

"You're already doing it. Didn't you just take control of the Loyalist cell network?"

"Yes. But just so we could protect the nanomites."

"Exactly. You can't help yourself. It's the Prophecy. You're taking control of the revolution and you don't even know it."

Leek sighed. "Do you really believe that?"

"Yes, and I think you do too."

"Well, sometimes I do things and then wonder what in God's green Earth was I thinking. It does at times seem like someone else is guiding me."

"Events are guiding you. You are just reacting to them the way the Liberator would be expected to. . . . Right now, what's most on your mind?"

Leek took a deep breath and thought about it briefly. "We've got to get some fighters if there's any hope at stopping the TGA before they reach Shini."

Captain Shilling's eyes widened. "True, but where could we get fighters in time to do any good?"

"I thought we'd steal them from Gallion."

Captain Shilling laughed. "That's brilliant, but how could you pull that off? I mean, steal fighters from the enemy!"

He told her of his plans to enlist the support of the seafolken, the mutants and the nanomites and to come up with a plan to steal hopefully a thousand planes. She loved the idea of it, but had severe doubts as to its feasibility.

"I don't know, but it's our best shot. Tam and Red have come up with an effective way to destroy hovertanks, but it requires three fighters working together to do it. There are over nine hundred hovertanks leading the TGA assault. We'll need at least a thousand planes to stop them—600 for the direct attacks on the tanks, 300 to fend off the TGA fighters while ours work, and a hundred to disrupt the supply lines so we can isolate their army and wear them down."

"What do you need from me? " Captain Shilling asked.

"I saw you have some seafolken aboard. I'm going to summon the seafolken generals when I go to Gallion in the morning to pick up Lorin.

William Manchee

Your seafolken crew members might be helpful in making contact."

"There were fifty-one seafolken aboard the shuttle. I released most of them when we landed. They were slaves and the Loyalist Assembly abolished slavery during their first session. A few didn't want to leave and enlisted in the Loyalist army—seven, I think. I'll assign them to you."

"Excellent. I'll need a transport plane. Did any survive the Battle of Rini?"

"Yes. There are two still operational."

"Good. I'll need them tomorrow morning."

"I'll have them ready for you at dawn, Commander."

"Commander?"

"Yes, with the command of the 3rd army comes the rank of Commander General. It's one rank below a full general. You are now the highest ranking officer in the 3rd army."

"What's left of it."

"Right."

A glint of a smile came over Leeks face. "Is *he* behind all of this?"

"Who?"

"Threebeard?"

"He *is* the Defense Minister," Captain Shilling said and returned to her file. "The fact that the 3rd Army is in shambles makes it possible for him to put you in charge. Under normal circumstances there would be a revolt amongst the officers you skipped over, but after such a humiliating defeat, Threebeard can justifiably say a radical change was needed."

Leek shook his head, turned, and left Captain Shilling's office. As he walked back to his quarters he ran his new title through his mind. *Commander General Leek Lanzia.* It had a nice ring to it, he thought, but instead of feeling exhilaration and pride he felt fear and trepidation. He'd just committed to an impossible and probably insane plan—stealing a thousand T-47 fighters from a highly fortified enemy military base. He swallowed hard. *Why does everyone follow me so blindly? Are they nuts?* His plan now seemed reckless and foolish and likely to get a lot of people killed for nothing. His hands began to shake. He stuck them in his pockets so nobody would notice as they passed him by.

Commander General? I'm not even old enough to drink back on Earth, but here they expect me to rebuild an Army and save them from the most evil despot in the history of Tarizon.

Tarizon: Civil War

When he got to his quarters he went in quickly and locked the door. He leaned against it and slowly slid to the ground, tears welling in his eyes. *What am I doing?* He wanted to go home—back to Earth and go to college. *Life was so much easier when nothing was expected of you*, he mused. There was a knock on the door. Startled, he jerked back and quickly wiped the tears from his eyes.

"Commander Lanzia? Corporal Lakey reporting, sir."

Leek took a deep breath, trying to regain his composure. "What do you want?"

"Captain Shilling told me to report to you. She said you needed some help from the seafolken onboard."

Leek got up quickly and opened the door. "Come in, corporal."

He turned away, fearing his eyes were red and the seafolken would notice. Motioning toward his desk chair, he said, "Sit down."

Corporal Lakee took a seat and smiled nervously. "Would you like a tekari?" Leek asked.

The corporal nodded, so Leek went to his refrigerator and pulled out two green bottles. He handed one to him and then sat down on the edge of his bunk.

"I don't know a lot about seafolken, corporal. So, forgive me if I say anything stupid. It's just that we're kind of behind the eight ball. That's an expression we use back on Earth that means our backs are against the wall. You know what I mean?"

"Yes, sir. The TGA is about to kick our ass. I've known quite a few Earth children. I've heard all of your expressions."

"Good. I'll get to the point. The seafolken have pledged to help in the fight against Videl Lai. I've summoned them once before on Lortec and I plan to summon them again at Gallion."

"Videl Lai is our enemy. He has murdered thousands of our people and enslaved tens of thousands. We will do whatever you ask of us to rid the world of him."

"Good. The problem I have right now is time. I've concocted a very complex plan that will require the help of as many seafolken as I can round up quickly. I don't know how you all communicate. I know at Lortec all I did was ask and fifty seafolken suddenly showed up. That's great, but I'm not sure it would work a second time. I'd feel better if I knew for sure."

Corporal Lakee nodded. "The seafolken are basically human but we differ in a few respects. Our feet and hands swell when we enter the water so we can swim as fast as any fish. Since it's difficult to talk under water we communicate telepathically. This telepathic ability, however, is only good for short range communication. When you summoned the help of the seafolken only those close by heard you. We use GCs just like you do for long-distance telecommunications."

"Oh, so you can get a message out to your leaders anytime?"

"Yes, if you have a GC and know their frequencies and codes."

"Do you?"

"Of course."

"Perfect!"

Leek told Corporal Lakee his plan and asked him to communicate it to Talhk, Rusht, and Quirken.

"You know our generals?"

"Only from my dreams," he said ruefully, "but that's not unusual for me."

"Dreams were how we communicated over long distances before there were GCs. It wasn't a very reliable method, though, since the dreams had to be interpreted."

"Yes. Let's use the GC. Do you have one?"

"No, sir."

"You can use mine until we get you one of your own."

Leek was feeling much better after talking to Corporal Lakee. One of his most worrisome questions had been answered. Things were beginning to fall into place and the fear and despair that had nearly strangled him earlier was gone and forgotten. Confidence restored, he was focused once more on the task at hand. It was a difficult plan, but not impossible. He could pull it off, he knew he could, he kept telling himself until he drifted off to sleep.

9
Responsibility

Lt. Hawkh was enjoying his battlefield promotion immensely. It felt great to have the crew salute him and call him sir. He was a career soldier but never had any expectations of becoming an officer. Mutants didn't become officers in the TGA when he joined up, so he had never thought about becoming one.

Early on he had proven himself a natural soldier and advanced from private to sergeant in just three cycles. His mutation, or enhancement as he liked to think of it, was a third ear on the back of his head that gave him the ability to hear sounds beyond the range of the normal human ear. He also had a superior intellect, which together with his audio enhancement made him an astute soldier. He was first noticed by Major Linz and was quickly assigned to his staff. At this point he'd reached the pinnacle of his career, so he thought. But now, he'd made a jump rarely seen in the Tarizonian military. He'd become one of the elite, an officer, a mutant officer at that. It was hard for him to believe it was true.

Now for the first time he realized the Loyalists were sincere in their beliefs about freedom, equality and the abolition of slavery—at least Captain Shilling and Commander Lanzia were. The thought of it almost brought tears to his eyes. But it didn't last. What did last was the weight of responsibility that had just been dropped on him like a lead pipe. He was in charge of re-establishing contact with all elements of the 3rd Army which was scattered all across the Doral Mountains—just a mere 10,000 square kylods to search!

The 3rd Army, the mutant army, had been comprised of sixty-three divisions: fifty-five infantry, five medical, two engineering, and one airborne. The airborne division by all reports had been totally destroyed at Rini. Only a half dozen fighters, a few copters and three transport planes had survived the battle, mainly because they stayed away from it. It was unclear what was

Tarizon: Civil War

left of the infantry divisions. What was clear was that hundreds of thousands of bodies had been left on the plains of Tributon. Those who were not obliterated by the hovertanks were mercilessly killed by the infantry that followed in their wake. Videl Lai was making good on his promise to rid Tarizon of what he called "its mutant cancer."

Of the sixty-two infantry divisions comprised of approximately 20,000 soldiers each, only eleven had been accounted for at the time Lt. Hawkh was promoted and given the assignment to locate them and reestablish contact. The eleven who had reported in had sustained losses of up to eighty-two percent of their personnel with half of the remaining soldiers left wounded and unfit to fight. Lt. Hawkh feared the reports from the other divisions would be worse.

The next morning he met his crew and took off in search of the fifty-one missing divisions. Their first destination was a hospital camp that had reportedly been set up by one of their medical divisions in the southern region of the Doral Mountains. It was about a forty-loon copter ride from the base. The flight would have been routine except that the TGA had decided they could spare a couple infantry and one airborne division to comb the Doral mountains for survivors of the Rini Massacre.

It was late summer in the Dorals and thunderstorms were a common occurrence. Due to the polluted skies it was often difficult to see a thunderstorm approaching, making flying somewhat hazardous. It was during one of these encounters with an unexpected storm that Lt. Hawkh and his crew had their first encounter with the TGA air force. They had just swung around a huge thundercloud, trying to avoid its strong winds and heavy rain, when they spotted three enemy fighters overhead.

The pilot looked at his radar screen and frowned. "Hostile at 1600!"

Lt. Hawkh looked up at the barely visible objects in the sky. "Do you think they've spotted us?"

"I don't know. I'm going to take us down to the tree tops just in case they haven't."

The fighters suddenly dropped and swung around toward them. "Skutz! They've spotted us," the pilot yelled over the rumble of thunder that shook the chopper.

Lt. Hawkh looked out over the hazy landscape for a place to hide. In the air they would be easy prey for the TGA fighters. Ahead he saw a narrow gorge that plunged deep into the mountain. "Take us down into that gorge up ahead. Maybe we'll be able to find a place to hide."

The pilot veered over to the gorge and descended into its depths. Almost immediately Lt. Hawkh realized he'd made a big mistake. The gorge was narrow but not so narrow the fighters couldn't swoop in and gun them down. He looked around nervously and froze when he saw the TGA fighter drop into the gorge behind them.

"Oh, God! We're done for," Lt. Hawkh moaned. "I'm sorry!"

Suddenly there was a flash of light, a crack of thunder and a downpour of rain that cut visibility to five feet. The copter began rocking and shaking violently. Lt. Hawkh strained his eyes but couldn't see the fighter. "Land! Land her right now!" Lt. Hawkh ordered.

The pilot looked over at Lt. Hawkh like he was a lunatic. "Land! Right now." Lt. Hawkh repeated.

The pilot cut the throttle and copter dropped quickly into the thick grey mist. There was a *swish* overhead, causing the copter to rock back and forth violently. Then another flash of light, but this flash wasn't from lightning but an explosion.

Lt. Hawkh looked at the pilot.

"Well that takes care of one of them," the pilot noted.

"See if you can find a place to land," Lt. Hawkh said.

The pilot looked at his instruments. "We're fifty feet off the ground. Hopefully we'll be able to see it soon and then I can look for a spot."

After a few tiks they saw the river raging below them. "Over there!" Lt. Hawkh yelled. "There's a sandbank."

The pilot nodded and swung the copter over and settled it down on the soft sand. They looked up overhead anxiously and were gladdened to see nothing but dark grey clouds. The storm eventually waned and the skies cleared, but Lt. Hawkh knew the enemy would be gone as they'd have to return to base for fuel.

"We'd better get out of here in case they send someone back here looking for us," Lt. Hawkh said.

"Yes, sir," the pilot responded. "Where should we go? Back to base?"

"No, let's get back on our original course. We've got to find that hospital camp before nightfall."

The pilot nodded and started the engines. In a few moments they were climbing up out of the gorge which was quite beautiful in the bright sky. Lt. Hawkh looked up and said, "You know, one of these days we're going to look up in the sky and see the sun."

"Wouldn't that be a sight," the pilot replied.

Then, as they climbed out of the narrow gorge where they'd escaped certain death, they saw it—miles upon miles of camocubes. Had they been a hundred feet higher they would have missed them, as they were designed to blend in with their environment. Each ulta-thin, lightweight, 10' x 10' sinalithic building block could be inflated in a few tiks and attached to other cubes to make almost any size structure that was needed. Since each soldier carried one cube in his standard infantry pack, there were always plenty of cubes to build whatever temporary structure was needed. Once inflated, the cubes were staked to the ground and could withstand gale force winds. Sound shields could also be placed on any square surface to provide privacy as needed.

Between the array of camocubes were campfires, ATVs, military equipment, armaments, and thousands upon thousands of wounded soldiers sitting around waiting for medical treatment. The copter cruised over the hastily built hospital compound. Lt. Hawkh's jaw dropped as he contemplated the suffering beneath him. He ordered the pilot to land.

Once on the ground the crew got out and began searching the compound for the officer in charge. The stench of death was heavy in the camp. Soldiers were loading bodies onto trucks while other wounded soldiers looked on with great trepidation in their eyes. Lt. Hawkh put his hand on one of the soldier's shoulders. "Corporal, who's in charge here?"

The soldier looked at Lt. Hawkh. "That would be Captain Buril, sir."

"Where can I find him?"

He pointed a southerly direction and replied, "The last time I saw him he was in the surgical cube—over there about half a kylod. It's the biggest cube in the compound. You can't miss it."

Lt. Hawkh thanked the soldier and went on with his crew in his wake. After a few loons they saw the large surgical cube in the distance. There was a scream from one of the cubes they were passing and voices arguing. Lt. Hawkh peered in at the dozens of cots lined up on both sides. The cube reeked of a combination of alcohol, blood and urine. A medic looked up at him.

"Can I help you, sir?" he asked.

"How long have you been here, soldier—this camp, I mean?"

"Seven days, sir."

"How many are in the camp?"

He shrugged. "I don't know"

"What unit were you from?"

"The 23rd Medical Division, sir."

"Thank you, carry on."

The group continued on to the surgical cube and entered it. It was an enormous array of cubes and appeared to Lt. Hawkh to house over a hundred beds. He grabbed the arm of a female nurse and asked, "Where can I find Captain Buril?"

The nurse gave Lt. Hawkh a once-over and asked, "You from Central Command?"

"Yes."

"Where in the name of Sandee have you been?" she said angrily.

"I'm sorry it took us so long to find you, but we've just got our new command center up and running. What's the situation here?"

"We have over eighty thousand wounded soldiers and we ran out of most of our medical supplies three days ago. The death rate around here is about five thousand a day."

Lt. Hawkh sighed. "I see. Why haven't you tried to make contact with us?"

"The hovertanks destroyed all our communications equipment and the sick and wounded have been flooding in so fast we've been too overwhelmed to try to rig up something. How did you find us, anyway?"

"We heard a report from a soldier that was treated here. He gave us an approximate location."

As they were talking, a grey-haired officer strolled up. "Sgt. Gittings, you're needed in surgery."

"Oh, Captain Buril. These men are from Central Command."

Lt. Hawkh extended his hand. "Hello, Captain. I'm Lt. Hawkh. We've had a difficult time finding you."

"Excuse me," Sgt. Gittings said. "It's been a pleasure, but I'm needed in surgery."

Lt. Hawkh nodded. "Of course, thank you." She smiled at him as she left.

"Well, I'm glad you're here now. As you can see the situation here is rather desperate."

Tarizon: Civil War

"Yes, I'll radio back to base and get you some help up here. In the meantime, I'd like to begin questioning soldiers to see what I can find out about our missing divisions."

"Sure. I'll get someone to take you around."

Lt. Hawkh divided his sixteen crew members into eight teams and got them started on canvassing the compound. He immediately realized he was going to need more manpower as the camp was so large. When he got back to the copter he got on the radio to call command.

"C1 calling base. Do you read?"

"H1 here," a voice said.

"Hi. Lt. Hawkh reporting in. Is Captain Shilling there?"

'Yes, one moment, please."

"Lt. Hawkh. Captain Shilling here."

"Yes, ma'am. We've located the medical compound."

Lt. Hawkh gave his report on the conditions at the base and advised that immediate and massive assistance would be needed.

"I'm afraid we don't have much to send them right away, but I'll start working on it."

"Good. I'm coming back to base. I'm going to need a lot more help reestablishing contact with our missing divisions."

He told her about the TGA fighters and his concern for the camp's security. The captain assured him she'd send some troops over for security and be sure they were equipped with portable Muscan missile launchers to deal with any fighters that might spot them. When he hung up he stepped outside again and looked out over the vast medical camp. He sighed in despair, wondering how many of these soldiers would survive this ordeal and go on to fight another battle.

10
A Bold Plan

Lorin's GC beeped, waking her from a shallow slumber. Looking out the window she saw nothing but clouds beneath them. She wondered how far they were from Gallion. When she was a child her father and mother had taken her there quite often to visit her aunt. Memories flashed through her mind of thousands of ships lined up along the docks, a relentless cold westerly wind, and strange scary people called seafolken. She shook away the sleep and answered the call.

"S1 here."

"Lorin, this is Senator Marcuzzi. I'm glad I caught you."

"What's wrong, Senator?" Lorin replied.

"Chancellor Mammett is very upset that you have left the capital. He found out somehow that the cells have been activated and he wants an explanation. He wants you to return at once."

"I can't do that, Senator. I'm about to get picked up by Captain Lanzia. There's no way I'm going back to Shini."

"He's issued an order for your arrest."

"My arrest? That's ridiculous."

"He and other members of the Assembly believe you are trying to subvert the new government."

"What government? They're all a bunch of worthless bureaucrats with no idea how to wage a war or run a government for that matter. I'm going where I can do some good."

"You'd better check your course. If your pilot's in contact with Loyalist Command they will surely recall your plane."

Lorin's heart skipped a beat as she looked out the portal again into the dense fog. Visibility was still zero. She jumped up and went into the cockpit. The pilot glanced over to her anxiously. Her eyes fixed on the compass reading of NW. They were headed back to Shini.

"Where are you taking me?" she demanded.

"Ah. I've been ordered back to base, Ma'am."

"Captain Lanzia is picking me up in Gallion. We have important business there."

"I'm sorry, Ma'am. I have my orders," the pilot said evenly.

Lorin slipped her hands behind her back and retrieved a C34 pistol. She aimed it at the pilot. "Your orders have changed. Take me to Gallion and pick up the pace, I don't want to be late."

The pilot stiffened up. "Yes, Ma'am. Whatever you say. Don't shoot."

"You have nothing to worry about if you change your course now and keep off your communicator."

"Understood. I won't cause you any trouble."

"Good. I'm in a bad mood and if you give me an excuse I'll blow your head off and fly the plane myself."

"You know how to fly this plane?"

"Oh, yes. My husband is a pilot and I've been up with him many times. He's taught me everything he knows."

The pilot raised his eyebrows but said nothing. Lorin wondered what he was thinking. "What will they do when they see you change course?"

He shrugged. "I don't know—maybe nothing. They don't really have any fighters they can spare to come after us."

"Good. I don't want any more trouble. How long ago did they call you?"

"About a half a kyloon ago."

"So, how long until we get to Gallion?"

"Less than a kyloon at the present course and speed."

"Can you go faster?"

"Yes."

"Then accelerate to maximum cruising speed."

"Yes, Ma'am."

Lorin found a place to sit down where she could hold the gun on the pilot and watch the compass. She didn't trust him to take her to Gallion voluntarily. She wondered if he had already somehow alerted Loyalist Command that the plane had been hijacked. If so, would the Chancellor have her shot down rather than let her rendevous with Captain Lanzia? The one thing she had going for her was that the TGA controlled the skies, so it was unlikely they'd risk sending one of their precious Loyalist fighters after her.

William Manchee

Lorin breathed a sigh of relief when the pilot began to descend for a landing. She prayed they were at Gallion and that Leek would be there to pick her up. It was still dark and foggy out when the plane hit the ground and screeched to a halt. She grabbed her things and started to deplane. Then she looked back at the pilot and said, "Better for both of us if you tell Central Command that you'd already dropped me off when you got the message ordering you back to base."

The pilot nodded and, just as soon as she was on the ground, closed the cabin door, spun the plane around and took off down the runway. She watched it take off, wondering what the pilot would do. When it was out of sight, she swallowed hard and looked out nervously into the darkness, gun in hand, wondering if Leek was out there somewhere. She feared that the pilot had tricked her and hadn't taken her to Gallion at all. In the distance she saw a building with lights in the window. Not knowing what else to do, she headed toward the building.

Halfway there she heard something moving to her right. She swung around and pointed her gun toward the noise.

"Don't shoot," Leek said. "It's me."

Lorin lowered the gun and exhaled. "Thank God."

"What's with your pilot? He just drops you off and leaves you here alone. What if I'd been delayed?"

"He was under orders to take me back to Shini. I had to convince him otherwise."

Leek gave her a wry smile. "I see. So, now you're an enemy of the Loyalists and the TGA?"

"Maybe. I suggested he may not want to admit he let a women overpower him. If he has half a brain he'll take my advice, but if he doesn't, then—."

"Well, I'm sure Chancellor Mammett must feel the same way about me."

"Yes, but he can't afford to arrest you. Threebeard and General Zitor wouldn't stand for it."

"Right. And as long as you're my administrative chief nobody will be messing with you either."

"Administrative chief of what?"

"The 3rd Loyalist Army. I'm the new commander."

"Really?" Lorin said, smiling broadly. "How did that come about?"

Tarizon: Civil War

Leek told her about Captain Shilling and his promotion to Commander General. He explained their plans to steal aircraft from the TGA air base at Gallion and how Tam and Red had figured out how to destroy hovertanks. She was excited and anxious to get working on the plan.

Leek took her to the building where Corporal Lakee and three other seafolken were waiting. They all climbed into a PTV and took off toward Gallion. Soon they could see the ocean in the distance and hear the waves breaking on the beach. About a kylod from Gallion they went off the road and drove along the beach. Finally, they stopped and everyone got out.

"This is where we are to meet them," Corporal Lakee advised.

"Good. Did you brief them on what we are doing?"

"Yes, sir. Briefly. I told them you would give them specific instructions."

"I see. Good."

The ocean in front of them began to churn and heads began popping up everywhere. Soon a dozen seafolken were walking out of the water toward them. Leek walked over to the first one out who seemed to be leading the group.

"Greetings," he said, bowing slightly. He didn't know whether to extend his hand or what. "I'm Leek Lanzia."

The seafolken likewise bowed. "It's an honor to meet you, Commander General Lanzia. I'm Grenz Lozich, General of the Dark Sea Defense League."

Leek glanced at Corporal Lakee and Lorin and said, "Do you know Corporal Lakee and Lorin Boskie?"

"We've never met Corporal Lakee in person, but I spoke with him last night at length. As for Lorin Boskie I have not had the pleasure of meeting her. I did meet her father once. My condolences, Madam Boskie. Your father was an inspiration."

"Thank you," Lorin said. "I've heard my father speak kindly of you as well."

The general bowed appreciatively then turned to Leek. "Congratulations on your promotion."

"Thank you. It was quite unexpected."

"Yes, events are moving fast and time is running out if Videl Lai is to be stopped. I'm grateful that you and Madam Boskie have stepped up to meet the challenge."

William Manchee

"Well, Lorin doesn't have much faith in Chancellor Mammett and I trust her judgement, so it didn't appear we had much choice."

"Yes, there is no time for political posturing," the general said.

"Okay, since Corporal Lakey has briefed you on our plan, you know what we need you to do?"

"Yes, you need a diversion while you steal TGA fighters."

"Exactly. I was thinking that we could kill two birds with one stone, as they say on Earth. Your attack will not only afford us an opportunity to steal the planes but will also strike a severe blow to the TGA navy. I suspect such an attack will catch them completely by surprise since they will be focusing on their own Rigimol offensive."

"Yes, you may be right, but TGA security isn't anything to take lightly. They will be on high alert."

"True. I don't want to downplay the danger involved in this operation, but I fear only a bold, if not brash move, will turn the tide of the war."

"You are the Liberator. We will not challenge your strategy as we believe it is the will of God and Sandee that we trust you."

"Thank you," Leek replied, "Although I've never talked directly to God or Sandee, I do feel driven by some overwhelming force that I cannot begin to understand or explain. I have to assume that what I am feeling is their hand guiding me forward."

"Tell us your plan then quickly, so we can proceed with the diligent preparation needed to make it successful," the general replied.

Leek explained what he wanted them to do and outlined the timetable for each segment of the plan. The meeting went on for half a kyloon before it ended and the seafolken returned to their domain. Lorin then took the opportunity to enlist the seafolken's help in Lortec. General Lozich agreed to contact the General of the Southern Sea Defense League and pass along Lorin's request.

The dark night provided them the cover they needed to explore the perimeter of the TGA base at Gallion. The base stretched along the Dark Sea coast some ten kylods and was five kylods deep. Gallion was the largest naval base in Lemaine Shane and boasted of at least two hundred ships in port on an average day. The air base encompassed the bottom one-third of the base and was the home of the TGA's 22nd and 223rd Airborne Divisions.

From their inspection they learned that the base was surrounded by

Tarizon: Civil War

a 10-foot electrified security fence and there were five access points to the base, each manned by a three-man security team. Each team member had a rifle and a personal sidearm. Although access to the base wouldn't be easy, Leek didn't consider it a serious problem. A more difficult issue was getting access to the planes without alerting base command that it was under siege.

"Have you or any of your men ever served with the TGA navy, Corporal Lakee?" Leek asked.

"Yes, I believe so. Luksa, weren't you a hand on a cruiser?"

One of the seafolken stepped forward, "Yes, sir. I served on the Teratom for three cycles."

"Were you stationed at Gallion?" Leek asked.

"Yes, sir."

"Are there any seafolken still enslaved by the TGA on the base?"

"Yes, sir."

"Do you know any of them?"

"I believe so, sir."

"Good. We'll need their help and if any of them want to join up with us, this will give them the opportunity to do so."

"I'm certain most will be delighted to be given that opportunity."

"You'll need to be careful, though. Only talk to those you trust. We must catch the TGA by complete surprise to pull off this mission."

"Sir," Corporal Lakee said. "If we do get our pilots on the base, how do you plan to get rid of the TGA pilots without alerting base command?"

Leek told them his ideas on that point and then suggested they return to base to make final preparations for the mission. They had but a short time before the TGA was expected to attack and they had to be ready when that happened.

It was after midnight before the PT22 touched down on the makeshift runway at the 3rd Loyalist Army's headquarters. Captain Shilling, Tam and Red were there to meet them. The population of the little valley where the Shuttle had burrowed in had doubled since Leek and his party had left. Red and John had already assembled several hundred pilots and more were arriving every hour. They were being housed in a growing array of camocubes that had been assembled at the north end of the base. Tam had brought in hundreds of mutant soldiers who were engaged in training exercises to the south.

"Lorin! It's been a long time," Captain Shilling said with a broad smile.

Lorin's face lit up in response to the captain. They embraced. "Yes, what has it been, ten or twelve cycles since we last met?"

"At least," she said.

"I didn't know you two knew each other," Leek commented.

"Oh, yes. The Captain's father, Arnell Shilling, and my father were friends. We used to hang out together as teenagers."

"Well, that's good. If you'll excuse me, I've got a lot to do in preparation for our mission."

"Go ahead," Captain Shilling said. "I'll show Lorin around the ship and take her to her quarters. I've scheduled an officers' meeting at 0600 tomorrow to coordinate our plans. If you need me before then my assistant will know where I am."

"Thank you, Captain. I'll see you later," Leek said as he started to walk briskly toward where Tam and the mutants were training.

"Come on, Lorin. I want to show you the command station I've set up for you."

Lorin nodded and followed the captain to the entrance to the shuttle which now was completely underground. From the air, only camocubes and soldiers in training could be seen. They walked down a metal flight of stairs to a long corridor. The pearl white walls along the corridor were soft to the touch. The floor gave a little with each step like a plush carpet. The soft, indirect lighting set a pleasant mood that was enhanced by the soft music in the background.

"So, your Liberator is working out quite well," Captain Shilling said.

"Yes, better than I first thought he would," Lorin replied.

"I like him. He's modest. All of this attention hasn't gone to his head."

"Well, he has a good heart like the Prophecy said he would."

The captain laughed. "Don't tell me you believe in the Prophecy now?"

"I don't know. He's a natural leader and the mutants and seafolken would die for him."

"What about the nanomites? Do you think he's really communicating with them or just pretending?"

Lorin sighed. "I don't think Leek would intentionally lie to us. If he says they are talking to him, then I believe him."

Tarizon: Civil War

The captain nodded. "That's my impression, too. . . . So, have you heard from Jake?"

"No. I was praying that you had."

"I'm sorry, but he's disappeared along with half of the pilots who went up that first day against the TGA."

Lorin closed her eyes and sighed. "If he were dead, I think I'd know it. I feel like he's alive somewhere. I just wish I could go look for him."

"After the next mission we'll get Leek and the Avengers to form a search party to look for missing pilots."

"The Avengers?"

"Yeah. That's what they're calling Tam, Red and John now that they've figured out how to destroy hovertanks. I sure hope our mission to Gallion is successful, so we have the air power to destroy every last one of them."

Lorin sighed. "You know, I'd like to believe Leek's plan will work, but frankly the odds are not good. It's a very imaginative plan but very complex as well, so something could easily go wrong. It depends on the coordinated efforts of so many different life forms, I honestly don't see how it could be pulled off even by our most brilliant generals, let alone a teenager with barely a cycle of military training."

"Why didn't you tell Commander Lanzia how you felt?" Captain Shilling asked.

"Because he doesn't need negative thinking right now. If he believes it will work, maybe it will. Who am I to second-guess the *Liberator*."

"So, you *do* believe in the Prophecy?"

"I guess I do," Lorin admitted, "as illogical as that might seem."

A wry smile came over Captains Shilling's face as they reached their destination. "Okay, right up here is where we've set up your command station." She stopped and looked into a retinal scanner. The door slid open and she motioned Lorin to go in.

"At—tention!" one of the soldiers said.

"At ease," the captain ordered.

Lorin looked around the rectangular room in awe. It was about twenty by thirty feet filled with electronic equipment of every sort. A long conference table split the room with two large video screens on one wall and workstations along the other. A large white desk and chair sat prominently at the far end of the room. Lorin smiled at Captain Shilling.

"Go try it out. I made sure it was comfortable since you may be spending every waking hour here for the next cycle or two."

Lorin went quickly to the desk and sat down gingerly. She took a deep breath and then settled back. The chair made a hissing noise as the material conformed itself to the shape of her body. She closed her eyes a moment. "Yes, I won't have any trouble sleeping in this chair."

They both laughed. "All right," Captain Shilling said pointing to various pieces of equipment. "You've got global communications, weather forecasting, local and regional radar, decoding equipment, computers, printers, and access to all media channels throughout Tarizon. There's also equipment to intercept or jam TGA communications."

"Very impressive," Lorin said, obviously pleased.

"Corporal Lindshill will be assigned to you. Whatever you need he'll get it for you."

"Thank you, Captain. This is wonderful."

"The corporal will introduce you to the rest of your staff."

"Right, I guess I should get to work. I need to follow up on the nanomite situation. I've been out of touch too long."

"Yes, go ahead. I'll come back later and show you to your quarters."

"Right. Thanks," Lorin said as she started punching in numbers into her new communicator. The captain smiled and left the room. Lorin was ecstatic with her new command center. It was more than she could have ever hoped for. Now she had lots of work to do. The green light on her communicator flickered. She picked it up.

"S1 here."

"Lorin? Where are you?" Senator Marcuzzi asked.

"In my new command center."

"Command center?"

"Yes, I'm Commander General Lanzia's new chief of staff. He's got quite a setup here."

"Commander General?"

She told the senator about Leek's promotion and what had happened to her in the hours since they'd last seen each other.

"Well, I'm glad you're okay. The new government here is in a frenzy over the expected TGA offensive and your disappearance hasn't helped."

"They need to quit worrying about me and concentrate on the TGA."

Tarizon: Civil War

"Should I advise the Chancellor of your whereabouts?"

"Yes, it's no secret. Tell him I've taken a job with Commander General Lanzia, so he won't have to worry about me anymore."

"Yeah, right. Somehow I don't think he'll be thrilled with that news."

"Probably not, so just tell him that you got a communication from Commander General Lanzia and that the 3rd Army will be continuing to disrupt the enemy's supply lines and will also be launching their own offensive at the same time as the TGA launches theirs."

"Launch an offenive? I thought the 3rd Army was destroyed."

"Not all of it. We're regrouping and plan to strike the TGA hard when they don't expect it."

"What exactly will *you* be doing?"

"I can't say any more. Someone may be listening in. I just wanted to keep the Chancellor apprised of the situation so he wouldn't be taken by surprise."

"Okay, I'll pass that on to him."

"I've got to go. I need to start calling cell leaders. I'll call you tomorrow."

"Thanks for the update."

Lorin hung up and began punching in numbers again. It was nearly dawn when she finished talking to the last of the cell leaders. All but three of the nanomite farms had been successfully moved and hidden from the TGA. Three were attacked before the cell leaders could organize transportation. Overall it was a successful operation but Lorin was sad that any had to die at Videl's hand.

While she had been on the GC with the cell leaders she told them it was time to begin expanding their operations by recruiting new members, making contact with mutant and seafolken leaders, and setting up an intelligence network. Once they were strong enough, she told them, they'd begin to build local militia to start sabotaging TGA and Central Authority operations.

As she was contemplating whether to find her quarters and try to get some sleep, Leek walked in. He looked fresh and alert but Lorin knew he couldn't have gotten much more than a kyloon's sleep.

"So, how are preparations coming?" she asked him.

"Slow but steady," he said. "There's something I need to check out."

"What's that?" Lorin asked.

"I understand you have a computer that's linked into the TGA web."

"Yes. Captain Shilling has given me everything I need for my operations. What do you need with a TGA web linkup?"

"I've got to see if I can make changes in flight schedules and substitute in new pilots."

Lorin laughed. "And how do you plan to do that? Even if you get onto their network, it would take a computer genius to get through all the passwords and security codes necessary to change a flight schedule."

"True. That's why I want to do a test run first—to see if I can do it. Fortunately the greatest computer genius on the planet has shared his knowledge with me."

Lorin gasped. "Threebeard shared his knowledge *and* memories with you?"

"Yes. So, I should be able to do whatever he can do and he was always bragging about being able to hack into any computer in the galaxy."

"Right. But does sharing his knowledge about computers give you the ability to manipulate them—that's an entirely different process."

"I don't know if it will work. My brain will have to process all of Threebeard's knowledge and experience. I haven't tried doing it yet, but in theory it should be possible."

Lorin squinted. "Okay. That makes sense, but—"

"No buts. Just let me try it. We'll know soon enough if I can do it. If I can't I could probably get Threebeard to do it himself, but he'll be pretty busy and I'd hate to have to distract him from preparations for the TGA offensive."

Lorin stood up and led Leek over to a computer workstation. "Have at it," she said and stepped back.

Leek sat down, took a deep breath, and closed his eyes like he was summoning the spirits to help him. Suddenly he exhaled and began typing at a furious pace. The computer screen burst into an explosion of images. Screens opened and closed quicker than Lorin could even read them. Then the screen froze, there was a loud beep, and a message appeared flashing: "AUTHORIZED CODE REQUIRED." Leek hesitated and then began typing furiously again. The screen went away and others began opening and closing until the home page of Gallion Naval Base and Air Station appeared.

Tarizon: Civil War

Leek clicked on "Today's Schedule" and then on "edit." He pulled out several sheets of paper and began making changes. When he was done he logged off the computer and looked up at Lorin with a grin.

"Boy, Threebeard is one smart mutant, huh?"

Lorin laughed. "Do you have any idea what you just did?"

Leek shrugged. "Not really. I couldn't write it down step by step. I just relaxed and let my subconscious mind take over."

"Well, how do you know if what you did worked?"

Just then the printer started up. When it was finished Leek pulled out the two sheets of paper in the printer. The first was the original flight schedule and the second was the revised schedule.

Leek looked at it with pride and handed it to Lorin. "Check that with my notes and see if all the changes were correct."

Lorin took the papers and compared them to Leek's notes. After a moment she shook her head and smiled. "It appears to have worked, but there may be some increased security on the day of the operation. I hope you can still do it then."

"Me too. If not, we're going to have to kill a lot of TGA pilots."

Lorin's stomach twisted. She didn't have half the faith that Leek possessed. She feared that something would go wrong and not only would the mission fail, but Leek and his men would be killed. If that happened, she thought, all would be lost!

11
Tam and the Mutants

While Leek was off to pick up Lorin, Tam set out with Lt. Hawkh to the camps where the remnants of the 3rd Army had gathered after fleeing from the TGA at Rini and Rizi. His task was to hastily assemble an elite squadron of soldiers to assist in the attack on Gallion. Tam was hopeful he could assemble a group as talented as the one Threebeard had let them borrow when they rescued Lorin and General Zitor.

"So, how many soldiers have you found so far?" Tam asked.

"About forty thousand, but I believe I'll have over a hundred thousand before I'm done."

"What's their condition?"

"They're tired and scared. It's going to take awhile to shape them up into a fighting force again."

"As I said, I'm looking for twenty or thirty soldiers with extraordinary abilities."

He told Lt. Hawkh about the platoon that had helped rescue Lorin and General Zitor and wondered how they might go about assembling a similar one.

"I guess we just need to talk to our platoon leaders and tell them what we're looking for. They'll know if any of their soldiers possess the skills you need."

When they got to the camp Lt. Hawkh summoned the platoon leaders close at hand for a meeting. About a hundred and thirty-five of them gathered in a crude amphitheater under an umbrella of pine trees. Lt. Hawkh told the group the purpose of the meeting and then turned it over to Tam.

"Thank you, Lieutenant. Very soon we're going to launch a very daring attack against the TGA. I can't tell you much about it, but it could be a deciding factor in whether we win or lose the war. What I'm looking for

Tarizon: Civil War

are soldiers with special abilities and talents that might be helpful in this new offensive such as telepathy, telekinesis, heightened senses, abnormal strength, etc."

One of the officers raised his hand. "I've got a man who can run faster than a leaprohd."

"Really? What's his name?" Lt. Hawkh asked.

The officer told him and then another hand went up.

"One of my men can lift up one end of a truck and hold it up with one hand for twenty tiks."

"Wow!" Lt. Hawkh said and took down the name of the soldier. Now hands were raising all around.

"Yes, Lieutenant," Lt. Hawkh said, pointing to another one of the leaders.

"There's a man in my platoon who can break the leg of a range deer without touching him."

Lt. Hawkh began to smile. "Really. Wow, that's excellent. I'll definitely want to meet that soldier."

"That's nothing," another officer boasted. "One of my men can jump over a PTV and land on his feet on the other side."

Lt. Hawkh's smile broadened. He was getting exactly what he wanted and more. The meeting went on for quite a while, and when it was over Tam and Lt. Hawkh were very pleased with the talent they had discovered. Now it was a matter of gathering these extraordinary soldiers together, testing them, and then figuring out how they could help with the mission. While Tam worked on that project Lt. Hawkh joined Red back at headquarters. He was studying his list of pilots he'd been able to locate and bring back to the base.

"Any luck yet?" Lt. Hawkh asked Red from the door of Red's office.

Red looked up and grinned. "Not a lot. I've found about three hundred and twenty so far and about half of them have made it here so far."

"That's not nearly enough," Lt. Hawkh groaned.

"Captain Shilling issued an order for all pilots to report to headquarters for assignment," Red replied. "Unfortunately, we don't know how many will be listening."

"So, what can we do in the meantime?"

"We need to process the pilots we have and teach them how to take out hovertanks. Once we have all of the pilots assembled we'll brief them together on Operation Gallion."

As they were talking, Lorin came over. "We just got a response to our call for pilots."

"What kind of response?" Tam asked.

"A request for transport. Apparently there are about eighty-five pilots in a camp 25 kylods southeast of here. I've got the coordinates."

"Great. I'll get a crew together and we'll go pick them up."

"I want to go with you." Lorin said.

"Why?" Lt. Hawkh asked. "I thought you'd be too busy for sightseeing trips."

Tam jabbed Lt. Hawkh in the ribs. He frowned and glared at him. "What?"

Lorin nodded. "It's all right. It's no secret I'm looking for Jake."

"Oh. . . . Sorry, ma'am," Lt. Hawkh said apologetically. "You're welcome to come with us."

"Thank you. We should get going. We don't have much light left today."

A few loons later they were flying across the treetops in new copters they'd just acquired from defecting TGA pilots. It was believed that there were a lot of TGA soldiers who wanted to defect to the Loyalist army but were just waiting for the right moment to do so. After the battle of Rini thousands of TGA soldiers had deserted their units, ripped all TGA insignia from their uniforms, and fled to the mountains with the retreating Loyalist forces. It was a strange but welcome development.

When the copters got close to the coordinates where the base was supposed to be located, Lorin leaned closer to the window to scan the ground beneath them. "There, I see smoke from a campfire."

The copter swooped down low and the soldiers below began to wave at them. The pilot flew by and landed in a clearing a few lods away. Lorin was the first out of the copter. She sprinted over to them, praying she'd see her mate's face amongst them. The soldiers looked tired and weak from their ordeal. It had been awhile since the battle of Rini and they'd nearly exhausted their food rations.

After mingling through the crowd of soldiers and not finding Jake, Lorin sat down on a log and closed her eyes. She wondered if she'd ever find him. A moment later Tam sat down next to her and put his arm around her. She looked up at him with tears in her eyes.

He smiled. "I sense that Jake is here," Tam said cautiously.

Lorin straightened up and looked around. "What do you mean? I've looked at everyone. I didn't see him."

"I have too, but I can feel his presence. He's around here somewhere."

Lorin knew of Tam's telepathic gifts. She also knew that Tam wouldn't joke about something as important as this. Her spirits soared. She got up, spun around and looked up into the trees. "We've got to search for him," she said.

Tam nodded. "Lt. Hawkh can supervise the transport of the pilots back to base. I'll get a few soldiers to stay here and help us search."

Lorin nodded. "Thanks. Where do you think he might be?"

"I don't know, but he's somewhere close. He may be injured."

Lorin went pale. "Injured? How do you know.?"

"I sense he's in pain. We should hurry."

Tam went off and returned shortly with three soldiers. He sent them all off in different directions and told them to fire their pistols three times if they found anybody. Lorin and Tam also began to search. They searched for nearly a kyloon when it started to get dark. Lorin looked at the darkening sky and feared that soon there wouldn't be enough light to continue the search.

"If he landed around here, why didn't he join the others?" Lorin asked.

"My guess is he was injured or fell some—look! Up in the trees."

Lorin looked up and saw a parachute caught high up in a tree. In the dim light she could barely make out a man swinging gently in the wind.

"Jake!" she screamed and began sprinting toward the tree. Tam pulled out his pistol and shot three times in the air. Lorin was halfway up the tree by the time Tam caught up with her.

"Be careful! Don't do anything. If he falls it could kill him."

Lorin looked down at Tam. "We've got to get him down!"

"I know. Wait for help. It's going to take all of us to get him down safely."

When Lorin reached him she turned his head and looked at his face. "It's Jake. You were right! It's Jake!" She stretched her hand over and felt for a pulse. "He's alive. We've got to get him down!"

"Okay, here come the other soldiers now."

William Manchee

One of the other soldiers climbed up next to Lorin and wrapped a rope around Jake's waist. Then Lorin cut the cord to the parachute and together they gently lowered Jake to the ground. Lorin knew there was a portable stretcher in the copter, so she had one of the pilots bring it to them. Two of the soldiers placed Jake on the stretcher and carried him to the copter. A few loons later they were in the air heading back to base. Lorin knelt over Jake's unconscious body, holding his hand in hers. She prayed he wasn't seriously hurt and would be okay.

When they got back to base they took Jake directly to the Shuttle's sick bay. The chief medical officer met them and took charge. Lorin wanted to stay but the medical officer told her she could do him no good, and promised he'd call her with regular progress reports. Reluctantly, Lorin left to go to her quarters to try to get some sleep. On the way there she ran into Lt. Hawkh.

"How is he?" Lt. Hawkh asked.

"I don't know. The doctor said he'd do a diagnosis and call me. I'm going to my quarters and try to get some sleep. I'm exhausted."

"I can imagine. You didn't sleep any last night, did you?"

"No. I don't have time to sleep."

"Yeah, I guess none of us do."

"What's your pilot tally now?"

"Four hundred and twenty-two."

"That's only a third of what we need."

"I know, but that's four hundred more than we had the day you set up this camp."

"True. Maybe the TGA will hold off a few more days on their offensive. We've been sending in fighters laden with cluster bombs every day since Rizi to raise havoc with their supply lines. Hopefully this will buy us the time we need."

"Hopefully."

"I'm going to my quarters if you need me," Lorin said wearily.

Lt. Hawkh nodded and went on his way. He was heading for a meeting with his division commanders to get an update on how the reorganization of the 3rd Army was going. As he climbed the stairs out of the Shuttle he looked out over the growing array of interconnected camocubes that had sprung up almost overnight. There was much anticipation in the air and he was beginning to feel hopeful that everything would eventually turn out all right.

The meeting was up on the ridge where Tam and Red had set up a strategic planning cube. From that vantage point it was possible to see the entire valley and the main passageways through the mountains. Tam, Red, several staff officers from the shuttle, and five division commanders were waiting when he stepped through the slit in the cube. Everyone looked over as he walked in.

"Gentlemen," Lt. Hawkh said. "Sorry I'm late."

Tam shrugged. "I was just telling everybody how my special op's team was shaping up."

"Oh. How do they look?"

"I've selected thirty-six men. They will be a force to be reckoned with."

"How are you going to use them?"

"That's up to Commander Lanzia. My job is just to get them ready."

"Right. . . . So, what's the latest on the TGA offensive?"

"The enemy hasn't shown any signs of movement yet. They seem to be regrouping and waiting for the right moment to strike."

"They're probably not in a big hurry. I'm sure they think they pretty much have the battle already won," Lt. Hawkh reasoned.

"And they might be right," Red reminded them.

"What's our troop strength now, Lt. Hawkh?" Tam asked.

"By my last count we have sixty-four thousand."

"Well, I hope that's enough," Tam said.

"Enough for what?"

"We've gotten a communique from our Defense Minister."

"Threebeard?" Red asked.

"Yes. He wants us to come down out of the mountains near Rhule and sweep in behind the TGA to cut off their supply lines and box them in."

"Sweep in behind them?" Red said. "Box them in? Are we talking about the same army that just ran over us like we were a sack of potatoes?"

"As unrealistic as that may seem," a voice from behind them said, "that's what we've been ordered to do, so we'll do it."

Everyone turned and saw Commander Lanzia standing behind them with two other officers they didn't know.

"Commander," Tam said and saluted.

William Manchee

"At ease," Leek said and turned toward his companions. "Gentlemen, I'd like to introduce Major Freelan and Major Oakril. They will be two additions to my staff. Major Freelan will be in charge of logistics and Major Oakril will be handling our intelligence operations." The two officers nodded and took a seat. "Also, I'd like to announce that Captain Tam Lavendar will command the 1st Airborne Division if we are successful."

Red raised his eyebrows. "Did you say Captain Lavendar?"

Leek nodded. "Yes, I did. Both you and Tam have been promoted to Captain."

Red looked at Tam. Tam smiled and said, "Thank you, sir. I'm confident we will be successful at Gallion."

"Then you'll have your work cut out for you knocking out hovertanks. . . . and the rest of you will need to get your troops ready to leave in the morning. It's imperative the 3rd Army be in position when the TGA offensive begins."

"Yes, sir," Tam replied. The others nodded in agreement.

"Lt. Hawkh will remain here on my staff as will Captain Levitur," Commander Lanzia added. "Well, that's all I wanted to tell you for now. I know the last few days have been difficult, but we can prevail if we stand together. Back on Earth there was once a great leader named Winston Churchill who led a battle against another evil tyrant named Hitler. When facing a similar situation to the one we find ourselves in today he said, 'never give in, never give in, never, never, never, never—in nothing, great or small, large or petty—never give in except to convictions of honor and good sense. Never yield to force; never yield to the apparently overwhelming might of the enemy.' And that's what we must do. No matter what the odds, fight for as long as it takes to restore freedom and justice to Tarizon. May God and Sandee be with you!"

12
Operation Gallion

Several days later the six divisions of the reorganized 3rd Army were in place in the mountains north of Rhule. In the meantime the number of pilots in the new 1st Airborne Division had swollen to six hundred and twenty seven. Although they had but a handful of fighters, each day they took turns flying sorties over the TGA supply lines and dropping thousands of cluster bombs on the long line of trucks and transport vehicles supporting the TGA army to the north.

The much anticipated TGA offensive into Rigimol finally started on the 8th day of the 7th segment at 0200 kyloons. It began by the most intensive aerial bombardment ever seen on Tarizon. At the moment the offensive began, Commander Leek Lanzia, Lt. Hawkh, Tam and his mutant platoon were on a hill overlooking the TGA Naval Base and Air Station at Gallion. Noticeably absent was Rhin, who hadn't been seen since she'd wandered off into the woods before Leek had arrived at headquarters. Before they'd left their base they'd coordinated their battle plan with the nanomites, the seafolken and the mutants enslaved on the base and Leek had hacked into the Gallion computers to alter the flight schedules.

A long line of fighters were backed up along the runways waiting to take off. Returning fighters from the front line were landing every few tiks. Commander Lanzia had planned to stay up on the hill and coordinate the operation. Tam and his mutant squad left to enter the base at the southern gate. At that same moment Red and the fighter pilots, dressed in TGA uniforms, were boarding a tram destined for the tram station that terminated inside the base. While this was happening the free seafolken were entering the harbor underwater and seafolken slaves already on board TGA ships were preparing to mutiny.

The mutant slaves were housed in barracks on the north side of the base. They were already in position to do their part in this most complex and

Tarizon: Civil War

dangerous operation. The nanomites swarms that lived surreptitiously in buildings on the base had been alerted and were ready to do their part as well. Security at the base was in place but not on high alert. It appeared at the onset that the element of surprise had been preserved.

The mutant called *Jumper* scaled the southern security fence with a single bound. He moved quickly to the guard shack and slit the throats of the two guards on duty. Two mutant slaves stepped out of the darkness and dragged the dead soldiers out of sight. Then they took up their stations at the guard shack. A truck containing the mutant platoon was the first vehicle to present itself at the gate. They pretended to check the drivers' credentials, inspect the vehicle, and then let them through. The truck drove along the main base roadway until it reached the road that led to the airport. It turned onto the road and proceeded to Hangar 2, the hangar farthest from the runways and out of sight of the control tower.

The several hundred free seafolken who had been enlisted for the operation swam into the harbor behind a battleship that was coming into port. Once they were inside the harbor's nets they split up into pairs and swam to various ships that had been preassigned to them. The slave seafolken aboard the ships did what they could to sabotage security and create distractions for their crews while their comrades set explosives at key points on all the ships.

The mutant pilots with their fake IDs arrived at the tram station and immediately were herded into trucks driven by mutant slaves toward Hangar 2. Traffic was heavy and soldiers and civilian personnel were everywhere, but nobody paid attention to the two trucks as they proceeded to their destination.

While the mutant slaves were busy helping Tam and his platoon, their mates were hosting a victory party at the base recreation center. They'd gotten permission from the base commander for the event to celebrate the expected victory over the Loyalist at Rini. The base commander was at first reluctant to approve the request but when reminded how important the morale of the troops was, he had given in. Unbeknownst to the base commander, however, fifty seafolken ladies had also joined the mutant mates to entertain the pilots coming back from Rini.

The most ticklish problem was getting rid of the pilots who were actually supposed to be flying the TGA fighters. Commander Lanzia's plan was to lure them to the victory party, get them drunk, and if they tried to leave, drug them. The job of luring the pilots to the party was given to the seafolken maidens who were very good at such things.

When the fighters started returning to refuel they normally went into a pilots' lounge to wash up and wait for their fighter to be refueled and readied for another trip. This is where Red, dressed in a TGA officer's uniform, waited to advise them they wouldn't have to fly anymore that day. He then suggested they might want to go to the victory party and steered them toward the seafolken women who were anxiously awaiting to escort them to it.

The plan went well and over a hundred and fifty planes with Loyalist pilots got off the ground before there was a glitch. This first glitch presented itself when one of the officers coming in was enjoying the slaughter so much he was anxious to get back in the air again.

"What do you mean I'm being relieved? I'm the best pilot in the division," he complained.

"It's no big deal. The commander just wants to give you a rest—save you for later. You've done enough for now."

"What are you talking about? I usually do three or four runs a day during an offensive."

"Listen," Red urged. "Why don't you go to the victory party. There's some sweet young ladies here that would love to escort you to it. Why don't you go talk to them?"

"You've got to be joking. You think I'm going to a silly party when a battle is underway?"

"Okay," Red said. "Go ahead inside and I'll arrange to get you back up in the air just as soon as I can."

The pilot mumbled something to himself and then stormed into the pilots' lounge. Inside Lt. Hawkh rapped him over his head with the butt of his rifle. The pilot collapsed to the ground. Tam and one of the mutant soldiers then gagged him, tied him up and dragged him into a closet. Several more ended up in the closet before the mission was over.

Meanwhile the party was in full swing with plenty of loud music, liquor and attractive women. For the first kyloon there were no problems and everyone seemed to be having a great time, but then some of the pilots wanted to leave. This obviously couldn't be allowed, so the seafolken escorts began luring the pilots into private rooms where they were drugged, tied up and taken to a secure room in the basement.

Tarizon: Civil War

Commander Lanzia stood at his command post watching fighters, one right after the other, taking off and landing. Since the operation began everything had gone exactly as planned. Unfortunately, Leek knew that would change abruptly when reports of the fighters attacking hovertanks got back to the base. He was expecting that to happen momentarily.

"R3, any problems?"

"No. These pilots love to party. Only a half dozen or so have given us any trouble."

"Well, brace yourself. All hell's about to break loose. I'm expecting it anytime."

"Understood. We're ready."

"S1, report."

"Yes, sir. Our men have set the charges and the seafolken onboard have abandoned ship."

"Good. I'll let you know when to start the fireworks. Once you do that get your men out of the harbor. I don't want to lose any of you. We'll be needing your services later."

"Yes, sir. Standing by for your order."

"R2. Are you there?" Leek asked.

"R2 here," Tam said.

"Are your men in position?"

"Yes, sir. Standing by to take control of HQ and the tower."

"Good. Any word on how the party is going?"

"There's a lot of traffic going in but nothing coming out, just as we planned."

"All right. Stay alert. The fun's about to begin."

Commander Lanzia peered through his binoculars at the base headquarters. All appeared normal. He turned and looked out at the office of the military police. Two officers were standing outside talking casually. Then suddenly a door flew opened and the two men were summoned inside. Commander Lanzia's pulse quickened. He swung the binoculars back to base headquarters. Officers were swarming out and heading for their transport vehicles. Commander Lanzia pressed the button on his communicator.

"M1. It's time to see some fireworks. . . T3. Secure your objectives!"

Just a few tiks later ships began exploding in the harbor like popcorn in a hot fire. Smoke billowed up from each of the blazes and soon covered the sky. Leek watched with admiration at the fine job the seafolken had done. Soon he saw a ship list and then sink into the harbor. Then he heard gunshots.

At the HQ a gun battle had started. The mutant platoon had entered the building and seemed to be facing some resistance. Leek swallowed hard, praying they'd secure the facility quickly. Finally, his communicator beeped.

"HQ secure," Tam reported.

"Good work, Lieutenant. Now shut down the tram station."

"On our way."

Commander Lanzia looked toward the airport. All air traffic had come to a stop. He strained his eyes to see what was happening at the tower. Mutant soldiers were climbing up the sides of it and trying to gain entry. Leek jerked his head to the right at the sound of copters taking off.

"M1. You've got some company on the way. Three copters."

"Understood. We'll be ready for them."

As the first copter approached the tower one of the mutant soldiers jumped out and gazed up at it. One of the blades began to twitch and gyrate violently. Suddenly there was a popping sound and the blade began to slow. The copter dipped and began to spin out of control. The pilot tried to stabilize it but it was too late. The copter crashed and burst into flames.

The other copters immediately landed after the crash and soldiers began pouring out of them. Three mutant soldiers stepped out in front of them and began blasting them with laser rifles. They scampered for cover and soon were pinned down. In the meantime the rest of the unit had secured the tower.

In the officers' barracks the communicators began to ring. Those who answered were told the base was under attack and they should report to their units for duty. They all rushed to comply, but when they tried to leave their barracks through the front doors, they found the doors wouldn't open. Frantic to get out and join the battle, they tried all the other doors but found them secured as well. Finally, when they went to the windows in desperation, they found they'd been covered by a hard white substance. Frustrated, they attempted to break the windows and doors but no amount of force would break them.

Lt. Hawkh and his men left Hangar 2 and one by one took out the TGA personnel operating the runway. Each man was replaced by a Loyalist soldier and soon fighters were taking off and landing again. Commander

Tarizon: Civil War

Lanzia had worried that somehow TGA command would get word to its pilots and instruct them not to return to Gallion, so Lt. Hawkh was instructed to cut off the Tower's power supply at the first sign of trouble. That had been done and the fighters kept coming in right on schedule. Two kyloons into the operation seven hundred and thirty-nine planes had been requisitioned into the 3rd Army's 1st Airborne Division. This was less than the twelve hundred Commander Lanzia had hoped to acquire from the operation, but that was all the pilots that could be located and readied in the short time they had until the TGA offensive began.

Commander Lanzia looked out over the base. Fires were still raging in the docks but the base appeared quiet. Fighters were still landing but takeoffs had ended since there were no more pilots to fly them. A transport vehicle drove up to the hilltop command center. Lt. Hawkh stepped out.

"Sir, we've run out of pilots."

"Yes, I know."

"Planes are still coming in. What should we do?"

"Well, we have two options. We've done quite well, so we could quit while we're ahead and get the hell out of here. The problem is eight hundred fighters won't be enough to get the job done. The other option is to figure out how to find four hundred pilots."

"Ah. . . . Yes, but that's not really an option, is it?"

"It wouldn't seem to be, unless we can do some recruiting right here on the base."

"But . . . do you really think any of the pilots would want to become Loyalists?"

"Yes, I'm sure there are some. The question is will there be enough?"

"Even if there are, how could we be certain they were really defecting to the Loyalist cause? They might just say they are defecting just to get into a fighter and escape."

"You're right, but I think between Tam and me we can determine if they are sincere. Let's gather them together in Hangar 2 and give them the opportunity to become members of the 1st Airborne Division."

Rounding up all the pilots wasn't an easy task, as many had been drugged, other had been tied up and gagged, and the rest were probably drunk. Fortunately the mutant mates knew where there was a stash of medicine that was specially formulated to negate the effects of alcohol. It took awhile but eventually they had over six hundred pilots assembled in

Hangar 2. Commander Lanzia stood on a chair and addressed them. Two lines of mutant soldiers stood between him and the pilots.

"My name is Commander General Leek Lanzia, commander of the Loyalist' 3rd Army. We have taken control of Gallion, destroyed all the ships in the port and seized most of your fighters. Although I am sure there have been casualties, our mission is not to kill soldiers. We're only interested in fighters. We mean you no harm.

"Now I know that this civil war was thrust upon you rather suddenly. I doubt any of you were given the opportunity to choose sides. You were part of the TGA and followed the orders that were given to you like any good soldier would do. I wonder, though, how many of you share the same political philosophy as Videl Lai.

"As a Loyalist, I believe in God, Sandee and the Supreme Mandate. I believe in freedom, human rights, and the abolition of slavery. I don't believe we need a dictator to tell us how to live our lives or that we have the right to destroy other life forms for our own gain.

"If any of you believe as I do, I want to give you, here this day, right now. . . I want to give you an opportunity to defect to the Loyalist movement and to become a pilot for the 1st Airborne Division of the Loyalists 3rd Army.

"Right at this moment almost 800 fighters are engaged in a desperate battle against your hovertanks. The hovertanks were the deciding factor in the battles at Rizi and Rini. It's estimated they butchered over 800,000 of the soldiers of the 3rd Army. Such a weapon should not exist. It is a threat to all humanity as well as the other life forms that live on Tarizon. Like your forefathers who banned nuclear weapons decades ago when the world was unified under one government, so should the hovertank, a weapon so devastating and so lethal to anything in its path, so should it be banned from Tarizon forever.

"Those of you who want to defect right now, here this day, step to the left of the hangar. You will be processed and given a test to determine your sincerity. Don't step to the left if you have any doubt. Don't think this is a way to escape with a fighter. It won't work and those who try it will regret it, I promise you.

"Now, make your move. Those who remain loyal to the TGA will not be harmed. We'll simply keep you under guard until we leave Gallion. Go now. Make your choice—will it be freedom and human rights or cheerful obedience to a ruthless dictator?"

Tarizon: Civil War

The room broke out in quiet conversation. Nobody moved for a moment and then one of the soldiers suddenly hurried past his comrades to the left of the room. A few tiks later two more joined him. Soon the left side of the room was filling up quickly with new Loyalist pilots. When the shifting stopped over half of the pilots had defected. Lt. Hawkh and the mutant soldiers removed the TGA pilots from the hangar and Tam and Commander Lanzia began screening them.

"Each of you will now be interviewed by Lt. Lavendar and myself. We will ask you two simple questions and if you sincerely answer them we will administer the oath, your TGA tracking chips will be removed, and you will become pilots for the 3rd Loyalist Army. When you stand before us, answer honestly. Don't try to deceive us. We will know if you are lying. If any of you change your mind before you are interviewed just advise Lt. Hawkh and he'll escort you to where the other pilots are being held."

Tam and Commander Lanzia began their interviews immediately. They each stood at the front of the line with the soldiers lined up to speak to them. A lieutenant was the first candidate to step in front of Commander Lanzia. A scribe took down the pilot's name, rank and serial number.

"Lieutenant. Do you believe in the principles espoused in the Supreme Mandate and the abolition of slavery on Tarizon?"

The lieutenant stood tall and replied, "I do, sir."

"Do you renounce Videl Lai and the Purist movement?"

"I do, sir."

"Look into my eyes, Lieutenant. Relax."

"Yes, sir."

Commander Lanzia looked into the soldier's eyes and touched his mind. He found no ambivalence or uncertainty. He smiled. "Congratulations, Lieutenant! Welcome to the 3rd Loyalist Army. Lt. Hawkh, please administer the oath."

"Yes, sir," Lt. Hawkh replied. "Lieutenant. Cross your arms."

The lieutenant crossed his arms and clinched his fists, as it was the custom when taking an oath on Tarizon. "Do you pledge to support and defend, with your life if need be, the Supreme Mandate and to faithfully obey the commands of your superior officers while serving in Tarizon's Loyalist Army?"

"I so pledge," the lieutenant replied and then saluted.

Lt. Hawkh returned the salute and then said, "The medic will remove your tracking chip, then get your gear together and report to the briefing room."

"Yes, sir," the lieutenant said and walked briskly toward the pilots' locker room.

The process was repeated with each defector until all had been processed. Thereupon the pilots were briefed on their mission, told how to destroy hovertanks and instructed on what to do when they had spent their fuel and needed to return to base. Commander Lanzia knew that he'd soon have to leave Gallion. It was just a matter of time before reinforcements would show up to retake the base. His forces were not strong enough to sustain such an assault, so they had to leave just as soon as the last fighter was in the air. While Red and Tam were getting the last fighters off, Lt. Hawkh and Commander Lanzia returned to their command post overlooking Gallion to make preparations for a hasty retreat.

As they stood overlooking the base Lt. Hawkh grew tense and slowly turned around. "There are soldiers coming. We've got to go!"

Commander Lanzia frowned. "I don't hear anything."

"Trust me, Commander, I've got keen hearing. They are coming. . . . Oh, God and Sandee! . . . They've got hovertanks."

Commander Lanzia's face became pale. He hadn't considered that the TGA might divert a hovertank from the front lines to respond to the attack on Gallion. He put his finger on the button on his communicator. "This is your commander. We've got an assault force and hovertanks coming down on us. Tell the remaining pilots to do their best to get in the air on their own. All units are ordered back to base immediately. Use the prearranged escape plan."

Lt. Hawkh and Commander Lanzia ran as fast as they could to where the PT22 was parked and standing by for takeoff. As they reached the ridge overlooking the abandoned road they used as a landing strip, they saw a hovertank coming straight at them. Suddenly the tank began firing at the aircraft until it exploded. Debris was shot in the air and began raining down upon them.

"Back to the base!" Commander Lanzia screamed. "We'll have to escape in a fighter."

As he ran Commander Lanzia pushed the button on his communicator. "Tam. Save me a fighter. They've blown up the PT22."

"Understood. One will be fueled and ready for you."

Tarizon: Civil War

At the perimeter of the base a transport vehicle was waiting. Lt. Hawkh and Commander Lanzia jumped in and the driver gave it full throttle. The hovertank was nearly overhead. The tank was quiet except for the deep pulse of its propulsion system. *Rummp...Rummp!...Rummp!* Commander Lanzia looked up and prepared himself for death. He'd done more than he could have ever imagined, but it hadn't been enough to win the war. He wondered why God had sent him there if he was just going to be one of a billion casualties? Rummp! ... Rummp! . . . Rummp! His life flew before him. He thought of his mother and father back on Earth—his brothers and sister. They wouldn't even know he had died. Rummp!... Rummp!...Rummp! What would become of Lucinda, his love? Who would rescue her now? *Rummp!...Rummp!...Rummp!*

The hovertank jerked left and shot at one of the fighters taking off. The fighter exploded, fell to the runway and skidded into one of the hangars. There was another explosion that rocked the transporter and nearly made it roll. A fighter shot past them. Leek turned quickly to watch it. The hovertank jerked toward it and prepared to fire. Decoys shot out from the hovertank in every direction. A missile followed one of them and exploded. There was another explosion behind them. Leek turned back to see it. *Rummp!...Rummp!...Rummp!* The hovertank dropped from the sky. There was a grinding sound as the stabilizer automatically swung out and hit the ground to stop the fall. The cannon swung toward them and took aim. Leek closed his eyes. There was another explosion. Leek waited for the shock, the impact, the pain. He waited for death's sting but felt nothing. He opened his eyes slowly and just in time to see the hovertank thrashing, burning and dying.

There was no time to stare at the fallen beast. There would be others coming soon and he might not be so lucky this time around. He wondered who'd saved his life but was pretty sure it was Tam, Red, and John. When his driver got him to his fighter, Leek jumped out and ran for it. A soldier handed him his flight suit and helmet and helped him put them on. Soon he was taxiing down the runway.

It was only when he was in the air that he thought about his destination. Should he go back to base? He was the commander of the 3rd Army. He was too important to be endangering his life going out on a mission. Lorin had begged him not go into battle. She'd reminded him that if he were killed the entire war might be lost. He doubted that was the case, but reluctantly set the computer for a return to base.

"R1 to R2. Are you there?"
"Read you loud and clear."
"Did everyone get out okay?"
"We lost one fighter."
"Yes, I saw that. Who was in it? Do you know?"
"It was Jake, I'm sorry to say."
"Jake! But Jake was in sick bay. He wasn't supposed to be on this mission," Leek argued.
"No. He showed up at the last minute. We were short on pilots so—well, he said he was feeling fine and the medic had given him clearance."
"Oh, my God! Did Lorin know he went on the mission?"
"No. I don't think so."

Leek's heart was pounding so hard he could feel his chest pulsating. He couldn't believe that Jake had come on the mission and was the sole casualty. Lorin would be devastated. He couldn't bear to think of the pain she'd be feeling.

"It's not your fault. It was his choice to go into battle. Don't report his death to anyone. I want to be the one to tell Lorin. I'm heading back to base now."
"Sure, I understand."
"Thanks for what you and Red did back there. I owe you my life."
"Nonsense. We just wanted to get in a little practice before we got to the front lines."
"You know I'd like to go with you, right?"
"Yes, but you can't. Go back to base. You're the Liberator. Think about your next bold move to save the world from Videl Lai."
"My next bold move will be to rescue Lucinda. I can't let Videl Lai continue to torture her."
"But she's being held in Shisk," Tam protested. "How could you possibly rescue her?"
"I don't know, but I have to try. If she's killed and I've done nothing to prevent it, how could I live with myself?"

Tam shrugged and said nothing. He knew there would be no use trying to dissuade Leek from trying to rescue the woman he loved. Even if it were impossible, he'd never tell Leek that for fear he'd be plunged into a hopeless depression.

13
The Battle of Shini

Threebeard looked up in the sky and gasped. Hundreds of fighters were overhead getting ready to unload their bombs on the Loyalist forces. It was routine strategy to soften up your opponent before you sent in the hovertanks and infantry, but this was unreal. Threebeard hadn't ever seen or even read about such an intense aerial attack. Fortunately, most of the Loyalist forces were not where the enemy thought they were. They had been carefully moved to each flank in anticipation of the hovertanks' invincibility. Now Threebeard was doubly glad he'd chosen that strategy. Had his troops been on the front lines most would have perished in the first few minutes of the assault.

After several kyloons the hovertanks began to move. They met only token resistance and blasted across the Rini River without breaking stride. When the infantry finally made it across the river the hovertanks were twenty kylods ahead of them. TGA command didn't seem surprised by the lack of resistance or, if they were, they didn't make any adjustments to their battle plan. The hovertanks just kept on blasting away at anything that moved, keeping up their breakneck speed.

As the infantry began to thin out, the main Loyalist forces attacked from both flanks. The infantry seemed stunned by this development and kept looking ahead expecting the hovertanks to come and protect them. They'd marched hundreds of miles, fought two major battles and were tired and confused by the civil war that had broken out. Morale was low because they'd seen unprecedented death and destruction at the hands of the hovertanks and because most of them had pledged an oath to defend the Supreme Mandate and yet they knew their new leader would soon renounce it.

The TGA's front line was hammered and pushed into a rectangular mass of infantry. They were getting crushed together by the unexpected attack from the highly motivated Loyalist forces. Although outfought and sustaining high casualties because of their superior numbers, they were

Tarizon: Civil War

finally able to dig in and stop the Loyalist advance. For almost two kyloons both sides fought hand to hand at great cost in blood and toil. Although they controlled the skies their fighters couldn't help them much due to the close proximity of two armies.

Finally the TGA command realized what had happened and recalled their hovertanks. They turned and moved swiftly toward the rear of the Loyalist divisions. General Zitor watched the battle on a big screen from his command post. He turned to Threebeard. "They're going to slaughter our divisions. I warned you this would happen."

"It would have already happened had we not moved our troops to the flanks. At least we have inflicted heavy casualties on the enemy."

"But isn't there anything we can do? I can't bear to see our soldiers ripped apart by the hovertanks."

"Pray to God for a miracle," Threebeard said softly.

A yellow spot started to blink on the screen. General Zitor squinted at it, seeming confused. "What's that?"

Threebeard smiled. "I believe your prayers have been answered, General."

"Huh? What do you mean?"

"Yellow flashes are Loyalist fighters," Threebeard explained. Several more yellow lights began to flash. "It's the 1st Airborne! They've come."

"What are you talking about? The 1st Airborne was destroyed at Rini."

"It's been resurrected—the Liberator has come through again."

General Zitor looked incredulously at Threebeard. "Even so, we know fighters can't stop hovertanks. All they'll be able to do is slow them down."

"I wouldn't bet on that. Remember the hovertanks that were destroyed at Rini?"

"I saw that report but it didn't explain how it was done."

Threebeard looked up at the screen again. Hundreds of yellow lights were now blinking. "Three Loyalist fighters destroyed fifteen hovertanks. I wonder what a thousand will do."

While Threebeard and General Zitor were watching the battle from their command station, Tam, Red and John were leading the 1st Airborne into battle. They'd hastily broken up the division into ten wings each with five squadrons of approximately 20-25 fighters. Three wings were offensive and would be attacking hovertanks. Two were defensive and charged with the responsibility of engaging any enemy aircraft that tried to interfere with the attacks on the hovertanks. As they approached the front line they were met by a dozen TGA fighters.

"R2 to 4th Wing Commander."

"W4 here."

"Take care of our welcoming party, would you?"

"Yes, sir."

Twenty-one planes peeled off and headed for the enemy craft. The others began dividing up and heading for their positions along the front line. The hovertanks were just starting to return when the assault began. From the deck of their command post, General Zitor and Threebeard watched the fierce battle raging over the plains of Rigimol. They screamed with joy when the first hovertank exploded. They sighed with anguish when a Loyalist fighter was hit and fell helplessly out of the sky.

It was difficult to determine how the battle was going but one thing was clear: both sides were inflicting serious damage to the other. General Zitor counted forty-four hovertanks destroyed and Threebeard advised he'd seen eighty-one Loyalist fighters shot down and an equal number of TGA fighters taken out. Reports from the infantry divisions were similar. In nearly three kyloons neither side had gained any territory, but both had suffered incredible losses. The battle seemed to be a stalemate.

"What should we do, General?" Threebeard asked. "Do we continue the battle until every last soldier on the battlefield is dead?"

"What choice do we have? We can't stop fighting. They'll run all over us."

"True, but our soldiers need a rest. They can't sustain this level of battle much longer. I'm sure the TGA soldiers are just as weary. If there is one thing that is clear, this battle will not be decided today."

"So, what do you propose?"

"It's getting late. The sun will be setting soon. Order a cease-fire and see if the enemy will let us rest for the night."

"All right. I'll contact our division commanders and so order."

The Loyalist rifles became quiet but the TGA continued to fight until they realized they were not getting return fire. Their officers apparently understood the gesture and welcomed it as the battlefield grew quiet and darkness enveloped them. It was a victory of sorts for the Loyalists as the

Tarizon: Civil War

TGA had expected to run over them and by this hour be fifty kylods into Rigimol.

As darkness approached, the 1st Airborne Division returned to their new Doral Mountain base. By their count they'd destroyed over eight hundred hovertanks but had lost nearly three hundred fighters. If you count in the destruction of twenty-one battleships, two cruisers and fifty other naval vessels it wasn't a bad day for the Loyalists. Of course, nobody knew what the body count was on the ground. Thousands had died although not nearly as many as expected. Threebeard's strategy had been brilliant and with Commander General Leek Lanzia's daring theft of nearly twelve hundred TGA fighters, the momentum in the Tarizon Civil War had once again shifted.

14
Bearer of Bad News

Major Freelan and Major Oakril were waiting when Commander Lanzia climbed down from his fighter. He had radioed in that the mission had been a success but they couldn't wait to hear the details. Commander Lanzia wondered why Lorin had not come out with them.

"Where's Lorin?" he asked.

"She's afraid to see you," Major Oakril said. "She's been sick ever since she heard her husband left sick bay to join the operation. She went to her quarters and nobody has seen her since."

Commander Lanzia sighed. "She was right to avoid seeing me. I've got bad news. Jake is dead."

Major Oakril shook his head. "She's going to be devastated."

"I wonder if she'll be able to go on after something like this," Major Freelan questioned.

"Oh, she'll go on. She'll have even more reason to fight Videl Lai. If anyone is to blame for his death, it's him. I'd better go tell her. I'll meet both of you in the command room in ten loons to give you a full report."

"Yes, sir," Major Oakril replied. "Sorry you have to be the bearer of bad news."

Leek shrugged and went off toward the shuttle. When he got to Lorin's quarters he knocked softly on her door. "Who is it?" she asked.

"Leek. I just got back from Gallion."

The door opened and Lorin invited Leek inside. He entered the room and took a deep breath.

"I hear you've been in your quarters all day. Are you sick?"

Her face was red and her eyes were swollen. She sat down on a chair and motioned for Leek to sit across from her. "No. I'm just angry at Jake for going on the mission. He's okay, isn't he?"

Tarizon: Civil War

Leek hesitated. . . . Lorin put a hand over her mouth and screamed. "No! No! Don't tell me he's dead."

"I'm sorry," Leek said, tears welling in his eyes. "He was taking off and a hovertank fired on him. He died quickly. He didn't suffer."

Lorin began circling the room erratically. Leek grabbed her and pulled her into his arms. "I'm so sorry, Lorin! I'm so sorry!" He squeezed her tightly and held her for a long time. When she'd calmed down a little, he took her to her bed so she could lie down. Before he left he called the medic and asked him to come and stay with her. Then he went to the command office to brief Major Freelan and Major Oakril on Operation Gallion.

"How's Lorin?" Major Freelan asked.

"Pretty upset. The medic is with her."

"That's a shame about Jake. He was a good man."

Leek nodded. "Yes, he was. I'll miss him."

There was a moment of uneasy silence and then Major Freelan said, "So, the mission went well, huh?"

Leek looked up. "Ah. . . . Yeah, it went quite well. Better than I thought it would, actually." Leek gave them a complete report and then went on to question them about the logistics of maintaining over a thousand new fighters and housing their pilots. Leek had no knowledge or training in logistics so he was happy he had Lorin and Major Freelan to handle it, but as Commander he had to be sure that it was under control.

"So, are you ready for the fighters arriving tonight? They should be here shortly."

"Yes, we've set up some temporary quarters, but Lorin suggested we contact the nanomites and ask them to build us something more permanent."

"Yes. They are great builders. I'm sure they'd be happy to do it," Leek replied. "I'll discuss it with them in the morning."

"Since you left I've been monitoring the TGA news stations," Major Oakril cut in. "There hasn't been much news about the raid on Gallion. The TGA is keeping a tight lid on it."

"Can't we get the word out somehow?" Leek asked.

"Yes, Lorin is in the process of setting up a worldwide news network available to anybody with a VC. Anyone interested in getting accurate news will be able to tune into it. I think she said she'd have it up and running by tomorrow."

"Can the TGA jam it or interfere with it in any way?"

"Not the way Lorin's setting it up. They'd have to confiscate every VC on Tarizon to stop people from tuning in."

"Good. The only way we're going to get defectors and new recruits is if they believe we can win, and that won't happen if Videl Lai controls the media."

"We'll make them believers, don't worry."

"Any word on how the battle at Rini is going?"

"Reports from the front line indicate that the advance has been stopped. I don't know how that could be, but that's what we're hearing."

"Excellent. Has Threebeard called for the 3rd Army to attack yet?"

"Not yet, but all divisions are in place and ready to move on a moment's notice."

Leek laughed. "God, I can't believe we just stole a thousand planes from the TGA. Videl must be livid."

"Yes, I'd like to be a Nanomite in his wall tonight," Major Oakril said.

"Does Chancellor Mammett know?"

"I'm not sure. Nobody here has told him. Perhaps you should call him."

"No, I don't want to talk to that slubdub. He hates me."

Major Oakril laughed. "Yes, I know, but after he finds out what you've accomplished today he'll have to rethink his opinion of you."

"All right," Leek said reluctantly. "I guess it couldn't hurt. Can you get him on the GC?"

"Yes, it will just take a few tiks."

Major Oakril motioned for one of his aides and whispered something to him. A few moments later the aide brought a GC to him. He punched in a code and waited.

"This is Major Oakril at the headquarters of the 3rd Army. I've got Commander General Leek Lanzia here. He'd like to talk to the Chancellor."

There was a moment of silence and then Major Oakril handed the GC to Leek. Leek hadn't talked to the Chancellor since his election so he felt rather nervous.

"This is Chancellor Mammett," a deep voice said.

"Hello, Mr. Chancellor. This is Commander Lanzia. I'm sorry to bother you. I would have called the defense minister or General Zitor but they're a little busy tonight."

"Yes. . . .yes, they are indeed. It's good to hear from you, Commander. How is the reorganization of the 3rd Army coming?"

"Excellent, sir. That's why I wanted to call you. We've just completed a very successful mission and I thought you should hear about it before anyone else does."

"What mission? I didn't know the 3rd Army was back in business."

"It had to be kept very secret since we were counting on the element of surprise."

"So, don't keep me in suspense, for the sake of Sandee. Tell me about it."

"We just appropriated over a thousand fighters from the TGA Naval Air Station at Gallion. The fighters are already in the battle at Rini as we speak."

"My word! A thousand fighters?"

"Yes, more than a thousand, actually and we also blew up every ship in port—sixty or seventy, I believe."

There was a moment of silence. "That's hard to believe. I haven't heard a word about it."

"That's why I called. I thought you should know. I'm sure the TGA won't give it to the media."

"Where did you get that many pilots? The 1st Airborne was annihilated at Rizi."

"True. We managed to locate about five hundred pilots who survived the battle. The rest are defectors."

There was a moment of silence. Leek could hear the Chancellor talking to someone in the background. "Sorry about that. I had to pass on the news to my staff. This must explain how Threebeard's been able to stop the offensive. We've been getting reports that over half the TGA's hovertanks have been destroyed."

"Yes!" Leek exclaimed. "I'm glad to hear that. That's great news. We've been working hard trying to figure out how to disable them. I guess we finally figured it out."

"I guess you did," the Chancellor said, sounding quite impressed.

Leek explained to the Chancellor in detail how they'd discovered how to destroy hovertanks. He also gave him more details on the mission and the status of the 3rd Army. He thought about telling him that Jake

Boskie had been killed, but then thought better of it. He didn't know if Lorin wanted anybody to know just yet.

"Well, thank you for the update," the Chancellor said. "Please keep me informed from now on. You don't have to go through the defense minister or General Zitor. You can call me direct anytime."

"Yes, sir. I'll do that."

Leek hung up and looked at Major Oakril. "Well, I think he was impressed. He said I could call him anytime."

"Yeah, I should think so after pulling off a miracle like that."

Later that evening fighters began returning to base and Leek got more details on the fighting on the front lines. Only seven hundred and eighty-seven planes returned from the battle but most of the pilots thought the enemy lost twice as many fighters as they had. After everyone had returned Red, Tam and Leek went to the mess hall for something to eat.

"I'm sure glad to see your ugly faces tonight," Leek said.

"Yes, likewise. We thought that hovertank was going to turn you into burnt toast."

"Yeah, well I kinda had the same thought."

"Well, we needed a warm up for the big battle."

"Glad I could oblige. . . . Did all the pilots find their quarters okay? Was everything satisfactory? Did they get fed?"

Tam nodded. "They all disappeared, so I assume somebody must have taken care of them. I haven't heard any complaints. Of course, if they are as tired as I am, you could toss me into a pile of leaves and I'd sleep like a baby."

Leek sighed. "Being commander general is for the dirkbirds. Every time I turn around there is something new I've got to worry about. Tonight I had to kiss ass to the Chancellor. I'd love to go back to being just a simple Lieutenant."

"The Chancellor?" Red asked. "You talked to him?"

"Sure, somebody had to brag about our mission, didn't they?"

Red nodded. "We've come a long way from Pogo, haven't we?"

"That we have," Tam agreed. "My father always said that responsibility will kill you if you let it."

"What do you mean, if you let it? How can I stop it?"

"Well, you can't worry about every detail of an operation. As the man in charge, your job is to see the big picture. Leave the details to the peons and the bureaucrats."

"Right, just concentrate on your next bold move,." Red added. "Didn't I hear you say we were going to rescue Lucinda?"

Leek smiled. "Yes, you did. Thanks for reminding me. I've got a lot of planning to do, but first I've got to help Threebeard outmaneuver General Bratfort and the 4th TGA Army."

"Good luck with that," Red replied.

They all laughed.

Before Leek went to bed he decided to take a walk around the compound. It was peaceful at night and every once in a while the sky would clear enough so you could see the moons and sometimes even the brighter stars. As he stepped out of the shuttle he saw a rhutz sitting beneath a tree. For a moment he thought it was Rhin but then he realized it was a bigger male rhutz. He reached out to it with his mind.

Do you know Rhin?

Follow me, the rhutz said silently and turned and trotted off. Leek anxiously followed it, wondering if Rhin were in trouble. The rhutz went deep into the forest and at times Leek had trouble keeping up. Finally the rhutz stopped on the top of a hill and looked back at him.

Not too much farther, the rhutz assured him.

Leek rushed to the top of hill and looked down into the mouth of a cave. The rhutz went inside. Leek rushed to the cave entrance and peered into the darkness. It was a shallow cave and in the dim light of Tarizon's two moons he saw Rhin and seven little pups fighting for their dinner. He started to approach Rhin but the male rhutz growled so he stayed at a distance and watched the incredible sight. The little beige pups were in constant motion fighting over their mother's nipple. Leek laughed at their antics and had the urge to pick one of them up and play with it, but he knew that wasn't possible. After awhile he reluctantly turned and went back to the ship.

When he got back there he decided to check in at Lorin's command center to see how they were doing without her. He was shocked to see her at her desk.

"What are you doing here?" he asked.

She looked up at him with her swollen eyes. "I can't sleep. I just need to keep busy."

Leek understood. He hadn't slept the night of Sy's death or the night of Lucinda's kidnaping. "Guess what? I found Rhin."

"Oh, my God! Where was she?"

"About a kylod from here in a cave. She's given birth to seven little pups."

She put her hand to her mouth. "Oh, I didn't even know she was pregnant."

"Nor did I. They are so cute."

"Oh, I want to see them."

"Tomorrow maybe. The father is a bit over protective. He wouldn't let me get too close and I don't think he liked me being there, but Rhin insisted I know what had happened."

"I understand."

"Can I help you?"

"No. Go to bed. I'm just putting together your mission report to broadcast in the morning over the Liberation Network."

"Yeah, I heard about that. That's incredible that you can do that. Videl is going to be very angry."

"Too bad. The people have a right to know the truth and I'm going to make sure it's available to them."

"What's been the reaction of the cell leaders?"

Lorin turned and tried to smile. "They'd like to make you king, I think."

"Really?"

"Yes, I'm sure Chancellor Mammett won't be pleased."

Leek frowned. "He sounded pleased when I talked to him."

Lorin turned sharply. "You talked to him?"

"Yes, awhile ago. I thought he should be updated on the success of our mission."

Lorin rolled her eyes. "That surprises me. I guess he knows he better embrace you before your followers trample him."

"Perhaps."

"Does he still think he's running the Loyalist government?"

Leek chuckled. "Yes, I believe he's still operating under that delusion, but that's okay. Let him wallow in his glory. When the war is over he'll be whisked aside like dirt on the kitchen floor."

"And then you can be king!"

They both laughed. Leek took Lorin's hand and squeezed it. "We better both get some sleep if we're going to be any good tomorrow."

Lorin sighed. "You're right. Thanks for cheering me up. Maybe I can sleep now. I hope so."

When Lorin got to bed she did sleep. Quite soundly, in fact, but that wasn't the case with Leek. He tossed and turned wondering what he should be doing to help Threebeard deal with the 4th Army. Then it occurred to him he should just ask him.

He took a deep breath and thought of the three-headed mutant. Their minds connected almost immediately since they'd been connected before.

"There you are," Threebeard thought. "I wondered when I'd hear from you."

"I hadn't realized we could communicate so easily."

"Well, I didn't want to rush it. I thought you'd eventually figure it out."

"I wish I would have sooner. I could have used your help."

"You seem to be doing quite well on your own."

"Not too bad, I guess. . . . So, you stopped the TGA. How did you do it?"

Threebeard explained his strategy and told him of the day's events. Leek then opened his mind and let Threebeard have his memories of the Gallion Mission.

"That was brilliant but very risky. I don't know if I would have been that bold. It's a good thing you didn't ask my advice. I am old and cautious. I may have discouraged you and we'd have five hundred more hovertanks to worry about tomorrow."

"We'll get rid of the rest of them first thing. Don't worry."

"Don't bet on it. I'm sure TGA command has made adjustments to their defenses to make it harder for you to take them out. You better come up with something new yourselves."

"Right, but what?"

"Just give it some thought. It will come to you."

"Okay. . . . So, what is your strategy for tomorrow."

"We were in a stalemate last night when it got too dark to fight, but it won't be that way in the morning. The hovertanks, what's left of them, will be back and the enemy will easily overrun us."

"What are you going to do?"

"We are going to retreat. In fact, we're doing it already."

"Retreat? How will that help?"

"It's a diversion. We want to spread out the 4th Army and then let your 3rd Army attack them from the rear."

"Right. I see. Then General Bratfort will have to make a critical decision—stop his advance and retreat to take on the 3rd Army or keep on advancing hoping his rear infantry divisions can handle the 3rd Army on their own."

"Without the hovertanks to contend with I think the 3rd Army will do okay," Leek thought.

"I agree, but he will probably hit you hard from the air, so it won't be an easy battle."

"If he does that we'll have any easier time knocking out hovertanks."

"True. That's what I'm counting on."

"Thanks, Threebeard. Now I know what I should be doing?"

"Yes, and whenever you need to communicate in the future just close your eyes and we'll be in touch."

"Yes, that's very comforting to know."

"How's Lorin?"

"Oh. You heard about Jake."

"I saw it though your mind a moment ago."

"Oh, right. She's devastated, of course, but she's dealing with it."

"Watch her. She's lost two loved ones in just thirty days. She'll need to lean on you until she gets through it."

"I'll be here for her, don't worry."

Leek cut the connection by thinking of Lorin. She was the closest thing to family he had on Tarizon—at least until his brother was born. He wondered about Tehra. He couldn't wait to meet her and find out how his family back on Earth was doing. Finally, he slept.

15
The Press Conference

The next morning Commander Lanzia ordered the 3rd Army to attack the TGA from behind and cut them off from their supply lines. They delayed their attack until mid-morning to give time for Threebeard's strategy to work. Initially they encountered very little resistance. A wing of the 1St Airborne was sent to soften up the enemy and then the infantry attacked. The enemy seemed confused to see troops coming at them from behind and ill prepared for the battle. Thousands were killed before the TGA air force showed up and started putting up some resistance.

Again the 1St Airborne came at the hovertanks on the front lines with a vengeance. But this time the enemy had heavy air cover and the Loyalist fighters had difficulty getting close enough to the hovertanks to disrupt their pulse. Then late in the day the air cover thinned as fighters were called away to help defend the attack from the 3rd Army. This was all that Tam and his pilots needed to start putting hovertanks out of commission.

When most of the hovertanks were destroyed Threebeard ordered his army to stop their retreat and engage the enemy face to face like the night before. Again there were heavy casualties on both sides, but at the end of the day the Loyalists had stood their ground. As night fell over central Rigimol the battlefield became as still as a graveyard.

After the last fighter had landed, Leek went back to the command center to talk to Lorin and see how she assessed the day's events. He was feeling pretty good about how his army had done but he wanted to get Lorin's assessment and to see how the media was reporting it.

The command center was a hive of activity. Leek was surprised to see so many new faces. Lorin was at her post so he walked briskly over to her. "Where did you get all these people?"

"Oh. Well, some of the senior staff had been hiding out in Quori and when they heard we had a new headquarters here they came at once. It's

Tarizon: Civil War

a good thing too. I don't need to be worrying about feeding troops. I've got the entire Tarizon underground to get organized."

"So, how do you think it went today?" Leek asked.

"Threebeard's a genius. We all knew that. He stopped them for the second night in a row."

"I thought the 3rd Army did pretty well too, didn't you?"

"Yes, considering what little time they had to get organized and trained, I think they did remarkably well."

"How's the media reporting it?"

"They're claiming the army is advancing as expected and that the Loyalists are in retreat."

"Nothing about Gallion or the destruction of the TGA's fleet of hovertanks?"

"Not directly. Videl did call the Loyalists a bunch of cowardly thieves today in an address to the General Assembly."

"Well, he may have a point," Leek admitted.

Lorin smiled. "He may have more to say about it tonight. He's asked the media for time to address the citizens of Tarizon."

"That's unusual, isn't it?" Leek asked.

"Yes. I think it's because of our new Liberation Network. I'm sure he was angry when our reporters pointed out the details of Gallion and our success at knocking out hovertanks."

Major Oakril interrupted them to say that Videl was about to go on the air. Lorin and Leek went over the big video monitor on one of the walls of the command center. The news reporter was advising the listeners that they were going live to Shisk for an address to the citizens from Chancellor Videl Lai.

An image of the Capitol Building came on the screen and the announcer said to stand by for the Chancellor's address. The screen changed to the Chancellor's ornate office. Videl Lai was seated in a large red and gold upholstered chair which to Leek looked a little like a throne. The Chancellor leaned forward and began to speak.

"Citizens of Tarizon. I asked for this time tonight to address you so I could dispel any concerns you might have about your security. There have been ridiculous reports from the Loyalists' new propaganda station that the TGA is being defeated on the battlefield. That is a lie. Since our campaign started on the Rini River we have stormed through Tributon and now are half-way through Rigimol. In a few days we will take the capital city of Shini and drive the Loyalist army into the sea.

"As I promised you when I took office I would not tolerate treason or desertion and anyone discovered aiding the enemy would be summarily executed. Unfortunately, there have been a few misguided officials, officers and soldiers who have gone over to the enemy and they have paid for their treachery.

"The first was Chancellor Garcia when he started this rebellion. Well, you saw what happened to him. He was choked to death in front of his family, friends and fellow traitors. He thought he was safe far away in Rigimol but he was wrong!"

Lorin gasped in horror. "That dirty skutz! I'd like to poke his eyes out." Leek took Lorin in his arms and held her.

"And then there was the, so called, Prophecy and Leek Lanzia suddenly appears, claiming to be the Liberator. Well, we couldn't get to him directly but we captured his mate, Lucinda, and she's confessed that Leek Lanzia is a fraud."

The screen dissolved into a view of a prison cell. Lucinda was chained to the ground like a zoo animal and looked like she was barely alive. Leek tensed at the scene and Lorin began to cry. In the background a voice asked, "Tell us, Lucinda. Is Leek Lanzia the Liberator?"

Lucinda coughed and struggled to speak. "No. He's Peter Turner from Earth. He's . . . he's—"

"Is he the Liberator?" the voice boomed.

"No! He's just an exile. He's nobody," she said, her voice trailing off.

Videl's picture flipped back on the screen. "You see what happens to traitors. They suffer and then they die! Rest assured, every last Loyalist and Loyalist sympathizer will be found and executed.

"Now, you've heard reports that the TGA is being defeated on the battlefield. Well, it's a lie and tomorrow the Loyalist soldiers will regret the day they deserted the TGA. Tomorrow they will pay as we will unleash a weapon so devastating that they will wish they were never born!"

The screen changed again to a prison cell. A soldier was being injected with something by a guard. He immediately began to thrash and writhe in pain. The camera panned in for a closeup of his swelling head, bulging cheeks and eyes that looked as if they were about to pop out of their sockets. Leek felt nauseous.

Tarizon: Civil War

"This is what is in store for every Loyalist soldier out there on the front lines tomorrow and there is no way to escape it. Good night, citizens of Tarizon, and sleep well. The enemy's days are few."

Leek looked at Major Oakril. "What's this new weapon? Do we have any intelligence on it?"

"No. It's the first I've heard of it."

"What do you think? Is it some kind of chemical weapon?"

"From the video, that would be my guess."

"How will they deliver it?" Leek asked. "Use a crop duster to fly over us and spray it on us?"

"More likely they'd fly over us and drop canisters of the toxin that would rupture on impact," Lorin replied.

"Then we can't let them control the skies tomorrow. We've got to stop them from delivering that chemical."

"I'm afraid that will difficult," Major Oakril replied. "There were new fighters streaming into Gallion yesterday and they have a full airborne division at Mapi. We'll be outnumbered at least two to one tomorrow, I'm sure."

"You should have blown up the runways before we left Gallion," Lorin said.

"We were going to, but our visit got cut short by the hovertank," Leek replied.

"We don't have chemical warfare equipment, but I know where we can get breathers for everyone. There's a warehouse full of them at Rhule. The 3rd Army found it on their way through town. I'll send someone back to get them."

"What about our soldiers in Rigimol?" Major Oakril asked.

"I'll make sure Threebeard is aware of the situation," Leek said. "I'm sure he can get his soldiers prepared for a chemical attack."

Lorin ran her hands through her hair and sighed. "What's wrong?"

"None of these precautions are going to do any good. Videl wouldn't have told us about this new weapon unless he was absolutely sure we had no defense against it."

"Maybe it's a bluff," Major Oakril suggested. "Maybe Videl just wanted to scare our soldiers—try to get some of them to desert."

"I don't think so," Leek said. "If he was trying get them to surrender he'd have offered them amnesty. There's no reason to surrender if you know you're going to get shot."

"I'm going to issue the breathers anyway," Lorin said. "It won't hurt to have them."

When Leek returned to his quarters he closed his eyes and connected to Threebeard. He thought about Videl's press conference, seeing Lucinda, and about the new weapon described by Videl. Threebeard felt badly about Lucinda and promised Videl would pay one day for his crimes. Then Leek asked him what his strategy would be for the following day.

"I want you to have Tam and his special unit available for a mission tomorrow. We have to control the skies tomorrow at all costs. If we face the TGA in a fair fight, I believe we can win, but if our troops are dodging cluster bombs all day, we won't have a chance."

After Threebeard and Leek had severed their connection Leek went to see Tam. He explained what Threebeard wanted them to do and asked him to get on it right away. Tam agreed and left immediately to make preparations. When Leek got back to his quarters, Lorin was there.

"I'm sorry about Lucinda. It must have killed you to see her like that."

Anger began to well in Leek again as the image of his mate chained to the wall of her cell came back to him. He'd tried to repress the thought because it was so debilitating. He couldn't show weakness in front of his troops. He had to be strong and focused. But now there was no reason to hold it in. He took Lorin in his arms and they both cried. They cried for her father, they cried for Jake and they cried for Lucinda. They cried and grieved for some time, but when they were done they felt a little better.

After Lorin left Leek slept, but it was a troubled slumber full of fiendish nightmares. In one of them he woke up with an angry snake hissing at him. Instinctively he grabbed it below its head and held it as far away from himself as he could. Then he found a stick and started beating its head over and over again. He woke up breathing heavily and shaking like a leaf in a hurricane.

He looked at his alarm clock and saw that it was almost time to get up. He didn't want to risk another dream so he turned on the light and got dressed. When he went outside, Tam's unit was preparing to board their transportation to Gallion and **Mapi**. Leek understood the importance of their mission, but feared Gallion's heightened security might make the mission there impossible. He knew the unit had little intelligence on Mapi,

Tarizon: Civil War

so the task there would be even more perilous.

Leek went over to Tam. "Are you ready?" he asked.

Tam nodded. "I think so. Wish us luck."

Leek smiled. "I will. If anything goes wrong just abort and get back here. Security will be tight."

"You know. I'm not so sure about that. They'll probably be more surprised this time than they were the last time we showed up. Besides, this time we plan to get in and out without being detected. All we have to do is tap into their fuel supply and let the contaminant do its job."

The contaminant was engineered personally by Threebeard. Only a small quantity introduced into the fuel supply would start a chain reaction that would change the chemical characteristics of the entire body of liquid and render it useless as a jet fuel. Once it was pumped into the fuel tanks the fighters would become inoperable. Only after removing all the fuel and cleaning out the residue could new fuel be pumped in. This was a slow process and would keep the fighters out of the sky for several days.

Of course, it was expected that the TGA would discover the problem before a lot of fighters were refueled, but that would still leave all the available fuel contaminated. To get the rest of the fighters in the air would require trucking or flying in fuel from another source. Either way the TGA would be out of the air for a day or two.

"Make sure that's what happens. In and out, no fireworks."

They embraced and then Tam started toward the plane. Just then a stout mutant soldier with hands like a spork climbed aboard. Leek stared at them. Tam smiled.

"That's Digger. He can dig a tunnel faster than a ground trencher."

Leek raised his eyebrows. The sight of the mutant with hands like the paws of a groundhog was unsettling. He couldn't imagine having to live with such a deformity. He wondered if Digger had been forced to endure a lot of ridicule over his odd-looking hands. He knew on Earth that would be the case, but because there were so many mutants on Tarizon he thought it might be different. At least he hoped so.

"Sounds like he'll come in handy," Leek finally replied.

Tam nodded and climbed aboard. Leek watched the two planes take off into the early morning sky and split off in different directions. He prayed the missions would be successful.

16
Viper Drop

Tam had split his special ops platoon into two sections for this mission. He would lead one to Gallion and Lt. Hawkh would take the other to Mapi. Lt. Hawkh had served at Mapi briefly while he was in the TGA before the civil war erupted, so it made sense for him to go there. The operation only required two soldiers to actually get onto the base. One to handle the contaminant and the other to stand watch and assist as needed.

The special ops team had three jumpers and Digger. This meant one team could jump the perimeter fence but the other would have to go beneath it. Lt. Hawkh elected to take Digger to Mapi as the ground there was predominantly clay, while the terrain at Gallion was mainly rock and sand. The plan was to find a secluded part of the perimeter, dig a tunnel under the fence and then proceed to the fuel storage units.

Before dawn the copter landed a kylod from the perimeter of the base. Lt. Hawkh and his men hiked toward the fence under cover of darkness. When they reached the fence Lt. Hawkh bent down and examined the soil.

"Okay, Digger. It's up to you now."

"No, problem, sir," he replied and began taking of his jacket and boots. "Just give me a few tiks."

Lt. Hawkh nodded and watched him as he bent down and scooped out a handful of dirt like it was sand on the beach. Soon dirt and debris started to fly. Soldiers scrambled out of the way of the deluge of earth as Digger tunneled effortlessly under the fence. Soon his body disappeared and the dirt began to cave in on the other side of the fence. When the ground gave way, Digger pulled himself out, looked back, and gave his comrades a dirty grin.

"All right," Lt. Hawkh said, shaking his head with admiration. "Under the fence. Let's go."

The rest of the platoon scrambled under the fence and followed Lt.

Tarizon: Civil War

Hawkh to the fuel storage area. When they were in place behind an equipment shed, two soldiers changed into workmen's uniforms and proceeded to the targeted fuel storage tank.

The tank was guarded by two sentries and there were several soldiers monitoring the flow of fuel in and out of the tanks. It had been decided the best place to introduce the contaminant was on a maintenance platform behind the tank, since it would be out of view of the sentries and workers monitoring operations.

Their plan was to drill a small hole into the tank and inject the contaminant. This required climbing the ladder on the side of the tank leading to the maintenance platform. The two risks were that they'd be spotted climbing up the side of the tank or someone might hear them drilling. The drilling would only take a few tiks so they hoped it wouldn't be noticed. If they were noticed the rest of the platoon was ready to cover them while they retreated.

The two disguised soldiers snuck around the back of the tank and began climbing. When they had climbed high enough they stopped and one stood watch while the other began drilling. The sound of the drill was much louder than they had expected and the two sentries immediately came around the tank and looked up at the two workers.

"Who goes there!"

"Hopsa Welders. Here to fix the ladder," one of the disguised workers replied while the other one continued to drill.

"We weren't informed of this."

He shrugged. "Yes. Sorry. We were supposed to do it last segment, but we've been very busy."

Lt. Hawkh signaled for two of his platoon members to target the sentries. He didn't want to kill them but if they tried to interfere with the operation there would be no choice. The drill suddenly broke through the tank's shell and there was a distinct splashing noise. The mutant soldier quickly injected the contaminant into the tank and stood up.

"What did you do?" the sentry demanded.

There were two silent laser shots and the sentries dropped to the ground. The two mutant soldiers climbed quickly down the ladder and began running toward the equipment shed. A worker witnessing their retreat sounded an alarm. Lt. Hawkh signaled for his men to retreat. Soon they were sprinting toward the fence where they had entered the base. Two sentries on hyper bikes came out of nowhere and cut them off. The platoon hit the dirt and began firing at the sentries. Lt. Hawkh looked behind and saw two more sentries on hyper bikes coming at them. Suddenly, Digger popped up from behind the sentries and began shooting. One of the sentries took a bullet in the chest and toppled over, but before Digger could fire again, the other sentry blasted him with his laser. Digger staggered a few steps and then fell over. While the sentry was watching to make sure Digger fell, Lt. Hawkh took aim and shot the sentry between the eyes.

With both sentries down, the platoon was back on the move and soon were scampering under the fence. Along the fence they dropped a dozen pellet mines that looked like common gravel. When the two sentries reached the fence and stepped on them they exploded, killing them instantly.

Back at the copter, Digger's lifeless body was lifted into the copter. Lt. Hawkh looked at him sadly. He'd given his life saving his platoon. As the copter flew low along the treetops toward the Doral Mountains, he wondered how Tam had done at Gallion.

At Gallion Tam faced a more difficult situation. The perimeter of the base was under heavy guard. He was glad he had the jumpers rather than Digger, as digging a tunnel was out of the question. The problem was what to do with the guards who came by frequently and not on any particular schedule. For this problem Tam turned to the telekinetic mutant. When the first two-man patrol walked by he mentally applied pressure to the soldier's chest, causing him to feel like he was going to have a heart attack. He turned white and let out a gurgling sound. His partner grabbed him.

"What's wrong?"

"I don't know. I can't breathe."

"Okay. I'd better get you to the medic," his partner said as he put an arm around him. Soon they were gone.

With the coast clear two soldiers also dressed in civilian worker uniforms jumped the fence and were out of sight almost immediately. When another patrol came Tam just watched them until they were gone. Meanwhile, the workers made it to the fuel storage tanks only to find them heavily guarded. They looked around for an alternative. They saw a pipe leading from the one storage tank to another. The end of it disappeared into the side of a concrete wall. They made their way over to the wall and were relieved to see they could work on the other side of it out of view of the guards. They quickly jumped the fence and began drilling.

After the contaminant had been injected into the pipe they realized the pipe was empty. They looked around for a valve. The valve would have to be opened or the contaminant wouldn't make contact with the main fuel supply. When they finally spotted the valve, they were horrified to see it was right next to one of the guards. They'd have to create some kind of diversion to draw away the guard, but not one that would arouse too much suspicion.

After giving it some thought, one of them ran and picked up a large wrench. He took it and then jumped on top of the tank with a single bound and ran to the other side where he dropped it so it would make a loud bang. When the guard heard the noise he scrambled to his feet and ran to the other side of the tank. While he was gone the other soldier turned the valve and the fuel began to flow through it. The sentry found the wrench and looked up but saw nothing. He shrugged and went back to his post.

When the jumpers returned to the fence they notified Tam that they'd successfully carried out their mission. When the next patrol came by, the telekinetic mutant caused one of them to trip and smash his head against a rock. This, of course, necessitated another trip to the medic who hopefully wouldn't wonder about the two incidents on the perimeter until it was too late.

The next day there was a noticeable absence of TGA fighters in the sky allowing the 1st Airborne to finish off the last of the hovertanks and the infantry to engage the enemy on an equal footing. By late in the day the TGA's northern front had been pushed back ten kylods and the 3rd Army had driven a wedge straight through the rear lines, cutting the TGA armies from its supply lines.

Leek was ecstatic with the news. He was with Lorin in the command center talking to one of the their division commanders when he noticed something strange on one of the VCs that was monitoring the battlefield. He stopped in midsentence and squinted at the image, trying to figure out what it was.

"What in the blazes is that?" Leek asked.

"What is it, Commander?" Lorin asked as she approached the monitor.

"There's something in the sky. It looks like a giant flock of birds. There's thousands of them. I've never seen anything like it."

William Manchee

"Oh, my God!" Lorin screamed. "They're falling from the sky. What are they?"

There was a low-pitched hissing sound coming from the receiver and then screams and sounds of panic.

"They're snakes. They're attacking everyone!" Leek yelled.

Hisszz. Hisszz. "Stop them. Don't let it in!" an unidentified voice exclaimed. . . . "Ahh! God!! No! Ohhh! Ohhh!"

The transmission went dead. Lorin looked at Leek horrified at what they had just seen and heard. Leek closed his eyes and linked with Threebeard, so he could see first hand what was happening. The general was running for his transport vehicle. Little snake-like creatures were hitting the ground and then suddenly attacking anyone who got close to it. The victims, once bitten, began to writhe and convulse in utter and unbearable pain. Leek remembered the video from the press conference. Somehow, Videl had been able to unleash this new weapon and he hadn't exaggerated its effectiveness. The defense minister got in his vehicle, slammed the door, and looked out the bullet-proof window.

Leek saw that the little vipers were attacking the hood of Threebeard's car. It suddenly occurred to him that these little monsters were guided by some sort of heat-seeking technology—heat-seeking vipers with a venom not only lethal but engineered to cause a slow, painful death. *What kind of a monster would even conceive of such a weapon?*

"Are you all right, Threebeard?" Leek thought.

"Physically, I'm in one piece, but I don't know about my mental stability right now. I've never seen so much human misery at one time as I've seen today. I'm going back to my command post to sort this out. Contact me later when I'm better prepared to discuss what happened here today."

Leek acquiesced and severed the link. Lorin was staring at him. He told her what he'd seen. She gasped and covered her face with her hands. Reports started to come in from the front lines. The vipers had been dropped from a high-altitude bomber, perhaps because the Loyalists controlled the skies. Strong winds had blown as many of the vipers over the enemy's own troops as had hit the Loyalists, so the death and suffering was felt by both sides. From a short-term standpoint the vipers were a disaster, but Leek knew the long-term effect on the morale of the Loyalist troops would be devastating. He wondered if he'd ever get his troop out on the battlefield again.

Tarizon: Civil War

For the next several days the battlefield was quiet. Both sides were still reeling from the last battle and tending to their dead and wounded. During that time scientists at Loyalist headquarters in Shini had dissected and reverse engineered one of the vipers. It was a small mechanical snake with short stumpy wings that allowed it to glide through the air rather than just drop. The technology that the scientists hadn't seen before was the heat-seeking magnet device in each of the vipers' heads. An object generating heat would attract the viper. If there were no heat-generating objects around it would lie on the ground in wait. The first time somebody or something strolled by, it would activate itself and attack the person or object. This made the weapon even more powerful, for it made a virtual minefield out of any area on which it was dropped.

Commander Lanzia decided if the war was to continue he'd have to take drastic measures to make his troops feel safe again—at least as safe as a soldier expects to be when he's facing the enemy. To do this he quickly proposed measures to ensure another viper attack wouldn't be nearly as deadly as the last. He insisted that all uniforms be upgraded to a puncture-proof material that the mechanical fangs couldn't penetrate. He also instructed the scientists working for the Loyalists to come up with a decoy shield that could be deployed to lure the vipers away from the troops. Finally, he challenged his scientist to come up with their own Viper, an improved version that included a guidance system that would allow each snake to change course to allow for wind currents and defenses employed against it. He called this new weapon the super viper.

Twenty-one days later General Bratfort launched several attacks on the 3rd Army and re-established his supply lines. He was clearly preparing for a new offensive. New hovertanks were seen moving toward the front lines. The air force was back in the air and had reclaimed control of the skies. New infantry divisions were moved to the front lines to replace the ones decimated by the Loyalists' attacks and the TGA's own errant vipers.

The 3rd Army had dwindled in size by one-third due to heavy casualties sustained since its counterattack. The defection rate was still good, otherwise the 3rd Army would likely have been out of business. Many TGA soldiers, however, were appalled by the use of an untested weapon that killed as many TGA troops as it had the enemy's. Many realized Videl Lai and their commanders had little concern for their lives.

Lorin attacked the reckless use of the Viper on the new Liberation

William Manchee

Network and called for TGA soldiers worldwide to defect. All over Tarizon Loyalist units began to form and secretly train for an eventual confrontation with their local TGA units. The largest and fastest growing units were in Lower Azollo and particularly Queenland, which locals claimed to be the home of the Liberator even though Leek Lanzia had never lived there. The logic was that his official record showed him to be from Queenland so, when the war was over, he'd no doubt would make Queenland his home.

Threebeard used this lull in the war to enlist and train new recruits and defectors. Every day soldiers were arriving to replace those who'd been killed in the previous battles and by the time hostilities began anew, the Loyalist Army was actually stronger than it ever had been. More importantly, however, shortly after the viper attack the Loyalist army opened up in northern Rigimol its first manufacturing plant for T-47s and within ten days was turning out ten new fighters a day.

When the TGA launched their next general assault they drove nearly fifty kylods into central Rigimol before their hovertanks were destroyed and the attack was stopped. Threebeard counterattacked, but the revitalized Loyalist forces could bend but not break the TGA's front line. They shifted back and forth slightly for several days, each side sustaining heavy casualties, until the battlefield became silent under an unofficial cease-fire.

Time, however, was on the side of the Loyalists. The overall size of the TGA army was declining, as well as its morale. Threebeard and Commander Lanzia knew eventually they would have the upper hand and would be able to drive the TGA off the continent. They just needed to stall and buy more time. Videl Lai also knew time was on the Loyalists' side, so he decided to play one last deadly card that he hoped would end the Loyalist movement once and for all.

17
Tribute

Commander Lanzia got a kick out of the locals' claim that Queenland was his home. He'd been telling people that ever since he'd joined the Loyalist movement but just as his cover story. Now he was curious about Queenland and wanted to visit it. Since Queenland had the largest and most effective Loyalist movement outside of Lemaine Shane, it made sense for him to go there and do what he could to propel the movement forward. When he asked Threebeard about it, Threebeard advised him to first go to Shini with Lorin to make some political hay out of the 3rd Army's recent successes. He said to use the excuse that he wanted to give a report to Chancellor Mammett and discuss a campaign in Queenland.

"But do you think Lorin will be welcome in Shini?"

"Not by the Chancellor but most everyone else will be glad to see her. If there were a vote for a new Chancellor today I'd bet she'd win. Nobody is happy with the Chancellor's performance, but nothing bad enough has happened to warrant a no-confidence vote. Everyone knows who's been running the war and who's behind the Liberation Network.."

"Okay, then. I've been wanting to go to Shini for a long time. There's someone there I need to see."

"Tehra?" Threebeard asked.

"Yes, you've been reading my mind again."

"You and I have no secrets anymore."

"Is that right? You can't tuck something away where I can't see it?"

"If I wanted to I could, but there is no need, and keeping such secrets with someone with whom you regularly share your thoughts is tedious work and I haven't the strength for it."

"My brother should be born by now. I'm anxious to meet him."

"I'll arrange a meeting. I've got more contacts in Shini than you do."

"Thank you. I can't wait to meet this woman who seduced my father. I still can't believe she did it."

"Don't blame your father. You know about seafolken women."

"Yes, I've heard the stories. How long do you think I'll have in Queenland before I'll be needed back here?"

"Not long. Don't linger. They only need your guidance and moral support. Evaluate their leadership and put someone in charge before you leave. Help them develop a general plan. Let them work out the details."

"Yes, sir. I'll keep you updated."

"No need. I'll be there with you in mind and spirit."

"Right. Of course."

When Leek told Lorin that he wanted to go to Shini and that he wanted her to come, she was resistant. First she complained she had too much work undone to leave her command station. Then she voiced her fears that if she went to Shini the Chancellor might try to sidetrack her and prevent her from returning to her post. But when she heard it was Threebeard's idea for her to go, she reluctantly acquiesced.

The Chancellor seemed pleased when Leek called and said he wanted to come to Shini to give him a report. He seemed equally delighted when Leek said he was bringing Lorin.

"Good. We wanted to have a memorial for Jake and give him a medal posthumously. With Lorin coming to town it will give us the opportunity to do it," the Chancellor said.

"I'm sure Lorin would appreciate that," Leek replied. "After the visit I'm thinking of going to Queenland to give our supporters down there a boost."

"I don't know," the Chancellor said. "That could be dangerous and with the enemy still on our doorstep it may not be a good time to go."

"I don't plan to stay long. Just a few days to let the people down there know we care about them."

"We'll talk about it when you come here. I'll start making the arrangements."

"Good. See you soon."

Several days later Lorin, Lt. Hawkh, and Leek arrived at Shini. They were met by Colonel Tomel, who had been given the assignment of planning the memorial service for Jake. Colonel Tomel had been one of Chancellor Garcia's trusted aides, so Lorin was happy to see him. On the way into town they talked and reminisced about old times.

When they got to their hotel, Colonel Tomel advised them of their schedule. The memorial service was to be early the following morning. In the afternoon they would meet with the Chancellor and then later with his military staff to discuss Leek's proposed visit to Queenland.

"Tonight I believe Senator Marcuzzi and General Zitor are taking you to dinner, Lorin," Colonel Tomel advised.

Leek looked at him. "What about me? I'm not invited?"

The colonel shrugged. "I don't know. I was told to take you to see a woman, ah . . . Tehra, I believe, is her name."

Leek smiled. "Oh, good. I definitely need to see Tehra."

"Who is this woman?" Colonel Tomel asked.

Leek explained the situation to him.

"I wanted to meet Tehra too," Lorin said. "I wish I could come along."

"Well, hopefully we'll be seeing a lot of her and the baby from now on. After all, they'll be my family."

Lorin smiled. "I'm happy for you, Commander. I know it's been hard for you to be so far away from your family on Earth. This will be nice having a family here on Tarizon."

Leek nodded appreciatively. Later that evening Colonel Tomel took Leek to Tehra's compartment. Leek pushed the intercom button and looked into the camera. A moment later the door slid open. Tehra greeted them and invited them inside.

"Oh, my God! You look so much like your father," Tehra said.

"So I've been told. How are my mother and father? I understand you've seen them recently."

"Well, it seems like just a segment or two, but I guess it was actually a little over an Earth year ago."

"Were they okay?"

"Yes, I guess you know your father finally told your mother what happened and it lifted her spirits immeasurably. She was still missing you, of course, but dealing with it much better knowing you were alive."

"So, where's my brother?"

Tehra smiled. "I know it must have been a great shock for you to hear about me and your father. I did a lot of soul searching before I decided to tell you about it, but I finally decided it wasn't fair to you or Sophilo."

"Sophilo?"

"Yes, it means hero."

Tarizon: Civil War

"So, where is he? I'm anxious to see him."

Tehra stood up and said, "Come with me."

Leek and Colonel Tomel followed her into the next room where there was a white crib. They walked over to it and looked down at the sleeping infant. Leek began to choke up.

"He's so beautiful," he said. "I can't believe he's my brother."

"Oh, he is, believe me. His DNA has been tested. You can see the report if you like."

"It won't be necessary. I can tell by looking at him that he's related. There are several Turner characteristics that I see right away."

She laughed. "Right. I know what you mean."

"So, what are your plans? I want to see a lot of you and Sophilo."

"I'd like that. I want you to be part of his life."

"Do you have a mate?" Leek asked.

"I did, but he died while I was on Earth. I haven't applied for a new one yet."

"Are you planning to?"

"I don't know."

"So, you're an Earthchild, right?"

"Yes, I was born in Texas like you."

"Wow," Leek said. "That's weird."

Tehra laughed. "Yes, it does seem a bit strange. The Dallas Metroplex has changed a lot since I was a child."

"I bet. We'll have to get Threebeard to loan us some of his video collection so we can watch them together."

"That would be nice," Tehra said. "I went to a movie with your father once. He's a great movie lover."

"Yes. He took us every week to whatever new shows were up. They don't have movies here on Tarizon. I wonder why."

"Not since the great eruptions. The world's been in too much turmoil, but there are old movies available. They run them on the VC sometimes."

"Really? I've never seen one."

"Well, the next time you visit I'll rent one and we can watch it together."

"Cool. I'd like that."

Leek liked Tehra a lot and stayed and talked with her all afternoon.

Sophilo woke up once during the visit and Leek got to hold him. Colonel Tomel grew weary of the visit and several times hinted that they had a big day ahead of them, but Leek ignored him. Finally, Leek reluctantly consented to be driven back to the hotel. They said their goodbyes in front of the PTV. Tehra held Sophilo in her arms and Leek kissed him on the forehead.

"Thank you for a wonderful evening. I really enjoyed talking with you. You have a wonderful son and I'm looking forward to watching him grow up."

Tehra smiled broadly. "I'm glad you came. I hope you can come back soon."

"I have to go on a trip for a few days, but I'll visit again when I get back. Now that I have a reason to come to Shini I'll do it more often."

"Good. I'd like that."

They embraced and then Leek and Colonel Tomel got in the PTV and drove off. Lorin was waiting up for Leek when he returned to the hotel. She was anxious to hear about the visit. Leek gave her a detailed report and told her how much he liked Tehra. Then Leek asked her how *her* evening went.

"It was great seeing Senator Marcuzzi and General Zitor again. They both send their regards."

"So, have they been able to keep your supporters in line?"

"Yes, apparently so and my political stock has gone up a notch since I teamed up with you."

"Good. So, how long until you're elected Chancellor?"

"Ah, well, that's a difficult question. We'll have to wait for the right circumstances. In the meantime, I'm quite satisfied doing what I'm doing."

"Yeah, I suppose you'd have a lot of distractions if you were Chancellor."

"I would, most definitely, but I'd put up with them if need be," Lorin replied with a sly smile.

"I bet you would."

The next day Colonel Tomel put on a great tribute to Jake Boskie. It was held on the parade field of Garcia Army/Air Force Base appropriately named after the late Chancellor Robert Garcia. A military band played stirring music, troops marched in impressive patterns, and Chancellor Mammett used the occasion to laud all those who had made the ultimate sacrifice to ensure the success of the Loyalist movement. The Chancellor got a moderate applause but when Lorin took the podium the big crowd gave her a standing ovation.

"Thank you," she said with a warm smile.

"Mr. Chancellor, Colonel Tomel, and all of you who came to remember Jake. I want to thank you for this wonderful tribute to him. I still can't believe he's not with us. I still wake in the night and reach for him—for his strength, his compassion, and his love. Then I remember that he is gone—stolen from me at such a young age because of a greedy, selfish, godless man who decided to make himself King of Tarizon.

"For so many cycles Tarizon was at peace under the Supreme Mandate. Most of us thought we'd seen the last of war and all the suffering it brings. Then the Purist Party sprung up and began spreading its message of hate and fear. It was unfortunate our planet was devastated by the great eruptions, but we had survived and were slowly bringing our planet back to life. There was no justification for scrapping the Supreme Mandate and suspending all the rights and freedoms that we all so loved and cherished."

There were shouts of approval. Chancellor Mammett nodded in agreement.

"My father, and now my husband, have given their lives to restoring peace, justice and democracy to Tarizon. We cannot let the loss of their lives, or the lives of the countless others who have died in this struggle, to have been in vain. We have to win this war! We have to rid our world of those who think they are superior to the rest of us and think they have a right to rule the world for their own pleasure and profit! It is our duty to stand up and say no! No, Videl! No more tyranny!"

Lorin smiled and concluded, "I better sit down or I'll be accused of campaigning for the next election." The crowd laughed. "Jake would love this tribute. I hope he's somehow watching us. Thank you again for being here."

Colonel Tomel got up, joined Lorin on the podium, and took the microphone. "And now it is my pleasure to award to Jake Boskie for his courage, determination, and sacrifice for the citizens of Tarizon, the Limbidium Pyramid which symbolizes the unbreakable bond between Citizen, Law, and God."

Colonel Tomel picked up a box and took out the Limbidium Pyramid. It was a small crystal pyramid that glowed from within and pulsated as if it were alive. Lorin's eyes widened as she saw it. The crowd let out a collective sigh of astonishment. Colonel Tomel handed the pyramid to

Lorin. She took it gingerly and held it up to the crowd. The pyramid had a calming effect on the viewer like a flickering fire. There were screams and applause as the pyramid glowed magnificently in response to the crowd's emotion.

After the ceremony there was a lavish luncheon in the officers' dining hall put on by the officer's wives. Leek and Lorin stuffed themself, drank tekari, and then watched as comics and jesters entertained the crowd. Finally, a band called Earth Jazz took over and played music that made Leek think of New Orleans. He wasn't a great dancer, but the music put him in the mood so he asked Lorin if she wanted to dance. She agreed and they took to the floor. Lorin felt good in Leek's arms. He imagined he was dancing with Lucinda. Lorin felt safe and peaceful in Leek's arms. She closed her eyes and imagined she was dancing with Jake. As the party wore on they danced closer and closer, brushing against eachother often and looking deep into each other's eyes. A few heads turned and eyes widened. When it was time to leave Leek and Lorin lingered, thanking the band for their wonderful music and their host for such a fine party. Finally, Colonel Tomel insisted they leave.

"The Chancellor and three generals are waiting for you, Commander," Colonel Tomel reminded him.

"Yes, we must go. Come on, Lorin," Leek said.

Lorin said one last goodbye and then they finally left and got into the PTV that was waiting outside. Colonel Tomel sat next to the driver and Leek and Lorin were in the backseat alone.

"Can I see that pyramid?" Leek asked.

"Sure," Lorin replied and passed him the box.

Leek carefully opened the box and pulled out the Lemdinium Pyramid. It was dark in the box but it lit up just as soon as Leek touched it.

"How does it work?" Leek asked.

"It's actually a real stone found deep under the ocean. Some say it's alive. Others believe it is a chemical mix that reacts to heat and other stimulation."

The pyramid was glowing softly. Leek took Lorin's hand. She looked up at him in surprise but didn't resist. The pyramid's glow intensified. He squeezed her hand and the pyramid responded with a burst of light. Leek laughed.

"This is cool. I wonder what it would do if I kissed you?"

Tarizon: Civil War

Lorin pulled her hand away. "Commander, what's gotten into you?"

"Nothing. I'm just trying to figure this thing out. I wonder if it's really alive."

"How could it be? It's a rock."

"I don't know about that. It has magical powers. Look at it. It turns a different color when our moods change."

"Magical? Don't be silly. I'm sure it's just some sort of chemical or heat reaction."

"No, it can't be that. It has to be something else."

"Like what?"

"I don't know. Maybe it makes some sort of psychic connection with the person holding it."

Lorin shook her head then changed the subject. "I'm nervous about this meeting. I know they'll be wanting information about our cells."

"Just give them a general report, no specifics. I'll try to protect you."

"You'd better. If they get that information they won't need us anymore."

"I'm not so sure about that. The cell leaders are pretty loyal to you. I doubt they'd be anxious to take orders from someone else. Besides, Threebeard's behind us."

"Yes, but I'm sure the Chancellor would like to dismiss Threebeard and appoint his own defense minister."

"Our coming today was Threebeard's idea, so I guess he's not worried about that."

When they arrived, General Zitor was there to greet them. They followed him into the huge conference center. Large electronic maps adorned the walls. Several staff members sat nearby at computer and communication stations ready to provide any information needed for the meeting. The Chancellor was seated at the head of a long black table with the Loyalist crest in the center. Three generals and six of their staff members sat across from Leek, Lorin, Colonel Tomel and General Zitor. Threebeard sat at the opposite end.

"Well, quite an enjoyable party, wasn't it?" the Chancellor noted.

"Yes, quite nice," Threebeard replied. "Now, unfortunately, we must again focus on the defense of our capital. Lorin and Commander Lanzia believe the time is right to open a new front in the war."

"So I heard, but do you think that is wise with the enemy still at our doorstep?" the Chancellor asked.

"There is a story often told to children. A man, his wife and their baby are traveling to another city to see relatives. On the way they are held up by a bandit brandishing a sword. The family is poor and they have nothing of value to steal, so the bandit tries to take the baby, for he knows he can sell it on the slave market at a good price. When the mother protests the bandit tosses her to the ground. The father has no weapons so he picks up a large rock and comes at the bandit. The bandit laughs at this and is about to strike a deadly blow to the father with his mighty sword when suddenly the mother lunges for him and grabs his ankle. He trips and loses his concentration just for a moment, but long enough for the father to smash the rock over the man's head and save his child from a life of slavery."

"So, you think if the enemy is distracted in Queenland that could help us in Rigimol?" the Chancellor asked.

"The enemy will have to divert troops and supplies from Lemaine Shane to Lower .Azollo," Leek replied. "We estimate it will weaken their offensive capacity by one-third for a cycle or more at almost no cost to us."

"What do you propose to do in Queenland, Commander Lanzia?" General Zitor asked.

"Meet with the leaders of our underground organization there, encourage them, and help them develop an effective strategy against the TGA. I'll also summon the seafolken, nanomites, and the rhutz down there and enlist their support for the war effort."

"Won't it be dangerous for you to go down there? If the TGA gets wind of your presence they'll try to assassinate you," Colonel Tomel warned.

"And if they are successful," the Chancellor added, "that will be a crushing blow to the Loyalist cause."

"I'm at risk no matter where I go. We'll just have to be careful who we tell I'm coming down there."

"I don't plan on telling them Commander Lanzia is coming," Threebeard explained. "I'm only going to say that we are sending a delegation to consult with them. Only the people in the delegation will know who they are and we'll swear them to secrecy until after we've gone."

"When will you go?" the Chancellor asked.

"Soon," Leek said. "I want to get back before the next TGA offensive."

"How will you get there?"

Tarizon: Civil War

"I haven't decided yet."

"When you do, will you tell us so we can provide more security?"

"That won't be necessary. The fewer who know about it the better. We all know there are spies about and I don't want to get ambushed before I even get there."

Chancellor Mammett sat up straight in his chair. "You think there are spies here?"

"Not in this room, but somewhere in your staff there probably is. I'm sure there are spies in my organization too. Don't you think it's inevitable when an army is split in two, like the TGA was, that a few stragglers would be left behind to spy?"

Chancellor Mammett didn't respond. He was wondering if it were true that he had spies in his organization. The thought hadn't occurred to him before. "How will you prevent your own spies from reporting your trip to Queenland to the enemy?"

"By not telling them about it. Only a very few will even know I'm gone and those will think I'm taking a short vacation."

"All right," Chancellor Mammett said. "It sounds like a prudent course of action. Keep us informed."

"I'll report to Threebeard and he can pass it on to you. It won't be safe to communicate by GC. When I come back I'll give you a full report in person."

"That will have to do then," the Chancellor replied. "Go and good luck to you."

Lorin and Leek left the base and headed for the airport. What they hadn't told the Chancellor was that the delegation was already on its way to Queenland and Leek was leaving that very day in his own fighter. His plan was to fly back to his base, refuel and then take off for Lortec. Along the way he'd refuel at the same refueling station Tam and Red had used when they escorted Earth Shuttle 26 to its new home. Although the access codes had been changed, Leek had been able to hack into the TGA computers and get the new codes. From Lortec he'd go across the Beet Islands, refuel once more at the new Loyalist base there and then on to Queenland.

18
Queenland

Major Freelan led the advance delegation including Red, Lt. John Sillmar, Sgt. Lindshill, the seafolken representative who'd been promoted since his part in the mission at Gallion, and Rhin the rhutz. They were met at a remote airstrip in Southern Queenland near the town of Rinfeld by a driver and three armed militiamen.

"Good afternoon," the driver said cheerily as Major Freelan stepped off the plane. "My name is Rohn Sulch. Tobeth Jons sent me to transport you to the farm."

"Excellent," Major Freelan said, wrapping his arms around himself. "Gee, it's cold down here."

"Yes, we're pretty far south. The winters are bad."

Major Freelan looked back at the delegation as they deplaned. He made brief introductions.

"Take a seat inside. I've got the heat on."

"How far is it?" Major Freelan asked.

"Just twenty loons or so. It won't take long."

As they started moving Major Freelan gazed out at the beautiful snow-covered landscape. It was late spring and he was surprised the ground was still covered with snow. They were traveling in a twelve-seat Korstar 7 commercial transport vehicle along a bumpy rural road. The land was flat with only a spattering of trees here and there. They turned off the main road onto a poorly maintained gravel one. When the road forked they went left several kylods through rolling hills studded with clusters of leafless trees. Two armed guards were posted at a gate before a long driveway. The driver spoke to the guards and they let them through. Armed men and women walked along the road and stared at them as they passed by. A few loons later they arrived at a large farmhouse with a half dozen barns and assorted outbuildings. The place was brimming with activity. A man and a woman came out to the Korstar and greeted them. The man was Tobeth Jons, a man of forty cycles, lean, with black hair. He was an advocate by trade and a former member of the Queenland Senate. Perona Guilin was a pretty brunette in her mid thirties. Her husband had been a lieutenant in the TGA when the war broke out. He had wanted to defect to the Loyalist cause but was killed in battle before he got the chance. Although she had no business or political training, she was personable, intelligent and had been instrumental in getting the Queenland cells organized.

"Welcome!" Tobeth said to Major Freelan as he stepped out of the Korstar into the chilly air. They shook hands and made introductions. The people, who had been busily at work when they drove in, gathered around the delegation. There was a gasp of fright when Rhin suddenly jumped out of the CTV. Everyone in her path scampered to get out of the way.

"Don't be afraid," Red said. "This is Rhin the rhutz."

"Commander Lanzia's companion?" Perona asked.

"Yes, we were told there are a lot of rhutz in Queenland, so we thought Rhin could help us communicate with them."

"Right. Well, we can talk about that later," Tobeth said. "Come inside. You'll catch a chill out here."

The spectators stepped aside, leaving a corridor to the main house. Major Freelan and the rest of the delegation followed Tobeth inside. The corridor widened as Rhin walked slowly through it.

"We've prepared lunch for you," Perona advised. "We knew you must be starving after such a long flight."

Red's eyes lit up. "I don't know about everyone else, but I could use a bite to eat," he said.

"Good then, the dining room is this way," Mr. Jons said, pointing straight ahead. "If you need to wash up a bit before you eat the washroom is down the hall to the right."

The dining room table was full of delicious looking meat, vegetables and desserts. All but Rhin sat the table and ate heartily. Rhin sat on the floor next to Red, who dropped an assortment of meats and bread onto a plate for her. While they ate Tobeth and Perona filled them in on the situation in Queenland.

"Fortunately, the TGA forces are small and scattered in this part of the world. Videl Lai isn't popular since it is believed he ordered the assassination of our senator, Sami San, just before the Senate was to vote for a new chancellor."

"Hmm," Major Freelan said. "I heard that."

"So, when Lorin told us it was time to get a militia organized it wasn't hard to find volunteers. In fact, we've had quite a time keeping this operation under wraps."

"What's its size right now?" Major Freelan asked.

"Almost two thousand," Tobeth said, "but that number could quadruple if they actually had something to do. Nobody is anxious to join an organization that has no purpose."

"Well, that's going to change now," Major Freelan said. "Loyalist Command has decided to open a new front in Queenland. We want to solidify control here and then move north and take control of all of Lower Azollo."

"That's what Lorin said in her communique," Perona said. "That's good news, but we're not quite ready to confront the TGA, I'm afraid."

"We know that our plan will take time and we will give you guidance and support while you prepare," Red assured them.

"How many soldiers would we need to recruit and train?" Tobeth asked.

"At least twenty-five thousand," Major Freelan replied.

Tobeth swallowed hard. "Even though the TGA is not strong here, the people are still afraid. They don't want them bringing hovertanks and vipers down here. It may be hard to get that many recruits."

"We know that. That's why Commander Lanzia is coming here tomorrow. He'd like to help you do some recruiting."

"Commander Lanzia is coming here?" Perona gasped.

Major Freelan smiled. "Yes, he's on his way."

"That's wonderful, but I'm shocked he'd risk coming down here."

"Well, he feels connected to the people of Queenland simply because for so long everyone thought this was his home."

"Well, this *is* his home and he's welcome here."

"He'll be glad to hear that."

"Now, say we go along with your plan," Tobeth said. "What if the TGA finds out and tries to stop us?"

"They *will* find out and they *will* try to stop you, but they have most of their resources tied up in Lemaine Shane right now. They will be reluctant to divert forces to Queenland. This will give you time to train your troops and prepare for battle."

"We don't have enough rifles and ammunition for that many soldiers," Tobeth noted.

"We'll provide the weapons, uniforms, and supplies along with personnel to help you train your recruits. Red here is going stay to help you set up an airborne squadron as well. You'll need air cover for your troops. We'll leave John here too as an advisor and liaison officer. Any orders or communications from command will go through them. Your outfit will be know as the 3rd Loyalist Army's 31st Infantry Division and 4th Airborne Wing."

Perona laughed. "Boy, you don't waste any time, do you?"

"We can't afford to. We need to get a second front opened within thirty days. If you will accept this assignment I am prepared to offer both of you commissions in the Loyalist Army."

Tobeth looked at Perona. She nodded, smiling broadly. "Yes, we'll accept the assignment and the commissions," Tobeth said. "We are anxious to get rid of the TGA, believe me."

"Good. Commander Lanzia will swear you in just as soon as he arrives."

"Speaking of Commander Lanzia, how does he plan to help us with our recruiting?" Perona asked.

"We were hoping he could give a live address on the Liberation Network here in Queenland tomorrow announcing the establishment of two new Loyalist divisions here in Queenland."

"Of course," Perona replied. "That's no problem. I can set that up."

"Good. In his address, he'll invite and encourage recruits to enlist immediately. He'd also be available for some impromptu appearances at various venues around Queenland to shake up the TGA and give the movement down here more credibility."

"That's an excellent idea," Tobeth agreed. "What type of venues did you have in mind?"

"We don't know yet. You'll need to help us with that."

"You know there is a field tournament in Guthlin tomorrow," Perona advised. "Athletes from all over Queenland will be competing for a spot on the national team. There will be thousands of spectators."

"Good. That sounds perfect for his first appearance. Can you arrange to commandeer the public address system for a few minutes?"

Tobeth laughed. "Yes, I think we can manage that."

After lunch the delegation was given a tour of the farm. The barns had been converted to barracks and the outbuildings were used for supplies and armaments. From the air the farm looked quite ordinary unless you started counting the number of farm hands working the property. About midway through the tour Rhin suddenly ran off into the woods.

"Where's she going?" Perona asked.

Red watched her thoughtfully. "Probably to make contact with the rhutz in this area. That's why we brought her. We won't know for sure until Commander Lanzia gets here. He's the only one who can talk to her."

"Do you think they'll be much help to us? I mean, what can a rhutz do against an armed man?"

"Ask Commander Lanzia about that. Rhin has saved his life more than once. I've been told she even took down a copter once."

"Really? I didn't realize they had that kind of abilities."

"Yes, besides being ferocious fighters, they are telekinetic as well as telepathic. You don't want to mess with a rhutz."

"I guess not," Perona agreed.

When they got back to the farm more people had arrived. Some of them were recruits but many were just ordinary people curious about what was going on. They lined the streets and cheered as the delegation went by.

"Who are all these people?" Major Freelan asked.

"I don't know. We weren't expecting them. They must be people from town who heard you had come."

"Well, I hope they don't plan on staying. They'll be in the way once you start training."

"They'll leave when it gets dark, I'm sure," Perona said.

At nightfall, however, the crowds didn't leave but continued to grow. By morning thousands had gathered around the perimeter of the farm and along the road leading up to it. After breakfast Tobeth took Major Freelan and Red back to the airstrip to pick up Commander Lanzia. They were shocked when they drove up and saw that the crowds had overrun the airstrip as well.

"I can't believe this," Major Freelan complained. "What do these people want?"

"When you arrived yesterday with the rhutz the people assumed that

Tarizon: Civil War

Commander Lanzia would be coming too. They're here hoping to get a glimpse of him, I am sure. After all, they consider the Liberator to be a holy man, sent by God to save them from Videl Lai."

"Well, if all these people know he's coming, the TGA will soon find out as well. This could be a dangerous situation for everyone."

"I've posted lookouts on all the roads. They are to call me immediately if they see any TGA soldiers."

They drove up the road to the airstrip slowly in order to avoid running over any of the spectators. When they got to the strip Major Freelan saw that some of the militiamen had cordoned off the airstrip and were keeping the crowds clear so the Commander's fighter could land. He watched the skies nervously, fearing he'd see TGA aircraft or copters investigating all the activity around the airstrip. But instead a fighter streaked by and turned around to come back for a landing. Major Freelan recognized Commander Lanzia's T-47 as it had the identification R1 on the wing.

The crowd began to yell and scream at the sight of the fighter coming in for a landing. Then they began pushing inward in defiance of the militiamen surrounding the runway. When the fighter rolled up in front of the crowd they pushed their way through and surrounded it. As Commander Lanzia climbed out of the cockpit the crowd began to chant *Seama lo dante! Seama lo dante! Seama lo dante!*

Commander Lanzia smiled and waved to the crowd. Red met Leek and took charge of the fighter. Several militiamen helped him move it into a hangar where it couldn't be spotted from the sky. Six militiamen surrounded Commander Lanzia to protect him from any direct contact with the crowd. He didn't seem to be in danger, but nobody was taking any chances, as spies and assassins were always a danger. Most who'd come just wanted to shake the Liberator's hand or just touch him. Leek shook as many hands as he could as he made his way slowly through the crowd. When he got to the awaiting Korstar 7 he slid in beside Major Freelan and shook his head.

"What is this? I thought my visit was going to be kept under wraps until my address tomorrow. Now the TGA will looking for me."

"Yes," Perona said. "I apologize. We didn't tell anyone you would be arriving, but apparently when they saw your rhutz they figured you'd be coming too."

"Hmm. I didn't anticipate that. I wouldn't have brought Rhin with me had I realized that would tip everyone off. Even so, I'm a little surprised that so many people have come out."

"Ha," John said. "Wait until you see what's waiting for you at the farm."

"Really? More crowds?"

"Yes, twice the size of this one."

"Wow. I guess that's good news for the Loyalist cause."

"It is," Tobeth said, then introduced himself and Perona.

"It's a pleasure to meet both of you. I've heard a lot of good things from Lorin about what you are doing down here."

"Oh, yes. Lorin has been our salvation. She's kept us informed and given us much hope."

"Good. Now we're going to give you more than hope."

"So, we've been told," Tobeth replied. "We are anxious to start building the 31st Division."

When Red made it back to the CTV they eased their way out of the crowd and onto the road. As they traveled back to the farm they realized they were leading a parade of vehicles. The crowd was moving with them back to the farm. The closer to the farm they got, the heavier the traffic became and soon they found themselves in a snarl. Tobeth tolerated the traffic jam for a while but at the first opportunity took a detour to try to avoid the crowds. Leek lost count of all the turns they made before he finally saw a cluster of barns and buildings in the distance.

"Here we are," Tobeth announced. "The house is just up ahead."

The spectators reluctantly moved aside to let the PTV go past. The windows were tinted so they couldn't see who was inside. When they got directly in front of the door to the main house a half dozen militiamen cleared a path and Leek stepped out.

"There he is!" someone screamed. "It *is* him!"

"Oh! Thank God and Sandee, it's Commander Lanzia!" another yelled.

Leek nodded and shook many hands as he walked slowly past his well-wishers. There was pushing and shoving as many wanted to shake his hand or, at least, get a good look at him. When he stepped inside the door he turned and waved. The crowd cheered and applauded again until he finally shut the door.

"Wow!" Leek said. "I wasn't expecting all this attention. I thought

Tarizon: Civil War

we'd just slip in for a few days and leave without much fanfare."

"The people have been following your exploits quite closely since you first stole the fighters from Pogo," Perona replied. "You've become quite a hero."

"Yes," Tobeth added. "I particularly liked your adventure with the Drogals."

"You heard about that? . . . I didn't realize that had been widely reported."

"Oh, yes. Everything you've done has been reported in detail in the media down here up until recently when the censorship began. Fortunately, the Liberation Network came on line pretty quickly, so I don't think we've missed much."

The two delegations talked and discussed plans and strategy the rest of the day. Leek was advised of the public appearance that had been arranged for him the following morning. When he inquired about Rhin he was informed that she had taken to the woods the first day and hadn't been seen since.

"That's all right. I'm sure she's just out making friends. I'll try to contact her later, which reminds me, Sgt. Lindshill and I need to go visit with the seafolken before we leave."

"Yes, we've scheduled that for right after tomorrow afternoon's address. After you talk to the athletes and fans at the stadium, we'll drive you and Sgt. Lindshill to Zangor. It's a seaport on the coast."

After supper, Commander Lanzia went to the window to see if the crowd had dispersed at all. To his alarm, it had grown. He wondered how long it would be before the TGA learned of his visit. Suddenly there were screams and the crowd began to scatter. Leek strained his eyes to see what was happening. Coming across the pasture he saw Rhin and a half dozen rhutz. They were barking and growling at the crowd and causing a panic. Leek ran to the front door, opened it and to his astonishment realized the rhutz were herding the crowd away from the house. He knew then what was happening.

He turned and yelled, "Get out of the house now! Get out! Get out now!"

Red jumped up and ran to the back bedrooms yelling and screaming for everyone to leave. Leek went upstairs and ordered everyone outside. Nobody argued or questioned Commander Lanzia's order as the urgency in his voice was clear. Just as the last occupant of the house staggered outside there was a loud screeching noise and then the house exploded.

After the air cleared, Tobeth got up, dusted himself off and ran for the Korstar. Seeing this, Leek screamed, "No! They'll blow that up next. Follow the rhutz into the forest."

Leek began running after Rhin and the other rhutz. The others watched and then began to follow him like sheep following a shepherd. As they all ran for their lives, three TGA fighters screamed over the farm dropping seeker bombs and blowing up everything in sight. When the bombs quit falling and the fighters disappeared over the horizon, the rhutz stopped under a canopy of trees.

When Leek reached the rhutz, he looked back and couldn't believe his eyes. The crowd was even larger than he'd previously estimated. A calmness came over the gathering even though the fighters could have come back at any moment. As they gathered around him he climbed up on the branch of a tree and spoke to them.

"Friends, citizens of Queenland, I appreciate you coming out to greet me, but as you can see my presence here is causing you all much danger. I've come to confer with your leaders to help them prepare to fight the TGA and eventually drive them from Queenland."

The crowd roared their approval.

"I know many of you were afraid of the rhutz who appeared to be attacking the compound. Actually, what they were doing was warning us that the TGA was coming. You see hundreds of kylods away there is a TGA air base called Torq Air Station. When my friend Rhin came here the first thing she did was to make contact with the rhutz in this area. So when the rhutz living near the air station saw three fighters take off in our direction, they communicated that information to Rhin who came with her friends to warn us.

"The reason I tell you this is so you won't fear the rhutz. They are on your side and will help you drive the TGA out of Queenland. If you ever meet a rhutz simply look into his eyes and he will know you are a Loyalist. But if you are a spy or not fully committed to freedom and the end of slavery on Tarizon, don't dare look into the eye of a rhutz because he will know you are the enemy and rip you to shreds!"

The crowd stirred at this warning. A man on the fringe of the crowd began to back away slowly. Rhin spotted the movement and looked in his direction. Their eyes met. Rhin began to growl and move slowly toward him. The man turned and started to run. Rhin took after him as the crowd gasped in shock. A militiaman stepped forward and cut off the man's escape. Two others grabbed him from behind, wrestled him to the ground, and bound him.

"So, now you have your first prisoner of war. Perhaps when you question him you'll learn something about your enemy. If he won't talk the rhutz can help you convince him otherwise. They will be a very helpful ally.

"So, now I need to find a quiet place to stay and continue talks with your leaders. That means I need all of you to go home. If you follow me around you'll make it easy for the TGA to find me and put my life and your lives in danger. So, thank you for your wonderful show of support, but now I need you to go home."

Nobody moved. They all seemed mesmerized by what had happened. Leek started to get angry. "Please, go home! Go home now! You're jeopardizing our mission!"

Finally, people began to grumble, turn around and start walking back to the road. Leek turned and looked at Tobeth. "Is there somewhere we can go until morning?"

"Yes, Molh Culberth has a boardinghouse up the road a bit. She can put us up until morning."

"Good. Let's go."

"The Korstar has been destroyed. I've called for someone to come pick us up in something else."

"Was anybody hurt back at the farm?" Leek asked.

"Two were killed. Six others were injured but they should be okay."

"The enemy is ruthless and cares little for human life," Leek said angrily. "I wonder if they had any idea who they were bombing."

"Probably not," Tobeth agreed. "If they get a tip about an illegal gathering they don't bother to check it out. They just do a preemptive strike. They don't care if innocent people die or not."

Soon two blue PTVs drove up and took the two delegations to the boarding house. Rhin and some of her friends kept watch outside along with a contingent of militiamen. After several hours of discussions, everyone went to their rooms to get some sleep as they had to leave early the next morning to take Leek to Guthlin.

Leek was so exhausted from his long journey from Shini and trek through the woods, he quickly fell into a deep sleep. When he woke up the next morning he felt good and was excited about the day's events. He knew he was pushing his luck making so many appearances in one day, but the warm reception he'd received from the people of Queenland had given him strength and courage.

They left that morning before the sky lightened. Guthlin was nearly 30 kylods away and they planned to stop at a studio to do the Liberation Network address and make an appearance at a factory before they went to the stadium. On this historic day everyone was dressed up in business attire so they wouldn't stand out. Beneath their clothes, however, they carried laser pistols, power knives, and stun guns. They were hoping to avoid trouble, but if they ran into any they didn't want to create a big commotion.

Making little noise, they slipped in the back door of the deserted studio and Tobeth led Leek to the broadcast booth where the program would be made. They'd planned to do the broadcast first because it would reach the most number of people. They knew the moment the broadcast hit the airwaves, the TGA would be out in force looking for them. During the broadcast, Red said he would prepare a surprise for the TGA when they got to the studio.

At the appointed hour Leek turned on the microphone and began his address. "Citizens of Queenland. This is Commander General Leek Lanzia talking to you today from your own homeland. Yes, I've come to Queenland to help launch the fight against Videl Lai and his henchmen who have stomped on the Supreme Mandate and stolen your right to life and liberty. I've come to Queenland because I know the citizens here are a proud people who love freedom and democracy. I know that you value all life forms and will not tolerate bigotry, genocide, or injustice.

"I'm happy to report the TGA advance has been halted in Rigimol. That is why I am able to come to you this day to encourage you to take up arms against Videl Lai and the TGA. While I'm here I will be enlisting the support of our friends the rhutz, the nanomites, and the seafolken in this effort. They have proven themselves invaluable in the struggle in Tributon and Rigimol and I'm sure that will prove to be the case here.

"Unfortunately, my visit will be short as I must get back to my duties as Commander General of the 3rd Army. Some of my staff will be staying on, however, to provide assistance to your leaders here in Queenland. Now is the time to rise up against Videl Lai and the TGA. If you are willing and able to fight, recruiters for the Loyalist Army will be around to enlist you in the fight for freedom and justice. If you are a TGA soldier who has been forced to serve Videl Lai, now is the time to defect and renounce both him and the Purist Party. Your enlistment will be simple and with no questions asked.

"Now I must leave as the enemy will soon be on my heels. May God and Sandee be with you!"

Leek turned off the microphone and looked at Tobeth expectantly. "What do you think?"

"Very inspiring, but we don't have time to talk about it now. Let's get going. It won't take the TGA long to find the source of the broadcast and when they do, we better be far away from here."

Leek nodded and they all rushed to the PTVs. Sirens could be heard in the distance. Just moments after they'd left, police and a squadron of TGA soldiers arrived at the studio. The police surrounded the building and the soldiers went inside. A few tiks later there was an huge explosion blowing glass and debris into the street. Fire quickly engulfed the building and billows of black smoke spiraled into the air. Those inside were Queenland's first casualties of the Tarizon Civil War.

Half a kyloon later Leek was shaking hands with factory workers on an assembly line at the Patrelin Electronics plant. "Leek Lanzia, good to meet you," he said for the umpteenth time. He climbed up a few stairs where he could be seen by a hundred or so workers. "Sorry to intrude on your work, but I wanted to stop by and tell you personally that the TGA's days are numbered!"

"Praise to God and Sandee!" a worker said.

Leek smiled. "I thought if you actually saw me here in Guthlin you might be more likely to believe me. I know when I see someone on the VC or hear them on the radio I don't always know if they are sincere or just reading a script. So, I want you to tell everyone you know that Commander General Leek Lanzia, Commander of the 3rd Loyalist Army, came to Queenland, came right here to Guthlin to personally deliver this message. So far the war against the TGA and Videl Lai has been taking place on the other side of the globe, but today it has come to Queenland!"

"It's about time!" someone screamed.

"Yes it is. For too long you have been living under the tyranny of Videl Lai and the Purists. They are as dark and evil men as you will ever see and if you don't believe me ask the friends and family of your own Senator

Sami San.

"Sami San was one of your most cherished leaders. He was a loving son, a devoted mate, a cherished father, a successful businessman, the mayor of your largest city, and finally Queenland's senator in the World Assembly. But being an honest man who believed in God and the Supreme Mandate, he was a well known foe of Videl Lai.

"So, when it came time to elect a new chancellor one of Videl's henchmen came in the night and slit the throat of your beloved senator, Sami San."

There were cries of anguish from the crowd. *Seama lo dante!* someone screamed.

"And this didn't just happen in Queenland but all over Tarizon. Good, righteous men were murdered to make the election of Videl Lai inevitable.

"We've all suffered by the deeds of this despicable tyrant. My beloved mate was kidnaped by Videl's own son and today languishes in a filthy jail cell, chained to the wall like a vicious animal.

"It's time to drive the TGA and Videl Lai out of Queenland. It's time to drive a knife through the heart of the tyrant!"

Seama lo dante! another person yelled.

"Yes, it's time for vengeance!" Leek screamed, raising his fist high in the air. He looked around and saw a steady stream of workers rushing into the room trying to get a look at him.

"I know that up until now there was nothing you could do. Videl and the TGA were too powerful. But now that's changed!"

The crowd screamed their approval.

"Do you want to avenge the murder of Sami San?" Leek asked.

"Yes!" the crowd screamed.

"Do you want to avenge the murder of Chancellor Garcia?"

"Yes!" the crowd screamed.

"Do you want a return to law and order, to justice and a free society?"

"Yes!" the crowd roared.

"Then find one of our recruiters and sign up for the Loyalist Army. We must purge Queenland of the TGA and the Purist blight!"

Seama lo dante! Seama lo dante! the crowd began to chant. Some of the militia passed out pamphlets describing how to contact a recruiter and then Leek and his entourage were off to their next stop. By the time they got there sirens could be heard all over the city and the sky was full of copters and low-flying aircraft. The TGA was looking for the Liberator as they were getting many reports of sightings. Most of these reports, however, were false reports called in by the local militia sending police and TGA troops to every corner of the city and steering them away from the places Leek and his entourage were actually going.

The two PTVs waited outside the stadium while their militia escort was securing a path to the press booth.

"How long will this take?" Leek asked.

Tobeth shrugged. "Not long. We have to get rid of the police and see if there are any TGA soldiers about."

"How will you get rid of the police?"

"Stun guns. We don't want to kill any of them, just put them out of business long enough for you to give your speech."

"You think the police are sympathetic to the Loyalist cause?"

Tobeth looked around anxiously. "Yes, but they must bow to the dictates of Videl Lai and Central Authority. They have no other choice. But when the time comes to choose sides, I think most will come our way."

Tobeth suddenly froze. "Skutz! There's a police cruiser coming our way."

Leek turned quickly and frowned. "Now what?"

"Let's see if he's goes by. He may not suspect anything."

"Ah, with the city on high alert, I doubt it."

"He's stopping," Tobeth moaned. "We have to abort the mission."

"Okay. I understand."

Tobeth gave a signal to his militiamen and they opened fire on the cruiser. Another backup cruiser was on the scene almost immediately and the two sides began exchanging fire. While the police were pinned down the PTVs made a run for it.

"Where are we going?" Leek asked.

"We've set up a relay station in case the mission had to be aborted. We're headed there now. The delegation will be split up, put in new PTV's and sent away in different directions. Each will merge into local traffic and the TGA won't be able to find us."

"Good planning," Leek said leaning back for the first time. "It's too bad I couldn't give the speech. I was starting to enjoy it."

"Don't worry. You're giving your speech right now. We paid an audio technician to put a copy of this morning's Liberation Network address on the PA system and then lock the audio booth so nobody could stop it before it was finished."

Leek laughed. "Who's idea was that?"

"Perona. She's pretty cleaver."

"I can see that. You two make a good team. I pity the TGA being up against you two."

Tobeth chuckled. "I am rather looking forward to kicking their collective ass."

Leek grinned. "I hope we don't have to abort our trip to Zangor. I really need to talk to the seafolken."

"No, that will be your next destination. We'll take the rest of the delegation back to a safe house to wait for you."

"Good. The seafolken will be invaluable allies. They may be able to help you communicate with the nanomites too. I'm hoping to teach them how to make contact with them. It's difficult, but must be done as I have little time for it anymore."

"Sgt. Lindshill is already there preparing them for the meeting. They should be ready for you when we arrive."

"Good. What about the nanomites."

"They are in exile at the Litel Cathedral. Of course, they don't know you are coming since we had no way of warning them."

"That's okay. In exile they won't be busy, right," Leek said with a smile.

"No. I suspect not," Tobeth admitted.

The PTV took a left down a street in the warehouse district. An automatic door was raising in a garage on the left. The two PTVs swung in and the door closed.

"Okay. This is where we switch transport vehicles and split up."

Leek stepped out into the spacious garage that appeared to be a repair shop for large dirt moving equipment. Four smaller passenger PTVs were idling. Tobeth pointed to a dark blue one and they both got inside.

"These are Grinden 230s. Top of the line passenger vehicles."

"Really," Leek said very much impressed.

"When we reach the tube the driver will open it up and we should be in Zangor in no time."

Tarizon: Civil War

The Grinden lurched left into a tube entrance and the driver opened up. In the time Leek had been on Tarizon this was the first time he'd driven in a tube. To him it was much like driving in a long tunnel except they weren't going through a mountain. He thought they must be going at least 200 mph.

"The tube is laid like a pipe in the ground, so there's never a problem with rain, wind or snow. Driving conditions are always optimal and there's no speed limit."

"These must be expensive to build," Leek noted.

"They are now with labor so expensive and supplies in high demand. This one was built before the great eruptions. None have been built since."

"That's a shame. Maybe when we get this war over, that will change."

"That's what we're counting on, Commander."

Leek noticed a sign indicating the Zangor exit was coming up. The driver exited the tube. Soon they were in the harbor district and Leek noticed many ships docked along the Reuhr River that spilled into the Dark Sea. They met the seafolken on the deck of a freighter. Sgt Lindshill introduced them to the six seafolken assembled for the meeting. General Quirken was leading the delegation.

"It's a pleasure to meet you in person, General Quirken. I want to thank you for your help on Lortec. I doubt I'd be here had you and your men not escorted us off the island"

"Yes, I'm glad you summoned us. We were anxious to help."

"Well, we're going to need your help again."

"Yes, Sgt. Lindshill has briefed us. The seafolken are glad to see that the Loyalist movement has spread to Queenland. As always, we are at your command."

"Good. I'm leaving Sgt. Lindshill here to act as a liaison between you and the 31st Loyalist Division which is in the process of organizing."

"As you wish, Commander."

"It will be awhile before the 31st gets fully operational. In the meantime I need your help with the nanomites."

"The nanomites?"

"Yes, they will be invaluable to the war effort if we can establish communications. I can talk to them, but obviously I don't have the time to consult with them everyday. We need someone down here to communicate on a daily basis with the local swarmmasters."

"How can we help?" Quirken asked. "I've never talked to a nanomite."

"It's not hard for someone with the gift and I know the seafolken are well endowed with that ability. Anyone who can enter a man's dreams surely will have no trouble talking to the nanomites."

Quirken smiled. "It was easy to enter your dreams, Commander. Your mind was openly searching for help."

"Was it?" Leek laughed. "Anyway, if you'll take a little ride with me to Litel Cathedral I think I can show you how to make contact pretty easily."

"I am at your disposal, Commander."

"Good. Then let's go now so we can stay a step ahead of the TGA and local police."

Leek and General Quirken were taken to the cathedral where many nanomite swarms had taken asylum. It was a beautiful crystal structure very similar to the ones Leek had seen in Shisk. When they arrived they were met by Bishop Bohd who welcomed them and invited them inside.

"The nanomites swarms were brought around to the back. I imagine they went immediately into the structure of the cathedral. I don't know how you'd find them. They only reason I can confirm that they are here, is by the fact that much needed repairs and maintenance has been done."

"Don't worry. They are so close, anywhere in the cathedral will be fine."

The Bishop led them to a quiet chapel and suggested it would be an appropriate location, out of the way and somewhere they wouldn't likely be interrupted. Leek thanked him and he left.

"Have a seat Quirken," Leek said and began explaining how he'd been able to contact the nanomites in the past. Quirken acknowledged the method and said he was ready to begin.

Leek closed his eyes and thought of his image of a nanomite. He only knew the name of one swarmmaster, so he concentrated on him and, in his mind, said, "Lunn of the nanomites. This Commander General Leek Lanzia, known to you as the Liberator. I summon your counsel."

There was a moment of silence and then Leek tried again., "Lunn of the nanomites. This Commander General Leek Lanzia, known to you as the Liberator. I summon your counsel."

There was no answer. Leek frowned and looked at Quirken. "Sorry, they weren't expecting us, so this might take awhile. I should have alerted my swarmmasters back at base to contact them and tell them we'd be coming."

"No worry," Quirken said. "Perhaps you're too nervous. It's been a trying day. Relax and let the world around you melt away."

Leek sighed. "Right."

Leek closed his eyes and took a deep breath. In his minds eye he saw the nanomite. He took another deep breath and let his limbs relax. Then he tried one more time.

"Commander? Is that really you," Lunn thought. "Or, am I dreaming."

"No," Leek thought. "It is me. Commander Leek Lanzia, known to the nanomites as the Liberator."

"We are honored that you have come to us. Thank you for warning us of Videl Lai's plans to exterminate our hives. Had you not warned us and helped us go into asylum we wouldn't be here today."

"I'm glad we were able to save you."

"What brings you to Queenland?"

Leek explained the expansion of the war to Queenland and the need for help from the nanomites. He told him he needed the seafolken General Quirken to act as a liaison between the nanomites of Queenland and the new 31st Division of the Loyalist Army.

"Of course, we will open our minds to him. Is he there now?"

"Yes."

Leek nodded to Quirken and the general closed his eyes. "Lunn of the nanomites. This is Quirken, General of the Southern Sea Defense League, seeking your counsel."

The connection came quickly and Leek was relieved that he no longer was the sole connection between the nanomites and the human race. After the three leaders concluded their meeting, Leek said his goodbyes and headed back to the airport.

When he arrived a huge crowd had gathered. Seeing the crowd he looked anxiously toward the skies fearing the TGA might show up at any moment. When the crowd saw him they began chanting. *Seama lo dante! Seama lo dante.*

Grateful for the show of support, Leek got out of his PTV and waded through the crowd, shaking hands and greeting as many people as he could. When he finally made it to the runway he saw Red had his fighter ready to go. They embraced and then two militiamen helped Leek into his flight suit. As he climbed into the cockpit of the fighter he waved to the crowd and they screamed in unison. *Seama lo dante! Seama lo dante Seama lo dante!*

Just then a fighter flew by so low it created a gust of wind that blew off hats and scattered papers everywhere. Leek closed the hatch and fired up the engines. Soon he was shooting down the runway and up into the air. The fighter swung around and tried to get on Leek's tail but it was too late. Leek gave it full throttle, put it in stealth mode, and disappeared over the Dark Sea.

19
Dalo Prison

Leek finally relaxed in the cockpit of his T-47 as he reached his cruising altitude of 55,000 ft. Above the clouds and shroud of pollution that encircled Tarizon it was dark and the stars were as bright as he'd ever seen them. He gazed out in wonder, wishing he could see Earth, but he knew it was not visible from Tarizon. He made a silent vow, as he often did, to return home one day. Of course, he was painfully aware that his return would only happen if the Loyalists were successful. If not, he'd never see his home or his family again. But, if he fulfilled the Prophecy, then the Loyalist government would owe him. They couldn't refuse his wish to go home. Eventually, Leek's mind slowed down and he remembered he needed to check in. He got on his GC and pushed Lorin's code.

"R1, reporting," Leek said.

"Go ahead, R1," Lorin said. "Good to hear from you."

"Likewise."

"Everything went well I see," Lorin said.

"Yes. How did you know?"

"I've been monitoring all enemy channels. You've been the topic of chatter all day. Videl is livid that you were able to get into Queenland so easily and move about at will. Heads will be falling tomorrow, I'm sure."

"I'm glad to hear it."

"I've been talking to Threebeard and he thinks you ought to go to Dalo on the way back. Some local cell leaders want you to make a few appearances as a diversion to their plan to seize one of the TGA prisons. They've guaranteed your safety."

"Dalo. I don't even know where that is."

"That's all right, I've programmed it into your flight computer. You can just sit back and relax."

"Okay, whatever you say. What's happening on the front?"

Tarizon: Civil War

"It's still quiet. There's no sign of an offensive getting under way anytime soon. Our air force is growing each day as more planes are coming out of production. Overall, everything is looking good."

"Well, I'm sure General Bratfort has something up his sleeve, so keep up your guard."

"I will. Don't worry."

"Who's meeting me at Dalo?"

"Rulsa Chinet. He's our cell leader. They plan to free five or so thousand seafolken and mutant leaders who are being held there as political prisoners pending execution."

"How do they plan to do that?" Leek asked skeptically.

"I'm not sure. They say they know how to do it, but just in case I sent Tam and his special ops team to help out. They should already be there."

"That's a relief. You had me worried there for a moment. Breaking into a highly fortified prison won't be easy, but I guess if the TGA is chasing after me that will give them an advantage."

"Sorry to spring this on you. I know you're probably exhausted from the tight schedule you've been on. If you want to come straight back here, I'll just have Tam run the operation without you."

"No. It's not a problem as long I can refuel on Dalo."

"You can. I've arranged a safe place to keep the fighter and they'll refuel it during your operation."

"Good."

"I heard about your heart-wrenching story about Sami San and what you told them about Lucinda. It's really stirring up support for our cause. How did you know about San?"

"It was one of Threebeard's memories that just came to me while I was talking."

"It was great. I'm going to have my staff research every place you go so you can tell more stories of local interest like that one. Since you left the city the recruiters have taken over twelve thousand applications and there have been three thousand defections with full military gear."

"Outstanding. What's been the reaction of the TGA?"

"They've been on a rampage, of course. Shortly after you left they wiped out the remains of the farmhouse and the airstrip we used. But luckily, these were only temporary facilities set up just for your arrival. The new 31st Division is being assembled and trained at over a dozen different locations, so that if they discover one it won't be a disaster for us."

"Well, I know you've got it well under control, so I'm not worried about it."

"Is there anything you need me to do here since you're going to be delayed getting back?" Lorin asked.

"Yes, have you been able to identify the prison where they're holding Lucinda?"

"Yes, it's called Pritzka Prison and it's about ten kylods from Shisk."

"I can't explain it, but I think time is running out for Lucinda. We've got to get a plan put together as soon as possible to rescue her."

Leek heard an audible sigh. "You're not seriously thinking of trying that, are you? It would be suicide."

"Yes. I've told you all along I was going to rescue her."

"I know, but I thought it was just wishful thinking."

"No. I'm not going to let Videl Lai kill her and the baby. I'm going to get her back or die trying."

"I understand. I'll get with Threebeard and we'll start working on a plan."

"Good. Contact Tobeth on Queenland and ask him to find out if there are any nanomites at Pritzka Prison. I've trained a seafolken general named Quirken to communicate with them."

"Okay. I'll get on it."

"I wonder where the baby is?" Leek said softly.

"I don't know, but we'll try to find that out as well."

Leek signed off, feeling better now that a plan to rescue Lucinda was in the works. He sank back in his seat and tried to make his muscles relax. He thought of Lucinda and their baby. He wondered if they were okay. He prayed Lucinda hadn't been tortured. That was too horrible a thought to even contemplate, but deep down he knew she must have been. He cringed at the thought. Anger swelled within him. He wished Videl were in his gun sights and he could pull the trigger and blow him into a million pieces.

As the fighter sped on autopilot to Dalo his thoughts turned to his friend Tam. Although it had only been ten days since he'd left, it seemed much longer. He'd missed his old friend and would be glad to see a familiar face. He finally fell asleep and began to dream. First he relived the video of Lucinda being chained to the wall in Pritzka Prison. Then it was his snake dream. He heard a snake *hissing* and when he opened his eyes it was hovering over him. Like before, he instinctively grabbed the snake just below its head to keep it from striking him. But this time he was horrified to see hundreds of more snakes coming from every direction—hissing, striking, and biting every inch of his body. Excruciating pain surged through him and he wailed in agony. An alarm on his control panel woke him up abruptly.

He sat up, opened his eyes and blinked a few times, trying to focus on the blinking light. There was a fighter within missile range, he finally realized. He took the fighter off autopilot and took evasive maneuvers. The fighter stayed on his tail but didn't attack.

"R1, is that you?" a familiar voice said.

"R2?"

"Right behind you. It's a good thing I wasn't TGA."

"Yeah, well I'm traveling in stealth. TGA couldn't have found me."

"You're right. Lorin gave me your flight path, so I've been waiting for you."

"How far to Dalo?"

"You should be coming up on it soon. I just came out to meet you. There's quite a lot of TGA traffic around the island so we'll need to wait for the right moment to land. I'll see if we're clear."

"Thanks."

There was a moment of silence. "All right. We're cleared for landing. You can put it back on autopilot."

"Okay, R2. I'm back on autopilot."

"See you on the ground."

Leek preferred to land himself but since he knew nothing of Dalo, and it was nighttime, it was safer to let the autopilot to do it. Once on the ground he taxied over to several PTVs with their projector lights shining brightly. He stopped and opened the hatch and climbed out. Tam's fighter was taxiing in behind him. A short man with a mustache stepped out of one of the PTVs and approached him.

"Commander General. It's such an honor that you have come to Dalo."

"You must be—"

"Rulsa Chinet," he said proudly. "Did you have a good flight?"

"Yes. Quiet and relaxing."

Tam walked up from behind and put his hand on Leek's shoulder.

Leek turned and smiled.

"Well, I'm glad you slept on the way here because your first appearance is in less than a kyloon."

"But it's still dark."

"It will be light soon. We want you to meet with dock workers on the far north side of the island. The prison is on the opposite end. When word gets around of your presence we expect all police and TGA forces to come after you. By the time they get there, of course, you'll be kylods away at your second stop, a major hospital on the island."

"Sounds good to me," Leek said. "How do you plan to break into the prison?"

"The local officials have bribed some guards into leaving a maintenance hatch opened and unguarded. Once inside we'll take out the perimeter guards and blow the cell blocks. We've got a dozen copters waiting once the guards are down."

"Sounds like I'm going to be missing the fun."

"Oh, I don't know about that. Having the police and the TGA breathing down your neck ought to get your adrenaline pumping."

Leek laughed. "True. Good luck to you."

"Thanks. You too."

The PTVs split up, each going in opposite directions. Dalo was a tropical island with a rugged terrain, lots of vegetation, and an abundance of trees and exotic birds. Toward the ocean side there were white beaches and many sand dunes. Toward the inner part of the island a smoking volcano lurked above them. The night air was warm and salty. It reminded Leek of his visit to Hawaii several cycles earlier. They'd taken a cruise from one island to the other and it had been quite tranquil and pleasant. Somehow he didn't think his visit to Dalo would be the same.

Just after the sun had risen, Leek and his entourage of local Loyalist leaders, security personnel, and the press made their way to the docks. A large crowd of workers had been gathered to meet the Commander of the 3rd Army. Leek waded into the crowd, shaking hands and exchanging pleasantries. The press snapped pictures and taped video for their local newscasts even though it was unlikely the TGA would let the footage be aired. The reports and video, however, would appear on the Liberation Network. In fact, there were reports that when it came to news, the Liberation Network was getting a much larger audience share than the

Tarizon: Civil War

private networks under the censorship of the TGA.

Leek and his party didn't linger with the workers but soon moved on to the hospital. It was just in the nick of time, as police and TGA soldiers soon were swarming all over the docks. At the hospital Leek visited fifteen rooms, talked to doctors and nurses and then left through a back door, again, barely escaping before a squad of TGA soldiers rolled up. At noon the reporter on the local news was reporting an assault on Dalo prison and reports of a massive breach in security. As he spoke Leek was shaking Rulsa Chinet's big hand and climbing back into his fighter. His part in the battle of Dalo was over.

After splitting up at the airport Tam and his platoon followed the local Loyalist militia to Dalo Prison. It was located on a small thin peninsula surrounded by huge rocks and a treacherous sea. This environment made escape almost impossible without help from the outside. In fact, only a handful of escapees had ever made it out alive. The prison was an ancient stone fortress with six main prison towers, each manned with two sharpshooters. It had been built as a military stronghold by the seafolken over a hundred cycles earlier but had been taken over by the TGA after the great eruptions and converted to a political prison.

Since this was a former seafolken fortress and many seafolken leaders were incarcerated there, Tam had enlisted the support of the local seafolken in the attack. While six seafolken swam in from the sea and waited in the rocks beneath the far tower, two mutants skilled in mountain climbing scaled the wall underneath one of the towers. When the guard saw the first soldier climb up onto the wall he started to scream an alarm, but the second soldier silenced him with his laser pistol. A second guard, responding to the alarm, suffered the same fate.

After the tower was secured the two soldiers dropped ropes for the seafolken waiting below. Together they systematically secured the rest of the towers using laser guns so as not to call attention to their assault. In the meantime Tam and the rest of the soldiers were entering in the maintenance hatch that had been left open for them. It wasn't until they blew the first cell block door that the sirens began to wail. The guards on duty were no match for the special ops team and the well-trained militia they were up against. Those who were not killed willingly surrendered.

A dozen Ritzoen 77 transport copters arrived, bringing in fresh troops and evacuating the prisoners. Hundreds of seafolken emerged from the sea and gathered around the perimeter of the fortress. Since the siege had gone so well, the seafolken and the militia decided to stay in the fortress and use it as a base of operations against the TGA. Before Tam and his team left they helped set up a Trisling missile defense system which included long-range radar and Muscan II missile launchers. The militia commanders thanked them for their help and asked if they'd do one more thing for them before they went back to Tributon. Tam agreed.

As Tam and his men were heading for the airstrip where their fighters were waiting, they heard several explosions and the sound of a battle raging in the city. They hurriedly put on their flight suits and climbed into their eight fighters. After they'd taken off they circled back over Dalo and while two fighters blew up the police station and TGA headquarters, the other six pounded the TGA air base and naval yards. When they finally left Dalo airspace, forty planes and twenty-one ships were ablaze. They'd fulfilled their promise and now it was time to get back to the main front.

"R2, are you there?" Leek asked.

"R2 here," Tam responded.

"Since you guys are so good at taking prisons, I've got another assignment for you."

"What's that?" Tam asked cautiously.

"Pritzka Prison. It's right on the way home. I've decided Lucinda's rescue can't wait another minute."

"But Pritzka Prison is in Shisk."

"I know. It's time to get her out. I don't know why I've waited so long. It just seemed so impossible, but her life is in danger. I can feel it."

"Do you have an actual plan? You've never mentioned one before," Tam asked skeptically.

"Lorin is working on a plan and if she gets it worked out in time we'll take a detour that way."

"Then I'll pray she gets it put together. You and Lucinda have been apart too long."

"Yes, and if we don't rescue her soon I think she'll probably die. You saw how weak she looked in that TGA video we saw before we left."

"I know. I'm sorry."

"All right. I'm putting it on autopilot so I can get some sleep."

"Confirmed. Catch you later, R2 out."

Tarizon: Civil War

Lorin had promised to contact him just as soon as she had completed her investigation of Pritzka Prison. Leek knew she would be giving it high priority, so he had no doubt he'd be hearing from her soon. He switched on his autopilot and yawned. He was exhausted and could hardly keep his eyes open. He slept for some time—a troubled slumber filled with dreams of past horrors and fears of impending doom. Sometime later an alarm woke him with a start. He looked at his radar but saw nothing. Then he noticed he was just about out of fuel.

Lorin had promised him a fueling drone at about the point where the Emerald Ocean runs into the Coral Sea. He flipped on his communicator. "R1 to S1, come in."

"I bet you're getting low on fuel," Lorin said.

"Yeah. My warning light's on."

"Look on your scope. You should be coming up on the drone any moment."

Leek saw a blip on his screen. "Got it. . . . Cutting it kind of close, aren't you?"

"Sorry, we've got a situation going on. It's been pretty hectic back here."

"What's happening?"

"The TGA hit Shini hard by air. They've punctured the dome and are dropping thousands of vipers on the city."

"Oh, my God! On the civilian population?"

"Yes, Threebeard says it's an act of desperation. Their infantry hasn't been able to advance any closer to Shini on the ground so they decided to hit it by air."

"How were they able to puncture the dome? I thought that was nearly impossible."

"The vipers were dropped to clutter the radar so that we couldn't see the missiles coming in. The city is in chaos. Loyalist headquarters has been destroyed and there are reports the Chancellor is dead."

"What?" Leek exclaimed. "I can't believe they'd stoop to such depths. Shall I alter my course to Shini?"

"Actually, Threebeard thinks this is the perfect opportunity for you to rescue Lucinda. He's getting the same feelings you are."

"What feelings?"

"That it's now or never. Her strength is failing."

Tears began to well in Leek's eyes. "I know. That's what I've been sensing."

"So, with Shini ablaze nobody would ever dream we'd launch an attack on Shisk, yet something like that is exactly what needs to happen to show we're still in this war."

"Okay, do you have a plan?"

"Yes, I'm programming your fighter now for a landing site just outside of Shisk. We've arranged for transport with our local cells in the area. Tam and his squad will meet you there together with some local militia."

"What about the nanomites? Are there any in the prison?" Leek asked.

"There were until your operation at Gallion. After the nanomites helped you there, as a precaution, Videl ordered all military buildings exterminated."

"Oh, my God! I forgot about the maintenance swarms. The poor nanomites."

"It was inevitable, I guess, that Videl would finally realize that all buildings constructed by the nanomites had a few swarms left behind. There were so many nanomite buildings there was no practical way to evacuate all of them."

"Right, but that doesn't make me feel any better."

"No. I've been sick over it too, but there's nothing that can be done about it now, other than to win the war and put Videl Lai in his grave."

"I know."

"I've arranged for Rhin to come. Perhaps she can summon some help from the local rhutz. We'll need all the help we can get. Red and John will try to make it too, if they can get there in time."

"Good. They're in Lortec right now helping plan a strike on Ock Mezan."

"Wow. Things are moving fast and furious."

"Yes, they are and we can't let this attack on Shini shift the momentum of the war. You've got to rescue Lucinda and then destroy every military installation in and around Shisk as a retaliation for the attack on Shini. You've got to make them pay for this atrocity."

"Any idea where we can find Videl? I'd love to pay him a visit while we're in town."

"We're working on it, but I don't want you trying to find him. It's too dangerous. If we discover where he is, we'll shoot a few missiles his way and hope we get lucky."

"All right. Let me know when you have a detailed plan. In the meantime I'm going to get some more sleep."

"Affirmative. Sweet dreams."

Leek relaxed as much as he could in his flight suit sailing at 55,000 feet over the Coral Sea. He was excited about the prospect of rescuing Lucinda, but was worried that the plan might fail. His mind raced over the news of the attack on Shini. He could just imagine the chaos the vipers had caused as they darted everywhere seeking out a defenseless victim. Even worse would be the nightmarish scene of people all around screaming in unbearable pain as they swelled up and contorted until a vital organ exploded and mercifully stopped the pain forever. An unbearable anger swelled in Leek and he hoped and prayed to God that one day he'd find Videl so he could make him feel the same pain he'd inflicted on so many others. Even that would be too kind to him, but he'd leave Videl Lai's eternal damnation to God.

20
Power Shift

Tears welled in Lorin's eyes as she watched the carnage on the streets of Shini on her remote monitor. Sirens wailed as fire trucks and emergency medical teams rushed from one disaster to the next. The smoke was so thick it was often hard to make out what the cameras were visualizing. With the dome collapsed, lethal toxins were streaming into the air, making it necessary for anyone venturing out of doors to wear breathers. Unfortunately, there were not enough breathers for everyone and those without them who were forced out on the streets by the fires or explosions immediately went into respiratory distress. First they'd turn red and then a ghostly blue until they'd collapse on the street. If they were not picked up quickly by the medical response teams and given oxygen they'd die. Lorin's communicator beeped.

"Yes."

"Lorin, it's confirmed," Senator Marcuzzi said. "Chancellor Mammett is dead. They searched the rubble of his home and found his body. It's been positively identified. The Vice Chancellor has been sworn in, but he's agreed to resign and force the General Assembly to elect a new Chancellor, if you'll agree to serve."

"Of course, I'll serve. That's what I've wanted from the beginning."

"I thought so, but I had to confirm it."

"Tell the Assembly that I'm already working on an appropriate response to this deplorable attack on our citizens. I'm going to make Videl Lai pay for this!"

"Good. They'll be glad to hear that."

Lorin took a deep breath. Finally, she'd be Chancellor, she thought. A great relief washed over her. Now she could come out of the shadows and take decisive action to rid Tarizon of Videl Lai. Nobody would question her authority now and she wouldn't have to answer to anyone but God and Sandee. Power felt good, she thought, almost intoxicating. A pang of guilt

Tarizon: Civil War

spoiled the feeling. *It would be so easy to let it overcome me, she thought, but then I'd be no better than Videl Lai.* She'd have to be careful and seek out Threebeard's and Leek's counsel to be sure she hadn't lost her perspective. She'd have the Supreme Mandate too; it would help guide her. She flipped on her communicator and punched in a code.

"Major Oakril here."

"Major, how are we coming on our plans to siege Pritska Prison?"

"They are almost complete and I've put the 1st Airborne on alert as you requested."

"Good. The siege is a definite go, so make sure the plan will work."

"Yes, Chancellor."

"Chancellor?" she laughed. It was the first time anyone had called her that. She liked the feeling. "You already know?"

"Yes, I'm your chief intelligence officer, remember?"

A smile came over her face. "Yes, of course. Carry on."

Lorin looked at the digital time readout in front of her. It was time to wake Leek and brief him on the mission. She hesitated, wondering if she was acting out of rage or intelligent assessment. She'd be putting the Liberator in great peril if she went forward with the mission. *What if he were killed? No, this is no time for cowardice or indecision. You know this is the right thing to do.* She did believe it; deep down she knew this was the perfect move to shift the momentum of the war toward the Loyalists and, as Leek and Threebeard said, time was running out for Lucinda. She flipped on her communicator and hailed Leek.

"R1 here," he said sleepily.

"This is the Chancellor," she said playfully.

"Huh? Lorin?"

"I guess I should be sad at Chancellor Mammett's death," she said thoughtfully, "but I never felt anything for that man."

"Chancellor Mammett is dead?"

"Yes, and the Vice Chancellor is resigning, so I can be elected Chancellor."

"Finally! Congratulations. That's wonderful. Now you don't have to be watching your back all the time."

"Exactly. So your Pritzka mission is a go and I've expanded it a bit to make sure it's an appropriate response to Videl Lai's cowardly attack on Shini."

"Excellent! What's the plan?" Leek asked eagerly.

Lorin explained the mission in detail and gave Leek a complete briefing on the situation in Shini. He was appalled at what he heard and had to fight an urge to go directly there to help out.

"There's nothing you can do there now," Lorin said. "The military has taken control of the city and General Zitor is personally supervising the cleanup. The dome is being repaired as we speak and should be resealed in a couple of days."

"How many casualties?" Leek asked.

"Over twenty thousand dead and eighty-five thousand have been treated for a variety of respiratory complaints. Of course, that's just the short-term ramifications of the attack. Those who were exposed to the toxins will be looking at a lifetime of disease and disability as a result of Videl Lai's act of desperation."

"Would you check on Tehra and Sophilo for me? I've been worried about them."

"I already have. They're fine. Their building has a filtration system and they stayed indoors during the attack."

"Oh, thank God."

"I'll visit them tomorrow when I get to Shini."

"Okay, tell them I'm coming up there just as soon as this mission is over."

"I will. Good luck tomorrow. I hope you find Lucinda and the baby okay."

Leek sighed. "Me too."

Lorin hung up and started making a list of what she needed to do before she left. She'd have to delegate much of the work she'd been doing in the past to subordinates. The duties of Chancellor would be time consuming and she'd have little time for the one-on-one relationship she'd developed with her cell leaders. Fortunately, many from her father's old staff were available and would jump at the opportunity to join her new government. Since she knew most of them quite well and they were experienced, it would mean her new administration would be up and running almost immediately.

Her most difficult decision was who should take over direct contact with her web of cell leaders around Tarizon. Her replacement would have to be intelligent, personable and compassionate. It was a delicate job that required much patience and tact. After carefully thinking about it she knew who she wanted to do it. She put in a call to Captain Shilling.

"Congratulations, Lorin, or should I say, Chancellor."

"Thank you. What a shock, huh?"

"Yes, Chancellor Mammett's death was unfortunate for him, but a lucky break for Tarizon."

Lorin stifled a laugh. "Well, I hope you're right, but only time will tell."

"What can I do for you, Chancellor?"

"You know the work I've been doing coordinating the resistance with all the cell leaders around Tarizon, right?"

"Yes. You've done an excellent job. I've watched you with great admiration."

"Well, I won't have time to do that anymore, so I'd like you to do it for me."

There was a moment of silence. "Really, but I'm the captain of Earth Shuttle 26."

"Yes, but Earth Shuttle 26 won't be doing any traveling until this war is over. In the meantime I could use your talents."

"I'm honored that you thought of me. I'd be happy to do it."

"Good. We'll contact all the cell leaders tonight and advise them you'll be coordinating their efforts in the future. Your title will be Deputy of Political Affairs. You'll also be in charge of the Liberation Network. Major Oakril will help you with that."

"All right," Captain Shilling said, tentatively.

"Don't worry, it seems like a lot but you'll do fine. If you need more staff just let me know and I'll arrange it."

"Okay."

"I'll see you in the operations room after dinner."

"I'll be there. Thanks again."

Lorin hung up the phone feeling relieved. She trusted Captain Shilling and knew she'd do a good job. Another important appointment would be her chief of staff. This person would have to be a very astute politician who could help her deal with the General Assembly, the Council of Interpreters, and the military. She wanted Senator Marcuzzi for the job but she wasn't sure he'd be willing to give up his Senate seat to do it. She thought about calling him, but decided it would be better to meet him in person since this was perhaps her most important appointment.

That night she couldn't sleep. She was finally getting what she wanted—to take over where her father left off. It felt good but it was also quite scary. Now she'd have nobody to blame if things didn't go the way she had planned. She thought of how close Leek had come to death on more than one occasion. What would she do if he were to die in the assault on Pritzka Prison? Every day the Loyalist supporters were relying more and more on his leadership and inspiration. Was it smart to rely so heavily on one person? She knew it wasn't but didn't know of an alternative. Leek the Liberator was too powerful a force to leave in the shadows.

The next morning Lorin was up before dawn packing and making final plans for her trip. At dawn she stepped on to her new PT22 along with eleven staff members she was taking with her to Shini. The trip was dangerous as she had to fly over enemy territory to get to Shini. A dozen fighters escorted her just in case she ran into trouble. Fortunately, the TGA didn't know she was traveling nor did they know about the Loyalist headquarters in the Doral Mountains.

Colonel Tomel, General Zitor and Senator Marcuzzi and a small crowd of well-wishers met her at the airport. They took her to the Linzcot Hotel where she was to live until repairs were complete on the Chancellor's Mansion. After she'd gotten moved in, she went to her office. The Chancellor's office was in the National Capitol Building. Rigimol's governor had graciously allowed the Loyalists to share his statehouse until Videl Lai was defeated and the government could return to Shisk.

Her office was quite lavish and spacious compared to her command center in Earth Shuttle 26. After she'd gotten her staff situated, she asked Senator Marcuzzi if she could have a private word with him. He agreed and everyone left to give them privacy.

"Well, this is a beautiful office but not too practical. I kind of liked my command center with everything I needed at my fingertips."

"Everything will still be available to you; you'll just have to ask for it. You won't have time to personally monitor everything that's going on."

"Yes, that will take some getting used to."

"You'll appreciate it in time."

"I hope you're right."

"So, what did you want to talk about?"

"I'd like you to be my chief of staff."

"Chief of staff? You want me to be chief of staff?"

Tarizon: Civil War

"Yes, I'm no politician. I need someone in charge who is astute and knowledgeable. You were the first person I thought of."

"I'm flattered, but I'd have to resign my Senate seat and disappoint a lot of supporters who worked hard to get me elected."

"They won't be disappointed if you become the second most influential politician in the government. They will be excited and happy for you."

"Perhaps, but—"

"You'll have a lot of responsibility. I promise the job will be both challenging and rewarding."

Senator Marcuzzi smiled. "Well, if you put it like that, how could I refuse?"

"You can't. So it's settled. Congratulations!"

"Thank you."

"I've appointed Captain Shilling as my Deputy of Political Affairs. She'll watch over our Loyalist cells around the globe and oversee the Liberation Network."

"Captain Shilling? But everyone thinks she's dead."

"I know. Let's keep it that way. Nobody needs to know about Earth Shuttle 26. One day we may want to use it in a covert operation."

"What do I say if anyone asks me who's coordinating the cell network?"

"Just say it's Major Oakril. He'll be working with Captain Shilling so he'll know what's going on and will play along."

"Very well. What's on your agenda for this afternoon? Anything in particular?"

"Yes, I'd like to meet with Threebeard and the Command Staff. We need to determine our next step in the war. Then I want to go visit Tehra and Sophilo. I promised Commander General Lanzia I'd make sure they were okay."

"Very well, I'll contact the Command Staff and get them here right away."

Senator Marcuzzi left and Lorin pushed her intercom button. "Cora, would you contact Tehra Connolly and see if it's convenient for me to visit her this afternoon."

"Yes, Chancellor. I'll get right on it."

"Thanks."

William Manchee

Cora had been her father's executive secretary. She was very capable and efficient but a bit overbearing at times. It seemed strange to Lorin, giving her orders after taking them from her for so long. Cora didn't mind it, though; she was just glad to be back in a position where she was respected and could contribute to the Loyalist cause. She'd been blackballed by Chancellor Mammett when he took power because of her loyalties to Lorin, so she'd been unable to get a decent job since his assassination.

Ten loons later Cora stepped in and announced the Command Staff had assembled in the conference room and were waiting for her. She thanked her, gathered her notes, and strolled down the hall to the conference room. A young secretary she hadn't met yet handed her a cup of sankee as she walked through the door. Everyone came to their feet and applauded.

Lorin was embarrassed at the applause as she didn't think it appropriate under the circumstances of her rise to the chancellorship. She took her seat at the end of the long crystal table.

"Thank you," she said politely, "but in light of the fact that two chancellors have been assassinated in the last 90 days and our capital city has just been ravaged by the enemy's vipers, I think the mood here should be of somber reflection and dogged determination to turn the course of the war."

The room quieted and the smiles vanished. Lorin continued.

"One man or woman can't defeat Videl Lai. It's going to take all of us and thousands more all working together for one purpose—the elimination of Videl Lai and the evil he represents. . . . Now, can someone give me a report on where we stand in this war as of this moment?"

General Zitor cleared his throat. "Yes, Chancellor. Let me do that for you."

"Very well," Lorin said.

"Let's start with Lower Azollo. Commander Lanzia's visit to Queenland has resulted in an avalanche of support for our cause. Our troop strength is expected to increase tenfold. Many of those soldiers are defectors such that we will soon have two fully operational divisions in southern Queenland. Of course, we also have several thousand seafolken, an unknown number of rhutz, and the nanomites.

"Again, with Commander Lanzia and Captain Lavendar's help, the militia on Dalo have secured the island nation. This will be invaluable to us

Tarizon: Civil War

as a staging area for an invasion of Azollo when the time is right.

"I'm also happy to report that with the help of the seafolken the TGA has been driven out of the Beet Islands, Lortec, and an invasion of Ock Mezan is in the works.

"Finally, just in the last few days I've learned there is a fully operational Loyalist Division operating out of the Weeping Mountains in Soni. As in Queenland, new recruits and defectors are flooding in so fast we're having trouble processing them."

General Zitor looked at Lorin and nodded. "Thank you, General Zitor. Now would anybody like to give me the bad news?"

"Yes," General Lugman replied. "Although nothing General Zitor said was untrue, he has sugarcoated things just a bit. In Lower Azollo the TGA is not asleep. They know we are gaining strength and intelligence reports show they're positioning themselves for a major assault on Queenland very soon. Since most of our troops lack both experience and proper arms and equipment, such an assault could prove disastrous. I don't deny that we are working on those problems, but we may be running out of time.

"In regard to an attack on Ock Mezan, I think the seafolken and our Loyalist command have greatly underestimated the difficulty in taking that island nation. If you study Ock Mezan you will discover that the enemy has four large military bases there. Two naval bases, one on each side of the island, an army base, and a large air station. The navy maintains heavy patrols along the coastline and the air space over the island is monitored very closely.

"Turning to Turvin, I doubt the militia hiding there in the mountains will last too long. That will have to be Videl Lai's first priority, to rid Turvin of rebel forces.

"Finally, I heard nothing about Tributon and the TGA armies poised to strike once again at Rigimol nor the devastating viper attack on this very city," General Lugman concluded.

"I was leaving Rigimol to our defense minister. I thought he'd want to fill you in on the situation there as well as the viper attack," General Zitor said.

All eyes turned to Threebeard. "Yes, I thank the General for letting me give that report, for I think that we stand today at a great turning point in the Tarizon Civil War. Although the enemy has devastated our capital city, they have not destroyed it. In fact, at this very moment the dome is nearly repaired, order has been restored and we now are busy mourning our dead.

"But when that is done the people of Rigimol and Loyalists all over Tarizon will be thinking of this evil deed perpetrated by Chancellor Videl Lai. They will be wondering what kind of man could launch an attack with no military significance simply to kill innocent civilians. As they think about this callous and shameful act they will get angry and their anger will turn to resolve, resolve to rid Tarizon of the despot, Videl Lai.

"I agree with General Lugman that Videl's number one priority will be to destroy the militia in Turvin. He will also be worrying about all the things General Zitor just explained to us. That is why tomorrow morning, with the Chancellor's permission, we will launch an all-out offensive against the TGA forces in Tributon and Rigimol. We have found out that General Bratfort has been called back to Shisk for consultation. This will mean someone less capable will be in command when we launch our offensive."

"Even so, do you really think we can beat the TGA with a force just half its size?" Lorin asked.

"Yes, Madam Chancellor," Threebeard replied. "I do believe that is possible, even likely, for three reasons. Number one, the morale of our troops is high and the enemy's is low. Secondly, our air force is much larger and better trained than it ever has been. Finally, thanks to Commander Lanzia's foresight and leadership in the development of new systems to defend against the viper and the hovertank, neither will be effective against our troops during this new offensive. Furthermore, we have developed our own weapon of horror, a super viper so lethal that it will decimate the TGA forces before we ever advance on them."

"Don't you think they will have developed defenses against a super viper attack, just as we have?" General Lugman asked.

"You would think so, but our intelligence sources have seen no signs of any defensive measures being taken to prepare their troops for a viper attack. We believe Videl thinks his attack on Shini has crippled us and that the TGA is close to victory. In fact, we have been intentionally sending out reports of our dire situation in hopes that the TGA will become overconfident."

"Thank you, Mr. Defense Minister. Your report gives me great encouragement. I wholeheartedly approve of your plan and will make sure you have the complete support of the government in implementing it."

"I appreciate that, Madam Chancellor. It would be helpful if you would ask your cell leaders all over the globe to organize as much civil unrest these next few days as possible. We want to shake the very foundation of the TGA until it cracks wide open!"

"Absolutely. I'll get that communique out immediately," Lorin said.

Threebeard hadn't mentioned the mission at Pritzka Prison, as surprise was an absolute necessity if the rescue was to be a success. Lorin had agreed that it should not be brought up and the fewer who knew about it the better. The meeting continued for another kyloon and when it was over and everyone had left, Lorin had her driver take her to Tehra's compartment.

The road along the way was cluttered with the debris left from the viper attacks. Lorin tried to imagine the horror everyone must have felt when the robot snakes fell from the sky and began attacking them. When they got to the building her security team checked the exits, searched the common areas, and then escorted the Chancellor to Tehra's compartment. Tehra bowed to the Chancellor as she stepped in the door.

"None of that," Lorin said. "I'm here as a friend. At least I hope we can be friends."

"Of course. I'd like that," Tehra said. "Come sit down. Would you like some sankee or luri?"

"Yes, a cup of sankee, please," she replied.

Tehra went into the kitchen and returned a moment later with two cups of sankee.

"Leek asked me to come check on you and the baby. He was worried about you when he heard about the raid on Shini."

"Oh. We're okay, I guess. At least we survived."

"It was bad, huh? Where were you when it happened?"

"We were in a taxi on the way home from the doctor. It had been a bright day but all of a sudden the sky darkened like an eclipse or a heavy thunderstorm. I was busy with the baby so I didn't think much about it until the vipers started falling and targeting their victims."

"Oh, my God! You saw them attacking people?"

"Attacking people, PTVs, tram cabs, taxis—one of them came at us and smashed through the windshield of our taxi. It was just inches from the driver's face. Lucky for him the taxi had shatterproof glass and the viper couldn't make it all the way through."

"What did he do?"

"He pulled out a gun he kept for protection and unloaded it on the viper's face. Then he pulled the taxi into a parking garage until the attack was over."

"Wow! You must have been terrified."

"I was afraid more for Sophilo than for myself. I would have died had one of those monsters attacked him."

"Oh, I'm so sorry you had to go though such an ordeal."

"That wasn't the worst of it. When we got back to our building the taxi driver parked out front and when he stepped out to open my door a sleeping viper suddenly came alive and attacked him. Of course there's nothing you can do once the viper sinks its fangs into you. He struggled and fought for a few moments until the poison took hold of him."

"How did you get into your compartment?"

"Two doormen came out and helped us out of the taxi. They carried garbage can lids as shields against the viper attacks."

Lorin shook her head. "Well, I'm going to make sure that never happens again. I promise you."

"Good. I'll sleep better knowing that."

"So, where's the baby?"

"Sleeping, but he should be waking up soon, so you can play with him."

Lorin smiled. "That would be great. I don't know how long it's been since I held a baby."

Tehra took a sip of her sankee and then offered Lorin a pastry. "Is Leek on a mission?"

"Yes, but it's a short one and he should be home soon. He'll come to see you right away, I'm sure."

"Good. I want him to spend time with Sophilo. He needs a man in his life."

"Don't we all," Lorin mused.

"Oh, I'm sorry. I forgot about Jake. I know you must have been devastated."

There was the cry of a baby from the bedroom.

"Ah, there he is," Tehra said. "Come on. Let's go get him."

Tehra got up and headed for the bedroom with Lorin on her heels. The nursery was beautifully decorated with a fancy white bassinet against one wall. She picked up the baby and held it close to her.

"Hey, little one. What's the matter," she said softly.

Sophilo quieted down in his mother's arms. She patted him gently and then asked, "Do you want to hold him?"

Lorin's eyes lit up. "Oh, yes. I'd love to."

Tehra handed the baby to her and she took him gingerly. Sophilo started to cry but quit when Lorin began rocking him.

"He does look a little like Leek, don't you think?" Lorin said.

"Oh, yes. Very much so. I hope they have a close relationship."

"I don't think you have to worry about that. Leek is always talking about you and the baby. You're his family now."

"I know. It did work out pretty well, didn't it?" Tehra asked.

"It almost sounds like you planned it," Lorin said wryly.

"Not exactly."

Lorin did a double take. "What?"

"I didn't know anything about Peter Turner or how he fit into the Prophecy, but I was a guide looking to get pregnant, so when I was assigned to Peter's father it was a pretty good bet I'd be returning to Tarizon pregnant with his child."

"So, you think someone planned for Leek to have a brother born on Tarizon."

"Exactly."

"Who do you think is behind it?"

"I thought maybe you would know? Your father comes to mind."

"No. Father didn't learn of Peter's exile until he was aboard the shuttle."

"Well, I may be wrong. It could just be a coincidence," Tehra conceded.

"No, I think you're right," Lorin said. "Someone has carefully planned this whole Prophecy thing and I'm pretty sure I know who it is."

"Who?"

"I'd better not say just yet until I've confirmed it and figured out what it means."

Tehra shrugged and took the baby. "I guess I better feed him."

On the way back to her new residence Lorin pondered her visit. She wondered if Tehra had designs on Leek or would be content to be a stepmother. Although she hadn't thought of Leek as a mate since she had always had Jake, now things were different. Still, Jake was in love with Lucinda, so it didn't really matter how Tehra or she might feel about him. He was off-limits. Now she understood why love had not been encouraged by Central Authority and Tarizon's citizens were mated by computer. Love was very complex and confusing and could only lead to discord and frustration.

21
Rescue

After the Chancellor had hung up, Leek's mind raced over the flood of information that had suddenly been thrust upon him. He was possibly facing the most critical and dangerous moment of his life. He took a deep breath and thoughts of his parents and siblings back on Earth flipped through his mind. Would he ever see them again or would he die this day millions of miles from home? Was it even possible to rescue Lucinda? Was she already dead or so emotionally scarred that she'd be a stranger to him?

Leek sat up and looked at his radar screen. He'd just crossed the Soni border and his autopilot was taking him in for a landing. The big domed city of Shisk glowed in the distance. It was just before dawn as he climbed out of his fighter and stretched. When he turned toward noises to his right he was astonished at the scene. Thousands of mutants and seafolken had gathered and were organizing and checking their weapons. Then he remembered Shisk was Threebeard's hometown. He'd have many friends and allies ready to do battle here. Fighters were landing one after another. He recognized the 1st Airborne and saw Tam in the distance. He walked briskly over to him and they embraced.

"Nice work back there in Dalo," Leek said. "I've heard our people have taken control of the island."

"Yes, thanks to you. Your diversion was perfectly executed."

"I can't take credit for that. I just shook hands and did what I was told."

"So, Lorin is our new Chancellor, huh?" Tam noted with a big grin.

"Yes, so we've got to make sure this mission is a success. We wouldn't want to blemish her new regime from the start."

"No. She'd never let us forget it."

A loon later Red and John joined them, along with the leaders of the local militia and the seafolken. Then Leek heard barking and smiled when he saw Rhin running toward him with a pack of rhutz on her tail. He knelt down and embraced his friend while Tam, Red and John backed off and watched them warily.

As Leek was stroking Rhin, a medic came up holding a small blue packet. "Commander?"

Leek stood up and gave the medic a hard look. "Yes."

"Ah, sir. I was told to give this to you," the medic said handing Leek the blue packet.

Leek took it and examined it curiously. "What's this?"

"It's a syringe containing a strong sedative. The doctor says you should inject Lucinda with it when you find her. She may be too weak to handle the trauma of her rescue."

Leek nodded. "But I've never given someone a shot before."

John took the blue packet from Leek. "I'll do it. I served in a medical unit before I became a pilot."

"Thanks," Leek said with a sigh of relief.

The medic left and with everyone there the leaders of the makeshift army reviewed their plans, made last minute adjustments and then moved out to make history.

From the Loyalist headquarters just inside Rigimol's southern border, Threebeard hacked into Shisk's master computer network and disabled the security on the city's primary entry points. This allowed the rhutz and militia dressed in civilian attire into the city. The troops were brought in on a tram that Threebeard managed to commandeer before shutting down the entire tram system along with the police communications network. The first strike came on Shisk's spaceport and adjoining air base. The 1st Airborne hit it mercilessly with Muscan missiles, cluster bombs, tactical flash bombs. The TGA was taken by complete surprise with most of its fighters on the ground.

At the same time three mutant militiamen armed with portable Muscan missile launchers blasted three large holes in the north wall of Pritzka Prison. The militiamen poured through the holes and headed for the cell blocks. Tam and his platoon engaged the guards and quickly neutralized the guard towers. Leek, Red and John began a search for Lucinda.

They had been told she was in cell block C, but when they got to it they found it locked down. While Red rigged a torch bomb to take out the door, Leek peered through the small square window searching for Lucinda.

Just as they were about to detonate the bomb, two guards attacked them from behind. Red went crashing into the bars then fell to the ground with the guard on his back. John pulled out his laser pistol and shot the man on Red's back point-blank in the head. He fell off to the side and didn't move.

In the meantime, the other guard had landed on top of Leek and knocked him to the ground. Leek struggled to get out the guard's grasp but the soldier was twice his weight and fought like a wounded bear. Finally, Red kicked the guard in the face and pried him off Leek's back. When the two were finally separated John shot the guard with his laser.

Red went back to his work rigging the torch bomb and, when it was ready, told Leek and John to clear out. They backed off and took cover. There was an explosion and the cell gate swung open. They all rushed in and began searching for Lucinda. In the last cell they found her lying on the cold stone floor, still chained to the wall as they'd seen her on the VC.

Red set another charge and the cell door swung open. Leek raced over to Lucinda and lifted her head. She was barely breathing and looked as pale as a ghost. John cut her chains with one laser blast about a foot from her hand. Leek picked her up in his arms, tears of joy and horror streaming from his eyes.

Lucinda's eyes opened slowly and Leek saw a faint smile on her face. "You came for me," she said, barely audible.

"Yes, my love, of course I came for you."

Her smile widened and then John took her arm and gave her the injection. Almost immediately her eyes closed and she went limp.

"Let's get out of here!" Leek said. "She needs medical attention."

Rushing back the way they came they immediately came under fire again. They took cover in a doorway and assessed their situation. Red had a heat-seeking grenade, so he pulled the plug and tossed it toward the source of the fire. The grenade locked on the heat signature of one of the guards and shot straight at him. The guard turned and tried to escape but grenade attached itself to his torso and exploded. The shock knocked the guards through a window and left them sprawled lifeless on the ground. Leek, Red, and John ran past the corpses and rushed toward the hole in the wall where they'd come in. As they broke through the wall they were horrified to see a line of TGA soldiers advancing toward them.

Behind them the militiamen were swarming out of the hole and, at the sight of the TGA, a firefight erupted between the two sides. Leek sank behind a disabled PTV trying to keep himself and Lucinda out of the crossfire. The battle raged for a long time and Leek knew each tik that went by would make their escape more difficult. Just when he'd thought all was lost he heard barking. Rhin and a pack of rhutz attacked the advancing TGA soldiers.

The soldiers turned and tried to fire on the charging rhutz but their laser guns were jerked out of their hands, leaving them confused and defenseless. The rhutz went for their necks and began tearing them to shreds. At this Leek saw his opportunity and ran through a break in the line. Red, John and Rhin followed them through the gap and ran to a waiting tram. They jumped in, pushed the close button, and the tram immediately left the station.

"How is she?" Red asked.

Leek looked down sorrowfully. "I don't know. She was lucid before we gave her the sedative. I think she'll be okay. She was very weak, though."

Red felt for a pulse. "She's still alive, but she needs immediate medical attention."

"There will be medics waiting just outside the dome. We'll be there in just a few tiks."

A short time later the tram stopped, the doors opened and they found themselves back in their staging area outside the city. Fires were raging in the distance and the sounds of exploding bombs permeated the air. Two medics came over and took Lucinda, put her on a stretcher, and began scanning her to determine her condition. Leek watched them anxiously.

A soldier rushed over and tapped Leek on the shoulder. "Commander. They've located the hospital where your baby is being held. We can take you there if you like, but we don't have much time."

"Yes, let's go."

Leek, Red and John followed the militiaman back on the tram and the doors closed. When it opened they found themselves in a commercial district. They got out and the militiaman pointed to a hospital down the street.

"Room 216c," he said.

They tucked their laser pistols out of sight and walked briskly to the hospital. No one seemed to notice them as they walked in, so they went directly to the elevators and punched the second floor. When the doors opened they walked out and looked around. There was a TGA soldier standing guard in front of one of the rooms. Leek assumed his baby must be in the room under guard.

John walked down toward the soldier. The soldier raised his laser and told him to halt. John raised his hands. "Easy comrade, I'm just looking for my sister's room, 218."

"This is a restricted floor. You must leave immediately."

John kept walking past the soldier. "It should be right down here."

"Stop!" the soldier ordered, turning to keep an eye on him.

Just as soon as he had his back turned, Red came up from behind and jolted him with his stun gun. Leek immediately rushed into the room. Inside there were six babies in bassinets. Leek studied them, wondering which one was his child. The first one was marked 216a. He looked at the one marked 216c and went over to it. There was a chart so he picked it up and looked at it. At the bottom a doctor had signed it and following his name it read: **Medical Officer, Pritzka Prison**. He turned the baby's head and immediately saw Lucinda's eyes. He nearly wept as he picked up the baby and held it close to his chest.

There was a commotion outside as a nurse was demanding to know what was going on. Red pulled her inside the room, tied her up and gagged her. Then they left with the baby. The militiaman was waiting at the tram station and opened the door when he saw them. A moment later they were on their way out of the city.

When they got back to the staging area the medics took the baby to prepare it for transport, then Leek asked them about Lucinda.

"I'm sorry to have to tell you this, Commander, but she's dead," the medic said.

Tears welled in Leek's eyes. "But, she was alive when I left here," he protested.

"I know. It looks like she was poisoned—there were traces of exicrin in the saliva we tested. It's a poison used to eradicate rats and other rodents," the medic added.

Leek shook his head angrily. "No! No! She can't be dead. Not my Lucinda." He staggered over to an ammunition crate and sat down. Red went over to him and put his arm on his shoulder. John looked away and closed his eyes.

"I'm so sorry, Commander," Red said.

"There were probably standing orders to kill her if there was a rescue attempt," the medic conjectured.

"Probably," Red agreed. "Well, at least you have your baby."

Leek looked up. "It's a boy, isn't it? I thought it was going to be a boy?"

"Yes, the medic said and it looks like they've taken good care of him."

John walked up and stood in front of Leek. "Sir," he said. "It's time to pull out. The TGA reinforcement will be here soon."

Leek nodded and looked up at the medic. "Take the baby back to base. Send him to Tehra in Shini. The Chancellor's assistant will know how to contact her."

"Yes, sir," the medic replied.

"Also, take Lucinda's body back to base. She should get a proper burial."

After the medic had left to carry out his orders, the others got in their flight suits and prepared to leave. As they were running to their fighters a hovertank suddenly appeared out of nowhere with guns blasting everything in sight. Panic overtook Leek as he realized the hovertank was on a collision course with the medic unit that had custody of his baby. He couldn't let them kill his son, but there was no way to take out a hovertank. It took three fighters to do that.

Then he remembered seeing Rhin take out a copter using her telekinetic powers. How had she done it? He looked at the hovertank and wondered what he could do to disable it. Then he saw several barrels of fighter fuel that soon would be directly under the hovertank. He shot the barrels with his laser and they exploded, engulfing the hovertank in flames.

The hovertank changed course to avoid the explosion. Leek continued to study it, trying to spot some vulnerability. Then it dawned on him. The pulse jet operated like a mechanical lung, breathing some kind of electronic impulse in and out. If he could throw something at the four pulse jets they might suck it in, causing an interruption of the pulse. He thought of airplanes on Earth crashing because they ran through a flock of birds. *It's worth a try.* He looked around the staging area and saw a large tarp that had been covering some boxes of ammunition. Focusing on the tarp, it suddenly sailed up toward the hovertank like it had been caught up in a gust of wind. One of the pulse jets sucked in the tarp and then spat it out. Leek concentrated and pushed it back into the jet. The jet sucked in the tarp again, this time jamming its mechanism. The hovertank tilted and began to list to one side. The tarp began to disintegrate and large portions of it were discharged. Leek looked at another tarp and willed it back into the pulse jet. For a moment he held it there, but it soon was discharged and fell to the ground. Leek cursed the mechanical beast. The gunner on the hovertank must have seen what Leek was doing because the big turret gun reeled around and began firing. A bullet pierced through Leek's shoulder, making him stagger backward. The tarp was about to hit the ground when it suddenly shot back in place. Leek looked over and saw Rhin, who looked back anxiously. Blood was dripping down Leek's flight suit.

Rhin returned her attention to the hovertank and growled angrily. The jet sucked in the tarp again and there was a rattling noise as part of the exposed pulse jet began to unravel. Soon the hovertank was spinning out of control. Before it hit the ground its stabilizer rod swung out to stop its fall but the momentum was too great and the monster went crashing to the ground. Leek saluted Rhin and then staggered for his fighter. Seeing him fall to one knee, a seafolken soldier grabbed his arm.

"Are you all right, Commander?"

"I don't know," Leek moaned. He could barely think, the pain in his shoulder was so excruciating.

There was a loud explosion. Leek and the soldier looked up and saw another hovertank bearing down on them.

"Help me to my fighter. I'll be all right."

The seafolken helped Leek into his T-47 and then ran off to catch up with his platoon. Leek sat in the cockpit trying to focus. He knew he had lost a lot of blood and had to stop the bleeding or he would die. He reached for his medical kit and pulled out a tube of healing gel and disinfectant wipes. He could hear the *wooof wooof wooof* of the hovertank coming at him fast. He cleaned the wound quickly with the wipe, squeezed the healing gel over it, and covered it with the bandage. He knew the gel would stop the bleeding.

Something exploded outside and rocked the plane. He started the engine, but couldn't take off yet without plugging the hole in his flight suit. As he was taxiing down the runway he opened a pocket in his flight suit and pulled out a patch. Pulling off the backing with his teeth, he slammed the patch over the bullet hole and gave the T-47 full throttle.

As he lifted off he saw the medical transport plane taking off on a different runway. He prayed it would make it back to base safely. Weakened from his loss of blood and shock of Lucinda's death, he just wanted to put the fighter on autopilot and go to sleep, but, he had one last task to complete. About fifty kylods south of Shisk was the huge Lutzva assembly plant where, among other things, the Lutzva Hovertank was manufactured. If they could destroy this plant that would go a long way toward winning the war. He swung around and soon was heading south.

"R2, are you there?" Leek said into his communicator.

"R2 here," Tam replied. "Are you all right, Commander. I saw you stumbling to your plane."

Leek stifled a groan. "Yeah. I'm fine. . . . R3, are you there?"

"Affirmative," Red said. "The rest of the wing is right behind me."

"Good. Lets put Lutzva Aeronautics out of business!" Leek commanded.

The three fighters dropped out of stealth mode and came in low over the industrial plant. They each dropped a line of cluster bombs directly over the plant. As they circled around for another run, twelve more fighters unloaded on the plant. Just as they were about to leave, a mass of TGA fighters appeared and opened fire on them. With the mission accomplished all the Loyalist fighters took off in different directions to divide up their pursuers. Unfortunately, this still left two TGA fighters for every one of the Loyalists.

Leek saw a fighter on John's tail and swung over to engage it. Before he could lock on and fire a Muscan, however, the TGA pilot launched a missile. John's decoys shot out and the missile followed one of them but the explosion was so close it clipped off part of his wing. Leek locked on the TGA fighter and fired. The fighter's tail exploded and the plane began to fall. The pilot managed to level out the plane but couldn't slow it down. It hit the ground, skidded and then crashed into a metal building.

A loud explosion jolted Leek's fighter. He looked to his left and saw a Loyalist fighter exploding. He watched in horror as the plane disintegrated before his eyes. His eyes started to blur. He felt disoriented. A harsh whining noise drew his attention back to John's fighter which was beginning to spin out of control. Leek tried to circle around and follow John but two enemy fighters were hot on his tail. He knew he was in no condition to outmaneuver them. There was only one way to escape. Reluctantly he gave his fighter full throttle, clicked on autopilot, and put it into stealth mode. As he flew off into the hazy sky, he wondered whose fighter had exploded. He prayed it wasn't anybody he knew. He turned on his communicator.

"R1 to R2, are you there?"

There was no answer.

"R1 to R3, are you there?"

Silence.

"L21. Are you okay?"

More silence.

"R1 here. Is anybody out there?"

"Commander, this is A16. I only count five of the attack team making it out."

"A16. Did you see the others go down?"

"No, sir. Just counted them coming out over the water."

"All right, A16. See you back at the base. Tell them I'll need a medic on landing. Lost a lot of blood . . ."

Leek's finger slipped off his communicator and he passed out.

22
Counter Offensive

When Leek woke up he was back in the Doral Mountains in a casualty bed in the new medical unit built by the nanomites while he was in Queenland. Captain Shilling looked down at him and smiled.

"Commander. How do you feel?"

"Like a shuttle landed on me," he moaned as he tried to sit up.

"No. No. Stay down. You've been seriously injured. It's a wonder you made it back alive."

"Really? Thank God for autopilots, huh?"

"Yes, and it's a good thing you had the sense to give yourself some first aid. I don't know how you managed it."

"My mother's a nurse back on Earth. She taught me a few tricks."

"It's a good thing."

"Hey, what about the Avengers? Are they okay?"

"Red's okay but we haven't heard from Tam or John."

Leek closed his eyes. "Oh. God! Not Tam. He can't be dead."

"I'm sorry. I know you two were close."

Tears welled up in Leek's eyes. He was relieved to hear that Red was okay. He hadn't lost all his friends, at least. He surmised that when John's plane went down Tam had circled back and tried to rescue him, but that would have been tantamount to suicide. He felt guilty that he'd left his friends behind even though he knew he had no other choice given the responsibilities that rested on his shoulders.

"What about the baby?"

"The baby is fine. Tehra is taking care of him."

Leek thought of Lucinda. She had spoken to him and then died in his arms. He figured Videl had planned it all along. He'd kept her alive for propaganda purposes and to punish the Liberator, but had given orders to poison her upon any attempt at escape. Except for the pain she'd been forced to endure, she'd been dead the moment of her kidnaping.

After Captain Shilling had left, Leek felt exhausted. He tried to sleep, but before he could doze off, Threebeard's thoughts came flooding into his mind. "Tomorrow morning we must counterattack. I've alerted the 3rd Army in your absence to be ready. This is our opportunity to cripple the TGA in Lemaine Shane. Your command staff has their orders."

"Yes, but the 1st Airborne has just returned from Shisk. I don't know if they'll be ready. I don't know if *I'm* up to it."

"You must be! This is the moment. The beginning of the end of the TGA!"

"All right! Okay! We'll be ready," Leek thought as he struggled out of bed.

A nurse tried to stop him, but he waved her off. He went to his quarters, took a shower and went to the command center. It was a hubbub of activity as the 3rd Army prepared to launch its most aggressive offensive of the war.

"Commander General! What are you doing here? I thought you'd be recuperating for a few days," Major Oakril said.

"I can't very well do that with the most important battle of the war about to begin. . . . What's our plan of attack?"

"Our army has occupied southwest Tributon since it reentered the war after the last TGA offensive began. We intend to start there and drive a wedge through Tributon and completely isolate the main TGA army to the north. At the same time the regular Loyalist armies will launch an all-out assault from their end and we'll squeeze them into submission."

"I see. So, all this came from Threebeard?"

"Yes. In your absence he has been giving us direct orders. . . . He also had us send two divisions to reclaim Quori."

"That shouldn't be too hard since its dominant population are mutants."

"Captain Lavendar's platoon has been sent to retake Gallion too. We intend to keep it this time."

"Without Tam?"

"Yes. Red was assigned to take his place. He's pretty familiar with the unit and the men know and trust him."

"Yes, I know they do, but they can't take Gallion by themselves?"

"Right. General Zitor is sending a couple divisions to help them out and the seafolken will be there too."

"So, I guess you didn't need me after all. Maybe I will go back to the casualty unit."

"Well, actually Captain Shilling told me you might show up, and if you did, to send you her way."

"Oh. Okay. Where is she?"

"In the studio."

Leek nodded and headed for the part of the command center where the Liberation Network broadcasted its messages all over Tarizon. Captain Shilling was at a desk writing. She smiled when she saw Leek enter.

"Well, look who's here. I figured you couldn't stay away. Don't you know it takes time for wounds to heal?"

"Sorry. Don't have time to lie around. Too much going on."

"Right. And idle time is no good when you're grieving."

Leek looked away, not able to reply.

"Anyway, I know this is a lot to ask, but we need you to announce our new offensive to the people of Tarizon. They need to hear the good news from the Liberator."

Leek nodded. "Of course. I'll try to pull myself together."

"I have a script I've prepared. You can look it over and make any changes you think are appropriate. Or, you can scrap it altogether if you don't like it."

Leek took the script from the captain and sat down in a chair across from her. He read the script and then looked up.

"This sounds great. I didn't know you were a writer."

"Before I joined the military I was studying to be a journalist. The lure of space travel got the better of me, though, so I gave up journalism and joined the TGA space program."

"When do we go on the air?"

"Well, not until morning, but since you're here now, why don't you tape it and then you can go get some sleep."

"All right. That sounds good. I am pretty tired. Let me read it a few more times so it will seem natural."

"Right. Take your time. It will take a few loons to get the studio set

221

up."

Leek reread the script and made a few changes. Then he read it again. When he felt he was ready he went into the recording booth and sat down. Major Oakril, Captain Shilling and the technical crew all crowded around to watch Leek as he began to deliver his historic message.

"Citizens of Tarizon. I am pleased to inform you that we are about to launch an ambitious assault on the enemies of Tarizon. At this very moment several major offensives are being launched in Rigimol, Tributon, Quori, Ock Mezan, Lower Azollo and, yes, even Turvin.

"This will be a turning point in our struggle to restore the rule of law on Tarizon. One day soon we will be governed by men who believe in God and the right of all life forms to live together in peace and harmony.

"I have just returned from Shisk and I'm proud to inform you we have destroyed the Lutzva assembly plant. As you may know, Lutzva was the manufacturer of our enemy's hovertanks that have killed so many of our brave citizens. Fortunately we have found other ways to destroy them but nothing as effective as preventing their manufacture. This is a major blow to the enemy and will save many lives.

"While I was in Shisk I led a raid on Pritzka Prison. Yes, we were able to penetrate TGA security in and around their own capital city and travel in broad daylight to Pritzka Prison where my mate, Lucinda, was being held. An assault team made up of portions of the 3rd Army and local militia penetrated the prison and rescued Lucinda and many political prisoners held there.

"I carried her from the prison in my own arms only to find out she'd been poisoned just before I arrived to free her. She died in my arms."

A tear welled in Leek's eye and overflowed down his cheek. He wiped it away with his sleeve.

"Unlike the coward, Videl Lai, who would have vipers dropped on our civilian population of Shini, we were in and out of Shisk with no civilian casualties. The only destruction we left behind was to Pritzka Prison, the space port, and the Lutzva assembly plant.

"That's the difference between the Purists and the Loyalists. We live by honor, integrity and justice. They live by lies, treachery and deceit. We believe in love, respect, and the sanctity of all life forms. They believe in strength, expediency and the dominance of the pure human blood.

"Tomorrow you will hear some shocking news. News of a devastating weapon that the Loyalists have unleashed on the TGA in Rigimol and Tributon. Regrettably the news will be true. Such a weapon will be used to put an end to this war. But this weapon will only be used on military targets and not on innocent civilians. This new weapon is similar to the vipers indiscriminately used by the TGA. Our new weapon, the superviper, is just as lethal as the original viper but will not cause the horrific, painful death that so delights Videl Lai and his cohorts. Furthermore, the super viper can be controlled in flight so that adjustments can be made if the wind shifts or the target moves unexpectedly. Finally, the super viper will not be worthless after just one attack, but can strike over and over again, seven times before running out of power and poison.

"All of us at Loyalist command abhor having to use such a devastating weapon but to fail to use it would be asking for defeat. For those soldiers in Tributon and Rigimol, I apologize to you and your families and pray that God has mercy on our souls.

"Fortunately, there is some good news this morning that I can share with you. While we were in Shisk we did manage to free hundreds of political prisoners and, on the way out of the city, I stopped by one of the hospitals and rescued my son. Yes, it's true. He's in good health and on his way to Shini as I speak to you today."

Leek smiled for the first time. He looked over at Captain Shilling and saw her wipe a tear from her eye.

"You know Tarizon has no monopoly on evil. Back on Earth where I came from we were battling evil constantly. Fortunately I lived in a time of relative peace between nations, but there were still plenty of tyrants and dictators around reigning terror on their own populations. For those unfortunate people who lived in those nations, life was indeed tragic.

"But what I've observed on Earth and know from the history of Earth and Tarizon, is that in the end all tyrants fall! Because evil benefits but a few, while goodness blesses the masses. This is why Videl favors genocide, because he knows that, no matter how powerful he might be, eventually the masses will overwhelm him.

"Citizens of Tarizon! Now is the time to rise up and take control of your destiny! It's time for the masses to rise up against the tyrant and smite him! We will start the battle but you must join in to secure victory!

"If you have not already joined the Liberation movement now is the time to make that call. We need you today. Right now. Drop what you are doing and join the battle against Videl Lai. Tomorrow may be too late!"

The camera lights went off and Leek took a deep breath. Captain Shilling walked into the booth and shook his hand. "That was great, Commander. Quite moving."

"Well, I just read the script. You put the words together."

"Yes, and I'm sure you'd have done just as well without my help, but there wasn't time."

"No. I think I'm going to hire you as my speech writer," Leek said jokingly.

Major Oakril stepped in and shook Leek's hand. "I'm already getting reports from our cell leaders that their recruiters are getting swamped with calls. It looks like your speech was just what we needed."

"Well, I hope so," Leek replied. "We've raised the hopes and expectations of the people; now we have to deliver what we've promised or suffer the consequences. I hope Threebeard knows what he's doing."

They all looked at him but no one said anything. He smiled and said, "I'm so exhausted now, I think I may actually be able to sleep. Wake me when reports start coming in from the fronts, okay?"

"Good idea, sir," Major Oakril replied. "I'll see to it that you are awakened the moment we know anything."

When he returned to his quarters, Rhin was there to greet him. He was glad to see her because she'd help him keep his mind off Lucinda. He thought about Lucinda's body and the need to plan a funeral, but with the new offensive it might be many days before he could get back to Shini to arrange it.

Leek sat on his bed rubbing Rhin's back vigorously. Then he put his arms around her neck and hugged her tightly. She didn't move, understanding his need for her. Then he wept.

23
Rescue

Tam decided to take one last run over the Lutzva assembly plant to make sure it had been completely destroyed and to get some footage of the burning rubble to play on the Liberation Network. Lorin had arranged for cameras to be rigged on his fighter for that very purpose and he didn't want to disappoint her. The TGA fighters had scattered, chasing their Loyalist prey and he'd managed to shake his pursuers, so the sky seemed clear.

As he was taking the footage he spotted a Loyalist fighter descending rapidly with a tail of smoke behind it. He broke off his pattern over the assembly plant and followed the fighter. He recognized it immediately as being John's. The fighter was missing part of its wing and having trouble leveling off for a landing but at the last moment managed to stabilize and hit the ground on its landing gear. The fighter's emergency deceleration chutes deployed, bringing the plane to a rapid halt.

Tam circled the plane and saw John had managed to land it in a freshly tilled field. He noted a farmhouse situated about two kylods away. There didn't seem to be anyone rushing to the crash site, so Tam decided to look for a landing spot and possibly make a rescue attempt.

He knew rescuing John was a longshot at best and if he landed his fighter he might never get it back in the air. The fighter required a hard surface and considerable running room for a takeoff. He doubted he'd find that out there in the country with narrow roads and most of the land covered with trees and vegetation.

His only hope would be to get to John before the TGA found him, and then try to hook up with the Soni militia that had teamed up with his platoon at Pritzka Prison. But that would be exceedingly difficult with the TGA swarming the area looking for them. He pondered if he should just point the fighter home, give it full throttle and put it in stealth mode. Then he remembered he didn't have to make this decision himself. He could

Tarizon: Civil War

consult with his mentor, Threebeard or his friend, Leek. He thought about it and decided on Threebeard since Leek, given their friendship, would be more likely influenced by emotion rather than logic.

He programmed his fighter to fly out to sea and then circle back to the spot where John had crashed. Then he put it on autopilot and closed his eyes. He thought of Threebeard and connected with little effort.

"What troubles you, my friend?" Threebeard thought.

"John has crashed and I wonder if I should try to save him. I've a little time, but probably not enough."

Threebeard searched Tam's thoughts and immediately understood the situation.

"You should try to save him. Destroy the fighter when you leave him. I'll find some rhutz to protect you until you can link up with the militia."

Tam hadn't thought of the rhutz. There would be some of their kind nearby.

"Actually," Threebeard thought. "This might be a stroke of luck. We needed someone like you to lead the militia on Turvin. I think God has sent you there for that purpose."

"Me? You want me to command the militia on Turvin?"

"Yes. As the closest friend of the Liberator they'll follow you without question. Tell them the Liberator sent you."

"All right, then. Thank you for your help. Would you tell Commander Lanzia that I'm all right? I know he'll be worried."

"I will," Threebeard promised.

"Thanks," Tam thought and opened his eyes.

He was unsure that he was the right man to lead the Turvin militia. He had never been much of a leader. You had to know how to follow to be a good leader and he'd never accepted authority too gracefully. That's why he had ended up on Muhl. Being Leek's friend, he'd been given much latitude and rarely had to take orders, but now he was expected to quickly build an army that depended on strict obedience to all orders without question. But then again, he thought, since he'd be giving the orders, perhaps he could do it.

As the fighter made its turn to go back to John's location he'd made up his mind he could command the 5th Army, as it would be named, and do his part in ridding Tarizon of Videl Lai!

Looking down over the crash site, Tam was delighted to see the cockpit door opened. He assumed John was okay and had left the plane. He immediately started looking for a place to land but saw nothing better than the field where John had crashed. Since he was going to destroy his plane anyway, he didn't need to worry about being able to take off again. All he had to do was to land without killing himself.

He circled again and started to descend for a landing. He was surprised he hadn't seen any TGA fighters yet, but he knew it was only a matter of time. Since he hadn't been flying in stealth mode he knew he'd be picked up on radar sooner or later. Sure enough, just as he was landing, he spotted two TGA fighters coming at him. Tam's fighter landed hard and the emergency parachutes opened. He blew off the cockpit window since he wouldn't need it and scrambled out of the plane just as soon as it came to a stop. Just moments after he'd hit the ground running the fighter blew up, scattering debris in all directions.

The blast threw him to the ground and knocked him unconscious. Fortunately his flight suit protected him from the searing heat of the blast. When he woke up, John was looking down at him with a worried look on his face. Tam struggled to a sitting position.

"You okay?" John asked.

"Me? How about you?"

"Just a headache. We've got to get out of here."

"You've got that right. There are copters all around. I can hear them."

John helped Tam out of his flight suit and they began running away from the sounds of the approaching copter. Before they realized it they were surrounded by rhutz. They followed the rhutz deep into the forest. A few kylods later the rhutz stopped, sensing their human friends needed to rest.

Tam looked the lead rhutz in the eyes and thought. "Thank you my friend. You got to us so fast."

"Yes. Threebeard said you'd need us immediately."

"What's your name?"

"Riddle," the rhutz thought.

"Riddle. I like that. Do you know where to take us?"

"Yes, to the place where the militia train. It will take us two days to get there."

Tam moaned. "That long? This air is killing me."

"It will be better in the mountains."

"What mountains?"

"The Weeping Mountains north of Shisk. We'll have to take an indirect path in order to avoid detection."

Tam and John sat on a fallen log. They hadn't talked much since they'd been going double time to stay ahead of the TGA. Now, however, John felt the urge to thank Tam for returning for him.

"You'd have done the same thing, brother."

"I don't know," John teased. "I'm kind of a dirkbird at heart. I probably would have hightailed it to safety."

"Well, that's true. You are a dirkbird."

"So, really. Why did you come back for me?"

"Threebeard said I should. He wants me to lead the militia here in Turvin."

"Really, so we're not going back to base?"

"No. We're meeting the militia in the Weeping Mountains and taking charge of the 5th Army."

"The 5th Army. I've never heard of it."

"It's just you and me and whatever militia we manage to convince to hook up with us."

Tam felt the rhutz in his mind. He looked over at Riddle.

"Sorry, friend," he said. "Time to move out."

John nodded and got to his feet. This time the rhutz slowed his pace a bit, indicating there wasn't any imminent danger lurking about. Soon it was dark but the rhutz didn't stop, and keeping up with them was often by sound rather than sight. The rhutz finally stopped on a hilltop where they could see many kylods in every direction. The glow from Shisk's dome illuminated the clouds hanging over the city. It was a magnificent sight that held them spellbound. The rhutz formed a circle around them and sat. Tam and John finally looked away from the city and prepared to camp for the night. They ate field rations John had retrieved from his fighter before he set the self-destruct mechanism and then they did the best they could to get comfortable and went to sleep.

Just as the sky began to lighten in the east the rhutz were on their feet. Tam sat up and rubbed his eyes. The air was thick and foul smelling. He wished he had a breather. He wondered why the air was so much worse here than in Tributon and Rigimol. He suspected it was because Shisk was so much farther south. The air seemed to be clearing from the poles inward.

After eating their rations Tam looked at the map of Soni that John had brought with him from his flight suit. He surmised from the map that they were on a course to bypass the city of Condati which was due east of Shisk. Looking at his compass, he saw that they were going almost due north and by day's end would be near the city of Blit. He'd heard of Blit as a resort town at the foot of the Weeping Mountains.

Riddle paced back and forth and barked.

"All right. We're coming." Tam said.

John and Tam put their packs on their backs and started after the rhutz.

"He's like the drill sergeants back on Pogo," John said. "Do the rhutz have ranks, you think?"

Tam laughed. "I doubt it. He's just doing his job like any good soldier."

"I'm glad they're on our side. I'd hate to have one of them mad at me. Did you see what they did to those TGA soldiers trying to keep us from fleeing Pritzka Prison?"

"Right. That was pretty gruesome. Their teeth must be razor sharp."

"I'll say. I've never seen so much blood."

"And it was all for nothing. They poisoned Lucinda before we got there," Tam said.

John looked away. "Right. Commander Lanzia must be a wreck. He really loves his mate. I'm fond of my mate, but I'm not obsessed with her like the Commander is."

"That's the way it is on Earth. You don't mate with someone unless you're in love with them."

"In love, obsessed with them so much you can't live without them, I don't know if that's so good, do you?"

"I don't know," Tam replied. "I've never thought about it much, but it seems to be good for the ones in love."

"I suppose."

Riddle and the rest of the pack of rhutz stopped. Tam looked around but saw nothing. John turned and scanned the terrain behind them. The forest was quiet. One of the rhutz suddenly took off running. Tam drew his sidearm. The rhutz was running toward a clump of brush. Just before he got to it two range deer shot out and started running. Another rhutz took off toward the others. The first rhutz overtook the range deer and went for its throat. It tried to shake the rhutz off but its grip was too strong. The deer finally stumbled and fell to the ground. The second rhutz soon had the second range deer on the ground and, after a brief struggle, it too went limp.

The rest of the pack trotted up to the first range deer and began feeding off of it but they left the second carcass alone. John looked at Tam and Tam shrugged.

"I guess it's time for lunch," Tam said. "Come on. You ever skinned a range deer?"

"No. They don't think we're going to eat it raw, do they?" John said.

"I hope not," Tam replied with a sour face. "You get a fire going and I'll cut out some good meat for us. We can't eat the whole deer. I'll give what's left over to the rhutz."

"Sounds good to me."

Tam got out his powerknife and began skinning a portion of the deer. After he'd cut out two good portions of meat he looked at Riddle and thought, *This is all we can eat. Thanks.*

Immediately several rhutz abandoned their kill and went for the second one. Tam watched them for a moment and then took the meat to the fire John had built. John produced two pointed sticks and they proceeded to cook their lunch by holding the meat over the fire.

The rhutz, who'd finished their meal, looked on with curious interest at the human ritual of burning perfectly good meat before eating it. When it was fully cooked John and Tam began eating with great delight.

"Wow. This tastes great," John said. "I think Commander Lanzia has the right idea. Everyone should have a rhutz to protect them and catch them great game."

Tam laughed. "Somehow I don't think the rhutz would go for that. They're only helping us because they hate Videl Lai and they're hoping we can kill the skutz."

"I know. Do you think they'd consider hiring out?"

"Well, you'd have to be telepathic to communicate with them."

"So, why don't you pick one out to be your friend."

"I wish I could, but Rhin is only the second rhutz to ever befriend a human being. I doubt I'd be so lucky."

Before long Riddle began pacing again, indicating their lunch break was over. John suggested they take a nap before going on, but Riddle growled when he started to lie down, so he abandoned that idea pretty quickly.

The hiking got more difficult in the afternoon as they began to ascend toward the foothills of the Weeping Mountains. Before long they learned how the mountain range got its name. A gentle mist began to fall and, judging from the moss on the rocks and trees, it was a permanent climatic condition on this side of the mountains. As they walked, some geography Tam had learned cycles earlier came back to him.

"The Weeping Mountains are a rain forest. I think they get rain almost every day. Moisture comes up from the Coral Sea and as it is forced over the mountains it cools and turns to rain. Very little moisture is left when it gets to the east side of the mountains. Have you heard of the Duesi Desert?"

"Sure," John said. "That's the place my flight instructor always said you didn't want to run out of fuel."

"Right. A hundred square kylods of rocky wasteland infested with poisonous snakes and deadly scorleons. And not a drop of water unless you happen to visit on one of the two days it rains during the cycle."

"Right. Too bad we can't kidnap Videl and drop him right in the middle of it."

"That would be too good for him," Tam said. "He needs to be tortured on live VC so everyone can watch."

"You know, I'm a little surprised we've managed to completely elude the TGA so far. They've got to have a massive manhunt out for us," John said.

"I know. I wondered the same thing. I haven't seen a single plane or a soldier since we lost the copters."

"Do you think they are keeping out of sight, hoping we'll lead them to the militia base?"

"Maybe, or they're afraid of the rhutz and don't want to confront them."

"But how would they even know the rhutz had joined us?"

"Good point. We better stay alert anyway. I'd hate to compromise the 5th Army before it ever got organized."

As they climbed the foothills of the Weeping Mountains Tam stopped at every opportunity to look back with his binoculars to see if there was any sign of someone following them. But he saw nothing unusual. Before nightfall on the second day a platoon of militia intercepted them.

Tarizon: Civil War

"Halt! Identify yourselves," their leader demanded.

Tam raised his hands. "My name is Captain Tamurus Lavendar, Commander of the 1st Airborne Division of the 3rd Loyalist Army. This is Lt. John Sillmar, one of my pilots."

"State your business here," the leader said.

"John's fighter was hit and went down and I tried to rescue him, but we couldn't get back in the air."

The soldier relaxed and cracked a smile. "Yes, we were expecting you. My name is Lt. Borros. Captain Shilling advised us to be on the lookout for you. Where did you get these rhutz?"

"Defense Minister Threebeard summoned them to provide security and lead us to your camp."

"Hmm. We've been told they are to be our allies but we've never been able to communicate with them. You'll have to tell us how you do it. We could use their help."

"It won't be a problem any longer. I can communicate with them quite easily."

The soldier raised his eyebrows. "Then welcome them to our camp and thank them for bringing you to us safely."

"Certainly," Tam said and looked over at Riddle to deliver the message. Riddle sat and bowed his head slightly. "The big rhutz over there is named Riddle. He's the leader of this pack. He says it was his duty and no thanks are necessary. He also advised me that their job is now done so they will be returning to their home."

Lt. Borros shrugged. "Okay then, follow me and I'll take you to Captain Belmoht. He's anxious to meet you."

Lt. Borros started off through a clump of trees. Tam, John and the rest of the platoon followed. It was a rugged climb up into the mountains, across several meadows and streams until they were standing in front of an impressive pile of large boulders. There didn't appear to be any way around the mass of rocks, but Lt. Borros entered a hidden passageway and then navigated them through a maze of dark paths between the boulders. When they emerged they gasped at the lush valley before them.

An endless configuration of camocubes stretched out as far as the eye could see. Soldiers marched to the left on a parade field and thousands of ATVs, jetcycles, and copters were parked and ready to transport the troops on a moment's notice. Smoke rose from several campfires and Tam recognized the smell of range deer.

Lt. Borros pointed to a large camocube ahead of them. "We should go to the command cube over there."

Tam nodded and followed Lt. Borros. When they got to the cube Lt. Borros told them to wait and went inside. A moment later Captain Belmoht stepped out.

"Captain Lavendar," he said enthusiastically. "We are honored to have two of the Avengers in our camp."

"Yes, well, we're happy to be here."

"So, you've come to relieve me of my command?"

"Well, not exactly. I'm here to officially organize the 5th Loyalist Army and invite you and your militia to join. If you accept you'll be second in command and, in actuality, continue to run things pretty much as you have in the past."

"I appreciate that, Captain or should I say Commander."

"Commander?"

"Yes, I believe once the 5th Army is officially activated its commanding officer would be Commander General."

"Oh, yes. You're right. That means I've caught up with Commander General Lanzia."

"Yes, quite impressive."

"And, you will no longer be Captain Belmoht but Colonel Belmoht."

"Excellent."

"So, tell me about my new army."

They all laughed and went into the command cube. Aides passed out tekari for everyone as Colonel Belmoht began filling them in on his militia. Tam was in a good mood. He liked Colonel Belmoht and, from what he saw of his militia when they broke into Pritzka Prison, it was a fine fighting unit. Realistically, however, the 5th Army was but a lone barracuda in a sea of sharks. It was hardly a threat and, if their location were discovered, Videl could destroy them in the blink of an eye.

24
The First Offensive

It wasn't Captain Shilling who woke Leek up the next morning, but Threebeard. His thoughts were like a dream as they came flooding into his mind. He was greatly relieved to learn that Tam and John were okay. He was excited and proud when he found out Tam would be leading the new 5th Army. The fact that Threebeard hadn't consulted him about the appointment bothered him a little, but he *was* the defense minister, so it was his prerogative.

Now his problem was who would he promote to take Tam's place as the commander of the 1st Airborne. He was considering that problem when his communicator buzzed.

"Yes," he said.

"We're getting reports in from the front line," Major Oakril said. "You may want to get some breakfast and then come up to the command center."

"Okay. Thanks, Major. I'll be there soon."

The mention of breakfast got Rhin to her feet.

"Yeah, I'm kind of hungry too," Leek said. "Let's go see if they're serving anything good this morning."

Rhin went to the door and it opened automatically. "Hold on a tik, girl. I've got to get dressed. You're lucky you don't have to mess with clothing."

Rhin backed up and the door closed. Leek went into the bathroom. A few moments later he returned fully clothed and they left. The dining hall was deserted with most of the soldiers out on assignment and the command staff busy monitoring the first wave of the offensive. The cook gave Rhin two big raw steaks from a pig-like animal called a treep and Leek an omelet made with squit eggs, assorted breads, and strips of range deer. Leek was anxious

235

to find out how the offensive was going so he gulped down his food and took his sankee with him to the command center. Rhin elected to stay behind and chew on her steaks awhile.

Leek felt the electricity in the air as he stepped inside. Every workstation was occupied and every piece of equipment was humming with activity. He went straight to his desk and sat down. Major Oakril came over to him immediately.

"Our forces have penetrated Gallion. The seafolken had a little trouble getting through the nets but they're up on the docks now and are engaging the enemy. Unfortunately after our last visit they removed all seafolken from TGA vessels and moved all of the mutants off the base."

"That figures. Where are Red and his men?"

"They've taken the tram station and are trying to take the control tower. The 84th Infantry Division is attacking from the east and are meeting heavy resistance."

"How's the 3rd Army doing?"

"They're holding back, waiting to see what's left of the TGA forces after the super vipers are done with them."

"How long ago were they dropped?"

"Just before dawn. The poor devils won't know what hit them."

Leek recoiled at the thought of one of the super vipers attacking from out of the darkness. He felt a little sick inside knowing he'd played an important role in developing such a ghastly weapon. What bothered him the most was that many of the soldiers in the TGA weren't there by choice but out of fear of the consequences of their desertion or defection. He took a deep breath.

"So, what about Ock Mezan?"

"The seafolken have established a beachhead on the south central part of the island. The 2nd Airborne has hit them from the air pretty hard and the local militia has secured one of the western provinces."

"So, any bad news?"

"There are reports of a large convoy of ships heading from Muhl to Ock Mezan. When it reaches land the local militia will be outgunned. Our only hope is the seafolken can figure out a way to delay or destroy the convoy."

"Hmm."

"There's been heavier than expected resistance in Lower Azollo. The offensive into the northernmost state of Morissee isn't progressing as rapidly as had been expected. They have a few hovertanks and a small number of fighters they haven't been able to take out."

"Get the rhutz up to the front line. Rhin and I took out a hovertank in Shisk by messing with the pulse generator."

"How did you do that?"

"It was Rhin mainly. All I could manage was to jam a tarp into one of the pulse jets but it wouldn't stick. Then Rhin came along and started dismantling the entire mechanism with her mind. Between the two of us the hovertank went down."

"Wow! I'll get in touch with Queenland Command and suggest they get some rhutz and seafolken up to the front line to see if they can duplicate what you and Rhin did."

Major Oakril rushed off and Leek looked up at one of the big monitors that was playing the broadcast over the Liberation Network. The image on the screen was footage of the attack on the Lutzva assembly plant. Then the image changed to a quiet military camp. Soldiers were coming out of their cubes and milling around, waiting for their morning rations. Suddenly the sky darkened. Many of the soldiers looked up to see what was causing the change in light. The camera panned upward to record what the soldiers were seeing. It was thousands of super vipers descending upon them.

Soldiers scattered in every direction when the vipers attacked. There were screams of anguish and horror that gave Leek gooseflesh. Soldiers were falling left and right never to see the light of day again. The vipers were relentless in the attacks and went from one victim to another. Although the victims felt no pain, the anticipation of instant death must have been the ultimate in mental anguish.

After awhile the scene was still. It didn't seem that anyone had survived the attack. Leek wondered if there would be any soldiers left to fight after the vipers were done with them. He turned away from the screen, sickened by what was happening. Captain Shilling saw his anguish and came over to him.

"Pretty awful, isn't it? We dropped in cameras beforehand so we could see firsthand how the vipers performed. It's not a film you'd want to see a second time."

Leek nodded. "Yes, I just keep thinking that not too long ago I was one of those soldiers."

Tarizon: Civil War

"Yes, we all were."

"I just wish Videl Lai could have been stopped before he took power so we could have avoided all this bloodshed."

"Yes. Don't we all. There have been numerous assassination attempts since he took power, but he's very smart. He rotates his security force so that no one is there long enough to plot against him."

"Do we have any intelligence as to where he is right now?"

"We believe he's in Shisk at the Chancellor's Mansion. It's very secure and he has a command center deep underground."

"Does he ever leave home?"

"Yes, to go to the Capitol Building and he has a ranch in Merria."

"If you find out at any time that he's left his mansion, let me know. I want to personally see that he suffers for his crimes."

"I know that you as much as anyone have been one of Videl's victims, but don't let your anger and longing for vengeance make you forget what this war is all about."

Leek winced at Captain's Shilling's warning. "Do you think I could do that?" he replied angrily. "Do you think I'm anything like Videl Lai?"

Captain Shilling nodded. "Yes. I'm afraid we're all capable of evil. It's part of human nature. You must be on your guard every moment. It can consume you without you even realizing it. Your mission should be only to bring Videl to justice. Let the councilors do the job of passing judgement."

Leek looked at Captain Shilling. He felt like he'd just been chewed out by his mother. "Okay. You're right, but if the squit gives me good cause, I'll melt his insides with my laser."

Captain Shilling gave Leek an exasperated look and then walked away. Leek looked back up at the quiet screen—still no movement. Suddenly a viper attacked the camera. Leek jumped back and someone near him shrieked. The screen went black. Leek swallowed hard and looked at Major Oakril who'd just returned.

He sighed. "Anything new to report?"

"We've disabled all the active vipers and the 3rd Army is on the move."

"How's it looking?"

"There's only been token resistance, so far."

"Good. How is the 1st Army doing?"

"There's been heavy fighting reported but the TGA is reportedly retreating."

"That's good news. Everything seems to be going as planned."

Major Oakril nodded. "Pretty much, but I'm sure General Bratfort isn't ready to surrender. He's an astute tactician and he won't be defeated easily."

"I'm certain that is true, so if you see anything unusual I want to be notified immediately."

"Yes, sir," Major Oakril replied.

Leek monitored the battles raging all over Tarizon very closely for the rest of the day. Nothing unanticipated had happened but he knew it would sooner or later. That night when he went to bed he thought of Threebeard and was able to see a brief visual of the day's activity on the northern front. Threebeard seemed content with the progress of the offensive, but he too warned that the tide could turn quickly and vigilance was the key to final victory.

When Leek did go to sleep his dreams turned unexpectedly to outer space. A hazy image of a spaceship filled his mind's eye. It was silver and black and shaped like an arrowhead. Occasionally a squadron of fighters would emerge from a hangar bay and fly out in space. He was watching it from behind and in the distance he saw a familiar sight—Earth. He awoke with a start. Rhin opened her eyes and looked over at him.

Leek sighed. "Sorry, girl. Go back to sleep. It was just a bad dream."

Rhin yawned and put her head back down. Leek wondered what the dream meant, if anything. His dreams often did have meaning and he was anxious to figure out what it was. Would he be returning to Earth? If so, wouldn't he be taking a shuttle? The ship in his dream was a war vessel and he was behind it as if following it or in pursuit.

The next morning when he got to the command center he described the ship to Captain Shilling and asked her if she'd ever seen anything like it.

"Yes, that's a Tarizonian attack cruiser. There are only three of them and they've never been used in battle."

"Why were they built?"

"Videl and his Purist Party believed the repopulation pact with Earth would fail and that eventually we would have to forcibly establish a colony on Earth. We had to have a hospitable place for propagating and raising healthy children for transport back to Tarizon. He convinced the World Assembly to build the ships just in case the treaty with Earth didn't work out. Ships like that take a long time to build so the Assembly went along with their construction as a precaution and a way to get his support for the repopulation project."

"I see. That makes sense. If Videl intends to kill all non-human life forms along with the mutants and seafolken, then he needs to be able to replenish the supply of purebred stock. Now that the treaty has been broken he'll probably send the warships back to establish a colony."

"Exactly, but this time he won't ask for permission."

"Where are the attack cruisers stationed?" Leek asked.

"On Clarion, the largest of Tarizon's moons. There's a base there where the ships are built and tested."

"How many deep space fighters does the TGA have?"

"Several thousand, I'm sure."

"Are they on Clarion as well?"

"Yes."

"So, even if we win the war on Tarizon, Videl will likely escape into space."

"I think you're right. That's what I'd do if I were him. It would be many cycles before we could build an attack cruiser to pursue him."

"We must work on a strategy to prevent his escape. I don't want him going to Earth and waging war there."

"I agree. Let me give it some thought. Perhaps there is a way we can get control of the base on Clarion."

"Do that. We must keep him on Tarizon so we can capture him and make him stand trial for his crimes."

Captain Shilling nodded and left to do a broadcast on the Liberation Network. Leek was sick at the thought of Videl Lai escaping to Earth. He had to find him so he could prevent that from happening. There was no way he was going to let someone from Tarizon attack Earth. He thought of thousands of vipers falling on Dallas or New York City. Although some technology had been given to the U.S. military, he was sure it was old and obsolete by Tarizon's standards. They certainly wouldn't have anything that could touch a hovertank, and he was sure they didn't have soldiers with telekinetic abilities like the seafolken or the rhutz. Leek's resolve to find and capture Videl Lai intensified the more he thought about the consequences of his escape into space. He had to capture or kill him. There was simply no other choice.

25
The Battle for Synclare

While the battle for Lemaine Shane waged on for several intervals Tam's 5th army grew stronger and stronger. John was promoted to colonel and put in charge of creating and building the 5th Airborne Division. It was started with the reassignment of one wing of the 3rd Army's 1st Airborne Division. With the production of new fighters at full throttle and defectors showing up each day at Gallion, the loss of the 2nd Wing's five hundred fighters was hardly noticed. Yet it was a fine nucleus from which to build the 5th Airborne Division.

Tam knew that sooner or later his army was going to have to come out of hiding and stake a claim to a portion of Turvin. He knew once he did this the TGA would launch an all-out assault to destroy his army. Still, he believed he had a majority of the population behind him and that once the 5th Army came out in the open there would be an outpouring of support for the Loyalist cause. The question was where to strike and when.

There was Tuht to the north, but its long seacoast would make it easy for the TGA to launch an attack. Obviously they couldn't attack Soni to the south, because Shisk was the world capital and its defenses were too formidable—particularly since the attack on Pritzka Prison. Rour to the southeast was a possibility but it too had a long seacoast. This left Synclare.

Synclare and Soni for centuries had been enemies and there had been many wars waged between them. In the last war, before the ratification of the Supreme Mandate, Synclare had been victorious and laid claim to a narrow strip of land between Tuht and Soni that gave it access to the Straits of Tributon and both the Coral and the North Seas. It was called the Tazi Strip after the port city of Tazi that was situated on its entrance from the sea. Tam knew that the people of Synclare hated Videl Lai and would stand behind the 5th Army if it decided to lay claim to it. In fact, most of army had been recruited in Synclare.

Synclare's mountainous terrain and heavy forests would also make it harder for the TGA to launch an all-out attack and would be much easier for the Loyalist forces to defend. Also, being in the center of the continent would allow expansion in any direction if they grew in strength as he expected they would. So the decision was made to attack Synclare's capital city of Roshaunda and declare Synclare the first Loyalist state on the continent of Turvin. On the eve of the attack Tam, John, Colonel Belmoht, and Riddle the rhutz met to go over their attack plan one last time.

"Just before dawn, two platoons from the 2nd Division will secure the Cathedral Street and Capitol Street entrances to the dome," Tam explained. "Each will have a rhutz with them to act as a scout and handle any police copters that might be called in. As soon as those entrances are secured the rest of the division will enter the dome and surround the Capitol Building. When the perimeter of the Capitol Building has been secured the 5th Airborne and 73rd and 89th Infantry Divisions will launch their attacks on the Sheelee Army Base south of the city.

"There are six entrances to the dome. The 37th Division will secure the three northern entrances. I'll enter the city with a platoon from 37th Division and go to the government's communications center. Two other platoons will surround the police station. When the attack begins outside the city we'll move in on the capitol building, the communications center, and police station. Now there are seventeen police substations that we'll have to deal with as well but we'll talk about those later," Tam concluded.

"Is there any indication that the TGA knows that something is in the works?" John asked.

Tam shook his head. "I don't think so. We've intentionally stayed away from Synclare so as not to alert the TGA there. The rhutz have been doing all our surveillance, and seeing a rhutz in these parts is pretty common."

"So, once we secure our targets, what next?" Colonel Belmoht asked.

"Then I go on the VC and the radio and welcome the citizens of Roshaunda as a new Loyalist state. Of course, we'll still have to secure the other eleven major cities in the state. Fortunately, the TGA has very little presence north of Roshaunda, so I don't think they'll put up more than token resistance."

"Very well, sir," John said. "If we're done, I've got a lot of work to do to get ready for tomorrow's assault."

"Yes, you're right. The time for talk is over. Now we must act to bring Synclare into the Loyalists' ranks!"

They all stood, shook hands and embraced. "May God and Sandee be with you!" Tam said as he escorted them to the door.

That night Tam connected with Leek's mind and conveyed the day's events and plans for the attack.

"Good luck to you my friend; I feel certain you will be successful. I've contacted the nanomites and they will be sure the doors to the Capitol Building will be opened when you begin your siege."

"How is your campaign coming?" Tam thought. He'd heard the official reports that the Loyalists had driven the TGA out of Rigimol and Tributon, but that was propaganda. He wanted to know the truth.

"The campaign has stalled along the Rini River where it all began. The TGA has almost two million men in Quori so it's going to be hard to root them out."

"What about the super vipers?"

"They've developed defenses against them just as we did. They're no longer all that effective."

"Well, perhaps if we're successful here in Synclare Videl Lai will feel compelled to pull some of his forces out of Quori."

"Yes, that would be a welcome result of your victory. Good luck to you. Are you sure there isn't anything I can do for you?"

"Well, I wish I had my special ops team and maybe a little of Threebeard's computer magic. I'm a little worried about getting bogged down at the entrances to the dome."

Leek sighed. "Yes, well I'm afraid the TGA has tightened their security and I'd be hard pressed to get the special ops team to you by morning."

"I know. Just wishful thinking."

"Don't worry. As they say on Earth, I think you're gonna kick their ass."

Tam laughed. "I hope you're right."

Tam broke off the connection and turned over to try to sleep. It didn't come easily but eventually he dozed off. When his alarm clock buzzed two kyloons later he woke up with a start. The enormity of the day hit him like a rock. For the first time he felt the real pressure of command. Today there could be no mistakes, no excuses; everything had to go as planned or the consequences would be devastating. He took a deep breath and began doing push-ups to clear his head and get his blood circulating.

After a quick breakfast and a cup of sankee he put on his uniform and then put a peasant's cloak over it. The plan was to approach the dome entrances as farmers taking their wares to market. Once they got inside the dome they'd take out the guards and open the gate to the rest of the army waiting in the woods not too far away.

The Black squadron was assigned the task of taking control of the Cathedral entrance to the dome. Their name came from their black robes they used to disguise themselves as clergy traveling to the Dothi Cathedral situated just inside the city. The entrance was at the end of a long bridge that spanned the Sheelee River. When the platoon arrived at the gate, however, they were stopped. Tam watched nervously from across the road amongst a group of farmers he'd joined.

"Who are you?" the TGA guard asked suspiciously. "I wasn't notified of any clergy visiting the Cathedral today."

"And, why should you be?" the platoon leader said indignantly. "The last time I heard, Synclare was a free state."

The guard laughed. "Don't they let you watch the VC? Videl Lai is Chancellor now. Things have changed."

"Well, one thing hasn't changed," the platoon leader said.

"What's that?" the guard asked cautiously.

"The Abbot is still a good friend of Chancellor Lai. If he learns the monks he summoned to help finish the new chapel were delayed by an overzealous guard, he'll be very upset. I wouldn't be surprised if he didn't make a call to the Chancellor to complain."

The guard frowned and looked around nervously. "Okay. Let me just call the rectory and verify that they are expecting you. It will only take a few tiks."

The platoon leader sighed and looked over at Tam. The guard picked up the communicator. Suddenly a rhutz stepped out in the open, and reaching with his mind, ripped out several wires within the device. The guard frantically pushed buttons trying to get it to work. He frowned and looked at the platoon leader.

"Well, I guess it's your lucky day. My communicator's not working. Go ahead on in, but go straight to the Cathedral. I'm going to call over there just as soon as I can get my communicator working again. All of you better be there."

"We'll be there," the platoon leader assured him.

Once the members of the Black squadron were spread out along the entire entrance to the dome they attacked the guards and quickly subdued them. The rhutz and the rest of the 2nd Division then left their hiding places and crossed the bridge. As they approached the entrance to the dome they heard fighters flying overhead and cluster bombs falling and exploding on the TGA air base to the southeast. After they'd made it inside the dome, they walked swiftly along the southwest perimeter of the city through the elite sector of Roshaunda where government officials, business owners, and professionals lived. People on the street gave them a hard look as they went by, but nobody challenged them or sounded an alarm. Most seemed just curious as to who they were and why they were in Roshaunda.

They heard gunfire and saw laser flashes behind them but there was no turning back now. When they got to the perimeter of the Capitol Building, six TGA soldiers confronted them but were easily taken out with lasers. Tam, one of the rhutz, and a squadron of soldiers separated from the division and headed for the communications center. A police helicopter swept down from out of nowhere and began firing on them. The rhutz stopped and began disassembling the copter's rudder mechanism. It began spinning faster and faster until it collided with a tree and burst into flames. They continued on until they reached the communications center. Two police pursuit vehicles were just pulling up. They bravely jumped out and confronted the soldiers but before they could shoot, the rhutz had them on the ground and were ripping them to pieces. Tam rushed by and entered the building.

The receptionist stood up and backed away. Tam went over to her. "We mean you no harm. Where is the government broadcasting studio?"

"Seventh floor," she replied.

Tam nodded and rushed to the elevator. The two rhutz remained on the first floor to keep a lookout. The receptionist watched them warily—terrified they'd attack her if she moved. On the seventh floor Tam and his squad found the government communications center and burst in the front door. They nearly tripped over two TGA soldiers bound and gagged on the floor. A young woman motioned to them to follow her.

"We heard you were coming so we thought we'd help out. The

soldiers were here to destroy the broadcast studio. We couldn't let them do that."

"Thank you. That would have been a disaster. How did you overpower them?"

"I hit one over the head with a brass statue and my friend used a flowerpot."

"Where's your friend?"

"Guarding the studio to make sure nobody messes with it."

They rounded a corner and saw another young woman standing nervously in front of a glass door.

"Mellie! They're here!" the girl yelled.

"Thank God!" Mellie replied and opened the door so Tam could go inside. He rushed in with his squad behind him.

"Is anybody in here?" Tam asked.

"No. Everyone left when they heard the building was under siege," Mellie replied.

"Why do you two want to help us?"

"We're part of the Synclare cell. Captain Shilling told us you might need our help. We can show you how to use the equipment."

"Good. I want to address the entire nation. Can we do that?"

"Yes. There's a prerecorded program playing right now, but we can interrupt it."

"Okay. Get it all set up and I'll tell you when I'm ready to go on the air. I need to check in with the other divisions first to be sure the operation is going as planned."

Tam got the GC and hailed John.

"5th Airborne, report," Tam asked.

"5th Airborne, eighty percent of mission accomplished. Two more runs ought to do it."

"73rd Infantry, report!"

"Yes, sir. We've taken the tower and set the fuel tanks on fire. We're heading for base headquarters now but are taking heavy fire."

"Keep the pressure on. You need to take the headquarters building."

"Yes, sir. Will, do."

"Black squadron, report!"

"Black squadron here. We've secured the Capitol Building, and the TGA has fled. Everyone left here is friendly."

"Good. I'm going to make my broadcast then."

"Yes, sir. We'll make sure everyone turns on their VC."

Tam turned to Mellie. "Okay, are you ready?"

"Yes, Commander," Mellie said. "Just take a seat and put on this headset."

Tam did as he was told and the green light on the camera came on.

"Citizens of Synclare. This is Commander General Tamurus Lavendar, Commander of the 5th Loyalist Army, speaking to you from the Government Communications Center in Roshaunda. Today is a momentous day for Synclare and for Tarizon. This morning we have launched an attack on the TGA military base at Sheelee as well as the main government offices in Roshaunda. I'm pleased to announce our mission has been accomplished and we now control the Synclare government and are in the process of driving out the TGA.

"What this means for the citizens of Synclare is that freedom and justice under the Supreme Mandate have finally been restored to this great state. Slavery is abolished and all life forms shall enjoy the same rights and privileges as human beings.

"Soon you'll be seeing divisions of the 5th Army beginning to occupy all regions of Synclare. In the meantime, any intelligence you can provide us as to TGA positions and armaments will be invaluable to us and hasten the day that you will be rid of Videl Lai and the beasts that support him.

"For those who have assisted in the invasion I thank you for your support and my friend, known to you as the Liberator, Commander General Leek Lanzia, sends his thanks and best wishes to you all. We pledge to you that, from here on out, we will do all that we can to defend Synclare from the tyranny of Videl Lai. Any of you who are willing and able to fight are urged to join the Loyalist Army, for we still have a lot of work to do to free Tuht, Merria and the other nations of Turvin. The war is far from over but today we've taken a dramatic step forward. Good day and may God and Sandee be with you."

26
Naming the Baby

It was some time before Leek was able to get away from his duties as Commander of the 3rd Army and visit his newly born brother and son in Shini. Tehra had graciously taken the newborn child in and treated it like her own. It was like having twins, she told her friends, since they were born less than six segments apart. Leek had hired a nanny to assist Tehra and they had everything they could possibly need to ease the burden of caring for two infants. Lorin and Colonel Tomel were regular visitors, relishing every moment they had with the babies and giving Tehra much comfort and support.

The question of a name for the baby came up often but Tehra insisted that it was Leek's responsibility and she'd leave that to him. Leek was nervous as he drove up to Tehra's compartment. The thought that he was now a father had scarcely crossed his mind as his responsibilities as Commander of the 3rd Army gave him little time to think of personal matters. Today, though, he had no choice but to consider the fact that he was a father and now had a child to rear. The thought of that overwhelmed him. What did he know about raising a child and how could he do it without Lucinda?

When he reached the building's security panel he hesitated. Finally, he raised his hand and placed it on the scanning panel. Inside her compartment a chime rang and Commander Leek Lanzia's presence at the door was advised. Tehra handed her baby to Ginger, the nanny and rushed to the door. She opened it with a broad smile and they embraced.

"Commander. You finally made it. It's so good to see you."

"Yes, I'm sorry it's been so long. I know I placed a tremendous burden on you. I hope you'll forgive me."

"Nonsense. Your son is a delight and all your support and assistance has been a godsend."

"Well, good. I'm glad to hear he hasn't been a burden. Can I see him?"

"Yes, I think he needs his diaper changed."

Leek gave Tehra a startled look. "Just kidding. Your nanny just changed him."

Leek laughed with relief. "Oh, the nanny. How is she working out?"

"Wonderful. She's a big help and great company. I don't know what I'd do without her. . . . Your baby's in here."

Tehra led Leek into the nursery and stood proudly over the baby's crib. Leek went over to it and looked down into his son's blue eyes.

"He's a lot bigger than when I first saw him."

"Well, they grow fast if you feed them right. I don't think poor Lucinda got a very good diet during the last of her pregnancy, so you're lucky he's as healthy as he is."

"He is healthy then?" Leek inquired.

"Oh, yes. The medic said while the baby is in the womb it takes whatever nutrients it needs from its mother, and it's the mother who is wanting if there aren't enough for both. That's why Lucinda looked so poorly when you found her."

"That and the poison."

"Oh, yes. The poison. How ghastly that must have been for you."

"My mind has repressed the image, but I still often dream of the moment."

Tehra took Leek's hand. "I'm so sorry. I know how much you loved Lucinda."

Leek forced a smile. "Can I hold him?"

"Of course, silly. It's your baby."

Leek picked up the baby and he began to cry. Leek looked at Tehra, horrified.

"Just rock him a bit and show him you love him."

Leek began rocking the baby and smiling at him. Soon he quieted down and a contented look came over his face.

"See, he likes you."

"You think so?"

"Of course he'd like you better if you gave him a name. I'm so tired of people wanting to know his name and not having an answer."

"Oh, a name. I'm sorry. I should have come up with something sooner, but—"

"I know. You were busy saving the planet. I understand, but now you need to give the poor child a name."

Leek took a deep breath and exhaled. "Hmm. Should I give him an

Earth name or come up with something more common on Tarizon?"

"Probably a combination of both since he has dual citizenship."

"Right. I could name him after my father, Stanley."

Tehra raised her eyebrow. "That would be nice. Do you know Lucinda's father's name? That would be a nice tribute to her to give him part of her father's name."

"Tokin. His first name was Tokin."

"That means *peace*," Lucinda said. "Tokin Stanley Lanzia—do you like that?"

"I don't know. It sounds kinda awkward."

"How about Tokin Leek Lanzia?"

"No. I think every child should have his own unique name."

"Okay."

"After all, he's such a miracle child."

"What do you mean?"

"Well, conceiving him was the last thing I ever imagined would happen to me after I was abducted to Tarizon. Then I thought he'd be raised by Lucinda and her mate and I'd never see him again. Lucinda getting unmated—that almost never happens on Tarizon. The kidnaping and Lucinda's being tortured and starved to death . . . yet somehow he survived and I was able to rescue him. The fact that he is in my arms right now is only after a long string of miracles. So, I think God wanted me to have him, so his middle name ought to be something holy. Perhaps his middle name should be *Sandee*, for only by the will of God and Sandee is he alive today."

"So, Tokin Sandee Lanzia is your choice?"

"Yes, I think so."

Tehra smiled and looked at Tokin. "I like it. *Tokin*. It has a nice ring to it."

"And his best friend will be Sophilo. He'll be like Tam is to me. I hope they'll both be telepathic so they'll always be connected."

"Can't you test them right now and find out?" Tehra asked.

"No, that ability doesn't come until they're five or six cycles old."

"Oh. Then we'll just have to wait and see."

Leek stayed with Tehra and the boys for three days before he had to go back to his Doral Mountains headquarters. He hated to leave. He'd become very attached to both of them and Tehra as well. Tehra was a few cycles older than Leek but he couldn't help but feel an attraction to her. He understood how his father had fallen in love with her and let her seduce him. He didn't blame Tehra for what she had done. He knew that on Tarizon the highest priority for any woman was to get pregnant. The survival of the human race depended on it.

Being responsible for two infants gave Leek a new perspective on the war. He hated the fact that he couldn't put a stop to it immediately. The cost of it was just too high. He thought of all the soldiers who'd already died and the millions of children who'd lost their fathers. This war was an abomination. It made the whole Tarizon repopulation project a joke. He was sure more people had died in this civil war than had been conceived on Earth and brought back to Tarizon under the repopulation project. He felt frustrated and helpless.

While he was in Shini, Leek met many times with Lorin and the command staff to discuss strategy and to set goals and objectives. After the last meeting he and Lorin had dinner at the Chancellor's Mansion. He'd never been there before so Lorin gave him the grand tour. They strolled into a large bedroom decorated in a lavish, intricate decor.

"This is French, isn't it?" Leek asked.

"Yes. The Chancellor was an Earthchild and he had several rooms decorated in popular Earth styles. Do you like it?"

"Yes, it's gorgeous. The French really know how to enjoy life."

"Really? What do they do differently than anyone else?" Lorin asked.

"They didn't worry about every little thing. They relaxed a lot, drank too much, ate voraciously and spent a lot of time in bed with their mates."

Lorin laughed. "Sounds like a good philosophy. Now I understand why they made their bedrooms so lavish."

Leek thought of Jake and how sad it was he couldn't be there to enjoy all this luxury with Lorin. Lorin saw the sadness in his eyes and took his hand.

"What's wrong?"

Leek forced a smile. "I'm so proud of you, Lorin. You finally realized your dream."

A tear rolled down her cheek. "Yes, it is wonderful but I feel so alone now. There's nobody to talk to. Jake and my father are gone and you're so far away."

"True. But we've got the GC. You can call me anytime."

"Yes, but we're both so busy. I wish I was telepathic so our minds could connect. You and Tam are so lucky to be able to do that."

"Why don't you apply for a mate?"

Lorin's mouth dropped.

"A mate? Are you kidding? I don't believe in computer mating."

"You don't? But, I thought everyone was mated by computer on Tarizon."

"Not me. I wouldn't stand for it. When Jake and I fell in love my father arranged for us to be mated."

"So, are you going to change the system now that you are Chancellor?"

"Not just yet. It does have one enormous advantage."

"What's that?"

"When a soldier dies and leaves a widow she can immediately apply for a new mate so the family unit can be restored quickly."

Leek raised an eyebrow.

"So, I'll wait for the killing to stop before I suggest to the Assembly that we abolish computer mating."

"Okay. So, is there anyone out there you could fall in love with?" Leek asked.

Lorin took a deep breath, giving Leek a penetrating stare. "Just one," she said softly.

Leek frowned, wondering who she was talking about. He was dying to ask her but then thought better of it.

"Well, I'm serious. Call me anytime. When do you go to bed at night?"

"Late. Rarely before midnight."

"That's about when I go to bed too. Why don't I call you every night. We can talk, but not about the war or politics. We'll talk about what mates talk about. You'll have to help me out though, Lucinda and I never got a chance to spend much time together."

"Nor did Jake and I. We were always going in different directions."

"Well, it will be a new experience for both of us."

Lorin nodded, already feeling excited about the prospect of a nightly chat. She smiled and led Leek into a small dining room where a lavish dinner was waiting. A waiter helped them get seated and then asked if they'd like some wine.

"Wine. Do you drink wine on Tarizon?" Leek asked.

"No," Lorin admitted. "This came from the experimental agriculture station, but I thought you might like it."

"I've actually never had wine. Well, except altar wine at communion."

"Never had wine? But I thought wine was popular on Earth."

"It is for adults, but I wasn't old enough to drink when I left Earth and my parents didn't allow experimentation."

"Well then, this will be a new experience for both of us."

They lifted their glasses and then took a drink. Leek shook his head. "Not bad. What do you think?"

"Very good. I could get used to drinking this. It's much sweeter than tekari."

They ate and drank for a long time, enjoying each other's company. When the bottle was empty they got another one and were a little drunk when Leek's driver rang the doorbell to advise them it was time to take Leek to the airport. Reluctantly, Leek got his things together and went to the door to leave.

"Do you really have to go?" Lorin complained.

"Well, you know my boss, the Chancellor. She's one tough lady. She'd give me hell if I was derelict in my duties."

"You're right," Lorin moaned. "She'd have to convene a court-martial."

"So, I best go."

She took a step and nearly stumbled. Leek caught her arm and steadied her. She put one hand on the doorjam and regained her balance.

"Don't forget you promised to call every night," Lorin reminded him.

"I won't. I'll talk to you tomorrow at midnight."

"And every night. Just like mates."

"Every night," Leek assured her then turned and left.

On his way to the airport he marveled at his evening with Lorin. He had never seen her soft feminine side. She'd always had a tough, impenetrable exterior, but tonight she'd turned it off and let Leek in for the first time. It was like being with another woman. He thought maybe it was the wine, but she had let down her guard even before they'd started drinking. He didn't know what it meant, but he was glad he'd be talking to Lorin on a regular basis so he could figure it out.

27
Mobilization

By fall, almost a full cycle into the civil war, the Loyalists had driven the TGA out of Lemaine Shane, Lower Azollo, Ock Mezan, Muhl and most of Turvin. In Turvin, only Soni and Tuht remained in TGA hands. They still controlled Azollo, since the Loyalists had yet to set their sights on the conquest of that last continent, but Loyalist militia units were actively engaging the TGA on a daily basis and growing stronger each day. It was clear to most observers that the TGA had been beaten but they stubbornly refused to accept their fate.

In the new command center in the Tunisu Islands off the southern coast of Turvin, Leek, Tam and the general staff were gathered to discuss a final assault on Soni and Tarizon's capital city, Shisk. All agreed that if Shisk fell, Videl Lai would have no choice but to surrender and the war would be over.

"The intelligence reports coming in from the area indicate the TGA is fortifying its defenses in expectation of our assault," General Zitor advised. "The battle for Shisk will be a costly one for both sides. As you know, General Bratfort's 4th TGA Army, which was driven out of Quori, has been transported to Soni where it is in the process of being reorganized, strengthened and refitted. Knowing the General, it will be a formidable army when we engage it. This force, along with the 24th Army which has defended Soni since the war began, will make our task doubly difficult."

"Why don't we do what the TGA did in Shini—drop a hundred thousand super vipers on the dome?" General Lugman suggested.

"No," Leek protested. "That would result in the death of a lot of innocent civilians and leave the city in ruins."

"I agree," Tam said. "We need to come up with a strategy that will minimize collateral damage. Remember, Shisk has been the capital of

Tarizon since unification. There's a lot of history there that must be preserved."

"What do you suggest then, Commander Lanzia?" General Lugman asked. "How are we to penetrate such a formidable defense? There must be over a million men in those two armies."

"I think we should mass on the their northwest perimeter and drive into Soni like a locomotive."

"What's a locomotive?" General Lugman asked. "I'm afraid I'm not an Earthchild, so I don't know these things."

"It's a means of mass transit on Earth similar to our trams but much slower and less efficient. But a locomotive is heavy and when it gets moving nothing can stop it."

"But that will cause much destruction as well."

"True. But we can restrict the assault to a narrow corridor that is mainly industrial and won't cause a lot of unnecessary deaths. We'll drive straight through to the Capitol Building quickly before they have time to regroup."

"What makes you think they can't and won't stop this locomotive?" General Lugman questioned. "They'll have the entire perimeter guarded."

"True. So, we'll have to create some diversions."

"What kind of diversions?"

"Threebeard said he could easily get the mutants living inside the dome to go on a rampage. This would pull defenses away from the perimeter to deal with the civil unrest. We could also mass troops at one or two other logical invasion points to make them think we're coming in there rather than at the assault point we ultimately pick."

General Lugman shook his head and sighed. "But we'll have to mass troops on our targeted entry point too, so they'll be expecting us there."

"No," Leek replied evenly. "At nightfall they'll be few, if any, Loyalist forces at the targeted entry point. The redeployment will be done quietly during the night."

"But they have night vision equipment. Someone will be watching the perimeter and will see the redeployment."

"Maybe, so that's why I thought it would be a good night for a celebration. The one cycle anniversary of the formation of the Loyalist movement will be here in seven days. I think that calls for lots of fireworks and loud music."

General Zitor began to laugh. "Brilliant, General Lanzia! The fireworks will blind anyone watching with night vision equipment and the music will camouflage any noise we make in the redeployment."

"It sounds like we've got our work cut out for us," Tam said. "Do you think seven days is enough time for us to get in position around the city? What if the TGA tries to hold us up at the Soni border?"

"We have to be ready. Reliable sources have advised us that Videl Lai will only be in the city another eight days before he goes to Dark Land for a conference with leaders of the Azollo nations. We must commence our assault before he leaves."

"Then I'd like the 5th Army to spearhead the attack, sir," Tam said.

Leek nodded. "Yes, my thoughts as well. The entry point I have in mind is closest to where your army will be situated when it arrives at the dome."

Leek went to a map on the wall of Shisk and the surrounding terrain. He pointed to a tram station and entry station on the northeast perimeter and then took a marker and drew a straight line to the Capitol Building. "If we follow this line we can create a narrow corridor for our troops to pour into the city with minimum destruction of life and property."

"What's to prevent the TGA from cutting through the corridor and encircling half of our troop?"

"I'm sure that's exactly what they would normally do, except, about the time they get that bright idea, we'll attack from the south. They won't dare weaken their defensive positions while under an all out attack."

General Lugman sighed. "Well, I could see your plan working if nothing went wrong, but it could well end up in a colossal disaster."

"Anything we do will be risky, but I like Commander Lanzia's strategy and move we adopt it," General Zitor said.

"I concur, "Tam said.

"Well, I'm sure Threebeard helped you concoct this plan," General Lugman replied. "So, it would be useless for me to oppose it, but permit me to play devil's advocate, as they say on Earth, so we can address the obvious weaknesses in your strategy."

"Yes, I appreciate your candor, General Lugman," Leek said in a sincere tone, "and I look forward to your keen observations as I tend to be an optimist like my father."

"Yes, your father. That reminds me, someone told me of how he helped the Loyalist on Earth escape the TGA. When this is war is over we'll have to honor him in some fashion."

Leek nodded appreciatively. He wondered what his father and mother were doing at that moment. Could they even imagine what he was doing here on Tarizon. He thought of his little sister Marcia. He yearned to tell her of all his adventures. He laughed as he imagined what her reaction would be.

"What was that?" General Lugman asked.

"Ah. . . . Nothing. I was just thinking of a game I played with my father as a child. It was called 'Axis and Allies.' Today reminds me of playing that game."

"Except today men will die if your strategy turns out to be flawed," the General noted.

"Yes," Leek replied confidently, "so we must do everything in our power to make sure it works. If you discover any other weaknesses, general, I want to hear about them."

"Believe me, I won't hold anything back."

"Good. Then I think we're done here."

That night Leek called Lorin as he had been doing for some time now. He looked forward to their little bedtime chats. Although they'd tried for a while to keep their conversations of a personal nature, that soon proved impossible as they valued each other's opinions and counsel on the war and politics. He punched Lorin's number into the GC. She answered at once.

"Is it midnight already?" Lorin said softly.

"Yes, the days are flying by, aren't they?'

"I should say so. How'd the meeting with the general staff go?"

"They accepted my assault strategy without much of a fight."

"That's because they'd rather you put your neck on the line than them."

"You think so? I got the impression General Lugman had a plan he'd have liked us to consider."

"Lugman's a git. He seriously considered supporting Videl when he took power. My father had a hard time convincing him that would be a mistake."

"An opportunist, huh?"

"To the extreme. I'd watch him carefully."

"Well, he should be happy your father talked him into siding with the Loyalists."

"Yes, but I'm afraid gratitude and loyalty aren't words in his vocabulary."

"Well, it would be stupid for him to betray us now when the tide is going in our favor."

"Yes, you'd think so, but nobody said he was very bright."

"I'm more worried about Videl Lai slipping through our fingers."

"I'm sure he's got an elaborate escape plan should Shisk be taken."

"What do you think it is?"

"If I were him I'd go to Azollo and try to solidify his power there. He still controls the entire continent so he'd be fairly safe for a while."

"But isn't his power slipping in Azollo? I thought our militia were about ready to openly oppose him."

"Yes, I said for *a while*. If we take Shisk his days are numbered no matter where he goes."

"What about Clarion? He's got an attack cruiser there."

"Yes, I suppose that would be his final destination if he thought all hope were lost."

"I'll put Captain Shilling on alert in case we need Earth Shuttle 26."

"Don't be ridiculous. You can't go chasing Videl to Clarion."

"I know, but maybe we can catch him before he gets to Clarion."

"No. Just let him go. I don't want you dying after the war is already won."

"Well, don't worry about it. Hopefully we'll capture him before he leaves Shisk."

"When do you leave for your staging area?"

"We're leaving for Rour in the morning. We hope to cross the Soni border in a couple of days, so we'll be at Videl's doorstep on the anniversary of the war."

Lorin knew the plan only too well. She and Threebeard had helped Leek develop it. She knew it was a bold and dangerous plan, but the best one they could conceive after much thought and consideration. They cared about the population of Shisk and the preservation of its treasured history which necessitated a surgical strike rather than a brutal show of force. They thought it important to show some semblance of human decency in this otherwise hideous war.

"So, how are you feeling?" Lorin asked.

Tarizon: Civil War

"I'm tired, of course. We've been working eight kyloons a day for some time now getting mobilized."

"I know the feeling. I've been working the same schedule trying to help new state governments get up and running."

"Yes, that must be difficult."

"It is. You know politics. Everyone is jostling for power and pleading for my support."

"Are they holding elections or are you appointing new state leaders?"

"I'm establishing interim governments by appointment for now, but the term of my appointees will be short. Elections will be held within a cycle."

"God! I don't know how you do it. That's a monumental task with so many states."

"And your task is easy?" Lorin laughed.

"Well, mine is more straightforward."

"I don't know about that, but it's really not so bad. I trust my cell leaders, so I'm appointing them or persons they recommend.... Hey, I saw Tokin today."

"Oh, you did! How is he?"

"Fine. He's growing fast. You won't recognize him when you get back."

"I bet. How's Tehra and Sophilo?"

"They're both doing well. They miss you. Tehra's worried about you. I'm worried about you, too."

"Hmm. Tell them I miss them a lot and not to worry. I'll be outside the dome in my command post away from all the action."

"Don't let your guard down. Videl would like to put a bullet in your head just as much as you'd like to put one in his."

"We're going to make sure he's too busy to be plotting my demise."

"I hope so. I'd die if anything happened to you."

"Nothing will. Don't worry."

Leek hadn't been worried about his own personal safety until Lorin had reminded him that Videl would be desperately trying to find and eliminate him in order to crush the Loyalist spirit on the eve of battle. He suddenly felt paranoid. Would someone in his own ranks try to assassinate him? He'd known there must be moles in his organization. He didn't trust General Lugman but would he plot an assassination? Leek looked around

William Manchee

for Rhin. She came to him, feeling his apprehension.

"Watch out for me, girl. There'll be enemies lurking about these next few days."

Rhin looked at him and their minds touched. "I know. I can feel treachery in the wind."

A chill came over Leek. He swallowed hard.

28
The Final Assault

Tam couldn't wait to get back to his army. He'd be leading the most important battle in the history of Tarizon. He was a little surprised that Commander Lanzia had agreed so readily to his request. Most men would have wanted all the glory for themselves; but not the Liberator. Leek Lanzia had never cared anything about glory. Tam had thought that might change after he had a taste of it, but it hadn't for Leek Lanzia. If there had been a change in him it had been the development of a sad demeanor brought on by the weighty responsibility of being Commander of the 3rd Army, being a witness to a shocking amount of bloodshed, and losing Lucinda, the woman he loved. If one thing was clear, Leek Lanzia would gladly give up all the power and glory to have his beloved Lucinda back, or even for a ticket to Earth. Tam often wished he'd been chosen to be the Liberator, for he would have no regrets and relish every moment of it.

When Tam arrived at his camp, John, Riddle the rhutz, and Colonel Belmoht were there to greet him.

"How did the briefing go, Commander?" John asked.

"Very well. You won't believe this, but the 5th Army has been selected to lead the initial strike on the capital."

The men smiled but didn't look as excited about the honor as Tam did.

"When?" John asked.

"We leave in three days. We must be in position in five days."

"That doesn't give us much time," Colonel Belmoht complained.

"We have no choice. The Chancellor is leaving the city in seven days, so we must strike before he leaves."

"Do you think we can get to the capital city in time? There are a lot of TGA troops between us and Shisk."

"True, but their morale is bad and without hovertanks they've proven to be no match for us. We must attack decisively and drive them back to Shisk by the anniversary of the war."

"Why that date?"

He explained to them at length about the battle plan and reasoning behind it.

"Fireworks and a party? Do you really think the TGA will fall for that?" Colonel Belmoht asked.

"Yes, I think they probably will, but that's not important. All they have to do is be sufficiently distracted so that they don't see that we are redeploying our troops."

"How can we get a hundred thousand troops through that tiny little gate at the entrance of the dome?" John asked.

"We'll have to punch larger holes on both sides of the gate so there will be plenty of room for the troops to enter the city. We'll use ATVs and copters once inside so we can move fast. We must clear a corridor straight through to the Capitol Building and then hold it."

"Won't that allow pollution into the city?" Colonel Belmoht asked.

"Yes, but the filtration system can handle it as long as there aren't any fires. No bombs or torches in the city. Use your lasers or rifles. Part of he mutant militia is already in the city and may join up with us during the battle. Initially they'll be stirring up trouble to get the police and the TGA Away from our point of attack."

"What if the TGA shows less restraint and lights the place up?" Colonel Belmoht asked.

"Then you'll have to break out your breathers and use them. They'll be no retreating once we're in the city. If we don't complete our objective we'll likely be surrounded and killed, so follow orders and be vigilant. And remember our primary objective is to capture or kill Videl Lai. He mustn't escape. If we get him the war is over. If he escapes it may go on for many cycles."

"What about the rhutz? They can't use breathers," John noted.

Tam looked at Riddle and thought, "What about that Riddle?"

"It's okay," Riddle said silently, "we're used to the foul air. We've been living outside the dome for many cycles."

Tam nodded and vocalized Riddle's thoughts. "The rhutz have adjusted to the bad air. Don't worry about them."

"All right," Colonel Belmoht said. "I'll notify the division commanders."

"Very good. I'll see all of you at dawn."

Tam and his staff disbursed to begin preparations for the mission. There was a lot to do in just a short time, but Tam's staff was used to being under the gun and reacted quickly and effectively. On the eve of the mission Tam felt they were as ready as they would ever be, but he was still too hyped up to sleep. He had a million things running through his mind. He had volunteered his Army to lead the assault on the capital and now he was wondering if he'd been rash in wanting to take point on the operation. If it failed the blame for the Loyalist defeat could well be placed on his shoulders. He quickly dismissed that thought as he had often told his men there was no room for negativism in the 5th army.

As he was lying in his bed tossing and turning Threebeard's thoughts came to him.

"Greetings my friend. I just wanted to give you my encouragement for the upcoming battle. I know it must be weighing heavily on your mind right now."

"You've got that right," Tam thought.

"Don't be nervous. Your army is well prepared for this battle."

"I'm just concerned about getting to Shisk in time. If the enemy engages us early on we may get bogged down and unable to reach the city in time."

"Don't be concerned about that. You'll be the last thing the TGA will be worrying about tomorrow. We've hit them hard all day from the south and from the sea and tomorrow the assault will even be more intense. I'm confident you'll have nothing but token opposition on the road to Shisk."

"Good. I'm glad to hear that. Once we get there I'm confident we can fulfill our mission."

"I know you can. Now sleep. You'll need your strength and a clear head tomorrow."

"Yes, sir. Thanks again for your encouragement."

Threebeard's presence ended and Tam felt much better. Before long he was asleep and slept soundly until he was awakened the next morning. After eating a quick breakfast and meeting with his staff one last time, the 5th Army was on the move and crossing the Soni border headed for Shisk.

Tarizon: Civil War

The 5th army's two airborne divisions had been working all night blasting anything that moved along the road to Shisk. By noon the army had progressed halfway to their destination and had yet to encounter anything but token opposition.

The plan was to make it appear that the army was joining up with 3rd Army to the south which had launched an attack the previous day and was in the midst of a fierce battle. But as night fell the army stopped and, to anyone observing, appeared to have set up camp. The truth was the army was merely resting and waiting to move on.

Just after nightfall the sky over Soni lit up with a magnificent display of fireworks, flares, and mortar fire. Loud music permeated the air and Loyalist supporters under the dome took to the streets to celebrate the first anniversary of the war. Under this cover the 5th army moved into position for the following mornings assault.

At dawn a thousand soldiers made fires and moved around the 5th Army's staged campsite to give the illusion that the army was still there. It was hoped that this charade would be effective for at least a kyloon or two so that the mission could be commenced before the deception was detected. The plan worked and at dawn Riddle the rhutz and a hundred and fifty of his pack raced through the TGA checkpoint at northwest gate 11. The guards watched the beasts run by in shock and awe until the last few of them turned on the guards and attacked. The guards went down without much of a fight. They were no match for the rhutz who went for their carotid artery leaving them lifeless in a pool of blood.

Tam's special ops team arrived next on the scene cutting two large rectangular doorways in the dome on both sides to allow for easy access into the city. As soon as they were done the 5th Army began its trek through Shisk toward the Capitol Building meeting very little resistance. Some marched, some rode in ATVs and others were ferried in by copter. Crowds of mutants and Loyalist supporters along the way cheered at seeing the Loyalist troops entering the city.

Tam smiled and waved at the people streaming out of the factories and warehouses as they passed. This wasn't what he was expecting. He'd anticipated heavy resistance. Something was wrong, he told himself. He picked up his GC to check with Lt. Hawkh who was running the special ops team.

"C1, report."

"C1, here. We're about to leave the industrial district and heading into the downtown area."

"Any resistance?"

"No. Just friendly crowds."

"Describe what you're seeing now."

"We're starting down a boulevard lined with skyscrapers on both sides. They're all quite magnificent. Conspicuous in their absence are the police and the TGA."

"Something is wrong. I think it's a trap. Don't go down that street."

"But—"

There was a tremendous explosion and the GC went dead.

"C1, are you all right? C1! Can you hear me?"

There was no response.

"S2, report."

"S2 here."

"What's happening?"

"Several large buildings up ahead have exploded and collapsed on our troops and the spectators who were cheering them on. There are fires raging and the dust and smoke has brought visibility to near zero. I can't see a thing, but I can hear people screaming and crying in agony."

"Oh, Sandee. Find out what happened and give me a casualty report as soon as you can."

"Yes, sir," S2 replied and signed off.

Tam felt sick. The TGA had been cagey. They hadn't put up a fight but instead set a trap and he'd fallen right into it. He wondered if he'd lost his rhutz and the special ops team. He closed his eyes, cleared his mind, and thought of Riddle. Pain and grief quickly overwhelmed him. Riddle was alive and looking back at the pile of rubble that covered half his pack. Riddle let out a mournful howl that forced Tam to sever his connection.

"S2, reporting."

"Go, S2," Tam said.

"We've lost the special ops team and over a thousand soldiers who were following close behind them. Our corridor is completely blocked. We'll have to take a detour to get to the capitol building."

"No, that's what they will expect us to do. Use the copters to get over the rubble and keep moving."

"What if another building explodes?"

Tarizon: Civil War

"I doubt they'd do that. The contamination from these fires will tax the city's air purification system to the limit."

"Very well. I'll call in the copters we have working the corridor now and see if we can locate some more to speed up the process."

"Very good, S2. Keep me posted."

Tam wondered if Lt. Hawkh was dead. He wanted to organize a rescue party to look for survivors but he knew that wasn't practical right away. He had to concentrate on his mission now and get to Videl before he escaped from the city. As he was contemplating the situation Colonel Belmoht approached him.

"What are we going to do now, Commander?"

"We'll use our copters to get our troops over the debris and then continue on to the capitol like we planned."

"But, sir. It will take many kyloons to get our troops over the burning buildings and the enemy will most likely put up a stiff resistance once we get moving again. I'm afraid there is no chance in Hell we'll be able to make our timetable."

Tam began to pace back and forth. "There must be another way," he said to himself. His face suddenly lit up. "The nanomites. Maybe the nanomites can build us a path through the debris."

Colonel Belmoht gave him a skeptical look. "But that would take time if it were even possible."

"I don't know. Commander Lanzia told me a story once about his first encounter with the nanomites. He said in a matter of a loon they reduced his fifteen-by-eighteen-foot bedroom to the size of a small closet. If they can move walls around that quickly, maybe they will be able to build us a path through the rubble."

"Too bad you can't communicate with them."

"I haven't been able to, but Commander Lanzia could do it. I'll call him."

He picked up his GC and summoned his old friend.

"Tam. Are you all right? We saw the explosion and the fires," Leek said. "What happened?"

"Someone must have leaked our plans. They rigged several large buildings to explode and block our path. We lost quite a few rhutz and the special ops team."

"Oh, my God! Rhin and I felt it, the betrayal, but we couldn't figure out who it was."

"I don't know either, but we're expecting an attack at any moment. We need to find a way to move on or we'll have to retreat. We can't afford to stand around like sitting dirkbirds."

"How can we help?"

"Can you ask your nanomite friends to build us a path through the rubble?"

Leek thought about that a moment. "I don't know. I'll see if I can contact them. The TGA fumigated a lot of the buildings so I don't know if there will be enough of them left to build you a path. Give me a moment."

Tam waited what seemed like forever, then the GC lit up and Leek's voice came pouring through. "I've contacted the nanomites. Most of the buildings built by the nanomites, including the ones blown up, were fumigated, so there aren't any nanomites close by to help you."

"Then I should order a retreat?" Tam asked.

"No! The nanomite leader I contacted spoke of an underground ventilation duct large enough for soldiers to get through. It's part of the city's air filtration system. He says there should be a maintenance entrance near each tram station. There will be fans and filter units along the duct that will block your passage but most of them have maintenance doors you can get though without any trouble."

"Thank you, Commander. That's great news. We'll give that a try and hopefully see you at the Capitol Building."

Tam barked orders to the men around him and they began to move toward the tram station. Several soldiers screamed that they'd found the entrance and soldiers immediately began pouring down into the tunnel. The dark, damp tunnel ran deep below the city, so an advance team was sent in to set up lanterns and light torches along the way. The tunnel was made of the same crystal-like substance that the nanomites used for their buildings, so the floor was smooth and the soldiers were able to move quickly two by two under the mayhem of the city above. Twenty loons later soldiers started coming out well beyond the demolished building. They were met by a half dozen rhutz, including Riddle, who'd survived the building's collapse. As they moved away from the tunnel's exit they saw several dead TGA soldiers strewn about.

Tam, who had yet to enter the tunnel, put his GC to his ear. "S2, report."

"S2, reporting. Some of us are through the tunnel. It will take a little while to regroup and then we'll move forward according to our plans."

"Good. I'll be taking a copter over there in a loon. Are there any survivors from the special ops team?"

"Haven't seen any, but there are a half dozen rhutz who made it through. Lucky for us they did. It seems the TGA had a welcoming party waiting for us when we came out of the duct."

"Really? Thank God and Sandee."

"They'll be leading the way once we get started again."

"Good," Tam said. "They'll warn you if there are any TGA soldiers ahead, but I think Commander Lanzia's diversion has worked for the most part. This building demolition seems to be a defensive maneuver to buy them time to get some troops over here to protect the Capitol Building."

"And Videl Lai, if he hasn't already left the city."

"Oh, I'm sure he's still here. He's a proud man and he won't leave the capital city unless it's a matter of life or death."

"All right. I just got word that we're ready to move out. Anything else, Commander?"

"Yes, the contamination level has gone red. You'll need to break out your breathers."

"Very good, sir. I'll give the order."

As Tam turned off the GC he heard a copter coming. He looked up and watched it land a hundred strides away. When it was on the ground he and Colonel Belmoht ran for it and climbed aboard. It took off and rose high above the rubble and the heat draft caused by the fires.

Riding a copter was nothing like a fighter. A fighter had a smooth, quiet ride, whereas the copter was noisy and vibrated terribly. But with its transparent exterior, the copter provided a view that was breathtaking. Although visibility was poor, the sky was clear enough that Tam could see the massive battles raging outside the city to the south. He could also see crowds fighting police and soldiers all over the city. He felt encouraged by what he saw until he spotted a space shuttle landing on the beach just west of the city. He picked up his GC and punched in a code.

"R1 here," Commander Lanzia advised.

"This is R2. I'm in a copter over the site of the building demolition."

"Did you get through the ventilation ducts?"

William Manchee

"Yes, the nanomites were correct. We're back on track, but I've just observed a space shuttle landing outside the dome to the west of the city. I suspect it's Videl's ride."

"Understood. We'll have to move quickly to head him off and prevent him from leaving the dome. I'll contact the seafolken. They're coming in from the west. Perhaps they can intercept him. In the meantime, urge your men to move quickly to the Capitol Building. We can't let Videl escape! He's got to be captured, dead or alive!"

29
Desperate Pursuit

Grenz Lozich lived with his wife and three children in a shack on the north shore of Pogo Island. There were few inhabitants on this part of the Island and that was one reason Grenz chose to live there. He'd been separated from his family at an early age when the slave traders captured his father and mother and transported them to Shisk to be sold at auction. His elder brother and a sister, who'd been away when the traders raided their seafolken village, provided him some comfort and protection while he was growing up, but Grenz pretty much raised himself.

At age fourteen Grenz joined the TGA and served on a battleship for six cycles. During that time he became a master seaman and soldier. When his tour of duty was up he went to Shisk to try to find his mother and father. He searched for half a cycle before he finally faced the reality that he'd never see his parents again. Although they had been taken to Shisk to be sold at the slave markets, he realized their buyers could have taken them anywhere on Tarizon.

During his search for his parents he met a seafolken girl named Drina working in a tavern. She was seventeen and as pretty a seafolken maiden as he'd ever seen. Unfortunately, she was one of the tavern keeper's slaves. Part of her job was to entertain the customers, so Grenz found himself returning often to the tavern just to flirt with Drina.

One night their flirtation went a little too far and the tavern keeper told Grenz to leave and never come back. Grenz couldn't stand the thought of never seeing Drina again so he went back the next day and waited across the street, hoping to catch a glimpse of her and to get her attention. When he finally did see her, he was appalled to see she'd been severely beaten. He rushed over to her, anger welling within him with each step. For the first time in his life he really wanted to kill someone.

"Did your master do this to you?" he questioned.

"Yes, but leave him alone. If you hurt him they'll arrest you and put you in prison."

"But I can't let him get away with treating you like that."

She laughed. "Why not, I'm just a slave girl."

"Slavery is wrong. The holy man Sandee said so and the Supreme Mandate forbids it."

"Yes, men are free but we are seafolken."

"So what? We're just as human as any pure blood."

"So, why do you care so much about my honor that you'd risk the freedom you hold so dear?"

"Because I love you," he blurted out, surprising even himself.

Drina gave Grenz such a tender smile that he nearly melted right there on the spot. They embraced and kissed passionately. "I love you, too," Drina said excitedly. "When you go back to Pogo will you take me with you?"

"Yes, I won't leave you here to be mistreated and beaten."

"But if we're caught they'll likely kill us."

"Then we can't let them catch us. We'll leave tonight after your master goes to bed. That will give us three kyloons to get to the docks. I have friends in the navy who will help us get on a ship to Pogo. Once the ship takes off we won't have anything to worry about."

Drina agreed and that night snuck out of the tavern and joined Grenz who was waiting across the street. They walked to the nearest tram station and took a tram to the west entrance to the dome. Soon they were stowaways on a freighter bound for Pogo. When they got there they were married and Grenz and his family and friends helped him build a little house on the beach far away from any authorities who might be looking for him or his bride.

To combat the growing slave trading business, Grenz formed the Dark Sea Defense League and enlisted seafolken from all lands adjoining the Dark Sea. He trained them to attack slave ships, free the seafolken slaves, and kill the slavers. The slave ships were either sunk or refitted for use by the Defense League to pursue slave traders.

When Videl Lai became Chancellor Threebeard requested they join the Loyalist movement and take part in the campaign to rid the world of the Purists who would kill or enslave all seafolken. Of course, they were aware of the Prophecy, and when Peter Turner came to Tarizon and was identified as the Liberator, they waited anxiously for his call to arms.

William Manchee

It first came when they were asked to help drive out the TGA in Lortec and later there were the very successful raids on Gallion. But today Grenz and his soldiers had been called to help in the most important operation of the war. They were advancing on the capital city of Shisk to find and arrest, if possible, the man who'd ordered that all seafolken be taken as slaves or be killed, the tyrant Videl Lai. If they couldn't arrest him, so he could be tried for his crimes, then he was to be killed but under no circumstance could he be allowed to leave Shisk.

The seafolken, who could swim at sea as fast as any man could run on solid ground, were big and strong and made great soldiers and seamen. The average TGA soldier was no match for them in hand-to-hand combat. In the past they had managed to subdue them with bullet bombs. A simple bullet couldn't penetrate the tough seafolken skin, so they developed a bullet that stuck in the seafolken skin and then exploded. The TGA had been expecting their attack from the sea, but Threebeard had told them to land north of the city and transportation into the city would be provided.

They came to the shores of Soni, most by ship, but some straight out of the water. When they were all gathered together they were transported by nearly a hundred copters to a staging area just outside the northwest entry into the dome. When the 3rd Army launched its massive attack from the south and the fireworks began, the seafolken silently took out the sentries and entered into the city undetected. During the night they were taken into mutant homes and kept out of sight. Then at dawn, they regrouped and headed in three columns for the Capitol Building from the north.

When Grenz saw several huge buildings fall along the corridor the 5th Army was supposed to be advancing, he knew he and his men were the only ones left to find Videl Lai and prevent his escape from the city. He communicated this information to his platoon leaders and told them to let him know immediately if they saw any TGA transport vehicles moving through the city. Just as he hung up his GC, it buzzed again.

"DS1 here," he responded.

"DS1, this is R1. Did you see the buildings collapse?"

"Yes, what happened?"

"Three buildings were taken down, presumably to block the 5th Army's attack. We've found a way around the rubble, but I'm afraid we'll be late for the rendevous. Your men are going to have to find Videl. It looks like he'll be heading for a space shuttle that's just landed west of the dome.

Tarizon: Civil War

It shouldn't be that far from your position. Find it and make sure Videl doesn't escape!"

"Yes, sir. You can depend on us. DS1 out."

Grenz hung up the phone and swallowed hard. He knew it was all up to the seafolken now. He was glad that they'd have the opportunity to avenge the death of so many of their fellow seafolken and to kill the man who had ordered their extermination. *God is just.* He heard barking and was surprised to see a half dozen rhutz coming toward him. He concentrated and made contact.

"You can call me Riddle," one of them said to him silently.

"And you can call me Grenz," he thought.

"There are six of us and you have three columns. We'll split up in pairs and scout ahead for each of your columns."

"Your assistance is accepted. Take your positions. I'll inform my platoon leaders. We must not let Videl escape!"

The rhutz ran off to take their positions scouting ahead of each column. Tam had informed Riddle of the space shuttle's position so he led his column straight in that direction and told the other rhutz leading the other two columns to veer to each side to box Videl in when he arrived. Suddenly Riddle looked up. He could hear fast-moving transport vehicles approaching. He concentrated on Grenz.

"Videl is on the move. He's on Avenue West which leads to the dome's due west exit. If your third column takes the next street left they can intercept him. We'll meet you there."

"Thanks, Riddle. May God and Sandee be with us."

Grenz ordered his left column to take the next left and move double time to Avenue West. When they arrived they could see the Korstar 7 surrounded by several escorts coming at them. They hid behind PTVs and in between buildings until the escorts leading the procession had passed by. Then they stepped out and opened fire. The seafolken were armed with old rifles they'd stolen from slave traders, but a few had lasers they'd stolen from fallen TGA soldiers. The bullets bounced off the fortified vehicles but the lasers disabled the first PTV. The second one smashed into it. TGA soldiers jumped out and began returning the fire. Then there was copter noises above and two TGA copters landed, dropping dozens more TGA soldiers to help defend the Chancellor.

While the battle was raging the two rhutz had singled out one of the government vehicles and disabled it. A TGA soldier fired on one of the rhutz with his laser and the rhutz whimpered off and fell to the ground. Before the soldier could turn to fire on the second rhutz, it was at his throat and blood was gushing out the neck of his uniform. He staggered and fell to the ground.

The door to the vehicle opened and Videl Lai and two bodyguards dashed out toward one of the copters that had just dropped off troops. The rhutz came after them and tried to leap on Videl but one of the bodyguards got between them and they went down hard. The seafolken began firing on the two fleeing men, but their aim was poor and soon the men had reached the copter and climbed aboard. The rhutz wiggled out of the soldier's grasp, ran to the copter but it was too late. It took off quickly and disappeared between several buildings.

Grenz and the other two columns of seafolken had continued toward the west gate where they encountered several TGA platoons. They battled for several loons before they were able to make it outside the dome. As they left the city they saw in the distance the lights of the huge space shuttle. Both columns moved swiftly toward it, hoping they weren't too late. As they took up their positions around the craft they heard copters approaching. Grenz knew it must be Videl Lai as he'd gotten a report from his platoon leader that Videl had gotten away in a copter.

Grenz knew this was his last opportunity to get the revenge he so wanted. He called his platoon leaders and told them to try to shoot the copter out of the sky as it went by, but if that didn't work to attack it just as soon as it landed. He didn't want to give Videl Lai an opportunity to even step out on the ground.

When the copter finally flew overhead the seafolken opened up on it but none of their fire connected and the copter proceeded to land near the spacecraft. As they had been commanded, the seafolken opened up on the copter. Bullets and laser blasts flew over the copter and Grenz just knew one of them would have to connect, but none did. Suddenly, the ship's giant laser guns emerged from behind sliding turrets and began blasting the seafolken positions. There were screams and cries of agony from the soldiers who were felled. Grenz raised his fist in anger and frustration as he feared Videl Lai was about to escape! He'd failed in this most crucial mission and now how many thousands would pay the ultimate price for his incompetence?

30
Clarion

Captain Shilling had been disturbed when Leek told her of his dream. She'd worried about the attack cruisers the TGA had built and the fleet of space fighters designed to support them. There had been no specific plans to use the cruisers as a treaty had been worked out peacefully with the United States government, but now she was certain Videl planned to use the cruisers if he were to be forced off of Tarizon. Since that possibility seemed more likely each day, something would have to be done to thwart his plan.

She knew that neither Commander Lanzia or the new Loyalist government knew anything about the Tarizon space program as it had been overseen by Videl and the generals he had in his pocket. Therefore, she was the only one she could think of with the knowledge and experience necessary to concoct an effective plan to thwart their efforts. She was honored that Commander Lanzia had so readily given her the task, but she was already so busy with the Liberation Network, she didn't know if she could handle both jobs. When she told Lorin of her predicament, Lorin agreed the problem of the attack cruisers had to be her first priority and that Major Oakril could, in the future, handle the Liberation Network alone.

With her assignment now clear she began to consider options for dealing with this most dangerous situation. The first task would be to move the 3rd Army's headquarters off her ship so she could get if off the ground and ready for space flight again. Once she'd done that she would at least have the capability of traveling to Clarion and observing the TGA operation there. She wasn't sure what she could do once she got there, but she was hopeful she'd get some inspiration once she saw what she was up against.

Fortunately, the nanomites had been busy building all types of structures to accommodate the growing 3rd Army so Captain Shilling was sure they could quickly build a headquarters building to replace Earth

Tarizon: Civil War

Shuttle 26 when it took off for its new assignment. In the meantime all their operations would have to be moved to temporary quarters. With the assault on Shisk rapidly approaching, Captain Shilling knew there could be no delay. Within ten days she'd managed to move all operations off her ship and ready Earth Shuttle 26 for takeoff.

It was a cool day and hundreds of soldiers and staff gathered to watch the big ship come to life. The first task was the counterclockwise rotation of the craft which would ease it out of the ground like a giant screw. Once it was free of the ground its engines would be powered up and the craft could take off.

The earth shook and vibrated as the ship's lower section began to turn. The vibration was so intense most of the spectators backed away, afraid the ground might open up and swallow them at any moment. Soon the ship lifted up off the ground like it was being hoisted by a crane and slowly rose above the treetops. The big blue light at the front of the ship started to glow and then blasts of light exploded from it.

Inside, Captain Shilling barked orders and soon the ship began a forward motion and quickly accelerated until it was cruising across Tributon at an impressive speed. For the next few kyloons Captain Shilling put the shuttle through a long series of stringent tests designed to determine its readiness for space travel. When she had completed all of them successfully, she was satisfied Earth Shuttle 26 was ready for its assignment and they returned to base. As a precaution she parked the shuttle in a different location in case the enemy had observed the shuttle take off.

The next morning she gathered her crew together and advised them they were going on a sightseeing trip to Clarion. "The purpose of the trip is to gather intelligence on the TGA space facility and the fleet that is stationed there," she told them solemnly. "There is a distinct possibility that Videl Lai may try to escape into space should the situation on Tarizon become untenable. Some believe that he might take the fleet to Earth and try to set up a Purist government there. Another possibility is that he may try to exact revenge on the people of Tarizon for rejecting him and driving him away. There is a fear that he might try to destroy the planet."

"Is that possible?" Sgt. Ponde asked.

"Yes it is. Although nuclear warfare was outlawed by the World Assembly at the time of unification and all nuclear warheads were destroyed, the technology still exists. There is nothing to stop someone with the proper resources and technological expertise from building nuclear weapons. It's even possible that nuclear weapons are being built on Clarion as we speak."

"I understand the TGA has three attack cruisers and hundreds of fighters. With that kind of fire power will it be possible for us to get close enough to really see anything?" Lt. Lakee asked.

"That's a good question," Captain Shilling replied. "Our only hope is that nobody knows Earth Shuttle 26 exists. Most think our ship was destroyed on reentry after returning from Earth nearly a cycle ago. If that is the case the TGA probably won't be trying to conceal what they are up to or be on the lookout for enemy ships."

"Still, if we are detected we'll be—"

"In deep trouble without a doubt," Captain Shilling admitted. "But I don't see any alternative. We are the only spacecraft in service to the Loyalist government. That means we must do what we can to assess this threat and come up with a strategy to deal with it. So, I'll give you one kyloon to ready yourselves and then we'll be taking off. . . . Dismissed!"

While the crew was making last-minute preparations Captain Shilling decided to call Lorin and update her on the ship's performance and advise her they were ready to begin their mission. Lorin was glad to get the call and relieved that the ship checked out okay.

"Try not to be spotted. I'd hate for anything to happen to you."

"Don't worry. I know our limitations. This is strictly a sight-seeing trip."

"Good. While you've been planning this inspection mission, I've been working at this problem from another angle."

"Oh really? What's that?"

"If we defeat the TGA on Tarizon we might be able to spark a mutiny against Videl Lai on Clarion and peacefully seize control of the attack fleet."

"I don't know. Videl is ruthless. I'm sure his men know if they betray him, and the insurrection fails, they'll likely suffer a painful death."

"That's true, so we have to convince them it won't fail."

"How do we do that?"

"I haven't worked that out yet, but I'm working on it. So far, I've gone through the files of all the officers assigned to the attack fleet. What I'm hoping to do is find a few officers who are Loyalist sympathizers or opportunists who might want to switch sides before the TGA is defeated."

Tarizon: Civil War

"I'd like to take a look at those files too. I may know some of the officers."

"Sure, I'll send electronic copies to you so you can browse through them while you're traveling."

"Thanks."

"Good luck, Captain. Call me just as soon as you return."

"I will, Chancellor."

The next morning as scheduled the big ship took off, but this time it was set on a course for Clarion. Captain Shilling felt a little edgy. She didn't know if it was because she hadn't been in space for nearly a cycle or if she was worried about what she'd find on Clarion. She looked out her side portal and observed Tarizon getting smaller and smaller. She didn't know if it was her imagination or not, but the planet looked better than it had when they had approached it a cycle earlier. The dingy yellowish tint that she remembered was a shade lighter and the poles were lighter yet. This cheered her up again until Clarion came into view.

Captain Shilling had been out to the TGA moon base several cycles earlier when it was just a refueling stop and resort for tourists. She suspected there wouldn't be any tourists there anymore. As the base came into camera range she ordered it be magnified and displayed on the big screen on the bridge. When it came up she nearly gasped. The tiny little camp she had remembered had been transformed into a huge military complex. She quickly counted attack cruisers and came up with six rather than three.

"This is worse than I had expected," Captain Shilling said soberly.

"How could Videl Lai have built such a vast spaceport without the government knowing about it?" Sgt. Ponde asked.

"That's a good question. This hasn't been built in the last cycle. Videl has obviously been working on this for some time."

"So, now what?" Lt. Lakee said. "We obviously can't stop the fleet from taking off."

"True, but we can stop Videl Lai from getting here. That's our only hope. Once he makes it to Clarion he'll be off with his fleet and we won't be able to stop him."

"I wouldn't suggest we linger, Captain," Sgt. Ponde said. "They'll be aware of our presence soon."

"Yes, you're right. Take a full set of recognizance photos and then let's return to base."

"Very well, Captain."

On the trip back to Tarizon Captain Shilling felt sick. How could the Loyalists challenge such a formidable fleet of warships? Even if they captured or killed Videl Lai, there'd be a second in command who might be just as bad or worse. She hoped Lorin would find some soft spots in the space fleet's command that could be exploited. She hailed Lorin on the GC and patched in Commander Lanzia who was with the 3rd Army just inside Southern Soni getting ready to attack the forces defending Shisk. Lorin filled Leek in on the situation.

"How could this have been kept secret?" Leek asked.

"I don't know," Lorin replied. "I suspected there was more to the space program than the World Assembly was led to believe. Frankly, I'm not shocked by any of this."

"So, what should I do?" Captain Shilling asked.

"You need to come to Soni in case Videl tries to escape to Clarion," Leek replied. "If he gets away we'll have to go after him and make sure he doesn't make it there."

"We? Does that mean you want me to pick you up?"

"Absolutely. I want to see that skutz die so I can tell my grandchildren about it."

"I don't think that's a good idea," Lorin interjected.

"Don't give me any of that Liberator nonsense. We've won the war. I'm expendable now and I wouldn't miss the demise of Videl Lai for a trainload of gold bullion."

There was an awkward moment of silence and then Captain Shilling said, "Don't worry, Lorin. I was the best shuttle pilot in the fleet. If Videl can be stopped, I'll do it and without getting blown up in the process. I promise."

"I know. I have complete faith in you, Captain. I just hope we get Videl on the ground so we don't have to worry about chasing him to Clarion."

When the conference call ended, Captain Shilling ordered the course change to Soni and then she sat back and tried to digest everything that had transpired. Shuttles were not warships and had only limited firepower. Six short-range laser cannons were evenly positioned around the ship's hulk so that no matter where the enemy attacked there would be at least one cannon available to return fire.

Tarizon: Civil War

The shuttle's hulk was made of lemdinium, the strongest and most durable of metals known to exist in the universe. It could withstand most any type of conventional attack for quite a while. The biggest problem was the fragile crew. Even if they were strapped in, they could only take so much jostling before they became disoriented or lost consciousness.

When the shuttle reached Soni airspace Captain Shilling called in to Loyalist command for landing instructions. Once on the ground she was escorted to Commander Lanzia's cube.

"You made it just in time," Leek said as he picked up his flight jacket. "Videl is on his way to rendevous with the shuttle right now. We'll need to leave immediately if we're going to intercept him."

"Okay, we're ready. What's our plan?"

Leek explained his plan as they walked briskly to the shuttle. Before they reached it they were intercepted by Major Oakril. "The seafolken cut off Videl's escape from the city but he managed to get in a TGA copter. He'll be reaching the west gate very soon."

"Thanks, Major. We're heading that way right now."

"Can I come along, sir? I can keep a communications link open with Central Command in case there is any new intelligence."

"Sure, come on. We can use all the help we can get."

They all climbed aboard and closed the hatch behind them. Captain Shilling went straight to the bridge and began giving orders. Soon the ship was rising and gliding forward around the dome to the west entrance.

At the west gate seafolken were rushing through and heading for the shuttle craft in the distance. There was an explosion and then a crash as a large chunk of the dome fell to the ground. Suddenly a copter shot through the hole and raced for the space shuttle. The seafolken opened fire but their bullets couldn't penetrate the copter's bulletproof exterior. Then Riddle the rhutz jumped on top of a truck and glared at the copter. The rotary mechanism began to smoke and the big copter began to spin out of control.

Loyalist soldiers began streaming out of the west gate and with them were Tam and Colonel Belmoht. They saw the copter spinning out of control ahead and raced to help stop Videl Lai from escaping. They saw the pilot miraculously regain control of the copter and land it safely. Videl and two soldiers jumped out and began running toward the space shuttle which was just two lods away. There was a burst of blue light, causing Tam to look

284

up. A second space shuttle was landing right next to the one sent to pick up Videl Lai. Tam knew it was Captain Shilling and, he hoped, Leek Lanzia.

As Videl Lai and his guards made it half-way to the shuttle Commander Leek Lanzia, the Liberator, stepped in his path with Rhin, Captain Shilling and Major Oakril behind him to back him up. The two soldiers pointed their weapons and were about to fire when their guns shot out of their hands. They looked around frantically wondering what happened and then raised their hands in surrender.

Videl scowled at them in disgust and glared at Leek. "So, you think you've won. Well, you've underestimated me from the start. Do you think I care about this dying planet with all its mutants and half-breeds? Well, you can have it! I'm ready to move on to a much better place. A place where my authority will never be challenged and my armies will be invincible! You can have this cesspool of a planet. I'm through with it. My fleet is ready to take me to Earth."

Leek looked around and saw seafolken and Loyalist soldiers on every side. He raised his eyebrows and replied, "Well, I'm afraid your fleet will have to go without you. You're going to be turned over the Council of Interpreters to be prosecuted for your war crimes."

Videl laughed. "Get out of my way!"

Rhin growled and Leek pointed his laser at Videl Lai. "Arrest him and take him to Earth Shuttle 26." Two soldiers close by started to carry out Commander Lanzia's orders when Major Oakril stepped up behind Leek and pointed his laser at his head. "Stand down, soldiers!" Major Oakril ordered.

Startled by the betrayal, the soldiers hesitated and stared at Major Oakril and the laser pointed at their Commander's face.

"Don't worry about me," Leek ordered. "Take him down."

The two soldiers started to advance. "I will kill the Commander if you take one more step."

The two men stopped and Videl let out a wicked laugh that sent chills down Captain Shilling's spine. Videl Lai rushed past her and broke into a run toward the shuttle. Rhin followed him but didn't attack.

"Stop him!" Leek yelled. "It doesn't matter if I die. Don't let him escape!"

Major Oakril began pulling Leek toward the shuttle, making sure his laser was always out of Rhin's view so she couldn't pull it away from him with her mind. Soldiers and seafolken closed in on him from all sides as he stumbled backward toward the shuttle.

"So, you're the traitor who has been feeding information to the enemy?" Leek asked as he was dragged toward the ship.

"I'm the one who has stood by our Chancellor. I'm not a traitor like the rest of you," Major Oakril spat.

"You're the one who called in the air strike against me in Queenland, aren't you?"

"Yes, I did everything I could to stop you. I only wish I could have done more."

"Why didn't you kill me? Surely you had ample opportunity."

"Not with a rhutz at your side. I would have liked to, though."

"You are so gullible," Leek said. "Do you think Videl appreciates your loyalty?"

"He's taking me to Earth with him. I'm to be promoted to captain and given my own ship."

"You'll never make it off Tarizon."

"Yes, I will. You're my ticket off this planet. With you aboard they won't try to stop us."

"I'm sorry, Major Oakril, but I'm not coming," Leek said, jerking himself free and diving for the ground.

Major Oakril fired but the laser blast narrowly missed Leek and before he could aim and shoot again he was hit by more bullets and laser blasts than anyone could have possibly counted. Rhin, taking advantage of the distraction, launched herself at Videl and caught his left wrist. He cursed her as he tried to extricate himself from her grip. Blood squirted from a severed artery as Videl watched in horror. Then Riddle leaped into the air, landed on Videl's chest and knocked him to the ground. Rhin let go of his arm, lunged for his neck, and sunk her teeth into it while Riddle ripped off an ear.

Leek rushed over and watched the two rhutz maul Videl. Finally, he said in his mind, "Okay. He's dead. That's enough."

Rhin looked up and then walked a few steps away. Riddle sunk his teeth into Videl's torso one last time and shook it back and forth. "That's enough!" Leek ordered.

Riddle dropped Videl and then trotted off. There was a long moment of silence as everyone just stared at Videl's lifeless body. Leek couldn't believe it was over. Videl Lai had finally gotten what he deserved—a painful, humiliating death surely to be followed by eternal damnation.

Tam walked up to where Leek was standing and yelled, "*Seama Videl!*" Which in English meant Videl is dead!

Others joined in yelling, "*Seama Videl! Seama Videl! Praise to Sandee. Seama Videl!*" Soon all the soldiers and citizens who'd poured out of the city to bear witness to this historic event were laughing and rejoicing at Videl's death. But before the real celebrating could begin, the jubilation was interrupted by the intense noise of the space shuttle's engines firing. The space shuttle began to lift and as it did, its laser cannons began shooting. Everyone within range of the cannons ran for cover. Commander Lanzia and Captain Shilling ran for Earth Shuttle 26 but before they could get aboard they were blinded by the ship's big blue beacons.

Later when Commander Lanzia awoke, he was shocked to see Captain Shilling on the ground out cold. Then he noticed she wasn't the only one. Hundreds of soldiers seemed to have been rendered unconscious by the shuttle's blue light. Soon others began to wake up. Leek felt disoriented and tried to remember what had happened. Captain Shilling stirred and then opened her eyes and sat up abruptly.

"Oh, skutz. The memory light," Captain Shilling groaned. "I should have known they'd hit us with that."

"Yes. I was the victim of the blue light once before back on Earth," Leek noted, "when my father and I first discovered the Tarizonian presence on Earth."

"That's right. On Earth we used the blue light to disorient people and make them forget they'd ever seen us. It scrubs off a couple of loons of memory from anyone exposed to it. Since we were so close, it probably took a little more. No telling how long the shuttle's been gone. Luckily Videl wasn't aboard."

"Yes, but who's in command now that Videl is dead and why didn't they surrender?"

Captain Shilling shrugged. "I wish I knew. I haven't been able to find much out about the space fleet on Clarion, but I'm sure now that Videl is gone that will change."

"I hope so," Leek said. "We can't let the fleet take off."

"Without Videl, I doubt it will, but if you want me to follow the shuttle and try to capture or destroy it, I will."

"No. You'd never catch it now. We'll have to deal with the space fleet another day. Right now I need to find General Bratfort and see if he is willing to surrender. With Videl dead I think he'll give the idea serious thought. I hope so. I'm sick of this war and now that Videl is dead, I'd like to wash my hands of it."

When Leek got back to his command cube he immediately got on the GC and called Lorin. He felt profoundly relieved that Videl was dead. He had to share his joy with someone.

"Have you heard?"

"Heard what?" Lorin asked.

"Videl is dead!"

"Oh, thank God and Sandee! That is such incredible news. I was so afraid he'd get away and this war would go on forever."

"I'm trying to contact General Bratfort now. Hopefully he'll have the good sense to surrender."

"Yes, I certainly hope so. Either way, with Videl gone I can't see the TGA being able to survive much longer. In the last few weeks we haven't been able to process all the defections."

"If he does surrender, I want to come back to Shini immediately."

"Yes, you should," Lorin agreed. She wanted to add that she missed him terribly and couldn't wait to see him, but she knew that wouldn't be appropriate.

"I've got to give Lucinda a proper burial and I have a son I need to get to know."

There was a moment of silence and then Lorin replied evenly, "Yes, of course. Tehra is taking good care of him. I visit them nearly every day."

"I appreciate that, especially as busy as you must be."

"It's something I really enjoy. Tehra is wonderful. She's become a good friend."

"I'm glad to hear that. I hope you two will stay close. I know that it will be difficult now that you have so much responsibility rebuilding the government."

"Fortunately, thanks to you, we've got the basic framework already in place. If you hadn't protected me from Chancellor Mammett and helped me activate the cells around Tarizon, we'd be facing cycles of anarchy and civil unrest."

"There wasn't much else I could do. If it wasn't for you and your father, I wouldn't have survived my first week on Tarizon. It seemed pretty obvious to me what had to be done."

Tears welled in Lorin's eyes. "I can't believe it's over. Videl is dead and you have fulfilled the Prophecy!"

"I know. Neither of us expected that, did we?"

Lorin laughed. "Yeah, I guess you can't fight fate."

31
Shocking Deception

With the news of the fall of Shisk and Videl's death, the people of Tarizon took to the streets to celebrate. In Shisk, mobs of people lined up as the 3rd Army entered the city and marched to the Capitol Building which had already been secured by the seafolken. Within a few days Commander General Tamurus Lavendar met General Bratfort and accepted the TGA's surrender, and the 3rd and 5th Loyalist Armies took control of Shisk and the state of Soni. Under the terms of the surrender all TGA soldiers were stripped of their weapons and sent home after taking an oath never to take up arms again unless they were accepted into the Loyalist Army.

When Leek finally arrived in Shini he was met by a small contingent of government officials, soldiers, and airport personnel. Leading the welcoming party was Threebeard. Lorin was noticeably absent. After they'd embraced and congratulated each other, Threebeard took Leek aside for a private conversation. Leek was surprised at this and couldn't imagine what Threebeard had on his mind. Normally Threebeard would have connected with him telepathically had he wanted to have a private conversation. His mood seemed somber.

"There is something I must confess to you. You no doubt will hate me for what I have done. I can only hope after careful thought you will agree I was right to do it."

"What are you talking about? Videl is dead. The war is over. What could you have possibly done that would require an apology?"

"I have lied to you, deceived you and caused you much pain and suffering."

"Lied to me about what?"

"About Lucinda."

"Lucinda? What about her?"

"I know you loved her with all your heart and loathed Videl for taking her away from you. Love and hate are great motivators, and during those times that we connected I could feel the intensity of your anger and despair. You were focused on one thing, and one thing only—rescuing Lucinda. But you knew that would only be possible if Videl were defeated."

"So, I was obsessed with rescuing Lucinda? I still don't understand."

"When you found out where she was and went to rescue her, I feared your success would cause you to lose your focus and diminish your ability to lead the Loyalist Army to victory."

Leek frowned. "What are you saying? I don't understand."

"What I'm trying to tell you is that I made sure Lucinda's rescue was a failure. I couldn't afford to have you distracted at such a critical time in the war."

Anger welled up in Leek. He glared at Threebeard in shock and disbelief. He was confused and couldn't imagine what Threebeard had done. "What exactly did you do?"

"Do you remember when you went to rescue Lucinda from Pritzka Prison and John gave her a sedative?"

"Yes. She was so frail the medic didn't think she could stand the trauma of the rescue."

"Yes. And when you came back from the hospital with the baby the medic told you Lucinda was dead."

"Yeah. A lot of good the sedative did."

"Well, actually it did just what it was supposed to do—make it appear that Lucinda had died."

"Huh? What are you saying?"

"What I'm trying to tell you is that Lucinda is alive."

"What? . . . Lucinda is alive!"

Threebeard smiled. "Yes, Lucinda is alive."

Leek felt a jolt of joy like he'd never felt before. Tears welled in his eyes and his knees began to buckle. Threebeard took his arm to steady him.

"Only a few people knew of my deception—John, of course, the medic and a nurse who has been taking care of her since her rescue."

"Did Lorin know?" Leek asked angrily. "Tell me she didn't have any part in this."

"No. I just told her about it this morning. That's why she's not here to meet you. I'm afraid she took the news rather badly."

"Huh?"

William Manchee

"You don't know?"

"Know what?"

"She's in love with you, obviously. You two have been acting like mates ever since you thought Lucinda was dead."

A tinge of guilt swept over Leek. He knew he'd gotten very close to Lorin, but hadn't realized she was in love with him. It was understandable, he thought, since they had worked so closely together, that they'd become close, but had he betrayed his Lucinda? Had he crossed the line? He felt confused and conflicted. He couldn't think clearly. His mind was still trying to get around the fact that Lucinda was alive! *His Lucinda was alive!*

"So, where is she? I want to see her. I want to see her now!"

"Of course. A PTV is waiting. She's with Lorin at the Chancellor's Mansion."

Leek and Threebeard rejoined the welcoming party and then went outside the terminal to a string of PTVs waiting to take the Liberator to the Chancellor's Mansion. As they left the military base Leek noticed crowds of people along the street watching the procession of PTVs and waving wildly. As they got closer to their destination the crowds got bigger and more boisterous. Soon the PTVs were forced to travel at a crawl to keep from running down citizens celebrating the Loyalist victory and the restoration of the Supreme Mandate.

Tears welled in Leek's eyes as he felt the surge of emotion and thought back to all he'd been through since his arrival from Earth. It was almost like he was waking from a dream now that it was over. Someone was pushed against his window and Leek jerked back, startled by the jolt. He looked ahead anxiously to see how much farther it was to the Chancellor's Mansion. They were going so slowly he could hardly stand it. He saw the gate up ahead and wanted to open the door, jump the fence and run to the front door, but he knew the instant he did he would be mobbed by the crowd.

Eventually they turned into the driveway and made their way to the Chancellor's Mansion. Once they'd stopped, an attendant opened Leek's door and he quickly stepped out. A cluster of people stood by the front door. He spotted Lorin first, then saw Tehra holding her baby. His eyes swept over many familiar faces until they landed on Lucinda. She smiled, and he ran toward her and swept her off her feet. They embraced and kissed passionately.

Tarizon: Civil War

Tears welled in Lorin's eyes. She tried to hide them but soon she was sobbing out loud. Tehra put her arm around her. The people around Lorin thought she was happy that Leek and Lucinda were together, but her tears were of sorrow, not joy. At one moment, Leek looked over at her and smiled, but then the nanny brought over the baby and Leek took him in his arms, feeling a pride he'd never known before.

32
Conquest Earth

Evohn Cystrom watched in horror as his father was ripped apart by the two rhutz. He wanted to go to his aid but his father's orders had been quite explicit: if I'm killed, take the shuttle back to Clarion and implement Operation Conquest Earth. But he couldn't just sit there and watch the Loyalists murder his father, so he ordered his crew to fire on the crowd with the ship's lasers and sweep them with the blue light.

While the soldiers and citizens were fleeing in panic, the shuttle lifted off the ground and quickly accelerated for a rendezvous with Clarion. Evohn knew that the blue lights would disable his enemies for at least five loons. This would give him enough of a head start to make it nearly impossible for them to catch him. He was angry and sickened with grief that his father had been killed. Although Videl Lai was only his adoptive father, he had been good to Evohn, as good as any son could have expected. When he managed to kidnap Lorin Boskie, General Zitor, and the Liberator's mate, Lucinda Dimitri, and deliver them to the TGA, Videl had rewarded him with a promotion to Captain and had given him command of a space shuttle.

"I'm sorry, Captain. I can't believe Videl is dead," Rohr Lethrow, his first officer, said.

"Nor can I. Why didn't he leave the city yesterday? I don't understand why he had to hang around Shisk while it was under assault."

"I don't think the general staff thought the Loyalists had a chance of piercing our defenses so quickly. They thought, even if it such a thing were possible, it would take many days and Videl would have plenty of time to escape. The assault from the north was so quick and decisive. How do you defend yourself from thousands of seafolken suddenly appearing from the depths of the ocean?"

Tarizon: Civil War

"There are ways, but I don't think my father had his heart in this war."

"What do you mean?" Rohr asked.

"Tarizon has been so spoiled by war and natural disaster that its future is dim at best. I think my father knew the Purists' future was on Earth."

"Really. You mean he never intended to stay on Tarizon?"

"Oh, if it were possible he would rule it, but his ultimate goal was the conquest of Earth."

"I knew that was a secondary plan, but you're saying it was his primary plan all along?"

"Exactly. Although Earth has some ecological issues, it is nowhere near as bad off as Tarizon. That's why my father engineered the building of the Intergalactic Fleet. Once it was built his only problem was getting control over it. To do that he had to become Chancellor and then abolish the World Assembly. Once he'd done that, the Intergalactic Fleet was his."

"Right. It all makes sense now. So, had the civil war not broken out so quickly, his plan would have worked out perfectly."

Evohn sighed. "It still would have, had he not lingered in Shisk."

"Yes, that's unfortunate. So, what now?"

"Well, there is no future for us on Tarizon, is there?"

"Obviously not."

"Then we carry on with his plan. We have no other choice."

"What plan?"

"Operation Conquest Earth."

"That sounds like a pretty ambitious plan."

"Oh, yes, but quite feasible if we follow my father's instructions."

"You think so?"

"Yes, but first we must rescue Rupra Bruda. He's being held in Shini for the alleged assassination of Chancellor Garcia. His trial was to be the first order of business of the Council of Interpreters when it convened for its next session, but that session had been delayed indefinitely due to our devastating viper attack."

"Is that really necessary? Won't that alarm the new government and alert them to our plans for the Intergalactic Fleet?"

"Perhaps. But we have to rescue him."

"What makes Bruda so important?" Rohr asked.

"He's the founder and soul of the Purist Party. Videl Lai was its political leader. My father can be replaced by another strong leader like General Bratfort or one of the senators who sided with the TGA during the civil war, but without Rupra Bruda's resolve and determination, I fear the TGA command on Clarion will surrender to the Loyalists. When we get back to base I'm sure that will be the prime topic under consideration."

"So, what should we do?"

"We must postpone the surrender of the Intergalactic Fleet to the new Loyalists government to give us time to rescue Rupra Bruda. We are lucky he's still alive. He almost died during his interrogation by Leek Lanzia after the assassination, but for propaganda purposes the Loyalists wanted him alive to stand trial for his deed. So, they provided him with the best medical attention available and he recovered. Such foolishness. If they had just let Rupra Bruda die, our party would be dead and we'd have no choice but to surrender."

"So, how are we going to break him out?" Rohr asked.

Evohn explained his plan to rescue Bruda while he was in transit from Shini to Pritzka Prison in Shisk. Evohn felt certain this action would take the Loyalists completely by surprise and ultimately be successful. He planned to volunteer for the mission himself as he would have the best chance of pulling it off.

"After all, I was the closest person to Videl Lai. He personally trained me to some day take his place. I knew Leek Lanzia and the Loyalists better than anyone. I trained with the Liberator and many of his fellow officers. And before the war I successfully deceived them by pretending to be a defector."

"So, if we are successful, then what?" Rohr asked.

"Then we travel to Earth and build a perfect world."

Rohr nodded. "A very ambitious plan, indeed."

"But one that I am pledged to fulfill. And once I control Earth, I will come back to Tarizon and exterminate each and every rhutz that lives on the planet and kill Leek Lanzia and all who have conspired with him. For my father's murder *will* be avenged!"

THE STAN TURNER MYSTERIES
by William Manchee

Act Normal
Volume VIII August 2006 $14.95
Trade Paperback ISBN 1-929976-40-2

Stan is asked by the CIA to defend a woman accused of killing her alien husband and three children. The only problem, however, is the alien isn't from Mexico but from another planet. While Stan struggles to keep the government's secret under wraps, one of his oldest clients faces bankruptcy due to the embezzlement of hundreds of thousands of dollars by a trusted employee. When the embezzler is caught and sent to jail, he promises to destroy his former employer.

Cactus Island
Volume VII August 2006 $14.95
Trade Paperback ISBN 1-929976-36-4

Stan is called out to Possum Kingdom Lake in central Texas where there has been a tragic Jeep accident and a boy scout has died. When the junior assistant scout master is charged with negligent homicide he asks Stan to defend him, but Stan is reluctant to do so because the boy's excuse for the accident is tat he was distracted by an alien spacecraft hovering overhead. For Stan to get his client off he must prove aliens have landed at Possum Kingdom Lake!

Black Monday
Volume VI Lean Press Aug 2005 $13.00
Trade Paperback ISBN 1-932475-08-7

It's the October 19 1987, the stock market has crashed and banks and savings and loans are falling left and right. There are three murders in Dallas that night. The chairman of a failed thrift and his girlfriend are found with their throats slashed and and old lady is found asphyxiated along with her eleven dogs. Paula ends up defending the accused in the double homicide and Stan discovers he's the executor over the old ladies' estate and must figure out who killed her and why.

Deadly Distractions
Vol. V, April 15, 2004 ISBN 1-929976-22-4

Stan is called home from his vacation when his client is found standing over the body of a dead IRS Agent with shotgun in hand. Although it looks like Dusty Thomas is guilty, he professes his innocence leaving Stan with the greatest and most dangerous challenge of his career. When the radical Citizens Defense Alliance decides to provide Dusty a generous defense fund, Stan finds himself at odds with the FBI and the media. If this isn't enough of a distraction, his best client is kidnaped and Paula is accused of leaving the scene of an accident.

Cash Call
Vol. IV, September 2002, ISBN 0-9666366-8-6

Stan and Rebekah's good friends, Don and Pam Blaylock, are in deep trouble. An imprudent investment in a *Golden Dragon* franchise and their son's arrest for DWI triggers an avalanche of misfortune culminating with the murder of Luther Bell, the smooth talking restaurant promoter responsible for their impending demise. While Stan conducts a preemptive investigation to prove his clients are innocent, he is inundated with lawsuits and claims from their growing list of creditors and must deal with the inevitable marital strife that threatens these once proud families. Then one of Stan's old flames resurfaces and makes a play for Stan's affections sending Rebekah in a rage that culminates in a confrontation with the intruder and a .38 Special. A wrongful death suit worth millions, ancient Peruvian pottery filled with diamonds and a confrontation with the Mob round out this nail biting legal thriller.

Second Chair
Vol. III, June 2000 ISBN#0-9666366-9-4 Trade

Stan takes on the defense of a young college student, Sarah Winters, accused of murdering her own baby. Stan knows this is way out of his league so he convinces his old criminal law professor, Harry Hertel, to be second chair. Much to his dismay, however, midway into the trial Harry disappears. Bad goes to worse as Stan is stalked by a religious fanatic who calls himself Doomsayer. Then he narrowly escapes an attempt on his life and suddenly is the main attraction in a media frenzy. Despite all these distractions, Stan never loses sight of his goal to find out the truth about Sarah's baby. And when the truth is finally revealed it's not at all what anyone expects.

Brash Endeavor
Volume II, June 1998 ISBN#1-884570-89-5 Trade

Step into the shoes of Dallas attorney Stan Turner in the late 1970's as he begins the practice of law. Broke but determined to get his practice going, Stan starts with only a $2,000 cash advance on his American Express Card. It's the late 70's, a boom time in Dallas, and there are a lot of shady oil and gas and real estate promoters around. It isn't long before a couple of Stan's clients get him in serious trouble. When Stan's wife, Rebekah, is arrested for murder and a client turns out to be a ghost, Stan turns in his legal pad for a detective's notebook and goes to work to solve these most perplexing mysteries.

Undaunted
Volume I, June 1997, $12.95 ISBN#0-9666366-0-0

As a youngster Stan Turner has a brush with the law, gets interested in the legal system and decides he wants to be an attorney. He is mysteriously forewarned, however, that the path to his dream will be difficult and fraught with danger. At every turn Stan is confronted with seemingly insurmountable obstacles, yet he pushes forward, undaunted by the unknown forces that seek to derail him. Forced into the United States Marines by a vicious twist of fate, Stan leaves his wife and family and reports for duty. On his first day he unwittingly befriends a serial killer and soon finds himself charged with the murder of his drill sergeant.

REVIEWS

"*Undaunted* proves it to me; William Manchee is a master at story telling. He has a way of spinning a tale that will leave you breathless every time...." (Pam Stone, MyShelf.com)

Brash Endeavor "...fabulous-a real page turner-I didn't want it to end!" (Allison Robson, CBS Affiliate, *KLBK*)

Second Chair "...appealing characters and lively dialogue, especially in the courtroom..." (*Publisher's Weekly*)

Cash Call "...Richly textured with wonderful atmosphere, the novel shows Manchee as a smooth, polished master of the mystery form..." (*The Book Reader*)

Deadly Distractions "...each plot line, in and of itself, can be riveting..." (*Foreword Magazine*)

Deadly Distraction "...a courtroom climax that would make the venerable Perry Mason stand and applaud..." (Crescent Blue)

Black Monday "...Settle down to a good mystery from an excellent writer. I became a fan of William Manchee with his novel Plastic Gods. One of the tightest plots and best writing styles I had seen in quite a while..." (Harold McFarland)

Cactus Island "...if you like shows like X-Files and books with paranormal or science fiction elements, read "*Cactus Island*," and you will be in heaven! I sure was. (Paige Lovitt, Readerviews)

Act Normal "...a fascinating science fiction legal thriller in which the government trades children for advanced technologies." Harriet Klausner, The worlds most influential and prolific reviewer according to Time Magazine.

Act Normal "...Readers who like to mix their legal thrillers with a bit of science fiction will enjoy Manchee's... latest Stan Turner mystery, in which the Dallas attorney, grief-stricken by the kidnapping of his son by aliens, is asked by the CIA to defend a woman accused of killing her husband and three children." (Library Journal)

OTHER NOVELS BY WILLIAM MANCHEE
Twice Tempted
Death Pact
Plastic Gods
Trouble in Trinidad

Twice Tempted "...Manchee provides an awesome adventure for the thrill-seeking reader...." (Rapport Magazine)

"*Death Pact* "...one of the most exciting fiction novels of the year." Harold McFarland, Amazon Top 50 Reviewer (#39)

Plastic Gods "...this stunning work as writer Manchee offers the reader a peek into a side of banking and credit most of us never realized might exist. (Molly Martin Reviews)

Trouble In Trinidad "...It's terrorist suspense at its best!" MyShelf.com